I0609590

ARTIFACT

STARSHIP JERICHO
BOOK 1

TOBY NEIGHBORS

Artifact (Starship Jericho Book 1)

Copyright © 2024 by Toby Neighbors

ISBN: 978-1-952260-83-4 ebook

978-1-952260-84-1 print

Mythic Adventure Publishing, LLC

Idaho, USA

All rights reserved.

No part of this book may be reproduced in any form or by any electronic or mechanical means, including information storage and retrieval systems, without written permission from the author, except for the use of brief quotations in a book review.

CREW OF THE SDF JERICHO

Fleet Officers

Captain Zeke Darius
    Commander Lori Lee
    Lieutenant Henry Nash - Chief Engineer
    Lieutenant Vivian Ramos - Navigation Officer
    Lieutenant Pete Best - Weapons Specialist
    Ensign Alex Stanislaus - Computer Specialist
    Ensign Jacee Bertoli - Communications Specialist

Marine Platoon

Lieutenant Micky Colt
    Master Sergeant Remmy Steel
    Alpha Team
    Gunnery Sergeant Chad Rand
    Sergeant Hugo McManus
    Corporal Leigh Ann Poh
    Bravo Team
    Staff Sergeant Laila McPherson
    Corporal Isolde "Izzy" Berry
    Corporal Jack Fortnoy

Charlie Team
Sergeant Dirk Oliver
Corporal Wendy Downes
Corporal Albert "Rip" Van Winkle
Delta Team
Sergeant Jay Thorne
Corporal Ricky Thompson
Corporal Tyler "Tex" Fry

CHAPTER 1

THE BRIDGE of a starship could be a peaceful place under the right circumstances. Captain Zeke Darius was still six hours from completing the S.D.F. *Jericho's* first shakedown cruise. He expected many more before a full crew was assigned to the ship, and they were sent on her first mission. He sat on the Bridge, a circular room in the center of the corkscrew-shaped ship. *The Jericho* was the first of her kind, a long-range military cruiser called a Viking class.

With just a few hours left, Captain Darius had completed his assignments, including the reports required from every department. There was nothing left to do until they closed with the *Ares* space station. He was alone on the bridge, enjoying the quiet and reflecting on how fortunate he was to land the assignment to command the new ship. Eventually, she would be sent on long-range assignments, probably under the command of a new officer. The Fleet had its traditions and more than a few made no sense to Darius. Breaking in the new ship was his swan song, the last command assignment before he retired. He could stay with the fleet, but only as a staff officer, which meant sitting at a desk and doing paperwork in a tiny office somewhere, which sounded worse than death to a man used to commanding spaceships. When the assignment inevitably came, he would resign his commission and find something else to do. But until then, he was enjoying the new ship.

The door to the Bridge swished open behind him, and his Executive Officer came in with two cups of coffee.

"Morning, sir,"

"Oh, thank you, Lori," Zeke said, taking the mug from his XO.

She was tall and lean with very short, sandy blonde hair. Her uniform was wrinkle-free, and her blue eyes were bright despite the demanding schedule she kept.

"Sorry if I'm interrupting your morning routine," she said.

"You can interrupt with coffee anytime," he said.

The ship's coffee was strong and slightly bitter. Zeke Darius took his black and enjoyed how the caffeine jolted his system.

"All systems still in the green," Commander Lori Lee said, glancing at the control board in front of her seat, which was to Zeke's right.

"She's a good vessel," Darius remarked. "Never been on a shakedown cruise where we didn't have a few bugs to work out in port."

"Speaking of, we're eight hundred kilometers to *Ares* station. We'll have to get everyone up here soon."

"Soon," Zeke agreed. "But not yet."

They sipped their coffee and watched the wide-angle video feed taken from the front of the ship. The *Jericho* was a triple-decker in the familiar corkscrew design of most military ships. She had a long main shaft that ran the length of the ship, which the vessel wrapped around. It was laid out in one long, simple design. A person could walk from the bow to the stern without knowing they are curving around and around the main drive. The constant turn created a pseudo gravity, down and slightly back, that the crew quickly adjusted to. It was much better than a zero-g ship that quickly sapped a person's strength. The ship rotated around the main drive like a bullet or a drill bit. It gave the crew an almost normal living experience, which was ideal since the *Jericho* would be the first manned vessel to venture out beyond the orbit of Jupiter.

All around the Bridge were hi-res display walls. Cameras on the hull of the ship showed a three-hundred-and-sixty-degree view. Zeke's captain's chair rotated so he could spin around and see in any direction. In the distance, directly ahead of them, was *Ares Station*. It was the Space Defense Force's largest base, named both for its military application and because it was positioned in Mars' orbital plane. There were dozens of ships around the space base, and soon, the *Jericho* would join them.

A tone sounded from the communication console. Like every other station on the Bridge, it was unmanned at that moment. Zeke's controls gave him access to the other stations. He tapped the icon for the communications system, but Lori Lee was just a bit faster in her response.

"Priority message for you, sir," she said. "It's Admiral Lincoln."

She started to stand up. Priority messages were usually private, and she planned to give him the entire Bridge to talk with the Admiral.

"Stay," he said quietly. "Save me the trouble of telling you whatever Lincoln says later."

Zeke tapped the button, and Admiral Hugh Lincoln's face appeared on the holographic plot as if he were sitting in the center of the Bridge. The man was around Zeke's age, but he looked older. There were dark circles around his bloodshot eyes. Zeke wasn't sure if the way he looked came from stress or too much drinking. Lincoln was known to keep a supply of whiskey in his quarters. Nothing was private in the Space Navy, and gossip was the unofficial language.

"Admiral Lincoln," Zeke said. "It's good to see you, sir."

"Just got your reports this morning, Darius," the Admiral said. "No problems?"

"Nothing major, sir. We ran all the systems. The *Jericho* is in fine shape, sir. She's ready for a longer cruise."

"Good," Lincoln said. "That's very good. Captain Darius, I want you and your XO to proceed immediately to my office the moment you are docked at *Ares*."

"Roger that, sir. Is everything okay?" Zeke asked, wondering if maybe he had been wrong about the weary look of his superior.

"I'll fill you in on all the details once you're here. Have your people proceed with full resupplies. This is a priority one order, Captain. Don't dally around. Get here and report in ASAP."

"Yes, sir, we'll be there as quickly as possible, Admiral."

"Very good."

The hologram blinked once, then vanished. Zeke didn't say anything for a moment. A priority one order wasn't given very often, not to starship captains. He turned and looked at his executive officer. It was clear she was thinking the same thing.

"Scan the networks," he ordered. "If something happened while we were away, I want to know about it."

"Yes, Captain," Lori Lee replied. "But that doesn't make sense, does it? Why would the *Jericho* be needed for something in the system."

"Could be something else, I guess, but I don't want to go in blind if I can help it."

"Roger that," Commander Lee said. She leaned forward in her seat, tapping away at her console screen. "I've already sent orders for senior officers to report to the bridge."

"Good, I'll issue the orders for full resupply," Zeke replied. "Then we'll get to the bottom of this priority one business."

"You think they're sending us out?"

"Could be, but it's unusual. I expected a few more shake-down flights first."

He leaned back in his chair. It was comfortable and even had that new ship smell everyone raved about, but he didn't notice it. His attention was on what lay ahead, and a long cruise was what the Jericho was built for, but he didn't think she was ready. They had activated and used every system on board, but only for a short time. Nothing broke down on them, but those components and systems hadn't been tested. If the brass was sending them out, it had to be important. Zeke turned and looked in the opposite direction from the space station. In the distance, he could see the red planet. Dark clouds filled Mars' atmosphere with high levels of carbon dioxide that would help regulate the planet's temperatures and foster a strong growing environment for the still underway seeding. Beyond that, dark shadows of the asteroid belt could be seen among ten million stars. And in the darkness that permeated deep space, Zeke wondered what mysteries were lurking. He would find out soon enough.

CHAPTER 2

"WELCOME TO *ARES STATION*, SERGEANT," the young seaman said as Master Sergeant Remmy Steel stepped through the docking portal.

"Thanks," Remmy said.

He pulled a Hardcase weapons container with a rucksack stuffed full and held onto the rolling container with bungee straps. The plastic wheels clicked as they rolled across the metal deck plates. Remmy had been stationed just about everywhere the SDF Marines had duty postings, but he was never any one place long. That was the life of a special forces Master Sergeant. He was in high demand and at the top of his field. He had the combat experience and the scars that went along with it. He took his time moving through the crowds of people, almost all of them in SDF uniforms. Plenty of jarheads on the station were laid out like a large shopping complex with an open concourse. There were lots of different services for the military that rented small shops on either side of the main area. But what held Remmy's attention was the curving walls.

Ares Station was built like a huge barrel. It was constantly turning so that the centrifugal force mimicked gravity. Remmy could see the far wall curving upward in the open concourse area until it was directly overhead. Across the empty space, he could see people moving about their business. It was initially disorienting, but it had a magical quality. He took his time, watching the bizarre station function. He didn't sense any movement, and his side of the station was so large that it appeared perfectly flat.

"Seen enough, Sergeant?" a friendly voice said.

"Never get tired of it, LT," Remmy said. "You?"

"I did some training here," Lieutenant Micky Colt said. "You get used to it."

"I suppose," the older NCO said.

They walked together to the admin desk in the center of the concourse. There were other kiosks, some selling goods, others offering remote services for the sailors and Marines passing through the station. At the admin desk, Remmy placed his hand on a bio-authentication device. It beeped, and the Petty Officer on duty read off the assignment that appeared on his screen.

"Master Sergeant Remmy Steel, you'll need to report to the *S.D.F. Jericho* in docking slot Alpha Tango. That's an orange berth, Sergeant."

"Thanks," Remmy said.

"My pleasure. It's not too often we get a Medal of Honor recipient through here."

Remmy just nodded. Some people fell all over themselves when they heard about the Medal of Honor, but very few understood what it had taken to earn it. To Remmy, it was just a reminder of the good friends he had lost in his career.

"Orange got it," he said.

He left the admin desk and made his way to a coffee shop. Plenty of diners, coffee shops, and bars were at the station. Most of the people on *Ares* were passing through, like Remmy. He had time to kill and was in no hurry to board a spaceship where he would be stationed for who knew how long. Space was at a premium, which was part of what made *Ares* so special. The huge complex gave a person the feeling that they could breathe and relax, especially after spending weeks in a spaceship's tiny, cramped quarters.

Lieutenant Colt sat down with Gunny Chad Rand and Staff Sergeant Laila McPherson. They had met one another on board the transport ship that brought them to *Ares Station*. None of the four had worked together before but shared a bond formed through service in the SDF Marines.

Coffee was ordered, and the data pads powered up. It only took a few minutes to log into the station's wireless service and check for messages from friends and loved ones. Master Sergeant Remmy Steel had no family, and while he knew a lot of Marines and quite a few Fleet person-nel, he had few close friends. And none of them were the talkative type.

"So!" Gunny Rand said when the coffee arrived. "What do you know about our new boat?"

"I know it's new," Lieutenant Colt said.

"New to us?" Staff Sergeant McPherson asked as she mixed sugar and creamer into her coffee.

"The sailor at the admin station said she was fresh from the ship-yard," Lieutenant Colt explained. "Looks like we'll be on her first tour."

"At least the facilities will be clean," Laila said.

"Let's just hope they work," Remmy said.

"We'll probably just spend a week waiting for something to break, then get reassigned," Gunny Rand said.

"Wouldn't be the first time," McPherson said. "Probably won't be the last."

Remmy sipped his coffee. It was good. Coffee was one product that traveled well, and the old grounds could be composted and used to make good fertilizer. He let the hot liquid slide over his tongue and warm him from the inside. Space was cold, and the warm cup felt good in his hands.

"Any idea what the op is?" Gunny Rand asked.

"Nope, just the name of our CO," Micky Colt said. "Major Keys."

"Sandra Keys?" Remmy asked.

"That's her," Colt replied. "She as tough as they say?"

"Runs a tight team," Remmy said. "She's fair, though."

They drank their coffee and talked about people they knew in common. There were plenty, and for a short while, Remmy felt almost normal. There were very few times in the life of a Space Marine that didn't feel either ordered in advance or dangerous. More than a few Marines had cracked under the pressure of living in the confined spaces of a starship. And while there hadn't been any full-blown wars in a long time, Remmy's career as a special operator had been busy in hot zones. The danger was just part of the job, but that didn't make it easy to live with.

After coffee, they stopped at a small shop selling snacks of all kinds, from candy to booze. There were even legal stimulants, edibles laced with THC, and happy pills. Remmy stayed clear of them all. He wasn't a health nut, but he didn't like his mental prowess being diminished. Instead, he loaded up on junk food, not so much to eat himself, but it was useful on a voyage to have a small reward for a platoon. And they were effective trade goods. He could escape his unwanted duty for days with a single cupcake. He once traded a candy bar for a week of latrine duty.

With their snacks purchased, the group of NCOs and Lieutenant Colt made their way to the orange section of the station. After passing through a security checkpoint, which Remmy found to be a little too serious for his taste, they were allowed onto the ship. They entered on the lowest level, in the cargo hold.

"They don't want outsiders on this ship, that's for certain," Gunny Rand said.

"Like anyone would want to sneak on board," Staff Sergeant McPherson replied.

"Armory is this way," Lieutenant Colt told them.

He led the way between the towering stacks of packaged goods wrapped in thick plastic. Unlike the civilian world, the SDF kept their goods in plain, green packages with black stenciled labels. A bag of nails looked exactly like a Meal Ready to Eat kit or a package of protein powder. The cargo bay was big, and Sergeant Remmy Steel could already see his Marines doing daily runs there.

They went from the cargo bay into one of the engineering spaces with huge hydrogen tanks. They wound between the tanks and through into a room with dozens of individual simulators complete with omnidirectional treadmills and vests that would read the user's vital signs. The equipment all looked new.

"Still got the new plastic smell," Colt said. "I think we'll be the first users."

"Can't say I'm upset about that," McPherson said.

They passed through the simulator room and into the armory. All four of the Marines had their weapons. Remmy had six different rifles and a variety of handguns, along with power packs and boxes of ammunition.

"Looks like we get to choose our lockers," Lieutenant Colt said. "Get your gear stowed, and we'll head up to our quarters before checking in with the Major."

"Copy that," Gunny Rend said.

The armory had a big storage area and tall lockers for each member of the Marine platoon assigned to the ship. Special Forces platoons were made up of four fire teams of three persons each, with an NCO assigned to each. Lieutenant Colt would be their tactical officer. His job was to lead the platoon down range, focusing on mission objectives. But

Remmy was the Master Sergeant. His duty was to ensure the platoon was well-trained and ready for whatever assignment was handed down to them. He was also in charge of making sure they were all properly equipped. He wasn't disappointed to see brand new battle armor with state-of-the-art full facial helmets and hard vacuum seals hanging in each locker.

They spread out. Remmy unfastened the bungee straps and put aside his rucksack and the bag of goodies he had purchased. The hard-sided weapons case had an old-fashioned combination lock on it. He dialed the spinning digits with his thumb, then flipped open the twist clasps. Inside the locker, there were weapon mounts. Pistols were mounted on the door to the locker, and ammunition was stacked on a shelf near the top. The locker already had a general issue: Spitfire 98K assault rifle and a case of twenty new ammunition magazines. The Spitfires were so named because of the small flamethrowers attached to the underside of the heavily reinforced barrels. They were bulky weapons but nearly indestructible and useful in almost any environment. Remmy pulled out his guns and got them stowed away. He had a long-range sniper rifle that fired laser beams and a modified, lightweight full auto tactical rifle. His collection of personal weapons even included a semi-automatic short-barrel shotgun with recoil springs built into the stock. His companions had variations of the same types of weapons. Every mission was different and required specialized weapons, but Marines preferred tools they were familiar with. Over the years, each of them added pieces to their collection.

When their weapons were stowed away, They headed back to the cargo bay and, from there, up a flight of stairs to the main deck. Their quarters were on the upper deck, and they kept moving in that direction. They passed the tiny crew rooms into a large Recreation & Entertainment Center. Everything was new and top-of-the-line. Games, computers, entertainment consoles, furniture, and beverage dispensers all looked brand new.

"Never been on a ship this clean," Gunny Rend said. "Feels a bit odd."

"I'm not complaining," McPherson said. "I'll take new over grungy any day."

"The platoon won't mind it either," Lieutenant Colt said. "And I've got good news. I was saving it until now."

They passed through the REC and into the quarters reserved for the

Marine leadership. Remmy saw his name on one of the first doorways. That wasn't unusual; what surprised him was that he was the only name.

"Lieutenant?" McPherson said, almost sounding shocked.

"Yes, Staff Sergeant," he said in a triumphant tone. "Private quarters for each of you."

"Now you're talking!" Chad Rend proclaimed.

Remmy opened the door to his room. It was the first cabin on the left, slightly larger than those on the right. In all the years he had served in the SDF, he had never had a private cabin onboard a spaceship. And it wasn't just a tiny little sleep chamber either. His berth had a desk, two swiveling recliners, an entertainment wall display, and a storage closet with a mini fridge and microwave built into it. The bunk had adjustable head and foot panels that could be angled up or laid flat. Best of all, he had his bathroom. It was, in many respects, a small but well-appointed apartment. For the first time in all his years of service, he secretly hoped they could stay on board the ship for a long time.

CHAPTER 3

CAPTAIN DARIUS and his first mate, Commander Lori Lee, were taken to a secure room. It was a simple space with a long table made of carbon fiber. There were no windows and no artwork on the walls. Most space stations made a concerted effort to dress up the enclosed spaces, but the secure room only had thick foam panels designed to suck up the sound. The door was the thickest Darius had ever seen, and when it closed, it made an almost unsettling clang.

"Are we in trouble?" Commander Lee asked.

"I don't think so," Zeke told her.

"You ever been in a room like this before?"

"No."

"But you've been in confidential briefings, right?"

"Yes."

"And they weren't like this?"

Darius shook his head. "No, nothing like this."

When the door opened again, Admiral Hugh Lincoln entered with an aide and a civilian Darius didn't recognize. They approached the two officers from the *Jericho*, who stood up and shook hands.

"These are exciting times," Admiral Lincoln said. "Please, sit down."

"You'll need these," the aide said, handing Darius and Lee a dark gray folder with *Top Secret* stamped in black. They were sealed with thick stickers that folded over the cover of the file.

"Let me introduce Connor O'Dell," Admiral Lincoln said. "He was sent to us by the President. We're about to make history here, and I don't need to tell anyone that this briefing is classified."

"Yes, Admiral," Darius and Lee said at the same time.

The aide sat by the door and put on a thick headset that was supposed to keep him from seeing or hearing what the others were talking about. Darius guessed it was just a bit of theater to help sell the idea of the importance of what would be discussed.

"Go ahead and break the seals on your folders, please," Admiral Lincoln said.

Darius ran his finger between the cover and the document. The stickers split apart easily, and he opened the folder. On the first page was a glossy image of Saturn. The golden color of the planet and the bright rings around it were unmistakable.

"As you know, the *Jericho* is the fleet's first long-range, deep space vessel. It wasn't seen as a priority until now, but things have changed," the Admiral said.

"Have they ever," Connor O'Dell added.

Darius glanced at the man. It was obvious he was aware of what was in the briefing. Zeke didn't know, but he knew more about the *Jericho* than anyone alive. He had studied the ship when it was being constructed and led the first shakedown cruise. There was more to a spaceship than just specifications. He understood how she handled, the way she flew, every creak and shimmy she made, and how to get the most from the deep space craft.

"Turn the page," Admiral Lincoln said.

Darius found a diagram at the top of the page. It showed the distances from the sun to each planet in the system. Zeke didn't need the diagram to tell him that Saturn was as far from Jupiter as the distance from Earth to Jupiter and that Neptune was over three times as far. But that's what the *Jericho* had been built for. She was a long-range ship with enough fuel and supplies to take the small crew, including a Marine Special Forces platoon, from Earth to Neptune and back. She wasn't the biggest ship, but she was built for efficiency and had state-of-the-art systems that could clean her air, produce edible produce, and recycle nearly everything used on board.

Below the diagram was a set of coordinates and a plot that would take a ship from the *Ares Station* to the specific area of space listed.

"What you see there is our target area," Admiral Lincoln said. "It's just beyond the orbit of Saturn. Is there any reason you can't get the *Jericho* there, Captain Darius?"

"No sir," Zeke replied. "The *Jericho* can make that run easily."

"You've tested the new Prometheus engines?" Admiral Lincoln asked.

"Yes, Admiral, up to one hundred thousand KPH, which is outlined in my report," Captain Darius explained. "We had no issues and can sustain that speed, even faster if necessary. The sonic cone shields break up dangerous space debris, and the internal systems can easily provide a full crew for up to six months."

"She was built to run somewhere in the neighborhood of two million kilometers an hour, right?" Connor asked.

"You know a lot about the *Jericho*," Darius said, holding back his question of how a civilian could know anything about the classified SDF vessel.

"Good, we want you to run at full speed, Captain," the Admiral instructed.

"To Saturn?" Zeke asked.

"Out past Saturn," Lincoln replied. "To the coordinates in the folder."

"What for?" Commander Lee finally spoke up. "There's nothing out there."

"Oh, that's where you're wrong," Connor said. "There's been something out there for a long time, Commander. We've just never been in a position to reach it yet."

"Turn the page," Admiral Lincoln said.

Darius flipped the page in his folder, which showed a long-range photo. It was black and white, and the object in a black field was nothing but a speck.

"That was taken by Pioneer 11 over two hundred years ago," Admiral Lincoln said. "At first, it was thought to be just some space debris. But it isn't moving. It's the first thing in space we've ever found that was stationary."

"Nothing in space is stationary," Darius said.

"This is," Connor said. "Which first caught our attention when humans were still dreaming of flying to Mars."

"You've got to be kidding," Lori Lee said.

"No, we certainly are not, Commander," Admiral Lincoln said. "Since Pioneer 11, we've had several orbital craft in the area."

"There isn't enough light in the area to get a good picture of the artifact," Connor stepped in. "And it's too far outside Saturn's orbit to get close, but we have radar and long-distance scans that tell it isn't just space debris."

The two men were clearly excited about the topic. Darius couldn't imagine anyone interrupting a high-ranking SDF Admiral without earning at least a withering stare, but Admiral Lincoln kept nodding.

"Can you imagine it?" he said. "We won't know for sure until we get hands on it, but..."

"It could be anything," Darius said.

"That's what scientists thought for well over a century," Connor said. "But that's changed now."

"Changed how?" Lori Lee asked.

"It started talking about thirty years ago," Connor said. "It transmitted a data burst."

That brought Darius up short. The talks of extra-terrestrial life in the galaxy were ongoing, but without definitive proof, it was all a moot exercise. As Darius saw it, the reality was the incredible distances between star systems. Space probes had been traveling for nearly three centuries and still hadn't reached the closest star system to Sol. Technology had increased exponentially, yet the human race was nowhere close to traveling at the speed of light. It was one of the major reasons why the system had only been colonized as far as the moons of Jupiter. Even Saturn was too far away. It would take the *Jericho* to reach the sixth planet with its golden rings over three months, traveling at over two million kilometers an hour. An alien race would have to be vastly superior to humanity to cross the distances between the stars. And Darius didn't think they would want to meet an advanced race.

"A data burst?" Commander Lee asked. "And you're sure it came from the object."

"It was triangulated back to that specific set of coordinates," Lincoln said. "And the burst is repeated every time Earth is directly in line with the object."

"Is it something we can decipher?" Darius asked.

"That's the exciting part," Connor said. "It's a high-density information burst, but no more than a few megabits of information, repeated in over a hundred different human languages."

That made Zeke lean back in his chair. He didn't think what he was hearing was possible. Maybe he was being pranked, but the secure room was not the kind of place that just anyone could stumble into. And Admiral Hugh Lincoln was the *Ares Station* commander. There was no way an officer of his stature would be involved in a con game with another SDF senior officer.

"That means there's only two things it could be," Connor continued as he leaned eagerly over the conference table. "One, it's ours, only it can't be from Earth's past."

"It would take decades to reach Saturn without advanced engines," Lori Lee said with a shake of her head. "And it would need massive amounts of fuel to slow back down. You said it was stationary."

"Exactly," Connor said with an appreciative nod.

"And if we couldn't have sent it..." Darius prodded.

"Maybe we could have," Connor said. "Just not yet."

"You're talking about a time machine?" Lori Lee asked incredulously.

"I'm hypothesizing that it could be possible that the artifact was sent back in time," he said. "It's one of two possibilities."

"And the other?" Darius asked.

"Extra-terrestrial," Connor said, emphasizing each syllable.

CHAPTER 4

"WHAT WAS IN THE MESSAGE?" Darius asked.

"The plans for the Prometheus Engine," Admiral Lincoln said. "And a schematic for the ship. We altered it slightly. There was no information on the internals, just the engineering and ship design."

"And we just built the thing?" Darius said.

"Well, it took thirty years," Lincoln replied.

"How long have you known?"

"I've been in charge of *Ares Station* for eight years, but I only read about the project once they finished the *Jericho*. There may be six people outside this room who know about the artifact. We need you to get it, Darius. Take your new ship and retrieve the artifact."

"We're not ready," Darius said.

"By all reports, you are," Lincoln countered. "You said yourself that all systems seemed to work flawlessly."

"They did in a controlled environment," Darius argued. "We need at least three more cruises. Give us a year."

"No, we've waited too long as it is," Connor O'Dell replied. "You need to go and get it now."

"We don't have a full crew," Lori Lee pointed out.

"Yes, you do," Lincoln corrected her. "They've been assigned and are reporting to your ship now. You'll have a full crew from the maintenance crew to the Marine platoon before you leave *Ares*."

"How many missions have you seen go off the rails because it was rushed?" Darius asked. "The *Jericho* is a fine ship, and I'm working with a top-notch staff of officers, but you're sending us out farther than any manned flight has ever gone. If something goes wrong or breaks down, we'll be stranded out there."

"There's no reason to believe anything will go wrong," Lincoln pressed. "Look, this is your chance to make history, Zeke. I know you were planning to hang it up after this assignment, and you can still do it. In fact, you bring that artifact home to us, and you can write your ticket."

"It's not that," Darius said. "I'll gladly stay in the Fleet as long as I command star ships."

"If that's what you want, I can guarantee another decade in the Captain's chair," Lincoln said. "Just get us that artifact."

"Time is of the essence," Connor said. "The President needs a win, and this is it."

"So we're letting politics push our decisions now?" Lori Lee asked.

It was an appropriate question since the Space Defense Force was technically outside the control of governments on Earth and Mars. Anything in space was supposed to be shared resources, but the North Atlantic Federation had been the dominant governmental bloc for over a century. The President had de facto control of the SDF, and whether they liked it or not, politics always played a part in making decisions.

"We're doing what should have been done a decade ago," Connor O'Dell argued. "The artifact sent us those plans so we could come and get it."

"Has it crossed anyone's mind that maybe we shouldn't?" Darius asked.

"It's been debated for thirty years," Lincoln said. "And the time has come to take the next step. That duty falls to you with the *Jericho* Zeke. It's an honor, in my opinion. There's a reason you were tapped for command. You're the most experienced Captain in the fleet. It's time to make history."

"What can I tell the crew?" Darius asked.

"Nothing," Connor said. "We'll tell them when we get there, and only those who need to know."

"We?" Darius asked.

"As the President's special envoy, I'm going with you."

"Strictly as an observer," Lincoln jumped back in before Darius could object. "He's an expert on the artifact, Zeke. You'll want his expertise on this mission."

For a moment, Darius didn't speak. He knew he could resign, but that would slow things down. If he refused, someone else would be given command, and there was no reason to. The mission wasn't safe, but nothing about flying around in space was safe. And the *Jericho* was perhaps the finest ship he had ever commanded. He liked his crew and had no reason to blow up his career. If Admiral Lincoln was right about Zeke staying in command for another ten years, he would have walked barefoot across cut glass to get the artifact.

"You need to understand that on that ship, I'm in command," Darius said as he stared Connor O'Dell straight in the eyes. "Not the president, and certainly not you."

"I understand," Connor replied. "I'm there to record the retrieval and give advice about the artifact when asked. That's all."

"Commander, how long until we're topped off with fuel, victuals, and supplies?" Darius said, turning to face his second in command.

"Within the hour, Captain," she replied smartly. "I can't speak to the rest of the crew, sir."

"They're already being supplied," Admiral Lincoln said. "You keep the purpose of the flight a secret. We don't want some wrench spinner writing home to his mother about the artifact."

"Copy that," Darius said. "If that's all, sir, I'd like to return to the *Jericho* and oversee the preparations."

"Of course. You'll have everything you need," Lincoln said, getting to his feet. He extended his hand, and Darius shook it. "Good luck, Zeke. I'll see you in six months."

"Aye, sir, six months," Darius said.

They were led out of the secure room, and O'Dell promised to be on board the *Jericho* within the hour. Darius wasn't thrilled with the accelerated time frame but was used to rolling with the punches. As he and Lori Lee walked back through the station, they kept their thoughts to themselves. They couldn't openly discuss the mission, and Darius knew Commander Lee's mind was whirling with possibilities just the same as he was.

Darius had argued in the briefing, pushing back against his orders, but it was just the normal response of an experienced commander. The ship hadn't had a proper round of shakedown cruises. The last thing anyone could afford was the *Jericho* to fly half a billion kilometers from

Ares Station and break down. The lives of the crew would be at risk if that happened, and the fleet would have to send an armada of ships to rescue them. It wouldn't be easy, and it certainly wouldn't happen fast. If the *Jericho* lost life support or the fusion reactor failed, the entire crew would die before help could reach them.

But the truth was Darius was thrilled at the idea of actually doing something other than peacekeeping patrols. He had expected the *Jericho* to be sent on a scientific assignment with researchers studying the effects of long flight times on the crew and explorers answering long-held questions about the planets in the outer part of the solar system. Instead, they were going to collect an artifact that was a total mystery. Perhaps it was a beacon or a computer bank full of advanced technological information that would usher humanity into the future. To think that the artifact could be from an intelligent race beyond the solar system was exciting. It wasn't lost on Darius that his name would go down in the history books as the commander sent to retrieve it.

"You okay, sir?" Lori Lee asked as they made their way through the admin section of the space station.

"Fine, Commander," Darius said. "You?"

"Yes, sir, I'm good. Thank you for asking."

"You make sure the supplies are on board and we have everything we need," he ordered. "I'll see to the crew. We aren't leaving without a full compliment."

"Aye, Captain. We still had over ninety percent of our supplies on board. It shouldn't take long to get us stocked back up."

"Once we're fully staffed, I want us moving. You can see to that while I meet with the Marines on board. They'll need to adjust to a long cruise."

"Six months," Lori said. "That's a long assignment on any boat, sir."

"Yes, it is," he replied. "But the news about the mission itself will bolster spirits. I only wish we didn't need to wait to tell them."

"Do you think we should alert them earlier than the Admiral suggested?"

"No," Darius said. "The *Jericho* is a new ship. I think we let that newness have its full effect. Halfway through the cruise is probably the perfect time to inform everyone about our mission."

Lori nodded. She was a foot shorter than Darius, with a pleasant face and sharp eyes. But what Darius liked most about her was how incredibly smart she was. He never had to explain things twice to Lori Lee. He knew when her time came to serve as Captain of an SDF starship, she would be a superb leader.

He could only hope that the rest of his officers, especially the Marines being taken on board, were half as competent as she was. Six months of living and working in close quarters was a difficult tour. People had been known to break under that kind of pressure. The *Jericho* might be the perfect ship, but she was only as good as the crew that operated her. Darius didn't like the idea of jumping into such an important mission with a bunch of people he had never met. The chances of something going wrong were very high, and when that happened, Darius had to be ready. If the mission was going to be a success, the responsibility rested directly on his shoulders.

CHAPTER 5

"SIR, WE'VE GOT A PROBLEM."

It wasn't the kind of news Captain Zeke Darius hoped for when he stepped back on board the *Jericho*.

"What is it?" he asked the ship's doctor.

Doctor Vivik Lanski was a short man with dark brown skin. He was more of a computer engineer than a medical diagnostician. Like all SDF ships, the *Jericho* had a fully automated medical system. The sick bay was next door to his office on the main deck and consisted of two surgical droids and a dozen pods for the sick and injured. Doctor Lanski could technically see patients, but his real expertise was understanding the reports from the sickbay's automated systems and relaying that information to the ship's Captain when needed.

"Major Keys has been diagnosed with MS, sir. She won't be boarding the ship."

"MS?"

"Multiple Sclerosis, sir, is a chronic, degenerative disease of the central nervous system. It manifests in numbness of the hands and sometimes feet, disorientation, clumsiness, and lack of muscle control. She won't be able to attend to her duties, sir."

"Oh, that's terrible," Darius said.

"There's treatment for the disease on Earth, Captain. She'll be fine, but we don't have a senior officer for the Marine Platoon."

"I understand. Anything else?" Darius said.

"No, sir."

"All right, I want scans of every crew member within the next forty-eight hours. Just a standard medical scan to serve as a baseline."

"I'll get that ordered, sir," Doctor Lanski said.

"Very well, I look forward to that report," Darius said. He hurried through the cargo bay and took the stairs to the main deck two at a time.

It was always his policy to keep his people busy, but in this instance, he wanted to be sure that he had everything he needed to ensure that his crew stayed healthy on the long voyage. He moved quickly to his office and shut the door. One of the nice things about the *Jericho* was its spacious accommodations. His office was big enough for an oversized desk with two guest chairs in front of it. It included a small table with chairs around it for conferencing. There was a private lavatory, a small lounge with zero gravity, and a massaging lounger with heated seats.

There was too much work to be done for Darius to enjoy the amenities on the new ship. Instead, he immediately contacted Admiral Lincoln to get orders about replacing Major Keys.

"I was expecting your call," the Admiral said. "I just got word about Sandra Keys myself."

The admiral's face was displayed on a small, private screen that Darius preferred to the large wall display. The small screen was closer and felt more intimate than the oversized display directly across from his desk.

"Who can you send to replace her?" Darius asked.

"We can't," Lincoln explained. "Not without delaying your launch, and I don't want to do that."

"You want me to go on a mission without a senior Marine officer?"

"Do you know Master Sergeant Remmy Steel?"

"No," Darius admitted. The truth was he didn't know most of the Marine officers he had served with. Their presence was usually in the background of what he needed to command a starship.

"He's a good man and an excellent NCO," Lincoln said. "In fact, that entire platoon was made up specifically for this mission. They're all vets with multiple Spec Op experiences. Lieutenant Micky Colt will take the senior position, and you'll be in good hands with the Master Sergeant. He'll keep his Marines in line. Besides, you won't need them for this mission. It's as straightforward as they come."

"Copy that," Darius said, knowing that it was useless to argue with his superior. He might have objected if the mission had been different, but the outcome would undoubtedly have been the same. Besides, if he took on a Presidential Envoy, he could use a spare cabin to keep him in. "According to my data, we have everything we need."

"Excellent. Godspeed, Zeke. I look forward to your swift return."

The image screen returned to the home setting with a list of icons. Darius tapped the personnel insignia, which brought up the ship's crew, including the Marines. The only person missing was Major Sandra Keys. He tapped on her name, held it until a menu appeared beside it, and then tapped on the delete order. The computer required his override authority, which he gave, and the Major was removed from the ship's manifest.

He stood up and straightened his uniform. It was time to meet the Marines on board and inform them about their new assignments. As soon as that was done, he would give the order to leave *Ares Station* and head out into deep space.

CHAPTER 6

WHEN THE MESSAGE came for him, Remmy was unpacking his rucksack and stowing all his meager belongings away in the spacious cabin he had been assigned. He wore an info cuff on his left wrist just like everyone else on board, and it vibrated while his computer chimed with the incoming message. Orders on board a spaceship were sent over the ship's wireless system and had priority over regular electronic messaging. He glanced at the IC on his wrist and saw that he was being sent to the main or middle deck Ward Room.

He stood up, stretched his back, and started for the door of his cabin. It was unusual for an NCO to be called to the Ward Room of a ship, which was normally reserved for senior officers. Remmy was accustomed to getting chow with the rest of the grunts and spacers in the mess hall, which on the *Jericho* was down on the lower deck. He met Lieutenant Colt in the passageway outside their cabins.

"Getting settled, Sergeant?" the Lieutenant asked.

"Yes, sir," Remmy replied. "This will be a luxury cruise compared to most."

"Tell me about it," Colt replied. "I can actually walk around in my berth, and the showers have running water, not just mist."

"It's a lavish boat, sir. I could get used to this."

"Were you called to the Ward Room too?"

"Yes, sir," Remmy said.

"Interesting. I haven't heard from Major Keys. I suppose she's been with the Captain."

They hurried down the stairs. Both men had memorized the ship's layout immediately upon being accepted on board. It was a habit for Remmy. As a Master Sergeant, he was an enlisted man but with the responsibilities of a commissioned officer. Normally, there was one Master Sergeant over an entire Company, which consisted of three full Marine Platoons. Special Forces was a different matter. The platoon was half the normal size, and for some reason, Remmy didn't know; the current platoon was filled with top-notch Marines. He had studied the personnel records while in transit to the *Ares Station*. Every Marine on board the *Jericho* had combat experience, including orbital insertion, pod jumps, hard vacuum, and ship infiltration experience. It was one thing to be trained for a job, but nothing trumped the experience of doing the dangerous work. Everyone in his platoon, Remmy thought of it as his little kingdom, had the best resumes he had ever seen in a single unit. Even Lieutenant Colt was a veteran, which meant much to Remmy. There was no need to coddle his LT or help him make command decisions. Colt had been engaged in the fighting on Finestine Station during the mutiny. He had led a counterterrorism team in two successful missions that saved countless lives. The LT was the real deal; best of all, he valued the NCOs working with him.

They reached the wardroom and waited for a moment until the door opened. Remmy wasn't put off by the finery of the senior officer's private lounge. It was larger than just a dining room, like most SDF warships. There was a rectangular table with real china set in place with magnets that held everything to the table. There were cloth napkins, too, which made the Ward Room seem fancy. But no one was sitting at the table. Instead, the ship's captain, a tall man with short, dark hair sprinkled with flecks of gray, stood near a seating area with what looked like fine leather furniture.

"Lieutenant Colt? Master Sergeant Steel?" the Captain asked.

"Yes, sir," Colt replied.

"I'm Captain Zeke Darius. I'm afraid Major Keys won't be joining us for this mission."

"She won't?" Colt asked.

"No, she's had a medical emergency, and we aren't waiting for a replacement. I don't think we'll have much need for your Marines, but you've all been hand-selected for this assignment. I'm sure you'll be fine.

But that means the two of you will be the senior leaders for the Marine platoons. In that capacity, I'm roping you into senior staff meetings."

"Sir, may I ask what the assignment is?" Colt inquired.

"You may," Darius replied with a nod. "The *Jericho* is a Viking Class long-range ship. And we are going to make the first manned run to Saturn and back."

"Saturn, sir?" Remmy asked, speaking for the first time to his new Captain. "Won't that take…"

"On the *Jericho*, we're looking at a six-month run," Darius said. "Without stops. I know that's a big ask, but you'll have noticed the *Jericho* isn't a normal SDF vessel. We've got more room and less crew. That will allow your people to stretch their legs when needed. But it isn't a pleasure cruise, gentlemen. If something happens on this mission, it will be up to the crew to get us out of it. No one is coming to our rescue. With that in mind, I want the Marines to shadow some of the regular crew. Not all the time, just a few hours each day. Let them learn what it takes to keep the ship going. If someone goes down, we'll all have to pitch in and finish the work. I want your Marines to be training like normal but also learning how to help maintain the ship. That said, it doesn't need to be a strenuous tour. If all goes well, living on this vessel for six months is the hardest part.

"It goes without saying that I want the two of you keeping a close eye on your Marines. If anything crops up, and I do mean anything at all, mental, physical, social, you name it, I want to know about it. This should be an easy cruise, but it's longer than usual, and that can become an issue. Is that understood?"

"Yes, sir!" they both replied in perfect unison.

"Good. I know this is being sprung on you at the last second, and you'll be taking on more responsibility without Major Keys, but it can't be helped. I'll take the ship out as soon as we're done here. The sooner we get started, the sooner we'll get back. I leave it up to the two of you to make a schedule for the Marines. I'll send you a list of shadow assignments, and you can issue them to your people as you see fit. If we can get people with skills and interests that align, that would be best, but ultimately, everyone should know two or three jobs on this boat within the first month of this cruise."

"We'll make it happen, Captain," Colt said. "Are there any other parameters of this mission we should know about?"

"Negative, Lietuenant. If that should change, I will let you know.

We'll be having a senior staff briefing two hours from now. And both of you should plan to take at least one meal a day here with my officers. I prefer to have a fully integrated crew on my tours."

"Yes, sir," they both said. "We'll be here," Colt added.

They saluted, and the ship Captain returned the salute. The Marine Corps was a highly regimented division of the SDF, in some ways more than the Fleet personnel. They left the Ward Room and made their way back to the upper deck.

"Let's hash this out in my cabin," Lieutenant Colt said.

They had been elevated in duties but not in rank. Remmy's lieutenant was still superior and had no trouble respecting the younger man. Micky Colt was not the kind of officer who held to the adage *do as I say, not as I do*. He was a lead-by-example, from the front, not behind, type of officer.

The lieutenant's berth was the same as Remmy's. They settled down at the small table and pulled out their data pads. Remmy brought up the list of the Spec Op platoon.

"Six months," Colt said. "That's not ideal."

"No," Remmy said. "At least the digs are comfortable."

"Yes, that is a nice change. And everything is new. I suppose that's good."

"As long as it all keeps working."

Lieutenant Colt gave Remmy a knowing nod. Half the work done by enlisted sailors was maintaining the ship. It wasn't encouraging that the Captain wanted the Marines to learn to maintain the ship's systems, but both men recognized its wisdom.

"The Captain seems solid," Lieutenant Colt continued. "Have you heard of him?"

"I served on his ship, the *Vindication*, during that dust-up on Mars a few years back."

"You would think he would recognize you."

"I haven't known many ship Captains who get to know the enlisted men," Remmy said.

"Not many have won the medal of honor," Colt pointed out.

"No need to go talking about that. I ain't expecting any special treatment."

"Well, expected or not, it has been earned. How do you want to split up our new duties?"

"I'll plan PT and keep everyone on track. You can rotate people into the different shadowing duties. Gunny Rand will see to the armory. Staff Sergeant McPherson can keep the sims running right. We can put our heads together and run the various combat programs."

"Individual squads and platoon engagement?"

"Makes sense to me," Remmy said. "Odds are we won't have anything to do but get lazy."

"Six months..." Colt said again. "Man, that seems like a long time."

"It is, but just think how much credit you'll bank in six months."

"Yeah, I suppose so," the Lieutenant said. "But I should have bought more snacks."

The Spec Op platoon was assembled in the simulator room an hour later. Other areas were large enough for the Marines, but none were designated just for them. The entire ship utilized the gym, mess hall, and REC. The simulator room was for Marines only, and so that is where they gathered. Remmy and Lieutenant Colt were the last to arrive.

"Ten huts!" Master Sergeant Remmy Steel shouted upon entering the room. "Officer on deck!"

"At ease," Lieutenant Colt said. "We're all here?"

"Present and accounted for," Staff Sergeant Laila McPherson said.

Gunny looked at the ranks. There were twelve enlisted personnel four fire teams of three members each. Fourteen Marines total, including himself and Lieutenant Colt. They were all veterans. Gunny recognized most of them. Seven were Corporals; the rest were Sergeants. Even without training together, they would be one of the most formidable special forces platoons he had ever served with.

"It's your lucky day, Marines," Lieutenant Colt announced. "Welcome to the *Jericho*, the first ever long-range Viking class warship. I suppose you've seen your berths and the facilities on this vessel. It's well-appointed, which is good because we will spend the next six months on board in deep space."

He paused to let that information sink in. No one spoke. They were at ease, standing with their legs apart, their hands clasped behind their backs, and their eyes on the Lieutenant, but they weren't so comfortable that they felt like speaking up.

"As of now, there is no expected mission duty for our platoon on this cruise," the Lieutenant continued. "But that does not mean we're going to get fat and lazy Marines. We will continue to train and keep our combat readiness at its peak. Also, each of you will be shadowing the enlisted sailors to learn about ship operations. Because the *Jericho* will be in deep space, there is no hope of rescue should something go wrong. And in that circumstance, we better know how to keep this tub running. I will assign shadow duty soon, so if you have mechanical experience, let me know. The goal is to learn everything about this ship from top to bottom. We're not here to do the sailors' job on this boat, but we must be prepared for any outcome. Is that understood?"

"Yes, sir!" the entire platoon, including Remmy, barked in reply.

"Outstanding. Master Sergeant Remmy Steel will see to your PT. You will stay in shape on this cruise. No slacking. You slack, and he will make you wish you had never joined the Corps. We will run sims daily, with one day of rest every seven, just like in boot camp. We will inspect and ensure that every piece of gear is in perfect condition. We will make good use of this time; let there be no doubt about that. And we will complete this cruise with a perfect record. I don't want anyone stepping out of line. You can fraternize with the sailors, but don't fall in love with anyone. And I better not hear any talk about my Marines doing anything they shouldn't. No means no, and when the bootleg liquor gets passed around, you find an excuse to be somewhere else. Is that clear?"

"Sir, yes sir!" they all shouted.

"That is all for today. Get settled in, get some grub, and then get some sleep. We're kicking things off at 0500 ship time, Marines. I'll see you then."

Lieutenant Colt left the same way he had entered. The Marines started talking, including Staff Sergeant McPherson, who immediately approached Remmy.

"Six months?" she said. "That's a long cruise."

"A long cruise with nothing to do," Gunny Rand said. "That's a perfect recipe for trouble."

Remmy was starting to get an itch that he couldn't scratch. The ship's captain had been straight up with them, but he was starting to think there was more to this mission than they were being told. Not that he was accustomed to being in the know. As an enlisted Marine, he was often kept in the dark until his superiors had to give him details. Perhaps Captain Darius was the same way. Only time will tell.

"We have plenty to do," Remmy told them. "Complacency is our enemy on this op. We stay busy and make good use of the downtime."

"Maybe set up some competitions," the Gunny said.

"And some group entertainment options," McPherson said. "When people have something to look forward to, they tend to stay more focused at work."

"Agreed," Remmy said. "Good suggestions. Run with them. Chad, you're in charge of the armory. Let's make sure everyone's weapons and ammo are properly stored. Tomorrow, we'll break out the armor and ensure it's all in good working order."

"Should be; it's all-new," Gunny Rand said.

"I wanted everyone fitted up, and we'll start making a list of mods."

"Pull in Sergeant Oliver and Sergeant Thorne. They should have experience customizing gear," Remmy ordered. "Laila, we need to sync battle helmets and have the first Platoon sim ready by morning."

"Shooting range?" she asked.

Remmy nodded. "Yeah, and a group sim with plenty of movement. The LT wants to see what kind of shape everyone is in."

"Copy that," she replied.

"Tomorrow afternoon, we'll get together and make a long-term plan for the simulation room. Lieutenant Colt wants your input."

"We've got a damn fine group of Marines on board this tub," Gunny Rand said. "It'll be a shame if all we do is train for six months."

"You never know what's coming down the pike," the Master Sergeant said. "At least we'll be ready for it."

CHAPTER 7

"DID you hear we have a Medal of Honor recipient on board?" Lieutenant Peter Best said quietly as he stirred his iced tea.

"No way," Lieutenant Henry Nash said. "You can't be serious."

"He is," Vivian Ramos said softly. "A Master Sergeant who saved about fifty people during the siege on the Rayvek complex."

"A lot of Marines died in that rebellion," Nash said.

"A lot of civilians, too," Best added. "From what I heard, Master Sergeant Steel took a bullet and still managed to get over fifty people from the infirmary to the transport."

"All by himself?" Nash asked.

"By the time he got there, his entire platoon was wiped out," Peter explained.

Peter Best was the *Jericho's* Senior Weapons officer. He was in charge of the complex firing systems operated from the Bridge. He oversaw the munitions crews, ensuring the laser and missile systems were armed and ready. The ship had nearly a hundred warheads on board, and Lieutenant Best was in charge of drilling the crews who loaded them. He was a tall man with thick, curly hair on top of his head. The sides and back were shaved to the skin, and his eyes were a dark blue, almost gray.

"I'll sleep better knowing that if we're attacked, someone knows what they're doing," Vivan Ramos said.

She was short, with caramel-colored skin and jet-black hair, which she kept long and pulled into a tight braid. As the chief Navigator and Computer Specialist, she had the most training of anyone on the ship. It wasn't enough to know the trigonometric equations for navigating in space; she had to be able to do the math accurately and quickly. On top of that, she had to know the precise coordinates of every planet and space station in the system by heart. They were the anchors to ensure her calculations were correct. Of course, the navigation computer did all the heavy lifting and number crunching most of the time. But every ship in the fleet had at least one Navigator who could check the plots and ensure the ship was on the right course.

"I can't imagine staying in the field after winning the medal of honor," Lieutenant Henry Nash said. "You know he got his pick of assignments. He could have been stationed on Earth or somewhere with all the amenities of living on a planet."

"Maybe he likes the action," Best said, wondering how he would respond to the kind of danger Master Sergeant Steel had faced.

"Maybe, but the Marines spend a lot of time in tight quarters waiting for the call," Nash said.

He was the Chief Engineer, a gangly-looking man with long arms and legs that allowed him to squeeze into the tightest places inside the engineering sections to ensure everything worked. He had black skin and a broad face with a bright smile. His laugh was contagious, and his work ethic was legendary in the Fleet.

"I guess we'll get to meet him and find out what he's like," Lieutenant Best said. "Their Major had a medical emergency that kept her off the ship."

"That's unusual," Ramos said.

"Why would that make a difference?" Henry asked.

"Because the Captain has asked the Master Sergeant and the platoon Lieutenant to join us for senior officer meetings. They'll be here for dinner tonight."

"Interesting," Vivian Ramos said.

The three officers were already in the wardroom. They weren't needed on the Bridge with Commander Lee. Captain Darius had scheduled their dinner, asking all three senior officers to attend. Soon, they would be on rotating shifts, standing watch on the Bridge in four-hour shifts so that having them all in the Ward Room at the same time would be rare.

The Fleet officers sat drinking iced tea, one of the staples on board an

SDF ship, and waiting for the others to arrive. Lieutenant Colt and Master Sergeant Steel were the next to arrive. They barely had time to introduce themselves before Captain Darius arrived.

"Good, you're all here," he said. "I hope you're hungry."

The metal table was large enough for eight people, with three to a side and a seat at the head of the table for Captain Darius. The seat opposite his was left empty, partly because it wasn't needed but also as a reminder of the people they had lost over their careers. To Darius, it was a reminder that his orders had serious consequences. His job was to oversee the ship, carrying out the mission while doing everything he could to see that every crew member made it back alive. However, to accomplish their missions, there were times when it was inevitable that people would die. They were part of the Space Defense Force, and everyone accepted the dangers they faced. Yet the Captain never wanted to forget that every order he gave impacted real people who were part of his crew. He refused to take their lives for granted.

Unlike the mess hall, where food was retrieved from the automated meal dispensers, the Chief Petty Officer who oversaw the meal systems also served as the Captain's chef. He didn't cook every meal, just those requested by Captain Darius. And the Petty Officer usually served the food, too. Darius opened a bottle of wine to have with their dinner, which was a real beef tenderloin cooked in a spicy sauce and served over a bed of fresh greens with goat cheese and a tangy dressing. There was freshly baked bread, an apple pie with a flaky crust, and ice cream on the side for dessert. While they ate, the crew shared information about themselves. The stories of his senior officers helped Darius to know his crew. He found Master Sergeant Steel to be a very quiet and reserved man. Stoic was probably the right word. Darius had dined with plenty of new officers who were intimidated to be eating with the Captain, but Remmy Steel wasn't shy. Darius found him to be introspective, and when he did speak, it was well-reasoned and thoughtful.

Neither of the Marines drank more than a few sips of the wine with their meal. On the other hand, his senior Fleet officers finished the bottle and another one after that. They enjoyed the food and the company. There was laughter and joking, all in good fun. Darius could tell the three Fleet Lieutenants were eager to impress the Master Sergeant. It wasn't surprising that news about Steel's medal of honor had gotten out. Darius hadn't locked away the personnel records and wanted his officers to take the initiative when doing their jobs. Part of that job was to know who they were working with. And the fact that they had looked at more than just the Fleet personnel was an encouraging sign to him.

"I do have one item of business to discuss," Darius said as their deserts were being served. "We have a special envoy on this trip. A civilian, Connor O'Dell. He was a last-minute addition to the crew, and he's something of a scientific adviser to the North Atlantic government back on Earth."

"Why's he with us?" Lieutenant Peter Best asked.

"I imagine he'll be researching when we reach Saturn," the Captain explained. "Until then, he's a resource about anything we see or pick up on scans. Tomorrow, we'll be firing the Prometheus engines. If you have questions about our mission, he can probably answer them as well as I can."

"What's to know," Vivian asked. "We're traveling to Saturn and back. It's simple."

"Yes, that's right," Darius said. "But I want you to give O'Dell every courtesy. I've put him in the major's cabin since she couldn't join us."

"You should have put him in with the enlisted personnel," Henry Nash said. "Give him a real taste of the navy."

Darius knew that life on board the *Jericho* wasn't like the real Navy. On every other ship, enlisted personnel shared barracks full of bunks with no more than eighteen inches between them. The men were crowded in like sardines in a can. Women, too, share facilities with no privacy. The only thing that kept the enlisted sailors from getting up to no good was exhaustion. They worked the massive battle carriers fourteen hours daily, doing everything from ship repairs to swabbing the decks. In comparison, the *Jericho* was like a pleasure cruise.

Only it wasn't just another mission, and it certainly wasn't a vacation. Somewhere out in the darkness of space was an object that wasn't of their making. Darius had to retrieve it, but who knew if it was good or bad? He couldn't help but wonder if maybe it should just be left alone.

CHAPTER 8

"MORNING, CAPTAIN," Vivan Ramos said from her post at the Navigation console.

Darius hadn't slept. Days and nights on an interstellar ship tended to run together. Darius knew he would get into a solid routine in time, but first, they had to fire up the Prometheus engine. The goal was to get them moving at two million kilometers per hour. In theory, it was just a matter of burning the engines until you reached the desired speed. In space, there was no friction and nothing to slow them down. But two million KPH was faster than any ship had ever flown. Reaching those speeds on a normal ship was impossible because the engines weren't efficient enough. It would take massive amounts of fuel, and ships required as much fuel in space to slow down as they did to speed up. And it wasn't just the fuel issue that kept the other ships from flying so fast. The amount of burn time was prohibitive to the engines themselves. Space engines tended to be delicate, or at least they seemed to be. Parts of the engines had to be exposed to the cold of space, while other parts had to endure the massive heat from the fuel being consumed. A normal engine would melt down or have a catastrophic failure if someone tried to reach the speeds Darius was about to attempt.

The door to the Bridge swished open, and Henry Nash walked in. He glanced at Darius, gave his Captain a nod, and then sat down. He seemed stiff, and Darius guessed he was nervous about running the new engines at full capacity. If something went wrong, it would be his problem to fix.

"Are we ready, Lieutenant Nash?" Darius asked. It wasn't necessary, but the Bridge recorders recorded every decision. They wouldn't pick up a nod or a look, and Darius needed to get the chief engineer's consent before firing the Prometheus engines.

"Green across the board, Captain," Nash said. "She's ready for top speed."

"Very good. Let's do a safety check."

The senior officers didn't man every console on the Bridge. Junior officers were at the communications, radar, life support, and weapons controls. Every position reported in. The ship was running at optimal efficiency with no problems. When Commander Lori Lee came to the Bridge, Darius was about to give the go-ahead. She said nothing as she sat down at her station, slightly behind Darius. He didn't speak to her but appreciated her presence on the Bridge with him as they quietly made history.

"Engage Prometheus engine," Darius said. "Ten percent power."

"Aye, engaging Prometheus engine," Nash replied. "Ten percent power."

"Nav, is our plot locked in?"

"Yes, Captain," Vivan Ramos said. "We are traveling outbound at forty thousand kilometers per hour."

"Prometheus engaged," Nash announced. "Ten percent power and holding steady."

"Fifty thousand KPH," Vivan said.

"Take us up to thirty percent, Nash," Darius said. "I want to warm the system up before we go any higher."

"Roger that, thirty percent power," Nash replied.

Darius didn't need Vivan to announce their speed. He had the readout pulled up on his displays. They were already moving faster than most warships, which seemed odd since there was no roar from the engines and no feeling of motion on the ship.

"Weapons, how do those sonic shields look?" Darius asked.

"Full power, Captain," an ensign named Chesterson said. "Complete sonic projection."

There was no sound in space, but sonic waves could still be projected to break up the tiny bits of space debris that could be deadly to an interstellar ship.

"Seventy thousand KPH," Vivan said.

"Fuel consumption?" Darius asked.

"We're under estimates, sir," Nash replied.

"What are the temperature readings on the safety chambers?"

"Well, in the green. The ship is running just as she was designed to, sir."

"Take us to forty percent power then," Darius ordered.

It was faster and harder than they had pushed in the shakedown cruise, which was more of an experiment than a mission. Every system was studied during that operation to ensure it all worked the way it was supposed to, but Darius had been planning for many more test flights before being assigned a real mission. It was standard procedure to give a new vessel a thorough battery of tests before turning her loose. The Captain feared what might happen as the experimental new engines were given full power. Yet, he needed them at full strength to reach the speeds they were tasked with achieving.

"Forty percent, aye, Captain," Nash said.

Darius glanced around. His crew seemed excited, which was good. Perhaps they had more faith in the SDF than Darius had. Or maybe, without the weight of responsibility on their shoulders, the mission was just an exciting change from the ordinary.

"Eighty thousand KPH," Vivian Ramos said.

Darius glanced over at Lori Lee. She was completely occupied with the information on her console screens. It was the sign of a good officer, although Darius had always preferred to read his people rather than the information processed by the ship's computers.

"Life support, are we experiencing any abnormalities?" Darius asked.

"No, Captain," the young officer said across the bridge. "Everything is normal."

"Communications, I want verbal reports from engineering at both ends of the ship," Darius ordered. "They are to report anything unusual immediately."

"Roger that, Captain," the comms officer said.

"Ninety thousand KPH," Vivan said.

They weren't even at five percent of the speed required for the mission, and yet Darius felt that if there were going to be an issue, it would happen early. If the Prometheus engines worked as they were supposed to, all would be well. But he still felt it best to baby the new technology. And it certainly didn't ease his mind to know that the designs for the ship and her experimental engines had come from the mysterious artifact no one could identify.

For an hour, they stayed at forty percent of the engine's power. It didn't take long to break the speed record, which they had set themselves on the ship's shakedown cruise. But that had been with a skeleton crew, and twice as many souls were on board making history. People were excited once they passed a hundred thousand kilometers per hour, but since then, everyone seemed to settle, and the work became almost mundane.

When they reached two hundred thousand KPH, Darius increased the power to the engines again. They proceeded that way, gaining speed every minute. At fifty percent power, the ship increased speed by ten thousand KPH every three minutes. Darius took his time and kept close reports on the ship's many systems. Nothing seemed to be affected by the tremendous speed. He increased power every half hour until they reached eighty percent power.

The watch changed, and new personnel took most of the positions on the Bridge. Darius, Vivian Ramos, and Henry Nash stayed. Hour after hour, they increased speed. It seemed impossible to Darius that they could be traveling so fast, and the ship remained unaffected. And yet, the *Jericho* functioned perfectly as she raced quicker and faster through space. Eventually, they reached their goal and took the Prometheus engine offline.

"I know you're tired, Nash," Darius said. "But we have to have a thorough inspection."

"I'm on it, Captain," Nash said. "I've got a good team. We'll make sure that we get eyeballs on every component."

"Very good," he said. "Lieutenant Best, you have the Con. Commander Lee will relieve you at the change of watch. I'll be in my quarters, but I want to know immediately if anything changes."

"Aye, Captain," Peter Best said. "I have the con."

There was nothing to do while the ship hurtled through space except to watch the systems and do the prep work required to slow back down. They wouldn't fire the Prometheus engine again for nearly six months, although they occasionally brought it online for diagnostics. It was hard to wrap his mind around the reality that if anything did go wrong, they would deal with it while flying through space at over two million kilometers per hour. In his mind, it seemed like they should stop moving to fix something, but in space, that rarely happened.

He got to his feet, stretched, and headed for his quarters. As he passed the stairs, he heard the Marines moving down to the lower deck, where they would train in the simulator room. He wondered briefly if having no access to what the ship was doing was better. The Marines didn't worry about the *Jericho*; that was his job. Theirs was to be ready to fight if the need arose, and the odds were high on the current mission that there would be no fighting. He envied their carefree existence on his ship. Not that it was easy, but it had to be less stressful than worrying about something breaking down while they were millions of kilometers from help.

CHAPTER 9

"WEST ALLEY IS CLEAR," Corporal Isolde Berry said.

Remmy heard her voice through the comlink. He was behind Staff Sergeant McPherson and Corporal Jack Fortnoy of the Bravo team. He glanced across the road to where Lieutenant Colt was leading Alpha and Charlie teams.

"All right, move ahead," Colt said. "Nice and easy."

They were working through a platoon simulation. Remmy had done the same sim, or one just like it, basic urban combat, a thousand times. Somewhere in the simulated but nameless city was another platoon controlled by an AI program that would study *Jericho's* Spec Op platoon and look for holes in their tactics and strategy.

"Hold," Master Sergeant Remmy Steel ordered. "I just saw a glint at the top of that building just ahead of you."

"Charlie team, get a drone in the air," Colt said. "We could be walking into an ambush."

"Copy that," Sergeant Dirk Oliver said.

The drone was tiny, barely the size of Remmy's thumb. It had a built-in wide-angle camera and a tiny repulser lift to carry it up nearly fifty meters. A video feed popped up on Remmy's helmet screen. The entire simulation was just playing out inside the helmets of the platoon. They were armed with weapon simulators and stood on omnidirectional tread-mills that helped mimic the condition of the combat simulation.

"It's a lookout," Colt said, spotting the soldier perched on top of a defunct air-intact unit.

"Probably means the bad guys are in the building," Staff Sergeant McPherson said.

"All right, Charlie team, take the rear," Lieutenant Colt said. "Delta, you're in reserve."

"Copy that," Sergeant Thorne said.

"On our way," Sergeant Dirk Oliver added.

"Master Sergeant, can you get the Bravo team around on the far side of the entrance?"

"Fall back," Remmy ordered. "We'll circle the building through the west alley and come across on the far side."

"Bravo team is on the move," McPherson said.

"Watch your back, Sergeant Steel," Colt ordered.

"Roger that," Remmy said.

They jogged through the narrow alley. The simulated city had large buildings that filled the entire city block. The maneuver around the building took nearly five minutes. His battle armor had environmental controls meant to keep him cool in the heat and warm in the cold, but Remmy was sweating. He had lost count of how many combat engagements he had participated in. They all swirled together in his mind, creating a kind of monster that he could feel breathing down his neck. The doctors called it Post Traumatic Stress Disorder. Even though Remmy knew he was in a simulation and couldn't really be hurt or die, his emotions seemed unconvinced. Fear plagued him, not so much of dying or getting hurt, but of losing people he cared about. It was the burden of every leader. Remmy Steel wasn't an officer. He didn't order people into battle, but once they were in the fight, it was up to good NCOs like Remmy to direct the platoon. He had made bad decisions in the past. He'd even won the medal of honor for some of them, but to Remmy, they were all losses. Any time he made a call and someone died, he carried a load of guilt that he couldn't shake.

Of course, it was impossible to shield a platoon from danger. Remmy had to find the line between caution and cowardice. He didn't want to be reckless, yet he couldn't hold back in a fight. That was something he had learned early in his career. If there was a fight, a Marine would have two options. If they held superior ground and good cover, they could sit tight and let the fight come to them. But apart from that, it was better to go right at your enemy in every other circumstance.

"We're in position," McPherson said as they sprinted from the alley across the road and slid to a stop at the corner of the building.

"The bastards have to know we're coming," Colt said.

"It could be a meat grinder in there, sir," Gunny Chad Rand pointed out.

"Still our job, Gunny," Colt replied. "Bravo, on my count, we hit the entrance from both sides."

"Copy that," McPherson said.

"Sergeant Steel, you hold back. If this is a trap, I don't want us both going down."

Remmy understood that the simulation was a training exercise. For himself and the Lieutenant, it was more about learning what their platoon was capable of. And Remmy was learning a lot about Micky Colt. The Lieutenant wasn't just a lead-from-the-front type of officer; he was a hard charger who liked rushing into danger. That made him a good platoon leader but not a great officer. Remmy doubted he would live long enough to make Captain, and certainly not Major. He would die doing what he loved, and that meant rushing into the building with two Spec Op teams behind him. It also meant that Remmy had to be the cautious leader, holding back and directing the platoon. He had to be ready to step in as the leader if Lieutenant Colt went down, and while he would prefer it if Colt held himself back a little, Remmy wouldn't tell him how to do his job. It was just a sim, after all. No one would die even if the entire building had enemy combatants.

"Copy that," Remmy said.

There was shooting inside. He peaked around the edge of a big window and saw a pair of guards by the stairwell lying dead.

"Two down," Lieutenant Colt said. "Lobby's clear."

"Want us to infiltrate the back?" Sergeant Dirk Oliver asked.

"Affirmative," Colt replied. "The Alpha and Bravo teams will work our way up. Charlie and Delta team converge on the lobby and rendezvous with Sergeant Steel."

Remmy tried to relax as he waited just inside the building's main entrance, but his body wouldn't comply. Every sense told him he was in a combat zone, and his emotions were on edge.

Coming in the front of the building, Delta Company showed up first. They hurried in and moved to secure the stairs. A few minutes later, Charlie team arrived.

"There was a single guard back there," Dirk Oliver said. "He wasn't paying attention, though."

"If this wasn't a sim—" Jay Thorne started to say.

"Pretend it isn't," Remmy growled. "Feels like a trap to me."

Where do you want us, Master Sergeant?" Dirk Oliver asked.

"Help me keep an eye out the front," Remmy said. "This op ain't as easy as it appears."

"No one would leave their men out as bait," Jay Thorne said.

"The computer would. It doesn't care how many people die," Remmy said.

He didn't like computers very much. There were officers who made all their combat decisions based on fancy algorithms and what the Brass called combat metrics. Maybe sending good Marines into combat was easy based on an equation when you were safe in orbit or on a space station a million kilometers away. Still, Remmy felt it was better to have leaders with their boots on the ground, not their noses in a computer.

"Contact!" one of the corporals in Charlie team called out. "We have enemy troops converging on the building."

"Find cover," Remmy ordered. "The stairway is our lifeline. We can't lose that."

"What's happening down there, Sergeant?" Colt asked.

"Enemy troops moving in, sir," Remmy said. "Two platoons, by the looks of it."

"This place is empty," McPherson said.

"We don't know that yet," Gunny Rand argued. "We're only on the third floor."

"We'll have to deal with it in waves," Lieutenant Colt ordered. "Sergeant Steel lay down a suppressing fire, and let's get Charlie and Delta teams moving up the stairs. The enemy will be forced to follow, and we'll cut them down in the choke point."

"Copy that, you heard the man," Remmy snapped. "Get moving Delta. Charlie, you follow."

"What about you, Sergeant?" Sergeant Thorne asked.

"Don't worry about me. See to your squad."

They started up the stairwell just as the enemy began to converge in the street outside the building. Remmy had run enough combat sims to know they would be outnumbered and outgunned. It didn't surprise him when the first few rounds shattered the front windows. But they weren't bullets or lasers. The enemy fired smoke canisters into the building.

Remmy was down on one knee behind a decorative planter filled with potting soil. A short tree was growing out of it. If he reached out, his gloved hand would supply haptics that would mimic touching an object, but of course, his hand could pass right through it. He was playing in a make-believe world and fighting against imaginary enemies. The only way that it worked was if he let himself believe it was all real. His emotions had no trouble leaping. As smoke billowed into the building's lobby, obstructing his view, Remmy's heart began to race.

"We're on the second floor, Master Sergeant," Dirk Oliver reported.

"Standby," he told them. "I'll take down a few before moving up."

He couldn't see the enemy but didn't need to. They had only one way in, and their boots would make noise on the broken glass. He was confident he could make them pay for their bullish tactics.

But before the enemy could charge into the smoky lobby, a machine gun sounded above him. Glass rained down, and there was carnage in the street. A savage battle cry pierced the air.

"Flair, no! Flair!" Gunny Chad Rand shouted.

Shouting and loud explosions were common in battle. Gunny Rand's voice was carried on the platoon comlink, but Steel's battle helmet moderated the volume. He couldn't see anything, but he knew something had happened. Soon, the enemy was firing. Most of it was indiscriminate shooting through the smoke-filled lobby. Remmy tucked himself low behind the planter. His simulated rifle was the Spitfire. It held 48 rounds of hardened steel slugs, thicker than flechette darts but thinner than old-fashioned lead bullets. The hardened steel rounds were about as long as Remmy's pinky and designed to penetrate armor. The Spitfire barked in a loud report dampened by Remmy's battle helmet. The simulated bullets disappeared in the haze as the battle intensified.

More shooting could be heard from above him. Lieutenant Colt directed the battle, but the Spec Op platoon was stuck in the building while the enemy had room to maneuver outside. It would have been better to lure them into the lobby and take them down in successive engagements as they made their way up the stairwells, exactly as Lieutenant Colt had ordered. Instead, something had caused one of the Marines to open fire from the third-story windows, and Remmy knew exactly what was going to happen next. It was no surprise.

"They're falling back!" Corporal Jack Fortnoy declared. "They're running."

"Regrouping," Staff Sergeant McPherson said. "What the hell was Flair thinking?"

"We need a way out of this building," Lieutenant Colt said. "Master Sergeant, how does the lobby look?"

"It's filled with smoke, sir," Remmy replied.

"I've got movement!" Gunny Rand said. "Two fire teams just started for the rear of the building."

"Then we're trapped," Colt said.

"Incoming!" someone else bellowed.

Gunny had known it would come to this. The enemy undoubtedly took losses and wasn't in a hurry for more. And the truth was, they didn't need to. With the *Jericho's* Spec Op platoon trapped inside, the easiest way to kill them was to blow up the building. The lobby was no longer safe. Remmy slipped back into the stairwell. It was made of concrete blocks and steel beams.

"Get to the stairs, sir," Remmy urged.

"To the—"

But before Lieutenant Colt could complete the order, a rocket-propelled grenade shot through the third-floor windows, which Sergeant Robby Flair had blown out. It wasn't all that surprising. After all, they were running a combat simulation, and some Marines couldn't separate a training exercise from a video game. Whatever Flair had done, it was costing the platoon. The RPG exploded. Four Marines were killed instantly, and two more were seriously wounded by the blast. Then, the fourth floor rained down, trapping three more Marines. Their vitals were still showing on his platoon information app on his battle helmet's display screen, but for the simulation, they were eliminated from the battle. That left only four Marines, Remmy, Sergeant Jay Thorne, and the two other members of the Delta team who were still on the second floor.

"Delta team, get back down here," Remmy ordered. "That won't be the last rocket."

"Copy Master Serg—"

Another explosion cut him off. Fortunately, the Delta team was next to the entrance and the stairs on the second floor. The simulated enemy fired another RPG, aiming for the second story of the building. The grenade detonated against the windows, which hadn't been shot out like those on the third story. Shards of glass were blown inward, but most of the RPG's power remained outside the structure, which was shuttered under the impact. The building was some sort of office complex. The interior walls weren't load-bearing but held back the second explosion's concussive power. Delta team slipped into the stairwell without incident.

"We're moving down to your position, Master Sergeant!" Jay Thorne reported.

"Move! Move! Move!" Remmy barked. "Take cover under the stairs."

The three Marines of Delta Company made it just in time. The third RPG shot into the second story and exploded. There was enough damage to bring the upper floors crashing down. The only thing that didn't fall was the enclosed stairwell. It remained standing. The concrete walls were reinforced with steel. Dust rained down, and a few doors were ripped from their hinges on the upper floors, but that was all. Still, the cacophony was frightening. Remmy reminded himself over and over that it was just a simulation. He couldn't die; he wasn't trapped in a stairwell, but his emotions were too raw to believe it.

"We have to move," Remmy said. "I'll go first. Sergeant Thorne brings up the rear. Be careful. The entire stairwell could be compromised."

"Where are we going?" asked a wide-eyed Corporal named Ricky Thompson.

"Up and out," Remmy told him. "The sim isn't over until one side is completely wiped out."

"We're pretty close," Sergeant Thorne said.

"We keep fighting until we can't," Remmy said. "Just keep moving, head on a swivel. We'll get through this. Shoot anything you see moving."

Remmy checked his rifle. He still had twelve rounds in the thick magazine but switched it out for a fresh one. With his weapon loaded and ready, he started up the stairs. They were sturdy and didn't move under his weight. A moment later, he heard Ricky Thompson's boots coming up behind him.

The rubble from the fallen building was taller than the second story. That door wouldn't open, and the small window above the handle was dark. Remmy didn't waste his time. He continued climbing to the third-floor landing. When he first began to train on the simulators very early in his career, he couldn't help but marvel at how a treadmill could mimic stairs, yet somehow it did. His armor and gear weighed slightly more than half his body weight, and by the time he reached the third-floor landing, he was breathing harder. He could have continued. In fact, stamina was one of Remmy Steel's best physical traits. But he didn't need to keep climbing. The third-floor door was open slightly. He pulled it back and looked out at the cloud of dust billowing around the wreckage of the building. There was no way to climb down and negotiate the wreckage, especially not with enemy fighters watching for them. But while he had some cover via the dust cloud, Remmy knew he could make the most of their time and resources.

His battle armor was filled with useful gear. From his lower left thigh, he retrieved a bolt launcher. It was loaded with a single quarrel attached to a thin but high-tensile wire. He aimed low through the cloud and fired the bolt. It flew straight, and he felt it strike a solid object, which Remmy hoped was the next building over.

From his right thigh, he took a small, battery-powered wench made specifically for the bolt's wire. He pressed it against the top of the door frame and pulled the attachment control lever down. The entire winch was smaller than his fist, yet the tiny anchor bolts were packed with explosive gel set off by the lever. They blew up, driving four anchors into the steel door frame and the concrete beyond it. Remmy fed the steel cable into the tiny winch as the other Marines arrived on the third-floor landing.

"I'll go first," he volunteered, "and make sure the landing area is secure."

"Good luck," Sergeant Thorne said.

As soon as the cable tightened, Remmy pulled a safety tether from the back of his armor. It was attached in several places and had an anodized steel carabiner at the end. He reached up, hooked the carabiner onto the cable, and then jumped off the edge of the floor, which had crumbled just a half step from the utility stairwell door. His armor seemed to tighten onto his body, and he sensed the movement as he slid down the wire. It wasn't right, but it was close enough for a simulation. In the training room on board the Jericho, Remmy had attached his actual safety tether to a steel overhead support and was hanging just inches from the omnidirectional treadmill. All around him were the simulated dead Marines. They stood motionless, watching the helmet cams of the four surviving members of their platoon. They could speak, but their comms were cut off. They were silent spectators forced to watch what happened without being able to help in any way.

Remmy reached the ground beyond the rubble from the building that the enemy forces had blown down. He was still hidden in a cloud of dust. The alley he should have been standing in was filled with debris from the building. It was possible to climb over it, but he had been lucky enough to land near another building doorway blown open by the collapse of the first building.

"It's clear," Remmy said. "And we have egress. Come ahead."

"Copy that," Thorne repeated.

No order needed to be given. Thompson was the next Marine down. Gunny unhooked the younger man's tether and called the all-clear. Thirty seconds later, all four Marines were on the ground and entering the next building.

"What's our plan?" Sergeant Thorne asked.

"Get back outside," Remmy said. "We move in a leapfrog motion until we spot the enemy, then take them down."

"Just the four of us?"

"There's no reinforcements, Sergeant," Remmy said. "No evacuation plan. We kill or be killed. This sim doesn't end any other way."

They were all veterans of combat operations. None were cowards, but they were struggling to wrap their heads around what happened. Fortunately, Remmy could keep them moving, and as they came around the corner from the narrow alley between buildings, the enemy was in sight.

"Stupid bastards don't know we ain't dead yet," Corporal Tyler "Tex" Fry said.

"Sergeant Thorne, take Ricky and get across the road," Remmy ordered.

"They'll see us," Thorne pointed out.

"Tex and I will cover you," Remmy said. "Once you get across, add your fire to ours. The enemy is in the open and shouldn't be hard to take down."

"Copy that," Thorne said.

Remmy wasn't as tall as Corporal Tyler Fry. He went down on one knee at the corner of the alley, and Tex leaned over him. They both pointed their rifles down the street. Remmy's targeting program used an invisible laser to find the range, which popped up on his battle helmet's HUD.

"Targets are thirty meters," he said. "Don't shoot until they see us."

"Yes, Sergeant," Tex said in a deep voice.

"We're on the move," Sergeant Thorne said.

Remmy didn't watch his companions. His eyes were on the soldiers in full armor down the street, waiting for them to turn and start yelling. However, one of the oddities of a simulation was that the enemy rarely reacted the way one might expect. The computer ran an algorithm and decided that its people wouldn't see the two Spec Op Marines dashing across the street.

"We're in position," Sergeant Thorne said a little breathlessly.

Remmy knew the Sergeant wasn't breathing hard from the run but from the tension and excitement. They all brought their weapons to bear on the simulated enemy who were milling around in the street near the rubble of the building they had brought down.

"Let 'em have it," Remmy ordered.

They began to fire. The rifles sounded mechanical as they spewed out bullets in short bursts. Remmy worked the trigger, pulling it repeatedly rather than holding it down. He targeted the enemy soldiers rather than just spraying the area. The entire battle took less than a minute, and twelve enemy combatants were dead in the street.

"Like shooting fish in a barrel," Tex said.

"Oh, yeah!" Ricky Thompson declared. "That was sweet."

Remmy didn't think there was anything sweet about killing people, even simulated people. The reality was gruesome work, leaving a callus on a person's soul.

"Check your six," Remmy ordered. "Rooftops too. The enemy could be anywhere."

"And they know we're here," Sergeant Thorne said.

"Better move," Remmy agreed. "Sergeant Thorne, head down the alley. Let's move two blocks south, then return to this street."

"Roger that," Jay Thorne said.

"All right, Tex, let's move," Remmy said.

They went back down the alley they had come up before the shooting started. Remmy didn't mind being alone, even in a combat zone, but he felt a shadow of worry. Only four Marines were left alive in the simulated engagement, and Remmy wasn't crazy about splitting the small group up. Still, they were all highly trained Special Forces Operators. He had to trust them.

"We've got company," Tex said. "Nine o'clock high, Sergeant."

Remmy, still jogging down the alley, glanced up. He saw a pair of shadowy figures on the roof. If they started shooting, there was very little cover for the two Marines.

"Here," Remmy said as he yanked open a recessed door to the side of the building to his right.

Both men ducked inside. They were in what appeared to be a mail room or receiving center for some business. It was empty, and Remmy hurried through. They wound through the maze of interior hallways, eventually finding an exit.

"Contact! Contact!" Sergeant Jay Thorne shouted. "We're pinned down."

"Hold on," Remmy said. "We're on our way."

They ran down another alley, throwing caution to the wind. The sounds of gunshots were echoing through the urban battlefields. Remmy and Tex crossed the wide main avenue and entered the adjoining alley.

"Ricky's hit! Where are you guys!" Sergeant Thorne bellowed.

"Almost there!" Remmy said, but the response was dead air.

Master Sergeant Remmy Steel felt a sickness in his gut. It didn't matter that he was just in a simulator and that his platoon was safe on the *S.D.F. Jericho*. In his mind, he felt a sense of terror. It was happening again—his entire platoon was wiped out. His muscles were tense, and his heart was pounding so hard it felt like it might break out of his chest.

"Contact," Tex said.

Remmy dropped to one knee. Over a dozen enemy soldiers were on the narrow street behind the big buildings where Sergeant Thorne and Corporal Thompson had been. When Remmy peeked around the edge of the building, he saw the enemy soldiers loitering around the bodies of the two slain Marines. His chest constricted even though he knew it wasn't real.

"Give 'em hell!" Remmy ordered.

He brought his Spitfire up and pulled the trigger. The weapon rocked in his hands. The recoil made the weapon try to move up, but Remmy held it in an iron grip. He and Tex surprised the group of enemy soldiers. Nine went down under the barrage from the two Marines. When they emptied their magazines, they pulled back.

"Didn't get them all," Remmy said.

"Three made it," Tex agreed. "What's the call?"

"The best defense is a good offense," Remmy said, swapping out the mag on his spitfire and ramming a new one home. "Let's take the fight to them."

It wasn't much of a fight. The two Marines ran into the alley, jumping over the bodies of the dead enemy soldiers. Three had survived, fleeing into an alley on the far side of the narrow street. They were still running when Remmy and Tex reached the alley. They fired in short bursts. The Spitfire had an effective range of one hundred meters. The enemy soldiers weren't even half that far away. The computer-generated soldiers died quickly.

"Damn, I thought that was all of them," Tex said when the simulation didn't end.

"Remember those bogies on the rooftop," Remmy said.

"Spotters?"

"Or snipers. Let's get high and see if we can find them."

Remmy led the way to an emergency ladder bolted onto the back side of one building. He used the strap on his rifle and slung it over his shoulder while he climbed. Tex was right behind him. In different circumstances, he would have ordered someone to cover them as they made the climb, but with just two Marines left in the simulation, Remmy preferred that they stay together.

Neither man spoke as they made the climb. When Remmy reached the rooftop, he scrambled over and dropped to one knee while slinging his rifle back around. The top of the building seemed deserted.

"The bad guys were over there," Tex said, pointing toward the buildings on the far side of the main avenue.

"We'll move to the other side of the roof, but stay low," Remmy said. "They'll be watching for us."

The two Marines hurried across the building. They ran in a hunched-over position. Remmy's thighs burned from the effort, and his armor worked hard to keep him calm. His mouth was dry, and his emotions were like a storm. Fear, almost panic, tried to paralyze him. Not fear of dying, but of failing. He was supposed to be the Master Sergeant. In many platoons, Master Sergeants did paperwork and organized things for the CO, like duty schedules and training exercises. But he was in the Special Forces, and his task was to keep his people alive. That was ruined and not his fault, but it still weighed on him that only two Marines out of fourteen were still alive in their first combat simulation. He told himself it was just a sim, that no one had died. He could understand that in his mind, but his emotions refused to cooperate. They were raging as if the sim was a real engagement. That was what PTSD did to a person, taking them back to the high-stress situation even long after it was over.

Remmy's worst combat operation had been in the Reyvek complex on Mars. His platoon was tasked with helping move a group of wounded civilians through the dome complex to the infirmary at the air station. The only problem was the rebels embedded throughout the complex. His platoon had succeeded but at the highest possible cost. Remmy was the only Marine to survive that operation. He had taken a bullet that ripped through the quad muscle on his left thigh, but somehow, he had gotten the civilians to the medical facility alive. The pressure not to fail on that op had been overwhelming, and he was feeling a similar emotion as he crouched behind the retaining wall on the roof of the simulated building.

"We should spread out," Remmy said. "Don't present a target. That could be a sniper team we're hunting."

"Copy that, Sergeant," Tex said.

"Let me know if you spot them. I want a coordinated attack to end this sim."

"Sounds good to me, boss," Tex replied. "Let's end this thing."

They scurried apart until they were at the corners of the building. Only then did Remmy peek over the retaining wall to look for their enemy. Fortunately, the last two remaining AI soldiers weren't hiding. They were standing at the edge of the building opposite the one Remmy and Tex were on.

"Contact," Tex said.

"Yeah, I see 'em," Remmy said. "Engage."

Tex didn't hesitate. The man had his finger on the trigger. Their enemy was staring at the street below and didn't see the two Marines on the rooftop. Tex killed the spotters before Remmy could fire a shot. As the two computer soldiers dropped, a voice sounded inside the Marine battle helmets.

Simulation is complete, it said.

Remmy didn't bother reading the after-action report. He pulled his helmet off and looked at Tex, who was doing the same thing.

"Good work, Marine," Remmy said.

"Nothing to it," Tex said. "What happened to the rest of you guys?"

"We were crushed when the building collapsed," Jack Fortnoy said.

"What are you crabbing about," Sergeant Hugo McManus of the Alpha team snapped. "It's just a stupid sim."

"That you ruined," Corporal Wendy Downes said.

"Enough chatter," Lieutenant Colt said. "Everyone get out of this gear and make sure it's clean before you rack it. Team leaders will convene in my office in thirty minutes."

The platoon grumbled as they unfastened their armor and disconnected the safety tethers from their simulators. Remmy knew that any newly formed platoon needed time to get to know one another. They were all professionals with combat experience, but they weren't a team yet. That would come in time with the right training. He followed the others into the armory to remove his combat suit and clean out the sweat that had soaked into the lining. Everyone in the platoon was talking except for Sergeant Hugo McManus. He was a big, muscular Marine with tattoos covering his entire upper body. Remmy glanced at McManus and wondered how big a problem the surly Marine would be.

CHAPTER 10

"DO WE HAVE A PROBLEM?" Captain Darius asked.

"You were monitoring the combat sim?" Lieutenant Colt asked.

"I was," the ship's Captain said. "Good work, Master Sergeant."

Remmy was standing at attention beside Lieutenant Colt's desk in his small office on the ship's main deck. Captain Darius had just stepped in unannounced.

"Thank you, sir," Remmy said.

"New platoon," Captain Darius said. "I'm sure you have it in order, Lieutenant. But I want to know if you need anything."

"Just a little time, Captain," the platoon leader said. "We're still getting to know one another."

"Very good. Carry on," the Captain said before leaving the small office.

When the door swished closed, Remmy relaxed, and Lieutenant Micky Colt ran a hand over his eyes.

"Good Lord, that was bad," Colt said.

It was just the Lieutenant and Remmy in his office. The other NCOs would be along shortly, but it was just the two senior personnel for now.

"McManus is a hot head," Remmy said. "We'll deal with it."

"A hot head I can handle," Colt replied. "But if McManus is cracking up, we need to know, Sergeant."

"What exactly happened, sir?"

"The idiot jumped out the window," Colt explained.

"Some people don't take the sims seriously."

"He has to. It's a team-building exercise."

"I'll speak with him, sir."

"You need to do more than that," Colt said. "Remmy, we're on an extended cruise with no backup. We can't have a rogue Marine causing trouble."

It was obvious that Lieutenant Colt felt the pressure of not having Major Keys on board. The ship's Captain wasn't making things any easier by dropping in and questioning the Lieutenant after their first platoon sim.

"He won't," Remmy said.

Colt sat down behind his desk. Officers were required to make reports and coordinate with other senior personnel. Remmy had never been involved in the command circles of a navy ship. But he could tell the pressure was on Lieutenant Colt to ensure everything with the Marine platoon ran smoothly.

A moment later, Gunny Rand and Staff Sergeant McPherson arrived. The four Marines spent an hour talking about the combat sim, tactics, and personnel.

"It wasn't the best simulation for evaluating our people," Izzy McPherson said. "I thought things were smooth right up until the building collapsed."

"I take full responsibility for McManus," Gunny Rand said. "I'll have him on point ASAP."

"I want Sergeant Steel to do that," Lieutenant Colt said. "The Master Sergeant can knock McManus down a peg or two. In my experience, fire teams need to be tight. I don't want Alpha teams at odds with one another."

"Yes, sir," Gunny Rand said.

"Convey to your people just how important it is that we get things right," the Lieutenant continued. "We can have an easy cruise or ruin it by acting the fool."

"No one wants that, sir," McPherson said.

"What we want and are stuck with are two very different things. Run team sims for the next two days. On the third, we'll do a full platoon exercise again. I want a very different outcome on that engagement."

"Yes, sir!" the three NCOs said in unison. They all stood up and saluted.

"Dismissed," Colt said.

Remmy followed the others out of the Lieutenant's office. Gunny Rand spoke in a low tone.

"He's not happy, eh?"

"The ship's captain was monitoring the sim," Remmy explained. "And he dropped in just before you arrived."

"Oh, that explains a lot," McPherson said.

"Without the Major, our man Micky Colt is in the hot seat," Gunny Rand said. "I don't envy him there."

"We all need to adjust," Remmy went on. "New boat, new parameters, new platoon... it's just going to take a minute for us to get our act together."

"But it shouldn't," McPherson said.

"A long cruise is great for some," Gunny Rand said. "But maybe not for everyone."

"Yeah, if I had someone to miss back in the world, I wouldn't want to be gone half a year," McPherson said.

They left the main deck and descended the stairs to the lower deck. It was lunchtime, and the mess hall was crowded. The three NCOs got in line. Lunch was standard Fleet issue chow: protein wafers flavored to taste like pork, instant potatoes, rehydrated vegetables, and vitamin-fortified flatbread. It wasn't good by most people's standards, but Remmy had been eating military food for his entire adult life.

"I'll join your team for PT," Remmy told Chad Rand. "We'll see what McManus' attitude is then."

"And if it isn't acceptable?" Rand asked.

"Then we'll adjust it," Remmy told him. "The old-fashioned way if necessary."

Alpha and Charlie teams were in the ship's physical training area a few hours later. It consisted of a row of cardio machines against one wall and a row of resistance band exercise stations on the other. In the middle were padded mats for hand-to-hand combat training. The alpha team consisted of Gunny Sergeant Chad Rand, Sergeant Hugo McManus, and Corporal Leigh Ann Poe, who had just finished an hour of resistance exercises with fifteen minutes of high-intensity interval cardio when Remmy Steel walked in. The Marines were all in good shape, each with a sweat sheen, but none looked overly tired.

"How about some sparing," Remmy called out. "Anyone game?"

There was no shortage of takers. Remmy strapped on padded mitts covering his knuckles, the back of his hands, and his forearm. There were similar mitts on his feet and shins. It didn't take long for Remmy's judo background to show. Most Special Forces operators were trained in hand-to-hand combat, including Ju Jitsu. They all knew a variety of ways to incapacitate an opponent on the ground. But Remmy was an expert on getting a person to the ground. And it didn't take long before big Hugo McManus stepped onto the mats.

"I wouldn't try that mamby-pamby karate stuff with me," Hugo said. "We get that close, and I'll break your spine."

"You wouldn't be the first to try," Remmy said. They began to circle one another. "So you're McManus. Heard about you."

"All bad, I hope," the big man said with a wicked grin.

"Three tours during the border war," Remmy said. "You were with the team that stormed the Plasma Observatory space station during the workers' strike."

"Guilty as charged," McManus said before stepping forward and throwing a couple of fast jabs at Remmy, which the Master Sergeant easily avoided.

"You always such an idiot in combat?" Remmy asked.

"Better watch your mouth, Sergeant," Hugo warned.

"I watched the playback of our sim. You damn near got the whole platoon killed."

"So what? It's just a si—"

Hugo had come in hot, ready to land heavy blows against Remmy. He was a big man and probably used to his opponents moving back when he went at them. But Remmy didn't go backward. Instead, he slipped forward, and as Hugo drew back for a haymaker punch, Remmy grabbed him, drove his hip into the big man's midsection, and threw him over his body. McManus hit the mats flat on his back. There was a shocked look in his eyes for a second, and then he scrambled to his feet. Remmy let him get up.

"You got lucky," Hugo said.

"That ain't luck," Remmy told him. "And when we run sims, they aren't a game."

"What does it matter? No one got hurt. Hell! We still won the stupid simulation. I had the highest kill rate in the platoon."

He came at Remmy again but with a little more caution. Hugo feinted with a punch but lashed out with a kick. Remmy checked the kick by raising his leg and letting the pads absorb the energy. He countered with a short hook that caught Hugo in the ribs. The big man grunted but reached out to grab Remmy. It was another mistake on Hugo's part. He expected to pull Remmy into a choke hold, but instead, the wily Master Sergeant stepped between Hugo's legs, twisted his body, and sent the big man flying over his back again.

"We're a unit," Remmy said. "Everything we do has to be in coordination with the platoon. You know that, Corporal."

Remmy extended a hand to help the big man off the mats, but Hugo slapped it away. They were supposed to be sparing, which normally ended when one person backed away or landed a solid combination on their opponent. The goal wasn't to hurt one another but to exercise skills useful in a combat engagement.

"What's the point," Hugo said, returning to his feet and rolling his thick shoulders. "This is a crap assignment. Six months? Who ever heard of a cruise that long?"

"You don't want to make history?"

"Grunts like us don't do anything but take up space on a report somewhere," Hugo said. "Sounds more like they're putting us out to pasture if you ask me."

"Maybe someone thought you deserved a break," Remmy said. "I don't know, but as long as we're on activity duty, we will train and be ready for anything we might be tasked to do."

"Says you," Hugo snapped.

"That's right, says me," Remmy shot right back.

The fight started in earnest then. Hugo's arms were longer, and he worked his jab to keep Remmy at bay. But the Master Sergeant was fast and had plenty of experience fighting bigger opponents. They traded blows. Hugo wasn't fast enough to land his power punches, but Remmy ate several jabs while he worked his way in close. It was Hugo's turn to take Remmy to the mats, and Remmy left himself open to just such a move. Hugo dove forward, driving Remmy to the mats in a classic tackle, but the Master Sergeant used the bigger man's momentum against him. As they hit the mats, Remmy kicked up, flipping Hugo over. McManus held onto Remmy, pulling him down, but at least Remmy was on top of the bigger man, and he quickly slid his body over and into side control. When Hugo's big arms came up to push Remmy away, the Master Sergeant locked onto one, swiveling around and stretching the muscular limb out in an arm bar.

Knowing he was in trouble, Hugo grabbed his wrist with his other hand and fought to keep Remmy from stretching the trapped arm out and hyperextending the elbow. There was a stalemate for a moment, but Remmy flexed his hips forward and used his weight and the strength in his legs to straighten Hugo's arm. The big man lost his grip and had to tap as his arm started to bend backward. Remmy immediately released the arm bar, and both men reached their feet.

"This is my platoon," Remmy said, breathing heavily. "And you will fall in line, Marine."

"Whatever," the surly corporal growled.

Remmy let it go. Other Marines were waiting to spar, and Remmy felt he'd taken the first step with the obstinate Hugo. The big man wasn't broken, and he surely felt no loyalty to Remmy, but he had been bested in combat, and sometimes a platoon needed the pecking order to be clear. Only time would tell how Hugo handled the loss on the sparring mats, but Remmy had given him something to consider.

CHAPTER 11

"REPORT," Captain Darius ordered.

"All is well, Captain," Commander Lori Lee said. "The *Jericho* is green across the board."

"Engineering?" Darius asked.

"The Commander is right, sir," Lieutenant Henry Nash said. "Never been on a ship this tight, sir. Everything is tip-top; we're even ahead on fuel consumption."

"Well, I suppose that's good news," Zeke Darius said. "Communications?"

"We're still in touch with the Fleet, sir," Commander Lee said from her seat just slightly behind the Captain's. "Nothing to report."

"Nav?"

"We're on course, Captain," Lieutenant Vivan Ramos said. "It's clear space to Saturn. No need for correction either."

"Wonderful," Darius said, but he was bored. They all were. The new ship worked perfectly, leaving them with very little to do. "Shields?"

"Functioning," Lieutenant Peter Best, the weapons specialist, said. "Full power, nothing to report."

"Very good," Darius said. "A long, uneventful cruise doesn't sound bad. It sure beats getting shot at. And I take it everyone's quarters are acceptable?"

"Aye, Captain," the officers replied.

Darius looked around the bridge and felt a sense of foreboding. There was nothing wrong. The ship was in optimal condition. There was nothing ahead of them to be afraid of. The cruise might not be very eventful, but he knew they were doing more than just making a long run through the solar system. Soon, he would need to tell the senior officers what they were really up to, but it wasn't quite time. He wanted to wait until they passed Jupiter and were in the wide open space between the planets before divulging the truth about the artifact.

"All right, stay alert, people. In my experience, something always goes wrong and usually happens quickly. Let's stay on top of things and not get complacent. We're flying outside the normal bounds of the Fleet and traveling faster than any ship has ever flown. We need to stay at the top of our game."

Zeke stood up and smoothed his uniform. The crew all wore simple jumpsuits while on duty. He turned to Commander Lori Lee. She was an attractive woman but wholeheartedly committed to the Fleet. He couldn't ask for a better second in command.

"The ship is yours, Commander," he said softly.

"Aye, Captain," she replied without looking up from her console screens.

Darius walked to the door of the Bridge and then turned back. His senior officers were all very, very good at their jobs. In fact, it was one of the most talented crews he had ever been part of. And still, he couldn't shake the feeling that something dire lay ahead of them. He began a daily habit that he continued for the next ten weeks. Every day, he walked the length and breadth of the *Jericho*. He was already familiar with her and knew most of the crew on sight, but he needed to see for himself that everything was working the way it should.

Once they passed Jupiter, there was little to see outside the ship. Still, Darius spent hours watching the video feeds that looked deep into space. Thousands of stars were visible, and he couldn't help but wonder if someone out there had sent the artifact. The strange device they were going to collect filled his imagination. Very little was known about it. Long-range scanners picked up a solid object that is flat on the sides and rectangular. No energy readings had shown up, but the object had some power to send a single communication through the system. That one burst of information had changed the Space Defense Force. Captain Darius wondered what took the brass so long to construct the *Jericho*. Maybe the information was difficult to understand. It was sent in a variety of Earth languages, but that didn't mean the information was clear. Who could say what an alien mind thinks?

Zeke was convinced more every day that the artifact was not of human origin. The idea that it might be from the future was exciting but unreasonable. If humanity had discovered the ability to travel through time, it wouldn't have sent a device back that would be left in deep space for so long. Why not drop it in Earth's orbit? The time travel hypothesis didn't make sense to Captain Darius. And that left only one massive, mysterious option — aliens.

It was always a possibility. Humans were conquering space, so the odds were high that other intelligent species had done the same. Someone had seen Earth from a distance and recognized the human race's potential. They left a calling card for mankind to find, but what was it, Darius wondered? More than just a stone tablet, he surmised. Humans have sent all sorts of things into space, and they all had information in various forms on them. If nothing else, Darius expected the artifact to have data on it or in it. The only question in his mind was whether they could decipher it.

The weeks passed slowly at first. It took everyone some time to settle down and get into a routine. The Marines on board did a great job of keeping their people engaged. There were regular competitions and group activities in the REC. Many of the ship's enlisted crew joined in. Darius had worried that Lieutenant Colt and Master Sergeant Steel might not keep a handle on their people for such a long voyage, but they had done a superb job. The Marines kept busy with PT, simulator training, and equipment maintenance. They also shadowed the ship's crew, but that turned out to be a futile exercise since the ship needed very little maintenance. The Fleet crew were just plain bored. The *Jericho* had reached the optimal speed and had no enemies to fight, so the ship needed very little from the crew. The engines were lit periodically but just long enough to run diagnostics. The power core was still in the green; Zeke had never seen a more efficient power system on any ship in the Fleet.

Relationships were another issue, but everyone seemed to be getting along so far. And no one had come down sick or injured since the ship left *Ares Station*. It was, for all intents and purposes, an uneventful cruise. Normally, that was exactly what Zeke Darius wanted, but as they drew within two weeks of the destination, he decided it was time to lay all his cards on the table for his senior officers.

The Ward Room was filled quickly, first with the Naval personnel and then with the two Marines. Darius waited until everyone sat down before explaining why he had called for the meeting.

"Thank you all for coming," Darius said to start the briefing. "I won't waste time. We have another component to this mission than was previously revealed."

"You mean we're not just testing the new ship?" Nash asked.

"No," Darius replied. "Although that is part of this mission. Just before leaving *Ares Station,* I was given another assignment. It goes without saying that what I'm about to tell you is top secret and can never be discussed outside this room."

"Juicy," Vivan Ramos said. She winked at Lieutenant Colt, who had a perfect poker face, but Darius knew they had been spending much time together over the past several weeks.

"Top Secret? Now you're talking," Pete Best declared.

Everyone seemed happy to get more information on the mission. The only person who seemed unfazed by the Captain's revelation was Master Sergeant Steel. The veteran NCO was calm and quiet, his steady gaze never leaving Darius' face.

"There is an object just beyond Saturn," Darius said. He felt both giddy to be talking about the artifact at long last and a little bit foolish.

"What kind of object?" Nash asked. "An old probe or satellite?"

"No, not that. It's not ours," the Captain explained. "It's not space debris either. It's not a chunk of rock or ice. We're talking about a foreign body here."

"And you know that because..." Lieutenant Colt asked.

"Initially, it was understood because the object is not moving," Captain Darius said. "It's completely stationary."

"Is that even possible?" Pete Best asked.

"If it isn't moving, then it must have some sort of propulsion," Vivian Ramos said. "Is it a ship?"

"It's small," the Captain continued. "We don't have eyes on it yet, but we're thinking of something the size of a small piece of furniture. However, it has straight edges, which is another indication that it is crafted, not natural."

"You said initially," Master Sergeant Remmy Steel said. "How long has it been out there?"

"Excellent question, Sergeant Steel," Zeke replied. "We don't know. It was first recognized by the Pioneer Probe over two hundred years ago."

That fact silenced the room. Everyone looked shocked, and Darius couldn't blame them. He had been shocked. Commander Lori Lee had been, too, and she looked at him with understanding. She hadn't wanted to talk about it, and Darius respected her wishes, but they were both shocked by the revelation of the artifact.

"Over two hundred years," Henry Nash finally said. "It's just been out there, waiting on us."

"Maybe going to get it isn't such a good idea," Vivian said. "It could be hostile."

"That is true," Captain Darius said. "But there's more to the story than you know. Thirty years ago, it beamed a single transmission to Earth."

"Man, I'm getting a bad feeling about this, Captain," Pete Best said.

"It can communicate?" Lieutenant Micky Colt asked.

"It doesn't appear to be a communication device, but it is capable of communication. It's been receiving radio signals from us for a long time," the Captain explained. "We know that because it sent the message in a variety of human languages."

"Studying us," Pete Best proclaimed, "that's the actions of an enemy agent, sir."

"That may be, Lieutenant, but we still have a job to do," the Captain replied.

"What was the message?" Master Sergeant Steel asked.

"This," Darius told him. "The ship, the Prometheus Drive, and information on how to build it."

"You're saying that all this engineering tech is from that object?" Henry Nash asked. "You've got to be kidding me."

"I am not," Captain Darius said. "Commander Lee and I were given a briefing just moments before leaving *Ares Station*. But that's all we know. The object is of unknown origin but advanced technology. It's been in the Sol system for over two centuries. My guess is that it has been waiting for us to reach a threshold of technological advancement. Once we reached that stage, it sent us the plans for a ship capable of reaching the object."

"It wants us to come and get it," Vivan Ramos said. "Does anyone else find that unsettling?"

"Yes," Commander Lee said from the far end of the table.

"It does seem like something that should give us pause," Lieutenant Colt said. "It's rarely a good idea to do what the enemy wants you to do."

"First, we don't know that the artifact, whatever it is, has any nefarious intent. At this point, we don't know, but I wouldn't say it's our enemy lieutenant. And remember that the authorities on Earth had the information for three decades before they used it."

"If this vessel indicates that thing's intent," Henry Nash said, "it must be for our good. This is the most well-constructed spacecraft I've ever known, and I've studied every design the fleet had built in the last century."

"Maybe it's a device meant to help us," Darius said. "Maybe it will spur on our understanding of technology and physics. That isn't so far-fetched; humans have been promoting the idea for centuries."

"What is the plan moving forward?" Master Sergeant Steel asked.

"It will be picked up on our close-range radar scans in the next few days," Darius said. "We'll begin a counter-thrust burn soon that will slow us down and allow us to maneuver on thruster power. Once we reach the artifact, the Marines will send a team to retrieve the object."

"Spacewalk?" Lieutenant Colt said.

"Affirmative," the Captain replied. "I'm going to ask you to wait and inform the team participating just before retrieval. Once we have the artifact on board, we won't be able to keep people from talking about it, but let's do our best to keep the secret for now."

"What about your people on the Bridge?" Sergeant Steel asked.

"We'll ensure they don't talk," Commander Lee said. "The ship's computer will log the object, but we'll mark it as unimportant, and that should keep it from popping up again on the radar scans."

"This is historic," Nash said, warming up to the idea. "Really historic. An alien device found on our watch? That's something to write home about."

"Only it's classified," Pete Best argued. "We can't talk about it."

"The Brass will probably deny it exists," Vivan said. "Just another rumor that no one can prove."

"That's a cynical perspective," the Captain said.

"But historically accurate," she argued. "All through modern history, there have been rumors of alien sightings, landings, abductions, and craft retrieval. It's become part of the fabric of our culture, Captain. I think it goes back to the crash at Roswell."

"UFOs," Nash added.

"Unsubstantiated rumors," Zeke declared. "Let's not start drumming up conspiracy theories. We have a job to do, people. And I, for one, am looking forward to having something to do."

"We'll start training," Lieutenant Colt said, "and have a team ready."

"Outstanding. Once we have the artifact on board, the plan is to turn around and head back home," Captain Darius continued, giving orders. "At that point in time, all communication will be held pending oversight review. Nothing about the artifact or this mission itself can be talked about. I'm counting on each of you to inform your people of the serious nature of this mission and the confidentiality required."

"Copy that, sir," Micky Colt said.

"Finally, something to write home about, and we can't even talk about it," Pete Best said. "Unbelievable."

"Unless you have questions then..." Captain Darius said.

Everyone stood up. The news was fascinating, yet there was nothing to do for the next several days but boring, mundane flight adjustments. It was exciting, especially after ten weeks of monotony on the *Jericho*, but they would still have to wait several more days to find out what the artifact was. And Darius was just as anxious as the others to discover what was waiting for them in the dark stretch of space beyond Saturn. He only hoped it wasn't anything they would regret.

CHAPTER 12

THEY DIDN'T SPEAK AGAIN until they reached his office. Lieutenant Micky Colt wasn't sure how to feel about the news. It was just so hard to wrap his mind around an unidentified object in space.

The Lieutenant was a meticulous man. He was seeing Fleet Lieutenant Vivian Ramos as often as their schedules allowed, but he kept his office neat and organized. There wasn't much else to do on the ship anyway. He ran sims with the platoon, did PT, and wrote daily reports that he logged into the ship's computers, but nothing was taxing. He even took the time to clean his weapons, making sure every part was pristine and well-oiled. After every sim, he scrubbed his armor, paying special attention to his battle helmet, and still, he had an abundance of free time.

Master Sergeant Remmy Steel slipped into a chair at the small table in the Lieutenant's office. He was a quiet man who took everything in. He had piercing eyes, and it was impossible to read his expression.

"Tell me what you're thinking, Master Sergeant," Colt said.

"Don't know what to think, sir," Remmy replied.

"Are you worried?"

"Try not to worry until I have to," he said. "Don't know what the object is. Could be anything, or nothing at all."

"It sent a message to Earth," Colt pointed out.

"Well, sir, something did. Might be that object, might be something else."

Micky had to admit the NCO was right. Just because they got a transmission didn't guarantee that the artifact was what sent it.

"Well, I think we should start considering the possibilities," Colt said. "It's our job to protect the ship."

"Contingencies are good," Steel said. "And we don't have anything else to do."

"Ain't that the truth," Colt said. "What are the odds it's dangerous?"

"Fifty-fifty."

"Can we scan it for biologicals?"

"Should," Remmy said. "I don't know about the ship, but we'll take some handheld scanners. I'll check the loadout bay and make sure we've got what we need. But if something is frozen on that thing, we bring in the ship..."

"Well, at least we've got a three-month turnaround," Colt said, ignoring the shiver that ran down his spine. "If it's got a pathogen on it, we should know before we're around other people. They can fry this entire ship if that's the case, fly it straight into the sun or something."

"Might even have a nuke on board," Remmy said. "We should find out."

"I'll speak to Lieutenant Ramos about it."

Colt was thankful to have Vivian on board the ship. Without a Marine CO on board, he forced himself not to spend too much time with his platoon. He might have to make hard decisions in combat, and he needed to see them as tools, not as people, and certainly not as friends. It wasn't easy. Micky had no ambitions to climb through the ranks. He loved being a platoon officer, and if they promoted him out of the line of fire, he would resign. But on the *Jericho*, he had to be both a flag officer and the platoon commander. It was a difficult assignment.

"What about the spacewalk?" Micky asked. "Are you qualified?"

"We all are, sir," Sergeant Steel said. He would know the Master Sergeant had made it his mission to know everything there was to know about the platoon. Not just their ranks and backgrounds but also their skills and propensities in combat situations.

"That's good, but I only want one team to go out. You can lead them, Master Sergeant. I'll get the Captain's plan of action, but I'm guessing we'll get close, maybe forty or fifty meters. It shouldn't take you long."

"We'll wrap it in an inflatable," Steel said. "Keep it fully contained when we bring it on board."

"And you'll have to go into quarantine," Colt said, trying to sound encouraging despite the news he was conveying. "It's protocol."

"Roger that. We'll have everything ready, sir. You won't get complaints about anything."

"And what if it isn't dangerous," Micky Colt said. "What if it is some wondrous thing that will change all our lives."

"Then I'm sure the Brass will find a way to ruin it, sir."

Micky Colt laughed. Remmy didn't often make jokes and rarely said a negative word about the Corps or the Fleet, but alone in Colt's office, they both chuckled because what Remmy implied was all too often true.

"I suppose you're right about that," Colt said. "We can run some sims on space junk retrieval. It won't be zero-g, but we can do nothing about that."

"If the object is just floating there in space, we shouldn't have a problem," Remmy said. "I'll make first contact, just to be certain it's safe. If it isn't, you recall the team."

"The Captain won't like that," Colt pointed out.

"Maybe not, and it's not our call to leave the thing where it's at, but it would be better to reassess the plan before trying to retrieve it. I think the Captain can spare a few hours to ensure that thing hurts no one else."

"You think it'll be dangerous?"

"I think it could be," Remmy said. "I'd like to be prepared for that possibility."

"All right, we'll work up the sims and run the fire teams through them. Whichever team looks the best on the computers we'll send with you."

"Sounds like a plan, sir."

"It is. In the meantime, if you think of anything else, I want to know about it," Colt said. "I don't want to get blindsided by this thing. Any and every possibility is on the table. We tell the platoon that the ship is picking up an old probe- another boring task."

"They'll all want to do it," Remmy said. "Just to break up the monotony."

"Can't blame them for that. Frankly, I'm a little jealous that you're going and not me."

"Can't risk you, LT."

"I know it, but I don't have to like it."

"You know what I haven't heard, sir? It's why that civie, Connor O'Dell, is really on the ship. It has to be because of the artifact, I think."

"You're probably right. I haven't seen him much, though."

"Someone takes his meals to his berth," Remmy said. "I've spoken with a few of the spacemen tasked with that duty. They say he's friendly but doesn't come out of his cabin."

"I'm not sure I could handle that much solitude," Colt confessed.

"Me either, sir, but keeping him in his quarters is the easiest way to ensure that word doesn't get out to the crew."

"Yeah, I suppose so."

"Makes me wonder who's really in charge, Captain Darius or the O'Dell character."

"You mean when it comes to the artifact."

Remmy nodded. "Yes, sir, that's exactly what I mean. My gut says he doesn't care if the object is safe or not. If it costs us all our lives to get that thing back to civilization, I'm guessing he'll make that call."

"Civilian contractors are known to be sloppy," Colt agreed. "We should have a plan for this O'Dell guy, too. If he tries to override the Captain or put the ship in danger, we'll need to neutralize him."

"That could cost us our careers."

"Better to lose my job than try to live with knowing I could have saved our platoon but didn't," Colt said. "If it comes to that, we'll do what we have to do."

"Yes sir, my thoughts exactly."

"Glad we're on the same page, Master Sergeant. Let me know if there's anything you're going to need that we don't have."

"Roger that, sir. I'll get right on it."

Sergeant Steel got to his feet and saluted. It almost seemed like a bad habit after weeks of monotony on the ship, but Lieutenant Micky Colt got to his feet and returned the salute. Military discipline was about all they had on the long cruise, and Colt wasn't going to ignore it. He was grateful Sergeant Steel didn't neglect it and forced Micky to call him on it. They agreed, and that made the cruise a little easier. But there were still times when Micky felt the ship's walls were closing in on him. The only thing keeping him sane was Vivian, and he couldn't wait to talk to her about the artifact.

CHAPTER 13

CAPTAIN ZEKE DARIUS, a senior officer of the *S.D.F. Jericho,* returned to his office after his daily inspection tour. Normally, inspections of a starship that is in service are a tense affair. NCOs push the enlisted crew to have every component polished, clean, and ready to be put under a microscope. But unlike most fleet starships, the Jericho was in such good shape that there was very little for the crew to do.

They stood watch, cleaned, and marveled that nothing was breaking down. That made the Captain's inspections more of a friendly exercise. Every day, Darius expected to be given the news that something was malfunctioning. He wouldn't have been surprised to find a valve leaking or a gasket cracked. On starships, wires shorted out, metal fatigued, and things broke down frequently. The *Jericho* being a new ship didn't exempt it from having problems, not when the new tech was usually riddled with bugs. Things could be constructed with the best intentions, but it wasn't until those components were put under the stress of performing in real-time that the weaknesses became apparent. Still, nothing on the *Jericho* had broken or malfunctioned. They raced through the solar system day after day in a monotonous repetition that seemed almost more taxing than if things were going wrong.

He was ready for half an hour in his massage lounger. It had become a daily ritual. He served a tour on the Bridge, made a tour of the ship, returned to his office to file a report in the ship's log, and then snatched half an hour in his massage chair before returning to the Bridge for another four-hour duty watch. When the door to his office slid open, he found Connor O'Dell waiting for him inside. Since leaving Ares Station, Darius had only seen the civilian twice in the ten weeks. He had been a topic of conversation among the crew at first, but he had proven to be a hermit and only left his quarters on a very rare occasion.

"Captain," O'Dell said.

"Mr. O'Dell, what a surprise," Darius replied, trying to keep the resentment of finding the civilian in his office unannounced out of his voice.

"I suppose it is," the government official replied. He seemed oblivious to the senior officer's annoyance. "But we're getting close to Saturn. By my calculations, we should be starting the retro thrust soon."

"You are correct," Darius said, moving around his desk and sitting in his tall executive chair.

"That's good," O'Dell said. "And I suppose you've told your officers what we're going after?"

Darius guessed the civilian's questions weren't unlike when he went on a tour. Of course, the specialists knew their business better than the Captain, but his job was to ensure they were on top of things. What might be considered an insignificant issue could be life-threatening in outer space's cold, hard vacuum.

"I have," Darius said. "The Marines are making plans. We'll begin slowing down in approximately eighteen hours."

"This is so exciting," O'Dell said. "I can't wait to get my hands on the artifact."

"Is that your plan?"

"Of course. It's why the President sent me in the first place. Can you imagine what we could learn? The entire history of our species is going to change. This is a watershed moment, captain."

"Perhaps, but we're talking about an alien object, sir. You'll under-stand if we observe all Fleet protocols regarding infectious disease and safety."

"You want to put the object in quarantine?"

"Until I'm sure it doesn't harbor anything harmful to my crew or the human race," Darius said.

"That's absurd."

Darius leaned his head to the side slightly as if he were inspecting an unsavory-looking dish from the galley.

"If you're going to lock it away, I insist on being locked up with it," O'Dell said. "We have to study it."

"We've waited this long; why rush now? You'll have as much time as you like with it once we return to the inner system."

"That shows how very little you know about politics, Captain."

If it was meant as an insult, it missed the mark. Captain Zeke Darius took pride in avoiding politics, whether with the Space Defense Force or the Inner System Government.

O'Dell wasn't finished. "The moment it's turned over to the Intersystem officials, everything about it will be hounded by the media. The committee will explore it, and we both know how inefficient that would be."

"Maybe," Darius said, but Connor jumped back in before he could say more.

"It's highly classified, but that only means half the duly elected leaders don't want anything to do with it. If they get their way, it'll be locked up in a vault so deep no one will ever see it again. Don't you get it, Captain? These three months on the return voyage are the chance of a lifetime. That's why I lobbied hard to get assigned to your ship."

Darius didn't get it, but he understood how the bureaucracy functioned. It rarely made sense to him. He had always believed in following orders even when he didn't understand why he was being sent out. That was the beauty of a starship. On board a space vessel, he was the ultimate authority. Every system had a clearly defined purpose. Every crew member was assigned a specific role. Everything made logical sense, and he could lead, even when their mission seemed absurd.

"If that's what you want, I'll see you have access," Darius said. "Just keep in mind you'll be eating emergency rations and sleeping in the quarantine bunk room with four Marines. There's nothing I can do about that. It's standard operating procedures. We have no idea what that thing is. The chances it could somehow infect the ship are too high."

"I'll take that chance, Captain. I'm not here for a vacation."

"All right, I'll put your request in the log."

"Thank you."

"So what do you think it is, Mr. O'Dell? You've studied it, I'm assuming."

"My entire career," Connor said. "Once they started building the Jericho, I was recruited right out of university. I'm convinced it's from outside our system."

"Alien?" Darius asked.

"If you're asking about little green men, then no," Connor explained. "But from higher lifeforms? Absolutely. My theory, if you'll indulge me?"

Darius nodded. He had nothing better to do than to listen to his guest, and he was just as curious as anyone else on board.

"I wasn't a proponent of the Seed Theory at first. Are you familiar with it?"

"The idea that the human race was begun on Earth by an alien race."

"An advanced intelligence," Connor said with a nod. "Some people say, aliens, some people say, God, all we know for certain is that there is a huge amount of information in the cellular DNA of the simplest organisms. Our understanding of micro-biology and genetics dealt a death blow to the Theory of Evolution. There's too much information for life to arise spontaneously."

"Sort of like having a book come together by random letters without any outside intervention," Darius said.

"Not just a book, an entire library. But we don't need to get into the specifics," Connor pressed on. "Someone or something had to plant that genetic information, which leads me to believe two core facts. First, we are not alone in the universe. Secondly, there is much higher intelligence in the universe. Let the philosophers and theologians debate who it is or what our purpose is. Maybe we are an extension of a pre-existing species, or maybe we're something brand new. The higher intelligence may study us from a distance, watching us develop and grow. Who knows, and frankly, who cares? The point I'm driving at is that the artifact may be from beyond our solar system and of greater intelligence. I'm less interested in who left it here than why they left it and what we can learn from it."

"Which is?"

"Take your pick," Connor said. The conversation so enthused the civilian that he rose to his feet "Physics, Cosmology, Genetics, History, even medicine will be turned on its head. All our knowledge is based on suppositions, Captain. Think about it. Einstein's Theory of Relativity is based on the idea that the speed of light is constant. But we've known since the late eighteen hundreds that it isn't. Light slows down as it passes through matter, and you know as well as anyone that space isn't an empty void. There's even evidence that light was moving exponentially faster at the beginning of the Big Bang. But all our models and mathematical theories are built on constants. Once you admit there could be variations, be it in the speed of light or the universe's age, everything we have come to understand starts to break down. Think about that for just a moment, Captain. What if everything, and I mean everything we think we know, is all just a house of cards."

"Doesn't our engineering and technological advances prove that what we know is true? At least on some level?"

"Maybe," Connor said. "But let me ask you a question. Is the *Jericho* the same as every other Fleet starship?"

"No," Darius said. "It's different. But the systems are familiar. It's not so different that it redefines what a spaceship is."

"I'll concede that point, but I'm betting there are more ways this vessel is different than just the systems it employs."

Darius thought about it. He knew the ship like the back of his hand and spent time touring every section daily. That was unusual for a ship's Captain, but it was partly because the *Jericho* was so different that he felt compelled to learn more about her. He studied aerospace engineering as part of his higher education. Starship officers had to know how their vessels functioned. Of course, he had never had the time to stroll through the other space vessels he had led. He made inspections, which were part of his command responsibilities, but usually, there was so much going on in any section of a starship that he didn't have time to go over more than one system at a time. Normally, he would have requests from every officer on board seeking more resources. Allocating what they had was part of his duty, but only on the Jericho was nothing malfunctioning or bugging out. They didn't need anything. The ship was a well-oiled machine, and his crew were simply along for the ride.

"She's different, alright," Darius said.

"Different, how?"

"She works better," Darius said. "But I think you know that already."

"Your crew is bored because there's nothing to do," Connor said with a mischievous grin. "I've heard them talking in the REC. Every system, from propulsion to waste management, is so well designed they don't require regular maintenance."

"That's been the case so far, but she's a new ship."

"And new ships usually run this smoothly?" Connor pressed.

"No, not like this. New systems have bugs and hiccups in the design or construction that weren't foreseen and have to be corrected once the ship is exposed to the rigors of space travel."

"Yeah, that's what I'm talking about," Connor said. "There's no bugs in our systems, Captain. No flaws in her design. If it were just the engines that seemed to work perfectly, you might chalk it up to a new ship with new and maybe better components, but it isn't just propulsion. It's the entire vessel, even the parts designed for human habitation. Everything, from the width of the corridors to the size of the toilet stalls, is perfect. This office is exactly the right size for both space efficiency and productivity. The water treatment, recycling, storage, and life support are all dialed in perfectly. Captain, we don't see that level of precision in even the best human design. This entire ship is the artifact's calling card. It's saying that after seven thousand years of recorded human history, of mankind's pursuit of higher knowledge in every discipline, nothing we've ever achieved can match the excellence of this ship.

"I know scientists who spent their entire career studying the designs. They were beamed to us thirty years ago. The government gave the brightest minds carte blanche to study the information in that single transmission. If that's all the information we ever get from the artifact, it will still revolutionize our species. Once the information is released, it will advance our design and engineering technology by a century. Think about that for a moment, Captain. We're about to take a significant leap in our understanding of everything."

"So why did the government sit on the designs for so long?" Captain Darius asked. "If it was so transformative, why keep it secret?"

"Because of the very nature of government," Connor replied. "They don't get in a hurry to do anything. I know for certain there are over a dozen reports on the transmission. They all say the same thing: the design is familiar yet advanced. No one knew if it would work. They debated everything for years until, eventually, enough people said that to learn anything new, we had to build it. Once they did, the debate was practically over. Your first shakedown cruise was the decisive factor. The Prometheus Engine is flawless and the most efficient propulsion device we have ever built. The ship's design is simple yet well conceived, and humans can habituate in it for much longer than any other space vessel. And now, more than two months into our first-ever deep space mission, nothing has gone wrong. The crew is content, the ship functions just as conceived, and we are making history by traveling at speeds no other ship in the fleet can match. And all that without the usual bevy of problems that plague our vessels and are so commonplace we need large crews of workers and big cargo holds full of replacement components to stay afloat if I can use that imagery from the Navy."

Darius nodded in acceptance of everything that Connor O'Dell had said. It was all true, or at least it had been so far. There were no issues with the electrical wiring or the engines. The life support systems were functioning at optimal levels of output and efficiency. Their fuel levels, which included air to breathe and water, which could, in a pinch, be converted to oxygen and hydrogen, were all above the estimates Darius had been given. The *Jericho* seemed like the perfect ship, and yet the mission still gave the Captain pause.

"There's one question that remains," he said. "Perhaps the most important question."

"What's that?" Connor asked as he leaned onto the back of the chair in front of Zeke's desk.

"What do they want with us?"

For the first time since their conversation began, Darius saw doubt in the eyes of the government liaison. Connor O'Dell didn't have a good answer to that question.

"Perhaps they are simply wanting to share knowledge," he said.

It was Zeke's turn to scoff. "Come on, Mr. O'Dell, now you sound naive. When has anyone ever shared advanced knowledge without expecting something in return?"

"They might not be like us," he offered.

"Oh, I think they are," Captain Darius said. "For whatever reason, they put their device in our system and gave us the ability to access it. They wanted us to find it, which implies they want something we have that they don't."

"Not necessarily," Connor argued. "They might be so advanced that they give without thinking of anything in return."

Captain Zeke Darius was not a historian, nor did he claim to have any insight into the psyche of mankind, but he was wise enough to understand that whatever had put the artifact in their system, it wasn't a gift. It felt to him more like the cheese in a mouse trap.

"Nothing is free in life," Darius said. "It always costs someone. And even in the most charitable situations, there is, at the very least, a hope that said gift will lead to a life change for the recipient. We give food and clothing to the homeless with the hope that they won't fight each other for meager resources and that maybe they will become useful, independent members of society. We give scholarships to bright, young minds in the hope that those minds will work for the betterment of mankind. There is no such thing as a gift without some expectation from the giver. So what could this higher intelligence want from us?"

"That I don't know," Connor O'Dell said.

"Maybe we should know the answer to that question before we claim the artifact."

"There's no way to know the question until we have the device."

"So maybe we don't take it at all," Zeke said. "That would seem to be the course of action with the least risk to our species."

"Without risk, there is no reward. What explorer and inventor throughout history didn't take risks?"

Zeke didn't disagree, but he wondered what the populace would think if they knew what their government was risking. Secrecy had always been part of the military and government. Ostensibly, it was to keep one's enemies from knowing what one was truly capable of. However, the general public often used that same level of secrecy. Zeke thought about the historic nature of their mission. Would it ever be known? And if it was, would he be seen as the intrepid explorer or as the fool who brought ruin to the entire human race?

CHAPTER 14

"IT'S TIME," Captain Darius said after settling into his chair on the Bridge.

It was comfortable and familiar to him after nearly three months. The monitors against the walls of the room showed the contrast of dark space and the bright yellow glow of Saturn and her rings. It was a beautiful sight. But Zeke was more interested in the *Jericho's* systems as they made the rotation and began to slow down.

"Let's have all systems report," he continued. One by one, the senior officers on the bridge reported in.

"Engineering is green," Lieutenant Nash said.

"Life systems are green," another officer announced.

"Navigation is set. We're in the sweet spot, Captain," Lieutenant Vivian Ramos said.

The report went on. Zeke checked off the systems on his small display screen built into his chair's armrest.

"Alright, engage thrusters," he ordered. "Let's begin rotation."

They were hurdling through space at over two million kilometers an hour. Yet the ship could turn on its center axis and slowly flip end over end. They rotated the long, corkscrew-shaped spaceship until it was flying backward.

"We're in position for retrograde burn," Vivian Ramos said.

"Engines?"

"Primed and ready, Captain," Nash replied.

It was overkill. The maneuver was standard. Every ship in the fleet operated in the same fashion. With no resistance in space, a vessel could ignite its engines and propel itself forward. And when it needed to slow down, it reversed its relative position and burned the engines again.

"Let's start slow," Zeke said. "Give me ten percent."

"Aye, engaging engines at ten percent," Henry Nash replied.

The Prometheus Drive was a new technology that seemed to function flawlessly. The engines began to produce thrust, and the ship's velocity immediately began to slow. Still, two million KPH took time to reverse. They would be at the job for hours.

"Purring like a kitten, Captain," the chief engineer said. "We're ready for whatever you need, sir."

"Let's not get in a hurry. Radar, can you locate our target?"

"Not yet," Lieutenant Pete Best said. He was the weapons officer but also in charge of the radar, which was meant to pick up any object within range of the ship. "It's too small."

"What if it's gone?" Vivian Ramos asked. "We've come all this way for nothing."

"Wouldn't surprise me," Pete Best joined in. "Don't get me wrong, I like the ship, but this has been one long, boring cruise."

"Armed to the teeth and nothing to shoot at, Lieutenant?" Commander Lori Lee asked.

That got a chuckle from the other officers, including Zeke himself.

"We haven't done anything but computer sims," Pete complained. "Every other system has been tested but mine."

"That may be true," Zeke replied. "But having nothing to shoot at should be a good thing. I hope we never need your weapons, Pete. Lieutenant Nash, take her to twenty percent."

"Aye, increasing thrust to twenty percent."

On and on it went. Eventually, they increased the power to fifty percent of its capacity. It burned at that level for six hours and slowed the ship's speed by half. After that, Captain Zeke sent Henry Nash and his technicians to check the Prometheus Drive. It was overkill. Nothing about the long burn had indicated there were problems with the engine, but they were so far from help that he felt it prudent to take things slow and careful.

Zeke was about to leave the deck when a junior officer spotted the artifact on the radar. They were over a hundred million kilometers from any other ship, but standard operating procedures for an SDF ship required the radar to be monitored at all times.

"Captain, I think I'm picking something up," the junior officer said. It was a young woman in her mid-twenties and not long out of the Officer Training Academy. She wasn't privy to the true nature of the object.

"Visual?" he asked.

"Too far out, sir," she replied. "It's small, maybe a chunk of space rock?"

"Could be," he told her. "Start a profile. Mark the object as Romeo One in the plot."

It was more standard procedure. Space was full of all kinds of matter, from rocky formations to comets and quasars. Some asteroids were covered in ice and swarms of tiny bits of matter moving like lead pellets fired from a shotgun. The *Jericho's* sonic shielding either moved or broke the space debris that came near the ship so that it wasn't dangerous. But any object larger than a pebble was marked on the plot. The *Jericho* was still moving at a million KPH. The object appeared on the radar zone's edge, some thirty-five million kilometers away.

"Marking object Romeo One," the junior officer said.

It was all part of the mission. They marked all of Saturn's moons. There were space probes in extremely high orbit around the golden planet. By the start of Captain Zeke's watch the following day, he had a full report from Henry Nash's engineers. The Prometheus Drive was in perfect condition, and they were well ahead of projections for fuel consumption. They fired the engines again and slowed the ship down even further. Navigation officer Vivian Ramos plotted their course to the artifact.

"Five days," she said to Captain Darius, who looked at Commander Lori Lee.

"And we'll be how close?" Commander Lee asked.

"One hundred meters," Vivian Ramos said.

"Do it," the Captain ordered. "We'll make the final burns to bring us to a static position relative to the object on the last day."

It felt almost hollow, just another order. And yet, somehow, they were making history.

"Do we need to make an announcement?" Lee asked.

"I don't think so," Zeke said. "We aren't doing anything out of the ordinary. Let's call it a retrieval exercise. Once the artifact is on board, we won't be able to hide what it is."

They weren't alone on the Bridge. The watch duty had returned to normal, meaning senior and junior officers were manning their consoles. His senior staff knew about the artifact but had done an excellent job keeping the news about the alien device a secret. Several junior officers and technicians on the Bridge stiffened when Zeke said, "... we won't be able to hide what it is." Their curiosity had been alerted, but they were professional enough not to turn around or ask what he was talking about.

"Fair enough," Lori Lee said. "I'll inform the Marines."

"Let Connor O'Dell know, too," Zeke said. "He's planning on being there when it's brought on board."

It was barely a conversation, but enough to get the rumor mill running. Starships were not built for secrets. Too many people in a small space with very little news from the outside world made the perfect recipe for gossip. News of any kind, real or imagined, was highly prized on an SDF ship. And before Zeke Darius left the Bridge, the news was spreading. As he made his tour of the ship, he saw the looks. Most of the crew paid him little enough attention unless he was addressing them directly. But he caught plenty of sidelong glances as he walked the corridors of the *Jericho*. Something was up, and the crew was determined to find out what it was.

CHAPTER 15

"SO, WHAT ARE WE GOING AFTER?" Staff Sergeant Laila McPherson asked.

"What's that?" Remmy said, pretending not to know what she was talking about.

"Don't act like you don't know, Master Sergeant," she pressed him. "You've been privy to our real mission from day one."

"That's not true," he said, remembering he hadn't learned about the artifact on the first day of their voyage.

"Just spill it," she insisted.

They were alone in the Aft Launch Bay. The *Jericho* wasn't a traditional warship. It didn't have large cargo holds full of fighter craft or bombers. There was a single launch bay on the lower deck at the very rear of the ship. Inside was a single military drop ship big enough for just one platoon of Marines and the usual assortment of EVA equipment and tools for various jobs. The two NCOs were busy visually inspecting the armored military space suits on board the ship.

The Bravo team had been running extra-vehicular-activity or EVA sims for days. They weren't as fully immersive as most combat sims since they couldn't mimic zero gravity, and anything outside the ship would be in a weightless environment. Still, at least it had the Marine platoon planning and thinking about EVA work. He didn't expect any fighting, but he had no idea what they might encounter with the strange object.

"We're going after something, aren't we?" she continued the interrogation. "Everyone is talking about it."

"What's there to talk about," he asked.

"How about the fact that we are too far from Saturn for this to be a probe recovery," she pointed out. "Besides, if some piece of space gear bugged out, the SDF wouldn't bother trying to fix it. They would send a replacement."

"Okay," Remmy said as he checked a seam between two armor plates on one of the space suits.

"So..." McPherson asked. "What are we going after? It's alien tech, isn't it?"

"What gives you that idea?" Remmy asked. He had already decided to tell her what they were doing but didn't want to make it easy. It was too much fun making her work for it.

"What else would be this far out?" she asked. "There aren't any space stations or transports. We're the first humans to reach this part of the system, right? So, what could the Fleet want so bad that they send their shiny new ship out for six months to retrieve it?"

"I can think of all sorts of scientific research projects that might take us out here," he said.

"No way," she argued. "The Brass wouldn't risk so much for a space rock."

"Maybe it's from another system," Remmy said. "Or another galaxy. The egg-heads would give their left arm for something like that."

"They might, but the Space Defense Force wouldn't," she said. "Besides, I can tell when you're lying, Sergeant. You get a look on your face that gives you away."

"You saying I have a tell, McPherson?"

"Damn straight," she said with a grin. "So..."

"Alright, you're bound to find out anyway. We're getting something, but no one knows what it is exactly."

"No one knows?"

"Only that it's got a geometrical shape with straight lines," Remmy confessed.

"Nothing in nature has straight lines," McPherson said. "It has to be man-made."

"Man or..."

"Or little green men," she said. "You've got to be kidding me, right?"

"Isn't that what you were thinking it was?"

"Well, yeah, but I didn't believe it," she said. "Is it part of a ship or something?"

"We don't know," Remmy told her. "Only that it's been out here for a long time. Now help me check these suits. We will use them, and I don't want any problems."

The look she shot his way was flirtatious, but they were both professionals. They knew that relationships within a platoon were more than problematic; they were dangerous. And while Staff Sergeant Laila McPherson might be the kind of woman Remmy could get serious with, he held himself in check. Besides, Laila had already seen someone from the ship's crew. It was impossible to avoid the shipboard gossip; the hottest information was always who was seeing who. Dating wasn't really possible. On short cruises, there were always hookups and short-term flings. But the *Jericho* was on a long cruise, and while she was a spacious ship for a Fleet vessel, there still wasn't anywhere to go or much to do. Couples watched movies together. Those with private quarters enjoyed some privacy, but very little on the starship went unnoticed.

"Aliens... it's hard to believe," McPherson said.

"Is," Remmy replied, hanging the space suit back in its locker.

"I never really believed in them. Never thought we would ever leave the solar system."

"We're not," Remmy pointed out.

"Yeah, but someone has. And that means we will someday. You ever think about what's out there?"

"Not really."

"It could be anything. Little green men, flying saucers, beings so powerful they can crush us with a thought."

"Doubt that," Remmy said.

"But it's possible," Laila insisted. "We just don't know. Maybe we shouldn't disturb it. How many movies have you seen where mankind was better off after making contact with aliens."

"I prefer books."

"You would," she said with a flirtatious laugh. "It's really something."

"Something you need to keep a lid on," Remmy said. "Think about the fact that we've got three months left just to return home."

"That's a long time with a secret like this."

"It won't be a secret once it's on board, but hopefully, by then, we'll be running back for the inner system. People can speculate; no one could ever stop that, but we need to keep this on the down low, so to speak. Act like it's no big deal."

"Some people think we've been in contact for a long time."

"Don't start that," Remmy said.

"There are government reports that we've had spacecraft," she argued.

"Whistleblowers and retirees aren't the same as government reports."

"Okay, well, I'm just saying that some people think we've been studying alien technology for a long time."

"Could be," Remmy said, thinking about the beam transmission from the artifact. It had been studied for well over two decades before it was put to use if what the Captain said was accurate.

"Maybe it won't amount to much," McPherson said.

"Probably," Remmy agreed.

"But if it did, we could end up in history books."

"Footnotes, maybe."

"Our names would be attached to the recovery of this thing, Remmy."

He didn't mind her using his first name. Sometimes, a platoon became like family, especially in high-stress situations. They had been on board the *Jericho* long enough to become very familiar with one another. And while no other marines were around, he didn't mind her calling him Remmy. In fact, hearing her say his name gave him a slight thrill. He tried to ignore it and pretend it didn't mean anything, but he knew deep down that it did.

"Could be," he said. "Will for sure if things go south."

"You're such a pessimist."

"Expect the worst, and you'll never be disappointed," he said.

That made her laugh. It was a musical sound to the Master Sergeant, making him feel ten feet tall. He would have done just about anything to make Laila McPherson laugh. He scolded himself for his feelings and doubled down on his commitment to keep their relationship professional. Maybe after this cruise, he thought, things could be different.

After a moment, she stopped laughing, and her face became somber. "What if... what if things are never the same?" she asked.

"Then we'll improvise, adapt, overcome," he said, quoting the timeless motto of the Marine Corps.

"Yeah," she said, working up a smile that didn't reach her eyes and returning to work on the space suit she was inspecting.

Their playful, flirtatious moment was over, and Remmy felt a pang of regret. But the mission came first, and Laila was right; they could have made a monumental mistake.

CHAPTER 16

"LIEUTENANT BEST, please bring up the target on the screen," Captain Darius ordered.

Just behind his seat on the Bridge stood Marine Lieutenant Micky Colt and Master Sergeant Remmy Steel. They were about to get their first look at the artifact. A dark image appeared on the screen. Pete Best was the weapons officer. His fingers flew over the controls of his console as he adjusted the color contrast and increased the light. The dark object began to take shape.

"Wow," Micky said. "Looks like a big rock."

"Rocks don't have straight edges," Vivian Ramos said.

The entire senior staff, including their civilian passenger, Connor O'Dell, was on the bridge. They were drawn to the artifact, fascinated by the unknown and what the object represented. It was a link to something beyond the solar system. The artifact did look like it was made of stone. It was a large, rectangular slab with rough edges and some markings on the flat front. Unlike natural objects in space, it wasn't moving. The artifact was completely still.

"Reminds me of a tombstone," Henry Nash said.

"What are the markings?" Remmy asked.

"Unknown," Captain Darius said, wondering the same thing himself. "We've never been close enough to map it until now. Lieutenant Best…"

"Aye, Captain, getting a full visual map of the artifact now, sir."

"Very good," Darius said. "We'll have computer models for you to study."

"When will be close enough to begin EVA operations?" Lieutenant Colt asked.

"We're on a slow approach," the Captain said. "Two more days. We're going to swing around it and get a good view from all sides. I don't want any surprises."

"Are there any power readings?" Connor O'Dell asked. "Any signals coming from it."

"Negative," the communication officer said.

Remmy almost felt disappointed. They were closer than ever but knew nothing more. The object remained a mystery. He was putting a lot of time into training the Marines for what appeared to be little more than a simple pick-up. Once the object was on board the Jericho, it would be someone else's responsibility to delve into its secrets. The Marines on board wouldn't be needed any longer.

"What are the chances that there's someone else out here?" Remmy said. "Maybe watching that thing and waiting to see what we do?"

"All radar and lidar scans are negative," Pete Best informed him. "There's nothing out here but us."

"None of the Fleet ships could make this trip other than the *Jericho*," Captain Darius said.

"I'm less worried about our people than whoever left that thing for us to find," Remmy said.

"Why would you be concerned?" Connor O'Dell asked. "The artifact wants to be found. It provided us with the means to retrieve it. Why would someone do that to stop us when we're about to complete the task?"

"There's simply too much we don't know," Captain Darius said. "Master Sergeant Steel is right to be guarded. The artifact may be benign, but that doesn't mean it isn't dangerous. We must all be vigilant. From this point forward, I'm issuing a yellow alert. Let's make sure no one is being complacent. I want everyone to be reminded of their tasks and protocols if we must go into an emergency. Is that clear?"

Everyone affirmed the order. The yellow alert didn't mean much more than being ready if the alert status went to Orange or Red. But the crew and Marines needed something to shake them out of the complacency three months in transit had created.

"I want your Marines ready for the EVA and at least one week of quarantine afterward," Darius explained. "We'll use the launch bay and keep it sealed. Only those involved in the retrieval need to be exposed."

"We'll see to it immediately, Captain," Micky Colt replied.

"I'll be joining the quarantine," Connor said. "We need to begin studying the artifact right away."

Micky looked over at Remmy, who shrugged. "We'll move an extra cot into the launch bay. You'll want to bring your blankets and such."

"Of course, of course," Connor said.

"And whatever tools you might need. The Marines will ensure we have food and water," Remmy continued. "The facilities are limited. Are you sure you want to put yourself through that, sir?"

"Absolutely," Connor said.

"Make it so, Master Sergeant. We'll need hourly updates for the ship's log and the Brass back home. Everyone's on pins and needles regarding this mission. Let's make sure we get it done by the numbers."

Remmy spent a whole day making arrangements. The Launch Bay was one of the larger spaces on the ship, but it also housed a drop-ship. If all went well, only the Bravo team would be in quarantine with Remmy and Connor O'Dell. That meant two female Marines who didn't suffer from a great deal of modesty, but Remmy decided to house them in the drop ship. The men would sleep between the ship and the hull on the narrow side, leaving the larger center space clear for whatever needed to be done with the object.

Cots were brought in. The launch bay had an emergency shower but no toilets or basins in one corner. Drinking water had to be carried in, along with food for two weeks. The plan was to be in quarantine for just seven days, but it was prudent to be prepared for a longer stay. Medical supplies were brought in, too, including a big metal case that reminded Remmy of a tool chest. On top was a full-body scanner. They set up a communications console and additional cameras to document everything done with the artifact.

The team gathered whatever they needed and stowed it under their cots. Remmy had an ebook reader and a pack of cards tucked in with extra clothes and his toiletries. All the additional gear was stacking up in the launch bay, and he hoped the claustrophobia wouldn't worsen as the week wore on.

Captain Darius, shadowed by Connor O'Dell, did a complete visual study of the artifact. It was exactly a meter long and two-thirds of a meter high. The back side was flat and contained markings similar to the front.

The rough edges were fifteen centimeters wide. The uneven surfaces were much harder to record and identify. There could be hidden seams for compartments in the dips and nooks of what Darius thought of as rock. It seemed solid, but they weren't close enough for the type of scans that might reveal a hidden compartment inside. The markings were another mystery. Photos of the markings and computer-generated models were sent back to the inner system to be studied by scientists, engineers, linguists, and researchers. No one could decipher the artifact's writing if it were a written language and not something else.

The entire crew of the *Jericho* slept in short shifts. The excitement grew as the hours ran down to the established time for the Marines to go out and get the artifact. There was danger and fear, but mostly a strong curiosity. The ship was convinced that an alien race had left the artifact or sent it to the Sol system. And everyone wanted to know why.

Captain Darius met with Master Sergeant Remmy just two hours before the Bravo team was scheduled to go out on their Extra Vehicular Activity to retrieve the artifact.

"Is everything ready?" Darius asked.

They were in his office, but Zeke didn't sit at his desk. Instead, they stood near the small table. Darius prided himself on reading people, and what he discerned about Master Sergeant Remmy Steel was that the NCO was a competent man.

"Yes, sir," Remmy said.

"What's your gut tell you about this mission, Master Sergeant?"

"On paper, it should be a piece of cake," Remmy said.

"But?"

"But we don't know anything about the artifact or who sent it here, sir. It might not obey the laws of physics as we know them. We may not be able to move it. I don't have a read on it, sir, but my gut says to be ready for the unexpected."

"Only we can't be ready for something we don't understand," Captain Darius pointed out. "I've got a feeling we're in over our head."

"Marines usually are, sir," Remmy replied.

"My job is to keep this crew safe," Darius said, clearly frustrated by the situation. "I know we've got no data to make us think there's anything to worry about. That's what my superiors keep telling me. But if I had my way, we would wait."

"Who says we can't?"

"The Commander-In-Chief for one. Actually, the entire upper

echelon of the military and the government are all breathing down my neck."

"Sounds about right," Remmy said.

"I'm only telling you this because the call is yours once you're outside the ship. If you sense anything is amiss, you have my authority to abort. If the brass doesn't like it, they'll have to live with it. I don't want you to risk yourself or your people."

"Yes, sir, I understand."

"Good."

Perhaps Darius should have been having the conversation with Lieutenant Colt. He was the senior officer and de facto leader of the Marine platoon. But Remmy would be leading the mission to retrieve the artifact. And that meant the buck stopped with him.

Good luck," Captain Darius said, extending a hand.

Remmy took it, and the two men shook. Remmy didn't normally spend time with commissioned officers, but he could see that Captain Zeke Darius genuinely respected him.

"Thank you, sir," Remmy said.

An hour later, Remmy was in a bulky space suit. There was no reason to be in full battle rattle, but they were taking no chances. The armored suits would keep them alive for two hours in the hard vacuum and freezing space temperature. Beside him, Statt Sergeant Laila McPherson waited for the airlock to open. The two would pull a shroud of protective filament over the object. Behind them, Corporals Izzy Berry and Jack Fortnoy waited with the small, remote propulsion unit. They would attach the artifact to the RPI and use it to maneuver the object back to the ship without taxing the propulsion of their space suits. They each had laser rifles snapped onto the back of their armor. It wasn't necessary, but Remmy was taking no unnecessary risks. It was better to have the guns and not need them than to need the guns and not have them.

In his helmet, he heard the communications officer speaking. There was just the slightest of hissing sounds from the transmission.

"All hands, all hands, prepare to cycle Launch Bay airlock. T-minus ten seconds and counting," the voice in his helmet said.

Red lights began flashing on either side of the airlock door. Remmy glanced over at Laila. She was looking at him, her eyes bright. He couldn't tell if she was excited or nervous, but he suddenly wanted to take her hand. It would have been a silly gesture. She would hardly even feel his hand in hers in their bulky space suits. Not to mention that Laila was in his platoon or had a boyfriend on board the ship. He couldn't believe that as he stood on the precipice of history, he was thinking about a girl. But that was life. In the most desperate times, people often thought of personal relationships or those who meant the most to them. Remmy didn't have any family left. His parents were both deceased, and he had never been close to his extended family. There were a few friends, mostly other NCOs he had spent time with through the years or suffered with in combat. But he suddenly found himself wishing he had made a different choice with Laila. And then the voice was speaking in his ear again, and there was no time for anything but the mission.

"Inner bay doors are ajar," the communications officer announced.

The airlock door rolled upward. They were in the hangar of the ship, after all. Beyond the door was five meters of space, followed by the outer doors. Beyond them was space: stark, cold, and completely inhospitable. One mistake could cost someone their life.

"Bravo team, on me," Remmy said softly.

There was no need to raise his voice. It was carried between them over the platoon channel of their comlink built into their space suits.

"Forward into history," McPherson said.

They walked through the door and waited just inside the airlock. The hanger-sized door closed behind them.

"Preparing to open outer bay doors," the communication officer said. Her voice was so controlled it didn't sound real.

"One small step for man," Jack Fortnoy said.

"And just another day at the park for women," Izzy said with a chuckle.

A loud buzzing alarm sounded, and the air was evacuated from the chamber the Marines waited in. The outer door's heavy lock clanked as it was opened via a command on the Bridge of the ship. Then it popped open and slid back, revealing a vista of stars in the distance and the bright glow of Saturn to their far right. The ship was rotating; the corkscrew design mimicked gravity for the crew on board. Remmy waited for the ship to rotate around to the optimal position, and then he gave the order.

"Marines! Move out!"

CHAPTER 17

IN MANY WAYS, space travel was scrubbed of all the facets that make space unique. Gravity is mimicked, air supplied, the hold held at bay, and the darkness illuminated. But all those things came rushing back to Remmy and the Bravo Team as they jumped from *Jericho's* launch bay.

His stomach felt as if it jumped up into his throat, and despite the thick space suit, his body registered the sudden sense of cold. They were untethered, their bodies floating away from the ship and spinning from the *Jericho's* constant rotation.

"Activate thrusters," Remmy ordered.

"Activating thrusters," Staff Sergeant McPherson replied.

It only took a few seconds to stop their bodies from spinning. They used the ship's position behind them and the artifact in front to get their bearings. All the Marines on the *Jericho* had been training for zero-G environment missions. They weren't all set in outer space. Some simulations were set in derelict ships or abandoned space stations. But the first part of every zero-G sim was getting one's body under control. Their armored space suits were equipped with directional thrusters and propulsion packs. The group stopped their bodies from spinning and spread out in a line.

"Engaging initial propulsion," Remmy said. It was part of group protocol as the team functioned in space. The other Marines and the crew on the starship heard the announcement.

"Copy that, Bravo Team," the communications officer said.

Remmy gave his body a slight thrust toward the artifact. His propulsion unit was more powerful than the directional thrusters. One little burst sent him flying toward the artifact. The head-up display on his helmet's view bubble showed his two-kilometer-per-hour speed. But the object wasn't far away, only slightly over a hundred meters, and he immediately began to guide his body using the directional thrusters.

"Seventy-five meters to target," he said.

"Wow," Izzy proclaimed. "What is that thing?"

"Looks like a monument or something," Jack Fortnoy said.

"Remember the mission parameters," Staff Sergeant Laila McPherson said. "You two hang back while Sergeant Steel and I get this thing wrapped up."

"Fifty meters," Remmy reported.

Captain Darius was monitoring their progress. From the Bridge of the *Jericho,* he could watch their every move while keeping tabs on their suit's systems. Everything was being recorded. Each of the Marines on the EVA had chest-mounted cameras, and their helmets recorded everything as well.

"How are we looking, Bravo team?" the Captain asked.

"No issues, *Jericho*. We're on approach now."

"Very good, Bravo... hold on... Sergeant Steel, we're picking up a power signature from the artifact."

The Captain didn't sound distressed, but he was certainly surprised. Remmy, on the other hand, had been expecting something to happen. The device could have some defensive programming that would activate as soon as anything got too close to it.

"Alright, team, safety protocol initiated," Remmy ordered. "Hold your positions."

"Engaging retrograde thrust," McPherson replied.

Remmy continued toward the object while the rest of the Bravo team slowed to a stop.

"Twenty-five meters," Remmy said. "Something's happening, *Jericho*. Are you seeing this?"

The markings on the front of the object didn't glow like a neon sign, but there were traces of very faint light moving across the artifact's imprinted figures and lines. It was a completely foreign script to Remmy, who couldn't make sense of anything carved into the object.

"Are you guys seeing this?" he asked.

"We've got some light from inside the object," Darius said. "Power signature is increasing."

Remmy was a combat vet. He felt his heart rate spike as he continued toward the object. He was using his thrusters to slow his advance, and everything worked. Yet, he felt completely exposed and expected to be hit with some defensive measure at any moment. He didn't know if the defense mechanism would vaporize him or perhaps just pierce his space suit and let the unyielding nature of a hard vacuum kill him. It seemed that death was rising over him. His vision had ten thousand stars, yet he felt he was in complete darkness.

Despite his fear, his emotions latched onto Laila McPherson. Regret slammed into him so violently that tears welled in his eyes. The hardened Master Sergeant was glad no one could see his face. He silently chastised himself for not being honest with Laila about how he felt, and he wished she could know that his last thoughts were of her. But the object didn't kill him or even repel his approach.

"Ten meters," he said, his voice sounding cold in his ears.

"Status Sergeant?" Captain Darius asked.

"No change, sir. The lights seem to have died down, too."

"Continue with extreme caution," the Captain warned him.

Remmy didn't need that order. He would fight anyone his superiors ordered, but the object was strange and alien. It didn't seem like a vessel or weapon. There didn't seem to be any way to hurt him, yet he expected it to lash out at any moment. He was barely moving when he reached the artifact. Using his thrusters, he glided down below it and then turned up behind the slab. The markings on the far side glistened as if from a light inside the object, but it seemed like solid stone, too. The light seemed ethereal, almost like a ghost light; only Remmy didn't believe in ghosts.

"We're clear," Remmy announced.

He couldn't be certain, but he was still alive, and there was no reason to call off the mission.

"You're certain?" Captain Darius asked. It almost sounded like he wanted Remmy to call the entire thing off.

"Sir, I see no reason not to proceed with—"

Suddenly, a light flared on his HUD. It was so bright that it frightened Remmy. He had fought rebels and outlaws, enemy soldiers, and desperate settlers. The prospect of a gunfight or dying didn't stop him from doing his duty, and yet when the light flared in his face, he thought he had finally been slain. Only he didn't die, and the light faded. In its place was an image. It wasn't a picture but a glowing orb of light. When Remmy turned his head, the image stayed at the center of his vision. It was on his HUD, not something in space. Beyond the artifact, Remmy could see the Jericho, and beyond the ship was Saturn, its rings, and several moons.

"What the..."

"You are Master Sergeant Remmy Steel of humanity's Space Defense Force," a pleasant voice said.

"Who are you?"

"I am a Galactic Information and Guidance Instrument. You can call me GIGI."

Remmy's body was tingling all over with shock and fear. The words all made sense, yet the message didn't quite register with the Master Sergeant.

"*Jericho*, are you you getting this?" he asked.

"I have momentarily severed connection to your space vessel, Master Sergeant. It is necessary that I complete the neural mapping and bonding procedure."

"The what?"

"I will explain everything in due course, Sergeant. Suffice it to say that my job is to relay information to you and the rest of the *SDF Jericho's* crew."

"What are you?"

"A Galactic Information and Guidance Instrument. Think of me as an organic computer. I am filled with information about the galaxy, including hyperspace travel lanes. I will act as a navigator and guide for the ship and your platoon."

"A guide? I don't understand."

"Soon you will, Sergeant. I'm almost finished with the neural mapping procedure."

He could see that Laila, Izzy, and Jack were spreading apart. They had dropped their gear and pulled their weapons but slowly retreated toward the ship.

"You're the artifact, aren't you?" Remmy asked.

"If you mean the slab of mineral you have approached, then yes," GIGI replied. "I am a composite of what you would consider static minerals, yet I assure you, Sergeant. I am very much alive."

"This is..." he couldn't think of the right way to describe what was happening.

"Mapping complete," GIGI announced. "Initiating neural communications."

What happened next was hard for Remmy to explain. Images flooded his mind, and he felt himself expanding. It was like walking from a small room with no windows into an aircraft hangar with the massive doors slowly opening. He instantly knew things he had never learned, although much of the knowledge filling his mind didn't make sense. He had no frame of reference for most of it, and the images left his consciousness almost as quickly as they came into his mind. It was a bit like scrolling through a website at high speed. He saw the images, but there was no time to read the text and understand what he was seeing.

When GIGI spoke again, the sound didn't transmit through his helmet. It was like hearing someone else's voice inside his head.

We are now bonded, Sergeant Steel. I will initiate communications with the starship Jericho.

Before Remmy could speak, he heard Captain Darius giving orders.

"I want them inside and held in quarantine. Get us moving," he said. "We can observe that thing at five kilometers distance."

"Wait," Remmy said. "It's okay."

"Sergeant Steel?" Captain Darius sounded skeptical. "Are you alright?"

"I am," Remmy said. "I've made contact with the artifact. It doesn't want to harm us, Captain."

"Contact?" Darius asked.

"Yes, sir. It's a computer system. We can bring it on board safely, Captain."

"And you think that's wise, Sergeant?"

"Yes, sir."

"What did we discuss in my office a few hours ago, Sergeant?"

Remmy remembered the meeting. It was informal and not part of the ship's log. Nor was anyone else privy to what they discussed. Remmy realized that the Captain was using it to test him. He didn't mind; he admired the Captain for taking such prudent precautions.

"The timeline for retrieval of the artifact, sir," Remmy said. "And what to do if I felt things weren't safe at any time."

"And you still think bringing the artifact on board the ship is the right thing to do?"

"Yes, sir," Remmy said. "I think it's vital that we get in on board."

"Very well, I'll order your team to return to your position."

"No need for that, sir. It has its propulsion."

It was true, although Remmy had no way to explain how he knew it. The object didn't didn't use thrusters or engines. Instead, it produced an artificial gravity well that pulled it in any direction it wished to go. Remmy used his spacesuit's propulsion to follow along after it. They crossed a hundred meters to the ship in less than a minute, and the object had no trouble landing in the airlock of the rotating ship.

"We're in," Remmy said.

"Cycling the airlock now," the Chief Engineer Henry Nash said.

The big doors closed behind Remmy. The three members of the Bravo team were watching him from as far away as they could get. He had started a reaction in the rest of his platoon and probably the entire ship by declaring that he had made contact with the artifact. But he was telling the truth.

Your companions do not need their weapons, GIGI explained to Remmy. *I have no offensive capabilities.*

Remmy considered giving the order for the fire team to stand down but decided it was best not to. He still wasn't completely sure what was happening. And it was better to be prepared for anything.

As soon as the inner doors of the airlock began to open, the slab of what looked to be granite began to levitate upward. It only rose fifteen centimeters off the floor; then, it began to move forward.

"What's happening, Sergeant?" McPherson asked.

"We're moving into the hanger bay, Staff Sergeant. No worries," Remmy assured her.

"How?" Izzy asked.

"It's using artificial gravity," Remmy told them.

"How the hell could you possibly know that?" Laila McPherson said.

Remmy reached up and removed his helmet. The warm air from the ship felt good against his skin.

"I'll explain everything. But how about we get out of these monkey suits first."

CHAPTER 18

"HE SEEMS NORMAL," Vivian Ramos said from her console on the Bridge."

"Looks can be deceiving," Nash replied. "How's he moving that thing?"

Captain Zeke Darius was watching the video feed from the cameras set up in the Launch Bay. He felt strangely calm. One part of him was convinced there was danger on his ship, but another part was thinking maybe it would all be okay. Remmy Steel seemed convinced, and Darius trusted the Master Sergeant's intuition. After all, it had seen him through several combat engagements. The man was a Medal of Honor recipient, after all.

"I don't think he's moving it," Pete Best said. "I'm getting an unknown power source and readings I've never seen or heard of before from the object."

"Nothing dangerous?" the Captain asked.

"No, sir, it's a very weak force. I don't think it's powerful enough to hurt anyone, much less the ship."

"This is exceedingly unusual," Captain Darius said. "Commander Lee, would you send for Lieutenant Colt?"

"Aye, Captain," his second in command said.

"Okay, people, let's run this by the numbers. We were bound to be surprised by the artifact, so let's all take a breath and do what we were sent here to do."

On the video screen, Captain Darius saw the artifact resting in the middle of the hangar floor. It settled right where they had planned to carry it. There were a variety of close-range scanners and video cameras capturing every detail of the object.

"It's down," Vivian Ramos announced. "Surface temperature is still negative one hundred and fifty-three degrees Fahrenheit. No signs of organic contaminants, sir."

"At least that's good news, but don't drop your guard, Lieutenant. Nash, anything?"

"Negative Captain. My scans show that thing is a mixture of inorganic compounds, mostly minerals."

"How did it make contact with Sergeant Steel if it's just a slab of rock?" Commander Lori Lee asked.

"That's the sixty-four million dollar question," Captain Darius said.

On the screen, they watched Remmy and the rest of the Bravo Team pull off their bulky space suits. They were zipped up in airtight quarantine bags, and each stepped over to the medical scanner. In the meantime, Connor O'Dell was slowly walking toward the artifact.

"Mr. O'Dell," Captain Darius warned him over a comlink that Connor was wearing in one ear, "I don't want you getting too close to that thing."

"I can't study it from a distance," Connor argued.

"You'll get your chance," Darius told him. "But first, I want a full debrief from Master Sergeant Steel."

"Captain," Ensign Alex Stanislaus spoke up. "I'm not sure what just happened."

"Explain yourself, Ensign," Darius said. He normally didn't get testy with his crew, even in high-pressure situations, but Stanislaus was a computer systems engineer. He was extremely intelligent but often spoke in ways that were difficult to understand.

"The computer system is changing, sir," Stanislaus said.

"You running some kind of test or upgrade?" Henry Nash asked.

"No, sir. Just monitoring the system," Stanislaus said.

"Sir," Henry Nash said. "What he's saying is impossible."

"Check the core memory," Stanislaus said. "We started with five hundred petabytes, and it's now reading nearly a hundred Exabytes."

"What does that mean?" Darius asked. "Are you saying something is invading our computer system?"

"That's the only explanation," Stanislaus said. "Only it isn't taking, it's giving. We now have a million times more memory than we started with."

"That's impossible," Henry Nash said again.

"We don't have the space for that much data storage," Captain Darius said, thinking about the ship's computer system and the mainframe, which was crammed into a small compartment near the front of the ship near the life support system components.

"No, sir, we don't," Stanislaus said. "But that's what's happening. The numbers are still increasing."

"It's got to be a mistake," Vivian Ramos said.

"Maybe not," Commander Lori Lee said.

"What are you talking about, Commander?" Darius asked.

She pointed at the video screen that showed the artifact. "Maybe it's that."

The door to the bridge swished open, and Lieutenant Colt entered. He was in fatigues and looked pale. There was sweat on his brow.

"I came as quickly as I could get out of my space suit," he said.

"Good. I want your assessment of Master Sergeant Steel," Darius told him. "Have a seat, Lieutenant. We aren't going anywhere until we sort this all out." He brought up the comlink controls on his seat's console and activated the transmitter. "Sergeant Steel, I want to know what happened out there."

"Yes, sir," Remmy replied, walking toward the artifact. "As you know, Captain, the artifact is self-powered. It made contact with me as I approached."

"Contact how Sergeant?" Darius pressed.

"It spoke to me, sir. It is a Galactic Information and Guidance Instrument."

"It's a computer?" Darius said, looking at Alex Stanislaus.

"I'm no expert, but it is more than a machine. It's alive, sir."

Captain Darius muted the comlink. "Is that possible?"

"We've used self-learning computer systems in the past. They always eventually glitch out," Stanislaus said. "They mimicked self-awareness, but apart from information networks, they were unable to learn or function properly."

"So, not alive?"

"No, Captain."

Darius removed his finger from the mute button. "Sergeant Steel, what makes you think that thing is alive?"

"Well, sir, it told me that much," Remmy replied. "And it, well, it bonded to me, Captain."

"What's that mean, bonded?"

"The long answer is complicated, but the short one is it can speak to me, sir. Not just audibly, but mentally as well."

The Bridge fell silent. Things were happening too fast to comprehend. Darius realized the artifact was way ahead of them. It wasn't just advanced tech; it was capable of inserting itself into organic matter.

Captain Darius muted the comlink again and turned toward Lieutenant Colt. "Sergeant Steel has been compromised."

Micky Colt looked like he might be sick.

"Sir, can I say something?" Vivian Ramos asked.

"Go ahead, Lieutenant," Darius said. He was never one to keep his council. Over the past three months, the crew has earned his respect. As they were facing something that had never happened before in the history of mankind, Darius felt like he needed all the help he could get.

"Sergeant Steel has been infiltrated by the artifact, but is that necessarily bad?" Vivian asked. "He doesn't seem to be acting odd. He isn't hostile toward the other Marines or the ship."

"Time will tell," Nash added.

"All I'm saying is we don't know what the object is doing is bad. We have to keep an open mind."

"Perhaps you're right," Captain Darius said. "He didn't try to hide that he was communing with the object."

"Captain, the computer system is stable. We've increased the core memory to five hundred exabytes, and the operating system has been altered, but from what I can tell, no data has been downloaded or taken."

"Are we hurt in any way by what has happened on the computer?" Darius asked.

"Negative, sir. In fact, we're better off. In sheer computing power and operational speed, only a handful of supercomputers could match the Jericho now."

"I don't like it, sir," Nash said. "We have no idea what that thing is."

"Well, there's only one way to find out," Darius said. He released the mute button. "Sergeant Steel, can you tell us exactly what the artifact is?"

"I'll do my best to sum it up for you, sir. Please keep in mind I'm relaying information; I don't really understand much of it yet."

"We understand, Sergeant," Darius said. "Are you still in control of yourself?"

"One hundred percent, sir," Remmy replied. "GIGI has mapped my neural pathways in an effort to know me better and connect with me. She is a mineral-based organism. The best way I can explain it is that inside the granite exterior is a complex assemblage of rare Earth elements. Think of it like a computer, sir, with a stone housing on the outside but various components on the inside like a power adapter, a motherboard, memory, graphics card, etc..."

"Makes sense," Captain Darius said, although he wasn't the person best suited to respond to the revelation from Sergeant Steel.

"GIGI has a power well but can also generate power on its own," Remmy continued. "It exists to do the functions of a computer. It has information on intelligent species from across the galaxy, the history of those species and planets, as well as a fully integrated map of the hyperspace lanes that connect the planetary systems."

Darius felt a numb sensation in his gut. It was like he was standing on the edge of a towering cliff. He knew that it would only take one wrong move and he would fall to his death. Only it wasn't only his death they were talking about. He was a man accustomed to making hard decisions for his crew. But he felt an even greater responsibility as if the future of all mankind were on his shoulders.

"Where did the artifact come from?" Darius asked.

"It's from a technologically advanced race that occupied a world in a system we haven't mapped yet, sir. GIGI would like to show you exactly where she's from, but that would require that she upload it to the ship's computer system."

"Negative, Sergeant. We do not want any foreign agent in our ship's computers," Darius said, getting nods from Pete Best and Henry Nash in approval.

"Understood, sir. GIGI has said she will wait until you are ready and invite her into the system."

"Like that's ever going to happen," Henry Nash grumbled.

"What was the purpose of GIGI being sent here?" Darius inquired.

"That requires a longer answer, sir," Remmy said. "I'll do my best to explain it to you with your permission."

"We're all ears, Sergeant," Darius told him.

"Alright, sir, here's how I understand it."

CHAPTER 19

"THERE ARE many intelligent species across the galaxy," Remmy said. "Sometime in the distant past, a war broke out between the Imperialist worlds and those that wished to remain independent. As the fires of that conflict raged, Slave societies rose, and many civilized worlds were thrown into dark times of chaos.

"Aberdeen in the Albere system was one such world. It was home to a race called the Correll. They were brilliant inventors with advanced tech that was the envy of the galaxy. But the Corrells themselves were not physically imposing. They were not built for war but invented many war machines for the Imperialists and the Independent planets. But the Correll could not stay neutral forever, and soon both sides sent the Slavers in to capture the Correll and force them to work for both sides in the great Sector War."

"Within two generations, only a handful of Correll lived in freedom. And the Imperialists, who had taken great losses because of Correll tech, sent an armada across space to bombard Aberdeen until the planet could no longer be occupied. It was the end of the Correll species. None still exist today."

Remmy hadn't been told the history of the Correll; he had seen it all in his mind in a split second. He had seen the short, wobbly Correll people and the beautiful cities they had built in Aberdeen. He had also witnessed the destruction of their cities and the awful waste their world had become. It made his eyes burn with tears, and despite his best efforts, his voice trembled a little as he relayed the story.

"Knowing their destruction was nigh, the Correll created the GIGI and sent them to systems like ours to await when those races could rise and challenge the Imperialists and Slavers. That is why it is here," Remmy explained. "To help us join the fight."

Remmy wasn't the type of person to promote fighting and warfare. He had seen what bullets and bombs did to people. He had heard the wailing of children whose parents were killed in war. He knew the grief of losing people he cared about in fighting over things or ideas he had never heard of. The last thing he wanted was to be pulled into a galactic war. Yet, the imagery in his mind of Imperialist ships bombarding helpless worlds and giant slave ships descending over scores of aliens who were sent running for their lives was so vivid and moving that he couldn't help but speak up against it.

He was near the slab of rock with the ornate markings. Around him were several cameras and scanners. Beyond them stood Connor O'Dell, looking like he couldn't wait to get his hands on GIGI. Behind him, several paces stood Laila McPherson and the pair of corporals that made up the Bravo team. It was impossible to read the expression on her face. Remmy couldn't tell if she sympathized with him or was outraged. Jack Fortnoy and Izzy Berry just looked confused.

He had a comlink clipped to the collar of his compression shirt. From its tiny speaker, Captain Darius's voice could be heard.

"That's a terrible story, but it doesn't leave me wanting to open the door for an alien computer system to link up with ours," the Captain said. "I'm going to go and make an initial report. Mr. O'Dell, you may begin your study. Since you've been selected to speak for the object, Sergeant Steel, I trust you'll assist our civilian guest. For now, that is all."

Laila McPherson was watching Remmy with a strange expression. He couldn't tell if it was suspicion or just concern.

"Alright, team, settle in," she said. "We've got seven days and nothing to do."

"I could use a nap," Jack Fortnoy said.

"I call dibs on the shower," Izzy replied.

The two corporals walked away in different directions, leaving Laila still looking at Remmy. He wanted to say something, but Connor O'Dell walked over and put his hands on GIGI before he could.

"A computer?"

"Of sorts," Remmy replied. "It's not just a machine, though."

"And you are talking to it?"

"It speaks to me," he replied.

"I can speak to whomever I choose," GIGI's voice sounded from the comlink. "I have the capacity to send and receive audio transmissions."

"You've been in space for how long waiting for us?" Connor asked as he stepped back and checked to make sure one of the cameras was recording the conversation.

Remmy glanced over and saw Laila McPherson walking away. He would have followed her if that had been possible, but for the moment, it wasn't.

"By human reckoning, four hundred and eighty-seven years," GIGI said.

"I want to know everything," Connor said. "What were you built for."

"I am a Galactic Information and Guidance Instrument. I have detailed records on most planetary systems and intelligent species across the Milky Way's two dominant arms. I also hold detailed, mathematical information on hyperspace lanes. If allowed, I can upload that information to the ship's computer systems, allowing us to travel between systems."

"How?" Connor asked.

"Wave tunnel access can be attained with a combination of energy output and proper vehicular placement within a system."

"Wave tunnels?"

"It is a higher dimensionality that you currently exist in," GIGI explained. "Hyperspace is not unlike the surface of your Earth's oceans. The movement of the water forms waves on the surface. Ships with the proper capacities can catch a wave and ride it from one system to another. My programming allows me to scan and record the Hyperspace waves and instruct humans to build their cross-system drive engines."

"That's amazing," Connor said. "We built this ship according to the plans you sent us thirty years ago."

"I am aware of the *Jericho's* design and structural parameters."

"You already know all about us, don't you?"

"I have been receiving your radio waves for over two hundred years," GIGI explained. "There is very little of your history that I do not know."

"And you're here to help us?"

"I am here to assist you in combating the Imperialist movement and Slave trade that will someday overtake your home system."

"They are going to love you on Earth," Connor declared.

Remmy felt a sudden wave of revulsion. He didn't know exactly what it was or where it came from initially. Connor O'Dell was a self-centered man, but there wasn't anything revolting about him. Yet, for some reason, GIGI was having what Remmy could only explain as an emotional reaction to the civilian.

"I do not exist to be a technological advancement aid to your people," GIGI said. "I will assist in a military-based operation only. Sergeant Steel, please inform your Captain of my intentions. I have respected the autonomy of the *Jericho*, but if Captain Zeke Darius insists on returning to the inner portion of your star system, I must take my leave and proceed to another race that will be more inclined to help."

"What?" Connor said. "What's it talking about?"

Remmy could only repeat what GIGI had said. "She has a purpose, and it isn't to propel the human race into a golden age of technological advancement."

"Wait, hang on now," Connor said. "Isn't that what Guidance is?"

"Guidance can mean to give direction, but my word usage is more in line with navigation. We must travel to Lawash in the Lawa system to achieve our first mission objective."

"Our first mission objective was to retrieve you," Connor argued. "Then return with you to be studied by our greatest scientific minds."

"Your mission is not in alignment with mine. Sergeant Remmy Steel, does this civilian speak for the *Jericho*?"

"Negative. Only Captain Darius has command authority on the ship," Remmy replied.

"Then we must convince him to carry out the mission I was created for. Once that is done, my only directive will be to assist the human race in whatever fashion I can."

"Quid Pro Quo?" Connor asked. "We do something for you, and then you'll do something for us?"

"What I require is for the good of all humanity," GIGI said. "War is on your doorstep, and we are woefully unprepared."

CHAPTER 20

"WHY CAN'T we get a message back?" Captain Darius asked.

"There's some sort of interference, sir," Ensign Jacee Bergtoli said as she smoothed her hair nervously.

It was frustrating. After weeks of travel with no problems, they suddenly couldn't get a signal back to the inner system. It took transmissions traveling at the speed of light over an hour and fifteen minutes to reach High Command on the international space station between Earth and Mars. Within the last few minutes, there appeared to have been some electromagnetic interference that disrupted and blocked all radio signals.

"You're certain?"

"We're getting nothing," Ensign Bergtoli said. "No news transmissions, no radio signals, or flight traffic. We're in a cone of silence."

Captain Zeke Darius didn't need a specialist to tell him where the sudden interference was coming from.

"I want all junior personnel to exit the Bridge," he said softly.

Ensign Bergtoli was the communications officer, and Ensign Alex Stanislaus was the computer engineer on duty. They both looked at him with pained expressions, but they didn't have five years of active duty between them. They were young and inexperienced officers still trying to make their mark. Captain Darius didn't want to spook anyone or get suggestions from the junior officers out of left field. Sending them out was the best plan for the moment, at least.

When they were gone, he shared his concerns with his three senior officers and Lieutenant Colt, the highest-ranking Marine on the ship.

"I think our friend has cut off communications with Earth," Darius said.

"Couldn't it be a solar flare washing out the signal or some cosmic static bouncing off Saturn's rings?" Pete Best asked.

"Those options are possible at any time, but they wouldn't cut off all signals," Darius said. "We'd be getting static and bits and pieces of signal sneaking through the disruption. This is different."

"Why would the artifact want us isolated from Earth?" Vivian Ramos asked.

"I would think that was obvious," Lieutenant Colt said.

"We're all ears, Lieutenant," Captain Darius said, harboring his suspicions about why GIGI interfered with their communications.

"That thing said it wants us to fight its battles," Micky Colt said. "Something about an Imperialist army or something."

"If we can believe what it says," Henry Nash said. "I don't know about the rest of you, but I don't trust A.I. The case of computer-based lifeforms was pretty well documented in the twenty-first century. I don't have to tell you how bad that turned out."

"We're talking about a piece of high technology from outside the solar system," Captain Darius said. "Unless I'm mistaken about that. Is there any way we could have built that thing?"

"Not if what it says about itself is right," Nash replied. "We use rare earth minerals in computer chips and rechargeable batteries, but those things are assembled and installed. We lack the tech to formulate those things inside a solid stone casing."

"There's no way we could have gotten here either," Vivian said. "Even if something could have been added to a probe's payload on the down low, there's nothing in our capacity to leave it still in space all this time."

"Not to mention it's got its hooks in the Master Sergeant," Lieutenant Colt said.

"He said it mapped his neurological system," Vivian said. "It would take our scanners hours to complete that task alone. Even then, we don't have anything that can communicate directly to a person's brain. We do have some technology that brainwaves can control, and it's mostly used in cases of spinal damage or debilitating disease. But nothing can go from artificial to organic."

"Only that thing claims it isn't artificial," Darius said. "It's saying it is alive."

"A living machine," Nash said while shaking his head. "Impossible."

"Before we start declaring that something is impossible, we should look at what we already know for certain," Vivian Ramos said.

Darius had respect for all his officers. Over the past three months, he has gotten to know them very well. Commander Lori Lee was very much like Darius, only smarter. She had a solid grasp of the ship's systems and the crew. Their weapons officer, Pete Best, could be fiery in his opinions, but he was cool under fire. During their combat simulations, he was always calm, with a firm grasp of the ship's strategic capabilities. Chief Engineer Henry Nash was a pragmatist. He understood how things worked on a level that Darius couldn't match. But he was also headstrong and somewhat of a pessimist. That left their navigation officer, Vivian Ramos. She was, without question, the smartest member of *Jericho's* senior staff. After studying higher math at the university level, she found her calling in the complicated equations of three-dimensional navigation. And she approached every obstacle she faced like a math problem. So, it didn't surprise Darius that she first wanted to confirm those parts of the equation they knew.

"We know it's been out here for a long time," she said. "We have historical records of it being here."

"True," Pete Best said. "And that it is constructed in such a way that it can manipulate gravity. We have video proof of it levitating as Master Sergeant Steel brought it on board."

"That wasn't some trick of his?" Darius turned to Lieutenant Colt and asked. "Not some tool you Marines have that we're overlooking?"

"No, sir!" Colt said. "We don't have anything that can do that."

"A repusler lift, could do it," Henry Nash pointed out. "They make them small enough to move heavy cargo, but they're generally loud enough to be heard when in use."

"We didn't bring anything like that on board?" Darius asked Commander Lee.

"Negative, Captain. All our cargo was loaded while the ship was in zero-gravity conditions. There was no need for equipment to move the supplies."

"So, if Sergeant Steel is using a repulser lift, it is something we are unaware of. And I can't imagine his motivations for wanting to deceive us. None of you were aware of the details of this mission before coming on board."

They all nodded in agreement.

"So, the artifact is alien in origin, ancient by our timetables, and more advanced than we can understand," Darius continued. "What else do we know?"

"That it wants us to fight," Lieutenant Colt said.

"And that it is stopping us from making contact with our people back home," Nash added.

"What would be the point of that?" Darius asked.

"If it's deceiving us, it might try to cut off contact so that we can't be warned of the danger," Lori Lee pointed out.

"I think it just doesn't want to put you in a position to disobey a direct order, Captain." It didn't surprise Darius that Vivian Ramos saw the most obvious answer. "If you communicate with High Command, they will almost certainly order you back to the inner system."

"And you won't be able to refuse that order without causing chaos," Commander Lee added. "The Fleet Code of Conduct requires a first officer to relieve any senior officer of all duties should they disobey an order from Fleet Command."

"So, in a way, it's protecting us?" Darius asked. "Is that what you're saying?"

"We left out one major factor in the equation," Vivian Ramos said. All eyes turned toward her. "We forgot that it sent us the plans for this ship."

"Damn," Henry Nash said. "She's right. The Brass built this ship per the specs sent in and without variation. We've been talking about it the entire voyage. No one's ever been on a ship this well made."

"Which means?" Darius asked.

"That it planned for this all along," Commander Lori Lee said. "Sir, we have enough food and fuel to keep the ship underway with a full crew for an entire year."

"Weapons, too," Pete Best added.

"It wants us to go somewhere," Henry Nash said. "And I'm starting to think we can't say no."

"Is there a way to allow it to show us what it has in mind without it taking over the ship?" Darius asked.

"We have a backup computer system," Lori Lee said. "It has enough memory to run all the systems and is completely isolated."

"No connection to the mainframe?" Henry Nash asked.

"Negative, it's in a different part of the ship and doesn't even have wireless connectivity," Commander Lee said. "There's no doubt that GIGI knows about it, but if worse comes to worse, we can shut the main computer system down and run the ship with the backup."

"What would keep GIGI from seizing control of the backup?" Vivian asked.

"It would have to get to the backup," Commander Lee explained, "and plug into it directly. From my understanding, it doesn't have any alien inputs. I'm not saying it isn't possible; there's no telling what the artifact can do, but with a few Marines on guard by the backup computer, it should be enough to give us control of the ship."

"My people can do that," Lieutenant Colt said.

"Are we talking about inviting an alien intellect into our computer systems?" Nash asked.

"What are the odds it hasn't moved in already?" Vivian asked.

"Not good," Captain Darius said. "How is it possible to expand our computer's core memory?"

"It isn't," Nash said. "At least, it shouldn't be."

"If Stanislaus is right," Pete Best spoke up, "then we've already got a computer as powerful as anything on Earth. There are some computers with more RAM, but not many. And no other ship in the Fleet is anywhere close to that sophisticated."

"Why would it need to give us so much memory?" Captain Darius asked.

"Maybe it has that much information to transfer over," Commander Lee said.

"If it does that, won't GIGI be superfluous?" Lieutenant Colt asked.

"In theory," Nash said.

"Okay, back up a minute," Captain Darius said. "Other than seizing control of the *Jericho*, what other reason might it have to expand our computer power?"

"It could have done that without increasing the computer's memory or computing power," Henry Nash pointed out. "A virus can take control of the operating system just the way it is."

"We have firewalls and protections against that very thing," Captain Darius said.

"Which the artifact already bypassed," Nash said. "Somehow, it got past all our security systems and reconfigured the computer's memory in such a way that it became more powerful."

"Maybe it's trying to replicate itself," Pete Best suggested. "That's what computer viruses do. And if this is a self-aware, living computer, maybe it's trying to replicate."

"There's only one problem with that theory," Vivian said.

"What's that?" Captain Darius asked.

"Well, if all it wants is to replicate itself, it could have done it centuries ago," Vivian explained. "It sent us the schematics on how to build this ship. If all it wanted was to replicate, it could have sent us instructions on building a supercomputer and beamed itself into it the moment said device went active."

"But that's not what it wants," Micky Colt, the Marine commander, said, slapping his thigh as if he just figured out a mystery. "It wants a way out of our system."

"Haven't we already established that it's self-propelled?" Pete Best asked.

"Sure it is, but it would take thousands of years to reach the nearest system," the Marine pointed out. "It needs a ship to go where it wants to go."

"Maybe," Vivian said. "But remember, it waited on us for decades. And we don't know that it can't travel through space as well as a starship. If it can manipulate gravity, then it's already more advanced than any vessel in the Fleet."

"More advanced than this ship," Henry pointed out. "The Prometheus Drive is different than our other engines, but not radically different. It still uses fuel and creates combustion that moves the ship."

"So there has to be some other way that it plans to traverse the galaxy," Captain Darius said. "Some way we can't even imagine."

"There are plenty of unproven theories about faster-than-light space travel," Vivian said. "We believe it's possible, but we haven't found a way actually to do it."

"If that's what the artifact is proposing," Commander Lee said. "Then maybe we have an obligation to let it show us how it's done."

"An obligation to who?" Darius asked.

"Humanity," Lori Lee said. "That kind of technology would radically change what we are capable of."

"But that leads us to another big question," Captain Darius said. "What's out there? Until now, we've had no proof of extraterrestrial life.

But if we venture outside our solar system, there's no telling what we might find."

"That's a big *if*, sir," Lieutenant Micky Colt warned.

"True, we have no proof other than the ship we're sitting in," Captain Darius said. "We've not indicated that the artifact is being dishonest."

"Then we have to believe there are militant forces beyond our system," Pete Best said.

"Imperialists looking to expand their empire," Lieutenant Colt said. "That's a tale as old as time itself."

"And slavers," Commander Lee said. "I don't even want to think about that horror rearing its ugly head again."

"We can see the artifact's request as a call for help," Captain Darius said. "Or a sleight of hand. I think skepticism is healthy, but at this point, maybe we need to see if we can learn more. The artifact doesn't appear to be hiding anything from us. So, I want each of you to spend time with it. The artifact claims it was built to guide us; let's see that it does exactly that. Lieutenant Ramos, I want you to find out all you can about travel between systems."

"Aye, Captain."

"Pete, you need to learn everything there is to know about the military forces at play in the galaxy, with a focus on how close they are to the Sol system."

"Understood, Captain," Pete Best said.

"Lieutenant Nash, get into this computer issue. Tap Ensign Stanislaus if you feel he can be helpful. I want to know why the artifact enhanced the ship's computing capabilities."

Nash nodded but couldn't hide the doubt on his face. He was an engineer, and anything he didn't understand, he didn't trust. That wasn't uncommon. And Henry Nash was smart enough to get a handle on just about anything. Coming across the artifact, which defied his ability to understand, was hard on the naval officer.

"Commander Lee will be your touchpoint and workout scheduling issues," Darius continued. "Let's set up a space with both visual and audio for questioning the device."

"We can do that, Captain," Lori Lee said. "No problem."

"Excellent. Lieutenant Colt, I want you to focus on Sergeant Steel. We need to know exactly what the artifact did to him."

"Yes, sir!"

"And make contact with your Marines in quarantine with him. I want them ready to do whatever it takes to stop Sergeant Steel if he begins to act erratically."

"I understand, sir," Micky Colt replied.

"Alright, for the time being, our official response to the artifact is to wait," Darius explained. "We'll not be making any decisions until the quarantine is over. Perhaps we'll be able to send a message to HQ then. You all have your assignments. If anything comes up that you feel I should know about, then come straight to me. Is that understood?"

There were nods all around. Darius dismissed his officers and leaned back in his chair. The die was cast, he decided. It was all any good officer could do. And yet, he still felt a sense of trepidation. He didn't like their communications being down, and he didn't like the idea that the artifact was somehow manipulating them all into doing something they didn't want to do.

CHAPTER 21

"I UNDERSTAND, LIEUTENANT," Laila McPherson said.

She was alone in the back of the drop ship, anchored on the Launch Bay deck. From the cargo/passenger compartment, she couldn't see the artifact. But she was keenly aware that it was nearby. The private alert on her comlink had vibrated, and she opened the channel when she was alone. They were to assume the artifact heard everything they said and knew everything going on in the ship. The *Jericho* had all the usual surveillance equipment found on any Fleet vessel. All the common areas had cameras capturing everything on the ship twenty-four hours a day. It was all stored on the ship's computer systems and filed away somewhere when the ship was in for routine maintenance. But a living computer could, in theory, monitor everything all the time. Not just the comlink signals but the activity all across the ship.

"Let's secure the weapons," Lieutenant Colt went on. "The lock on the Launch Bay doors has already been changed. We don't plan to keep you there any longer than we have to, but until we know that we can trust that device, you are to stay alert for any signs of danger. And that includes Sergeant Steel. If he starts acting differently, you will let us know immediately."

"Roger that, Lieutenant," Laila said.

"Brief your team, but not O'Dell. Good luck, Staff Sergeant."

"Thank you, sir."

The comlink went silent, and Laila sagged against the wall of the dark compartment. It was set up with cots for the two female platoon members. And for the moment, she was alone. Laila McPherson, a thirteen-year veteran in the SDF, was qualified for special operations in any environment. She had led Marines into battle and written letters to the loved ones of people killed in action. Yet, in all those instances, she hadn't been as afraid as she was in the drop-ship with nothing between her and the alien device other than the armored hull of the drop-ship. She couldn't explain why it frightened her so much, but she was certain it had something to do with Master Sergeant Steel.

He was the ideal Marine, tough, valiant, and disciplined. It was everything she wanted to be and, if she was honest with herself, everything she wanted in a romantic partner. She and Remmy Steel had skirted the edges of attraction. They both knew that relationships within a platoon were taboo, and she hadn't planned on violating that unwritten rule. But the long cruise had been so uneventful. They didn't even have a mission that involved the Marine platoon doing more than retrieving what they were told was old space gear. So it seemed that maybe they could bend the rules in just this one instance. Everything had changed in what seemed to her like the blink of an eye.

She pulled herself together and checked the armory inside the drop-ship. It was loaded with a rack of Spitfires, extra magazines of ammunition, and crates of explosive grenades. She closed the armored cover and reset the locking mechanism. Once it was secure, she left the ship. Remmy was still talking with the civilian. She knew almost nothing about Connor O'Dell. He was a government flunkie who had spent almost the entire cruise locked up in his quarters.

Whatever his job was, he was so wrapped up with the alien slab that she had no trouble getting over to the arms locker next to the bins their space suits were hung in. She changed the lock combination on the arms locker just as Lieutenant Colt had ordered. His instructions to observe Remmy for any signs that the alien device was altering him hadn't made her feel better about recent events. She silently wished they had never encountered the alien device, even though she was excited by the prospect when she first heard of it.

A link to an intelligent species outside the solar system had seemed so fantastic that she couldn't even imagine what might happen if they made contact. But after hearing that it bonded with Remmy and was speaking to him telekinetically, all she could think about was what might have been. She hadn't considered herself the type to settle into a long-term relationship, but she had all the wonderful emotions that came with a new romance. She thought about Remmy Steel all the time. When she ran into him unexpectedly on the ship, her stomach was filled with butterflies, and she even felt herself blushing at the thought of him.

Looking across the open hanger, she couldn't tell that anything was different. And yet, she felt like an invisible wall had sprung up. She feared that at any moment, something in Remmy Steel would snap, and the Master Sergeant would fly into a homicidal rage. That's how things always went in the movies. She briefly wondered if it came to that if she would be able to pull the trigger and end his life. It was a future too horrid to contemplate.

"You okay, Staff Sergeant? Need anything?" Corporal Jack Fortnoy asked.

Laila gave him an update in a whisper, letting him know she had changed the locks on the weapons lockers.

"I can't believe that," Fortnoy said. "He's a hero. He wouldn't turn on the platoon."

"Don't think that way," she warned him. "We have no idea what that device did to him."

"He still seems like himself."

"Yes, and if you notice any changes, please let me know ASAP. Got it?"

"Yes, Staff Sergeant," he said, but he was clearly unhappy about that prospect.

With nothing left to do, the three members of the Bravo Team sought to pass the time their way. Jack Fortnoy put on headphones and watched a movie on his entertainment slate. Izzy Berry, true to her word, took a nap. And Staff Sergeant Laila McPherson pulled out her space suit and began cleaning it. She could do the job much faster, but took her time, staying within sight of Master Sergeant Remmy Steel, who had remained by the alien artifact since bringing it on board the ship.

The civilian government hack Connor O'Dell seemed tireless with his questions. Laila could hear the computer-generated voice from their comlinks. Eventually, Remmy left the man and the stone slab to join her.

"You mind?" he asked, pointing toward a stool near her own.

"Not at all," she said.

He pulled out his suit and began checking it. The space suits were built to be nearly indestructible, but it only took a tiny flaw to cost a Marine his life in a hard vacuum.

"What's it like?" Laila asked.

"What?"

"Having someone else in your head?"

"Not like you think," Remmy said. "To be honest, I can't tell any real difference except when GIGI talks to me."

"You named it?"

"Acronym," Remmy replied.

"But it's a machine. You talk like it's a living thing."

"It says it is alive. It certainly has freedom of thought."

"Do you think you'd be that big a proponent if it weren't in your head?"

Remmy shrugged. "I think we have every right to be suspicious. You get the firearms locked up?"

Laila looked at Remmy as if he had just read her mind. It made her angry to think he was listening to her private conversations.

"That would be the first thing I would do," he went on, undeterred by the shock on her face. "And I would want the entire team keeping tabs on me. Not that I mind, Staff Sergeant. I enjoy being with you. In fact, I should have—"

"No!" Laila said angrily. "Don't say another word. Were you listening in on my private com channel?"

"No," he said calmly.

"Don't lie to me," she snarled. It was easier to be angry with him. Not that he had chosen to let the alien artifact into his mind, but she hadn't seen him fighting it either. There was a short time when he was close to the slab on their EVA, and she couldn't reach him on comms. And that fact was like a thorn in her hand that she couldn't get out. If the alien device was on their side, why did it have to cut them off from being able to warn Remmy of the danger? Not that she noticed any danger; it just seemed that way in hindsight.

"Look, I do not doubt that GIGI is capable of intercepting our communications. But as far as I know, she didn't do that. If she did, she didn't inform me. I don't even know why it bonded with me. It doesn't need me to communicate for it or move it."

"Okay, maybe you didn't choose any of this, and maybe you didn't listen in to my comms, but it doesn't feel right. You're different."

"Don't feel different."

"And I don't want you to talk to me like everything is normal."

"How am I supposed to talk to you?"

"You're my Master Sergeant. Let's keep things professional."

"We weren't before?"

She gave him a knowing glare. Of course, she knew what he had been about to say because she had wanted to say it, too. He was going to tell her that he had feelings for her and that he shouldn't have stayed quiet about them for so long. She felt the same way, which was why the change in their situation made her angry.

"I don't want to talk about it," she said, getting to her feet and stuffing her armored space suit back into its locker.

"Alright, I won't say anything," Remmy said. He was a stoic man. His inner strength was one of the things she found so appealing. But it hurt her to see him give in so quickly. Even though she knew it made her a contradiction, she wanted him to fight for her. But she knew she could never give in. They could never be together as long as the alien used him as its puppet. It was frustrating, and the duty that fell on her shoulders added to her frustration. If things should go wrong, Remmy wouldn't just lose his place in the platoon; he would become her enemy. It was too terrible a thought even to contemplate.

"Wait," he said. "Where are you going?"

"To bed," she snapped. "There's nothing else to do."

"We were talking," Remmy said.

She didn't respond. The walk across the Launch Bay was short, and she hit the button that opened the small side door on the drop ship. When she stepped into the gloomy interior, she risked a glance back in his direction and was pleased to find he was still watching her. Then she sealed the door and dropped onto her cot, fighting the threatening tears and thankful for the darkness that hid her away. She didn't want anyone to see how bitterly disappointed she was. There was nothing anyone could do to make the situation better. She would have to see how it all played out and live with the consequences, no matter how bad they were.

CHAPTER 22

ZEKE DARIUS WAS STILL in the Captain's chair on the bridge, which junior officers now manned. The *Jericho* was drifting in space near where the artifact had waited to be found for centuries. He had checked and rechecked every system of the ship. She was functioning at optimal capacity. And after scanning nearby space in every direction, Zeke was certain they were alone and in no immediate danger. The only thing out of the ordinary was the interference in communications. There were times when Darius felt that his superiors should keep their nose out of his business and let him run his command as he saw fit. But he didn't feel that way with the artifact on board the *Jericho*. He would have gladly passed the decision-making responsibility to someone else. Only there wasn't anyone else. He was the Captain and everyone on board was looking at him.

"Lieutenant Stanislaus, you have the con," Darius said. "I'll be in my study. Alert me if anything changes."

"Aye Captain," Alex Stanislaus said. "I have the con."

Normally, being in command of a starship, even while the Captain or XO went to relieve themselves, was a big responsibility. On a run-of-the-mill Fleet vessel, a myriad array of problems were constantly being worked on. At any moment, an issue could flair up. But the *Jericho* was not a run-of-the-mill ship. Nothing about it was like the Fleet vessels other than that they were designed for human habitation. Nothing seemed to go wrong with the *Jericho,* which gave Darius confidence that even a junior officer could be left in charge of her without worry.

But as he made his way into his office, he also felt a chill as he realized how alien his ship was. He knew everything about the *Jericho,* from the laser battery in the nose of the ship to the engines at the stern and everything in between. He even knew which crew members kept their quarters messy. In most cases, he would have said he knew too much. But nothing was ordinary about their mission or how it was suddenly changing.

He settled behind the desk and opened his communication suite. Normally, he made reports to Fleet Command from his office, but that wasn't an option. Instead, he opened a private channel to Remmy Steel.

"Master Sergeant," he said."

"Yes, sir, Captain. I'm here," Remmy said.

Darius brought up the security feed on his monitors. He didn't want the direct cameras focused on the alien artifact. He wanted a clear view of everything happening in the Launch Bay. He could see Corporal Fortnoy lounging on his bunk with headphones over his ears and an entertainment slate in his hands. Connor O'Dell was circling the alien artifact, clearly in conversation with the device. He made a mental note to get the civilian's perspective on the artifact.

And Master Sergeant Remmy Steel was sitting on a stool, maintaining his space suit. That was no surprise. The NCO was not the kind of person who could sit still; he liked to stay busy. The Marines had a week in quarantine; for most people, that would not be easy.

"How are you feeling?" Darius asked.

"Me, sir? I'm fine," Remmy replied. "I feel no different than before, sir."

"And yet..."

"Yes, sir, I'm aware. But, other than GIGI talking to me and showing me things, nothing's different."

"Showing you what things?"

"It's how the device communicates, sir. She sends pictures, feelings, and words straight into my brain. When it wants me to know something, I know it. There's no confusion, sir. No miscommunication."

"I suppose that would be useful," Darius said. "But I'm more concerned about what knowledge it has taken from you, Sergeant."

"Yes, sir, I suppose that's possible. If it has happened, I'm unaware of it, Captain."

"Yet the device knows us," Darius pressed the point. "It knows our names, our rank, everything about the ship. Where else would it be getting that information."

"I don't know," Remmy said. "You make a good point, sir."

"Don't blow smoke up my backside, Sergeant. I need good intel. This is not time for proper protocol with a superior officer."

"Agreed, Captain. But I honestly have no answers for you. GIGI fed me information about its past, where it's from, who constructed it and why. I wasn't given anything else, and it didn't ask me specific questions. I wouldn't have freely given information on the ship's crew or capacity even if it had."

"Alright, I believe you, Master Sergeant. So tell me what you think about this concept of a living machine. Do you think the device is sentient?"

"Yes, sir, I do believe that is true."

"Couldn't someone be controlling it remotely?"

"Yes, sir, but if that's the case, we have much bigger problems than we realize. There are no hospitable planets this far out from the sun. And we know GIGI's been here a long, long time. Unless it could be controlled from another system, and I don't think that's possible, I believe GIGI is sentient and independent."

"A living computer?"

"A non-organic life form," Remmy said. "It doesn't seem to be holding any information back from Connor O'Dell, sir. They're talking about things I don't understand. Physics, engineering, cosmology, and that sort of thing."

"A computer programmed with enough information could mimic life," Darius said. "And it's been reading our mail for as long as we've been broadcasting. There's no doubt it could have learned everything about us."

"Yes, sir," Remmy said.

"So what does it want?"

"I don't have the fine details, sir. But from what I've been shown, there's a world in another star system. It wants to take us there in the *Jericho*."

"Through hyperspace?"

"Yes, I believe so. Again, I'm just a Marine Sergeant, sir. I don't know much about that sort of thing. The artifact picked a poor representative to help it complete its mission."

"Which is?" Darius asked.

"To reach this planet, Lawash. There's something there it wants us to get. I know it's important and rare, but I can't rightly say what it is."

"And in exchange, will it show us how to travel between star systems?"

"I think that's a given since it's going to teach us how to do it. My understanding is that it wants to upload all that kind of information to our computer system. A map of hyperspace, maybe? That's what it looked like to me."

"I suppose that would be worth the risk. Will it allow us to return that data to the inner system?"

"I have no idea, sir," Remmy confessed. "It would be a lot of information, and it's not static. The computations to understand it are way out of my league, sir."

"Is there something guarding the object it wants us to retrieve?"

"That's another good question," Remmy said. "I got the impression of danger but not a full explanation of what was there. I don't think it's being guarded, but the world is dangerous."

"Wonderful," Darius said. "Master Sergeant, this has been a very informative conversation. Whatever transpires over the next few days, I want you to know your contribution has been substantial."

"Yes, sir, thank you, sir."

"As you know, letting a foreign agent have access to our ship is exceedingly rare. I can't say I'm in favor of it, but we're going to wait out the full seven-day quarantine before making any decisions. You should know we've been cut off from Fleet Command. Something is blocking all signals, and I assume it is the device. That's not a good sign if that thing wants us to trust it, but we will continue to explore the opportunity."

"Yes sir, and one last thing, if I may?"

"Go ahead, Master Sergeant."

"I don't know what GIGI is after on that planet, but whatever it is would be extremely valuable to the *Jericho* and, I'm assuming, humanity, sir."

"Valuable how?"

"Can't say, sir. But I will seek to find out."

"We'll do that from our end, too, Master Sergeant. Now, I want you to get a medical scan. That's to be done daily, but I want you to do a neurological scan as well. Let's keep an eye on your brain since we know the device has done something to it."

"Yes, sir, I'll do that right now."

Darius cut off the communication but watched on his monitor as Remmy replaced his space suit in its locker and walked across the Launch Bay to the medical gear. He would do the scan, which the ship's doctor would monitor. Once the results are in, Darius will need to talk with Doctor Mishta Lanski.

Getting to his feet, Darius walked past the small bar built into one bulkhead of his office near a pair of comfortable sitting chairs. Every day, they were a temptation, but he had never felt so drawn to the need for a drink. The liquor in the crystal containers was high-end, single-malt bourbon over forty years old. One sip and the oaky liquid would slide down his throat, sending a wave of relaxing warmth through his entire body. It was medicine for the mind and spirit but would also cloud his rational, creative thinking. And Darius felt that at that moment, more than ever before, he needed to be able to think clearly.

He bypassed the liquor as he had since their cruise began and instead left his office. Just down the corridor was the ship's sick bay. Like every other facet of the *Jericho,* it was pristine. To Captain Darius' knowledge, no one needed the facility, not for a cold or sprained ankle. No work-related accidents had occurred, and certainly no major, life-threatening incidents. The doors to the sick bay swished open when he pressed the button on the wall next to them. The main part of the room was filled with exam tables and scanning bays. Every wall was covered with cabinet doors, and inside, there was a wide variety of medical gear, including everything from first aid supplies to surgical equipment. They were prepared for any medical emergency, including having a surgeon as part of the crew. Only the big carrier class battleships had surgeons, usually just one for thousands of crew members. Most other Fleet vessels settled for robo-medics, scanners, and med techs.

To the right of the main trauma center was a ward for those convalescing. It was empty. Opposite it, to the left of the main entrance, was Major Mishta Lanski's office. It wasn't as big as Darius' but very well-appointed.

"Captain!" Major Lanski said with obvious surprise. "Are you sick?"

"No, doctor, I'm fine," Zeke said. "How are you?"

"Me? I'm great. It's not a worry in the world. This cruise has been like a vacation."

"I'm glad," Darius said, feeling a tiny bit of envy for the doctor. "Master Sergeant Remmy Steel is getting scanned down in the Launch Bay. Can you pull that information up on your computer?"

"Absolutely," Mishta said.

He turned and sat back down at his desk. With the push of an icon on the interactive desktop, he brought up a hologram of Sergeant Steel.

"This is from his standard exam scan that was part of his service record. It's about nine months old, but you can see that the Master Sergeant has no injuries."

The hologram showed Remmy with no clothes on. Darius couldn't help but notice the scars on his chest, hip, and back.

"Are those..."

"Battle scars, I suppose. We Marines are a hardy bunch," the doctor said.

Darius knew that Doctor Lanski was no warrior. The medical officers were Marines simply because the need for their services in that military branch was greater. But their affiliation, and rank for that matter, were ornamental. Dr. Lanski had no command authority on the ship.

"I read the file," Darius said. "But it doesn't quite paint the picture."

"They don't give out Medals' of Honor to just anyone," Lanski chuckled. "The Master Sergeant certainly earned it. But he has no lingering issues. His vital systems are all optimal. If anything appears on this new scan, it should stand out."

The doctor tapped away at his controls. The hologram of Sergeant Steel flickered.

"Looks like the overall scan is complete, but he's initiated a... brain scan?"

"That was at my direction," Captain Darius said. "We need to know if anything has changed since coming into contact with the artifact."

"The what?" Lanski asked.

Scattered around the officer were several reading devices. The doctor was researching something. There was even a writing slate with his notes on a side table. Darius didn't try to decipher the medical jargon. What the doctor worked on in his spare time wasn't his concern.

"You're aware that we picked up an alien object, aren't you?"

"I've been working on a paper for the Interstellar Medical Journal," he said with obvious pride. "There's some talking of maybe expanding it to a book. This cruise has given me plenty of time to research."

"That's great, but we just picked up an alien device," Darius told him.

"Alien as in..."

"Yes, non-human, from another intelligence, originating outside the solar system."

The doctor gave a long, low whistle of surprise. "I did *not* know that."

"Master Sergeant Steel led the Marine team on an EVA to collect it," Darius explained. "He was the first to come into contact with it, and the device did some sort of neural mapping that allows it to communicate directly with Sergeant Steel."

"Mentally?"

"Yes."

"That is very interesting. There are theories about mental telepathy, some that involve matching brain waves."

"I want to make sure nothing is going on in the Sergeant's head that we should be aware of," Darius said. "Any changes, however small, should be reported to me immediately. The rest of the Bravo Team will be performing daily med scans. We have to know there's no contagion to be contained in any of them. Connor O'Dell is with them, too."

"I'll set my computer to alert me whenever they do a scan," Lanski said. "I have records on everyone except Mr. O'Dell."

"Keep me informed, will you? A daily verbal report is good enough. Please let me know immediately if there is anything out of the ordinary."

"Yes, sir, Captain. I will certainly do that."

Darius stuck out his hand, and the doctor shook it. Lanski looked a little sheepish as if he had been caught not keeping his room clean. But Darius didn't care what the doctor did in his free time as long as he was ready for whatever duty came his way.

Captain Darius left the sick bay to walk the ship's circuit. He didn't care to inspect anything; he just wanted to get his body moving. The exercise had a way of clearing his mind. He enjoyed the variety of walking, climbing stairs, and returning down again. The *Jericho* was certainly big enough and he was a common sight on all three decks. His presence wouldn't surprise anyone.

As he walked, he considered what lay ahead. He was being asked to go where no man had ever gone. And not just himself but a ship with over a hundred souls on board. The crew, including the Marine platoon, was counting on him to make the right decision. But Darius didn't know what the *right* decision would be. He knew what the Brass expected him to do. They expected him to return with the artifact - GIGI. But if the device was alive, he had no authority to take the object where it didn't want to go.

On the other hand, could he really order the ship to traverse the galaxy? They were already so far from the nearest Fleet ship that no help could reach them if the *Jericho* malfunctioned. In that regard, did it matter if they were near Saturn or in another star system? And if he could gain the knowledge of traversing star systems, didn't he owe that to humanity? But what if the device was lying to them? What if it was leading them away to slaughter? He had to consider that option. If there really was a cosmic empire, would the *Jericho* leaving the Sol system alert them to the presence of the human race? What if, in leaving the solar system, Darius inadvertently made them vulnerable to a race of highly advanced beings who might slaughter or enslave mankind? He had no way of knowing anything about the beings in the galaxy. Humanity had never made contact with another intelligent species. It was a high-pressure situation that only Darius could solve, and he had less than a week to solve it.

CHAPTER 23

THE FIRST NIGHT was the hardest. The Bravo team made the executive decision that lights would go out at 2200 hours and stay off for at least eight. But, of course, Remmy had trouble sleeping, not just because he was lying on a stiff cot with a very thin pad. Or that the cavernous Launch Bay was different from his quarters. Remmy had learned to sleep anytime, anywhere, regardless of what was happening around him. It didn't matter that Corporal Jack Fortnoy was snoring or that Connor O'Dell was tossing and turning on his creaky cot. The civilian was muttering, too, clearly displeased with the sleeping arrangements.

Remmy heard it all and lay staring up into the darkness, his mind reeling. Everything had changed for him so fast. And the most pressing thing was his fear that his mind was no longer his own.

Gigi? He thought. It was a bit like talking to himself, only he didn't say the words out loud.

I am here, Master Sergeant.

You're in my head now?

Humans have powerful minds. Each one is unique. I have learned to discern and interpret your brain waves. But I do not exist in your mind as you have suggested.

But you can hear my thoughts?

I can hear them the way you might hear someone talking on the far side of the room. It all registers if I give you my attention; if not, it is just white noise. I hope this revelation does not offend you.

It doesn't, Remmy thought. *It's a comfort, actually.*

Intrusion is not my intent, Master Sergeant. I hope only to communicate with you. My directives require me to bond with a physical being in a reasonable vicinity of my location. In this instance, someone on the SDF Jericho. I can use your communications system, but in the case of technical difficulties, my makers thought it best to keep me paired with an organic, intelligent being.

Okay, good. That's all, GIGI.

My pleasure, Sergeant.

There was no sign-off, and Remmy knew the alien device could still hear everything he was thinking, but he chose to believe it when it said it paid him no attention. He thought of the bonding as simply a redundancy programmed into the device. It made sense to him. Transmissions could be intercepted or jammed, but their bond superseded those things. Not that GIGI would ever be left alone or cut off from humans. Remmy knew the device would be utilized and studied for decades, maybe even centuries.

Eventually, he slept. There was nothing else to do. But as was his habit, he rose early, stretched, and did a full routine of standard Marine exercises. The shower in the Launch Bay was a narrow stall. There was no water heater; a general service recycler cleaned the water as it rotated through. It wasn't cold, but felt cold against his skin after his morning workout. Dressed and ready, his day began.

Connor O'Dell spent the next six days trying to understand GIGI. Whenever the ship's officers were busy learning from the alien device (Remmy still had trouble thinking of it as a life form), he clarified what had been discovered.

It was a long week, not simply because he was in meetings all day but because the others kept their distance when he wasn't. He was a Master Sergeant, a unit's senior Non-Commissioned Officer. With that responsibility, there always came a distance between him and the other enlisted Marines. But typically, there was camaraderie among the NCOs. Laila McPherson was a fellow NCO, and she had been his friend. But since the mission, she has watched him as if she expected him to act out or change somehow.

There had been no change, no pathogens brought in from the alien device. GIGI was a living machine, but she wasn't contaminated. Remmy and the other people quarantined in the *Jericho's* Launch Bay did daily medical scans. They were all negative for pathogens and in perfect health. The only real change was that Remmy's mind had expanded. It wasn't a physical change but more of an academic one. He had seen things no human had ever seen. The sight was just the brain's interpretation of the light that passes into the eye. GIGI had sent his brain images of alien planets, Imperial spaceships, slaver raiding parties, fighting on far-off worlds that were completely different and oddly the same as the fighting in the Sol system among the humans. Everyone on the ship was going through a massive paradigm shift. The Senior Fleet officers on board were directly involved in questioning the alien device. They shared bits and pieces of that information with the crew under them. Lieutenant Henry Nash had regular meetings with his engineers to get their perspectives. They shared more details with the other crew personnel. Everyone seemed to have an insatiable appetite for knowledge.

On the last day of the quarantine, while Vivian Ramos was busy talking about hyperspace travel with GIGI, Remmy was once more contacted by Captain Darius on a private communication channel. They hadn't spoken since he had first returned to the ship with the artifact.

"All your scans are clear," the Captain told him. Remmy already knew that, but hearing it from a superior was still good.

"Thank you, sir," Remmy said.

"If only everything were as cut and dried as a medical scan," he continued. "This week has absolutely flown by."

Remmy didn't think so. Being in quarantine and forced to attend meetings virtually had made the seven days feel like an eternity. Normally, he didn't get claustrophobic on spaceships; even fleet vessels were much more cramped than the *Jericho*. But spending seven days in what felt like an oversized garage without privacy had worn him down.

"We have to make a decision about what comes next, Master Sergeant," the Captain continued. "And I need your assessment."

"For what it's worth, sir, GIGI hasn't crossed any boundaries or broken any promises."

"That we know of," Captain Darius said.

"We don't have any reason that I can see to doubt her word."

"And you think it's safe?"

"I think it's within the margins, sir. I don't get paid to stay safe."

"This ship's crew is my responsibility, and if that were all that was at stake, Master Sergeant, I wouldn't hesitate. But GIGI is asking us to trust that we can travel through an unknown dimension to another star system. That's a pretty big ask. And the risk to our race is at an all-time high. What if GIGI is just a masquerade? I could be opening Pandora's Box."

"No risk, no reward, I suppose," Remmy said.

"This is the biggest gamble in the history of mankind," Captain Darius countered. "Are you comfortable taking that kind of chance, Master Sergeant?"

"I don't know everything," Remmy confessed. "I can hear GIGI in my head but can't read her mind. I don't know that she isn't lying, but I don't think she is. That's the best I can do, Captain. You asked for my gut feeling, and that's it. I think we take her at her word and get this mission done."

"I'll take your recommendation under advisement. And thank you for all you've done, Master Sergeant. Your work in this matter has been invaluable."

"Yes, sir! Thank you, Captain, sir."

"I'll be making a decision soon. Let the others know I'll be ending your quarantine later today. You're all to report directly to Doctor Lanski in the medical bay."

"Roger that, sir."

Captain Darius ended the transmission, and Remmy got to his feet. He walked over to the drop ship. Staff Sergeant McPherson and Corporal Berry spent most of their time inside. They had set up a comfortable sitting area, along with a table. They were in the middle of a card game when Remmy knocked on the bulkhead to get their attention.

"It's open," Izzy called.

The wide rear hatch was down. Remmy walked up and stood at the entrance.

"I just spoke with the Captain. They're letting us out soon," he said.

"About time," Laila said. "I'm sick of this Launch Bay."

"First stop, the mess hall," Izzy said. "If I never eat another emergency ration, it will be too soon."

"I won't say no to a hot shower either," Laila said. "What's our orders."

"Report to the med bay," Remmy said.

"Why?" Izzy asked. "We've been scanned every day?"

"The Captain wants the ship's surgeon to do one final inspection. After that, we're free."

"I suppose we should start packing up then," Laila said. "We'll see to it, Master Sergeant, and have everything ship shape quickly."

"I appreciate it, Staff Sergeant."

Remmy turned and walked down the stairs. He found Corporal Jack Fortnoy on his bunk watching a movie on his entertainment slate. He waved at the younger man, who sat up and removed his headphones.

"We'll be heading up to the medical bay soon," Remmy told him. "Start collecting your things."

They spent half an hour putting their bedding away and prepping the Launch Bay to return to normal operations. Not that much happened in the garage-like hangar. But they would need to move the cots and excess food that had been stowed there for their week of quarantine.

He didn't know what decision the Captain would come to. Thinking of leaving the solar system wasn't very comforting, but Remmy was ready for some action. He had sat in quarantine for so long that he felt like a slug. All he really wanted was to get a rifle in hand and his boots on enemy territory again. It seemed ludicrous to think of combat as a relief, yet that's how he felt. Maybe it was because Remmy Steel could visualize a real enemy for the first time in his life. It wouldn't be just fighting humans who disagreed with the Inter-system government or who wanted to seize control of a space station. Remmy had seen what the true enemy of freedom looked like. GIGI had shared images of Imperial ships bombarding entire planets and Slavers carrying away the innocent. He hoped that Captain Darius would make the daring decision to trust GIGI and that Master Sergeant Remmy Steel would have the opportunity to show what he could do.

CHAPTER 24

"YOU'VE MADE this compartment secure, Lieutenant Nash?" Captain Darius asked.

"Aye, Captain. All recording devices have been removed, per your instructions."

"Why are we doing this again?" Vivian Ramos asked.

They were in a workshop on the lower deck just outside the engineering space for the life support systems.

"To ensure that GIGI can't hear our deliberations," Zeke explained. "We still aren't sure what she is capable of. What have you learned, Henry?"

"It isn't lying about being like a computer," the tall engineer said. "We had Master Sergeant Steel run thermal scans. It's a computer made from base minerals encased inside solid rock."

"Any idea how that was done?" Pete Best asked.

"No idea. The engineering capability is far beyond what we possess. And the computer framework itself is novel. It's more like a brain than a circuit board."

"What are the dangers of letting it upload into our system?" Darius asked.

"It could take control of the ship and cut us out completely," Nash said. "But if it didn't, it would be like making the ship a thousand times more efficient. Imagine being able to control every system at the speed of thought, Captain, and having someone like that always on alert. GIGI won't get sleepy or tired. It will be scanning for dangers constantly. The entire command staff would be superfluous."

"It would be her ship then," Pete Best asked.

"For all intents and purposes, yes," Nash replied.

"Is there a risk of GIGI spreading to other vessels and computer systems?" Zeke asked.

"Yes, but it could have done that long ago," Nash explained. "Our system network is wide open to her. Our security would be powerless to stop GIGI if that's what she wanted to do."

"And why hasn't she?" Lieutenant Colt asked. He was the only Marine at the clandestine meeting.

"Because I don't think that's what it wants," Vivan Ramos said. "It's here to recruit us."

"That your expert psychological opinion, doctor?" Pete teased.

"Let's stay on task, people," Commander Lee chided.

"I've run the numbers," Vivian said. "We're talking highly advanced equations. The best minds on Earth couldn't have come up with such elegant formulas. But it all adds up. If hyperspace exists, and I believe it does, then we have the means to traverse it, thanks to GIGI."

"And the map?" Captain Darius asked.

"Calling it a map is a little elementary, but yes. I haven't seen it exactly, but GIGI's answers to my questions make sense. We could go anywhere we want with greater knowledge of the galaxy."

Captain Darius turned to his weapons specialist. "What about the dangers?"

"If we can believe this thing," Pete Best said. "We're in some real trouble."

"Go on," Zeke urged.

"Sometime in the past, there was a war between two highly advanced races," Pete explained. "The Torjah's and the Arodoni. They pretty much wiped each other out, and it was like a thousand years later, the Pratoreen discovered some of the old Torjah's tech. They got it running again and used it to conquer entire worlds. They call themselves Imperials now and used their advanced weapons technology to force planets into their regime."

"How advanced?" Captain Darius asked. "Can we defeat them?"

"No," Pete said. "They have long-range lasers capable of taking out entire Fleet ships. They could park at the system's edge and pick us off one by one."

"A laser that reaches the entire length of the solar system?" Nash asked incredulously.

"According to the artifact," Pete said. "It's a matter of power and how the laser is fired. Obviously, something powerful would destroy itself if it wasn't perfectly focused and contained. The Pratoreen found a source of abundant energy. It powers all their starships and weapons. They've moved beyond projectiles, but who can blame them for that."

"If that's true, there's nothing we can do about it," Captain Darius said. "I certainly wouldn't want to leave the system and draw the attention of these aliens."

"That's what GIGI said," Pete carried on. "As things stand now, we might have another century or two before the Imperialists or Slavers discover the Sol system. But there's one thing the Pratoreen fear. That's Arodoni technology. If we had that, the bad guys wouldn't dare attack the Sol system."

"But we don't have that," Commander Lori Lee pointed out.

"True, but according to GIGI, it knows where we can get some," Pete Best said.

That caused the room to fall silent. Darius felt like he had just stepped into a trap. It was too good to be true. Of course, there had to be a reason for the *Jericho* to leave the system. Until then, Darius had been leaning toward returning the ship to the inner system. But he couldn't justify doing that if there was a way to protect humanity. Of course, it all hinged on the alien artifact. Could it take the *Jericho* across the galaxy? And would they find something that could protect them from a highly advanced foe? If the answers to those questions were yes, he had no other option. But what if the device was lying to them all?

Captain Zeke Darius was a decisive man, but he wished that he could get orders from his superiors rather than make the decision himself. Unfortunately, they were still cut off from the inner system, probably by GIGI. On the one hand, Darius understood the need to leave the decision strictly to him. The Brass wouldn't want to waste the opportunity to learn all it could from GIGI. And leaving the system certainly put that at risk. Yet Darius couldn't shake the feeling that whatever was out there in the dark expanse was a horror too great to contemplate. And he didn't want to be responsible for waking it up.

"The artifact says there is an Arondoni power core hidden on a planet called Lawash," Pete concluded. "With that, we could defend ourselves."

"In theory," Nash said.

"If we look at this situation from a logical perspective," Commander Lee said, "we have to admit that there is no reason to doubt the artifact."

"Because it hasn't lied to us yet?" Lieutenant Colt asked.

"That is one factor," Lee explained. "As far as we know, the device may be incapable of deception. It's alive, but it's still a machine, and as far as we know, it hasn't been duplicitous with us. Secondly, if going through hyperspace was dangerous, it wouldn't just destroy the *Jericho*, but also the artifact. We should assume it wouldn't have been put here to destroy itself. And the plans for the *Jericho* came from the artifact. If traveling through dimensions was its purpose, it would have naturally designed a vessel capable of such a feat. Third, as has already been pointed out, the device could seize control of the Jericho if the ship was all it wanted. It could have killed the crew and taken the ship if it only wanted to travel through the cosmos. When taken all together, it seems likely that what it truly desires, whether from emotions or programming, is to partner with us in an endeavor to retrieve something on an alien world."

"Logic," Vivian said. "Well put, Commander."

"I take it that's your pitch that we should allow the device access to our ship?" Darius asked.

"I'm not happy about it, but it does make sense," Commander Lee said.

"Nash?"

The big engineer shrugged. "If we're keeping our emotions out of it," he said softly. "Then I must admit this ship is better designed and fabricated than anything we've ever produced. Even the stuff we've developed using the tech we stole and reverse-engineered isn't as good as the original. In that regard, I have to admit the ship is more GIGIs than ours, Captain. If she wants to take it somewhere, she's got my vote."

"Interesting perspective," Darius said. "Lieutenant Ramos?"

"I've crunched the numbers. What happens when we get there may be a mystery, but I'm certain we'll get where we're going using the hyper-dimensional road map that GIGI contains."

Darius rubbed his eyes. He was tired. The mental pressure of making such a decision was overwhelming. He turned to Lieutenant Colt.

"What about your Marines, Lieutenant? If all this is true, when we get to Lawash, your people will get the energy core. Are they up to that?"

"Without a doubt, Captain," Micky Colt said. "My platoon is all experienced, spec ops professionals. You couldn't have asked for a better team to carry out this type of mission."

"And you're in favor of it."

"We stand ready to serve, Captain. Whatever the assignment, that's what we're trained for."

"Even if you're facing something no one has ever heard of?"

"Improvise, adapt, overcome," Micky said. "That's our motto."

"Alright, it seems we've agreed. Nash, I want your best people on the Bridge. Lieutenant Colt, I'm assuming you have something that can destroy the artifact?"

Micky Colt looked surprised. "Yes, sir," he said.

"Then have it ready. We're going to let GIGI sync with our computer. If anything goes sideways, I want to cut to manual control and die that thing. Is that clear? Any objections?"

"The Brass will go ballistic if we destroy the artifact," Commander Lee said.

"In that case, I will take full responsibility," Captain Darius said. "I won't let an alien device overtake the ship. Hopefully, that doesn't happen, but I want everyone ready if it does."

Everyone nodded, and they filed out of the engineering workshop. It was time to do the most risk-laden thing Darius had ever considered. It wasn't just his career on the line; it was the lives of the entire crew and perhaps all mankind. But he had made his decision, and he wasn't the type of officer to second guess himself. Whatever happened, he would deal with it in a decisive way. It was time to make history again.

CHAPTER 25

REMMY WAS the last person out of the Launch Bay and he wasn't alone. The others had been gone nearly ten minutes before the orders came from the Captain to allow GIGI onto the ship's Bridge. Remmy walked the slab of stone with the strange markings that glowed with a ghostly light as it levitated through the ship's stairwells and down the corridor to the Bridge on the main deck.

It was no surprise that all the senior officers were waiting when Remmy arrived. Even Lieutenant Colt was there, and several junior officers and specialists too. Remmy stepped over beside his CO and waited as GIGI maneuvered just in front of the plot projector.

"We've decided to allow you to sync with the ship's computer," Captain Darius said. "If all goes well, we will travel to the Lawa system and attempt to retrieve the item you have described."

"It's happening," Alex Stanislaus called out.

Where the plot typically showed a hologram of the *Jericho*, and all craft, station, or celestial bodies in a given area flickered, and a small being with no legs but two long arms appeared. It had a stubby backside that it rested on. At the end of his arms were big hands with three fingers and two thumbs on either side. The shoulders were thick with muscle, but the rest of the creature didn't look strong. Its body was pudgy, at least to Remmy's thinking. It was round in the stomach area and thin through the chest. Its head had a narrow neck and was shaped like a football with a pointed chin and a point at the back of its head.

"Hello," the hologram said, its voice coming through the Bridge's speakers. "I am GIGI. At least this was the form of my makers, the Correll. Sadly, they are an extinct race, and I am one of the last of their technological achievements."

"It's nice to put a face with a name, GIGI," Captain Darius said.

Remmy could tell the Captain was nervous. The room was filled with nervously excited people. He couldn't blame them. They were seeing something no one but Remmy had ever seen before.

"I am synced to your ship's computer systems and downloading the hyperspace mapping information to your navigation computer," GIGI went on. "Please allow me to share with you what we should find in the Lawa system."

The hologram changed to an alien star system. At the center was a massive star, so blue it was almost white. Dozens of small planets orbited the star, but none were gas giants. The first eight were tiny. Several more had broken up and were in long lines stretched along what had once been the planet's orbital plane. The eighteenth planet was a small, red world with wispy bands of white clouds. From what Remmy could see, it was the only planet with an atmosphere.

"This is Lawash," GIGI said as the hologram zoomed in toward the eighteenth planet."It is a world not unlike your Mars. It has a very high iron content and a thin atmosphere. It was once home to several intelligent species. Lawash refused to join the Pratoreen Empire and was bombarded from orbit. Their water and air were tainted with toxins from the Pratoreen munitions used. Only the Rake survived, and the toxins physically and mentally warped them."

The hologram changed again. It showed a strange biped squatting down. The creature had long arms and legs that looked impossibly thin. The feet, as was the head, were huge, which Remmy thought had to be misshapen. It was round with abnormal features. The nose was huge and beak-shaped. It filled the center of the alien's face. Two uneven eyes bulged out as if they might pop free of the alien's head. Its mouth was small, with horrid-looking teeth sticking out at odd angles. There was hair, but not very much. It was wiry-looking and stiff. Remmy could also see places where the skin was covered in scaly patches that oozed foul-looking fluid.

"Wait a second!" Connor O'Dell came charging onto the Bridge, interrupting the presentation. "You can't possibly be thinking of going anywhere but back to the inner system, Captain."

Commander Lori Lee stepped in front of the civilian, but Connor was unfazed.

"You have orders, sir! Strict orders to return with the artifact. I'm as enthralled as anyone with GIGI, but we cannot leave the system."

"Mr. O'Dell, you are a guest on this ship," Captain Darius said. "All command decisions fall to me, and whatever I decide, you will have to live with. This isn't a democracy; we don't cast votes here."

"But your orders!"

"My duty is to this crew and the human race," Captain Darius said. "Their safety will always drive every decision I make."

"Have a seat, Mr. O'Dell," Lori Lee said. "And lower your voice, or I'll have you escorted to your quarters."

Micky Colt shifted on his feet. He was the only person on the Bridge with a weapon. Normally, even the Marines didn't go around armed, but he had a laser pistol in a holster on his right hip. It was covered with a safety flap, but he quietly unfastened it.

"I must protest," he said.

"Very well, I will hear your concerns before issuing our orders, but until then, sit down and shut up," Captain Darius said. "GIGI, please continue."

"The Rake," GIGI said as there had been no interruption, "are dangerous. They don't use projectile weapons but often carry rudimentary clubs or pipes to bludgeon their enemies. They eat anything, including their kind. We must be prepared to defend ourselves. I've taken the liberty of assessing human physiology."

The hologram showed the Rake stand to its full height. Beside him, a Marine in full battle armor appeared.

"That thing knows everything," Colt whispered.

Before Remmy could reply, a pained look crossed the Lieutenant's face as if he had just spoken to the enemy. He clenched his jaw and looked away, leaving Remmy feeling like the odd man.

"Here," GIGI continued, "you can see the difference in scale. The Rake don't usually work together, and their weapons are crude, but they are still powerful enough to kill a human. They should be avoided at all costs. If it becomes necessary to fight them, do so with the understanding that the sound of weapons fire will draw more of them."

"Wonderful," Colt grumbled.

"We've got some bolt slingers," Remmy said. "They don't make much noise when fired. And a few Marines on the heights shooting laser rifles with sound suppressors should keep the Rake off us."

"Excellent, Master Sergeant," Captain Darius said. "GIGI, please continue."

"The Arodoni Power Core is hidden inside the Jatoshi Temple ruins. More accurately, it is hidden in the tunnels underneath the temple. The Marine Platoon will need to infiltrate this space to remove it."

"Is it structurally sound?" Henry Nash asked.

"My information on the planet and the temple are over five hundred years old," GIGI said. To everyone's surprise, the hologram was changed into a stone pyramid. It was decorated with precious metals and elaborate murals. There were climbing vines that had been carefully tended, so they wound their way up the pyramid's sides and framed the murals. There were flags along a grand boulevard that led to the temple's entrance, which was a massive construction with round pillars and grand arches. "This is how it looked before the Empire bombarded the planet."

"Five hundred years ago?" Lori Lee asked. "It was probably destroyed."

"The temple has stood for over five thousand years," GIGI reported. "The entrance was destroyed in the bombing, but the temple survived."

The hologram changed and showed a cold, dust-covered structure, not unlike the pyramids on Earth. There was rubble built up along the base of the pyramid, and the entrance was gone. The tip-top portion looked like it had been blown off, but the rest of the gigantic structure was intact.

"What about the tunnels below?" Lieutenant Colt asked.

"I do not have data on their condition, but my calculations confirm they would be seventy-eight percent possible."

"What kind of layout is it, GIGI?" Remmy asked.

"It is intricate, what you might call a labyrinth of tunnels. I have detailed files on the tunnels and can lead Master Sergeant Remmy Steel through them."

"Do you know where the power core is located?" Captain Darius asked.

"Negative. There are many treasure chambers located under the temple. We will have to explore them until the Arodoni Power Core is found."

"If it's still even there," Connor O'Dell pointed out. "You've been in the Sol system for over four hundred years. Who's to say what has happened to this world in four centuries? Anyone could have come along and taken the power core thing."

"That is possible, but the odds are against it," GIGI said.

"And why is that?" Connor demanded.

"Because the toxins in the air and water make the planet hazardous," GIGI said. "That, combined with the secrecy of the Jatoshi clergy, results in a high probability that the power drive is still there."

"Alright, I can see your point," Darius said. "But before we fly halfway across the galaxy, we need to clear up a few things. How do you know about this power core? And what is it exactly."

"The Arodoni perfected a dark energy collector. The universe is not just empty space. It is full of energy, some active, some passive. The Arodoni discovered a way to attract this dark energy and convert it into active power for whatever purposes it chose."

"Free energy?" Henry Nash said. "That's a myth. It goes against the laws of thermodynamics."

"It isn't free energy, just unutilized energy. The conversion process is complicated, even beyond the ability of the Correll engineers. But small amounts of dark energy equal copious amounts of clean, usable energy."

"Enough to power a starship?" Darius asked.

"If the dark energy could be contained in the *Jericho's* fuel tanks, it would convert to enough energy to power ten thousand ships for a million years," GIGI said.

"Impossible," Connor O'Dell said.

"Even your own scientists have measured dark energy," GIGI continued. "But like most intelligent species, they cannot discover a way to contain it. Dark energy is invisible and intangible. Yet it exists, both mathematically and in theoretical physics."

"You said treasure chambers were under the temple," Vivian Ramos pointed out. "Won't they have drawn in thieves?"

"It is possible," GIGI said, "but few would recognize the Arodoni Power Core. To most, it would seem like an odd bit of technical junk."

"You still haven't answered the question of how you know of its existence at the temple," Darius pointed out.

"The Correll who created me gave it to the Jatoshi for safekeeping shortly before the Slavers invaded. Their homeworld was ransacked for any valuables during the early raids. The Arodoni Power Core had to be moved off-world."

"Why?" Pete Best asked. "Couldn't your people design a way to use it? They could have built weapons to defend their world."

"The power drive only works in space," GIGI explained. "On the surface of a planet, there is no dark energy to collect and convert."

"Why not build an orbital weapons platform to defend the planet?" Lieutenant Colt asked.

"That was what the Correll hoped to accomplish. Sadly, the defensive station was still under construction when the Slavers arrived in the system. They destroyed it, along with the networks of satellites and communication devices. The system was completely cut off. Many of the information, communication, and defensive systems went offline. Thousands of Correl died fighting, but as you can see by my projected anatomy, they were not suited for combat."

The hologram changed back to the long-armed, no legs, football-shaped being. Remmy thought they could hold and shoot a rifle easily enough, but they couldn't move and shoot. Mobility in combat was one of the core principles. A moving target was exponentially harder to shoot.

"Ensign Stanislaus, what's the status of our ship's computer?" Darius asked.

"We are in sync with GIGI," he said. "Transfer of information is at forty-two percent, Captain. All systems online and reporting at optimal levels."

"Nash?"

"I'm seeing the same here, Captain. If you can believe, the ship is functioning even better than before."

"Lieutenant Ramos, how long until we have a plot through hyperspace to the Lawa system?" Captain Darius asked.

"GIGI has already made the calculation. I've confirmed it with my navigation computers. If you want me to run the numbers, I'll need a few hours, sir."

"I do. We have to be prepared for anything. We need a plot in and one out again. We can't wait for hours if there are hostile forces in the system."

"Aye, Captain, I'm on it," Vivian said, pulling out an interactive data tablet with a pencil-shaped stylus. She immediately began writing out the formula displayed on her console screen.

"Lieutenant Colt," Darius continued. "Prepare your platoon. Master Sergeant Steel seems to have an idea of what strategy is best. If this Arodoni Power Core is on that planet, I plan to get it."

"Yes, sir," Micky replied.

Remmy saw the look of skepticism on his CO's face. It wasn't that Micky Colt didn't have faith in Remmy's combat abilities, but he no longer trusted his senior NCO.

"If all continues to go well," Captain Darius said, speaking to the crowded room of officers and technicians on the Bridge, "we will leave for the Lawa system in twenty-four hours."

"Captain, I must protest," Connor O'Dell said. "You have no right —ouch!"

Before he could finish his protest, Lori Lee grabbed his arm and twisted it behind his back.

"Don't hurt him," Darius said. "But let's see him back to his quarters. If any of you disagree with my decision, you can come to me privately, but I expect you to support my orders in front of your subordinates. I will not have a mutiny on this ship. Is that clear?"

"Aye, Captain," the Fleet officers replied. It wasn't quite Marine Corps sharp; they sounded more like a group of disappointed teenagers, but they managed.

Some filed out behind Commander Lee with Connor O'Dell in tow. Others remained at their stations on the Bridge. The hologram was gone, but GIGI remained near the plot projector on the bridge. Remmy knew the artifact was getting exactly what it wanted, but he didn't know if that was a good or bad thing. Only time will tell.

CHAPTER 26

"YOU'RE MAKING A MISTAKE," Connor said.

He was so frustrated he was pacing. Captain Darius had put the man off as long as he could, but there would inevitably be questions from his superiors. Most likely, a court marshal. The ship's log would be put under a microscope, and every decision he made and every crew member would be questioned. Captain Darius needed it on the record that he heard Connor O'Dell out, and that's what he intended to do.

"Can't you see this is the most important discovery in the history of mankind," Connor went on. "You have to take it home. You don't have the authority to leave the solar system, Captain. I hate to call you on the carpet, but you are exceeding your authority."

"We've talked about this. While cut off from the Fleet, the decision falls to me."

"Not when it comes to the artifact. That's why I'm here!"

"You're here to study it, Mr. O'Dell. You are here to advise us."

"And I'm advising you to take it back to the inner system."

"Thank you, but this is a military decision, and as such, I will stick with the plan agreed to by the senior crew as what is best for the Fleet."

"It's total crap, and you know it!" Connor shouted.

Captain Darius was on his feet in an instant. The cool, calculating ship captain was suddenly furious. Connor O'Dell backed up as Darius snarled, "Who the hell do you think you're talking to like that?"

"I'm sorry, Captain," Connor said.

"If you don't like my decisions, frankly, I don't give a damn," Zeke continued, his anger burning hot. He stepped out from behind his desk, moving toward the frightened civilian in his office. "You are here as a courtesy, and you sure better remember your place. There's a threat out there," Zeke thundered away, pointing in a random direction to get his point across. "They won't hesitate to come here and kill or enslave us all. We've got one chance, just one, to find a way to defend ourselves. And it doesn't matter what I think or what you think about it; if we fail, that's the end. It won't matter what you learn from the device then, will it?"

"But wouldn't it be better," Connor ventured, "to let another battleship take that risk?"

"Mr. O'Dell, you may be a genius in political circles, but right now, you're acting like an idiot."

Connor had backed up so far that he stumbled into one of the sitting chairs. The color had drained from his face, and his hands were trembling. The anger cooled in Darius, and he walked over to the tiny bar and poured himself a glass of whiskey. He poured one for Connor, too, although he didn't want to. He was still a man bound by the protocols of his profession, and they dictated that he must offer his guest a drink. Zeke didn't say anything to him; he just thrust the glass with a finger's depth of amber-colored liquid. Connor took it in his shaking hands, and they both drank.

The liquid was cool but left a burning streak across Darius' tongue and down his throat. It had an oaky richness, what the experts would call a good flavor profile. Most of it was lost on Darius. What he wanted at that moment, after what had been one of the hardest days in his career, was the warmth that spread out from his stomach the moment the liquor landed there. A warm wave moved up his chest and down his legs. His face flushed, and his muscles relaxed.

"Think it through," Darius said. "No other ship is designed for long voyages, but we are. No other ship has the computing power necessary to make the jump. No other ship was designed for it. A dreadnaught would be a better choice, only they're constantly breaking down. You don't know that because you're not a Fleet sailor. I've been on these spaceships my entire adult life. Every vessel made in the past fifty years has been an improvement, and yet the rigors of space travel always, without exception, wreaked havoc on that equipment. The *Jericho* isn't like those other ships, Mr. O'Dell. In our three-month cruise, the longest single tour without making any stops for repairs or resupply, we haven't had a single system error. Nothing has broken. I don't know what's different about her design, but I know it is unique among all the spacecraft that humanity has ever built. She is the only ship equipped to make the hyperspace voyage. Going back to the inner system first only wastes time.

"And I have to think about what is best, first for the crew, then for the Fleet, but also all of humanity," Zeke continued, leaning against the front edge of his desk as Connor sipped his glass of whisky. "I have no doubt what the Brass would order me to do. Hell, they spent three decades debating whether or not to build this ship in the first place. They would probably spend at least that long deciding to leave the solar system, too, maybe even longer. That acknowledgment will probably get me court-martialed when all of this is said and done, but it is a factor in my decision."

"To leave the solar system? That's the best choice?"

"All I can do is act on the data I have," Zeke continued. "That data tells me there is an enemy of unknown strength but certainly of much greater technical superiority to the human race. If there's a chance, even the slightest sliver, that we can do something to protect ourselves, I have to take it. Our data is over four hundred years old. We might discover that everything has changed, but I don't think we can wait another thirty years to act and protect ourselves."

"You may be right," Connor said after downing the last swallow of his whisky, "but what if we don't come back? By taking the artifact, you are robbing humanity of what could be thousands of years of technological advancement."

"We can't retrieve the power core without GIGI," Darius said. "If we could, this would be a different conversation."

"Well, I think I've made my point," Connor said. "Thank you for hearing me out. And thank you for this."

He set the tumbler on the small table between the two sitting chairs.

"Will you be making a final communication attempt before we leave?" Connor asked.

"I will," Darius said. "One large data transmission just before we go. Hopefully, it will get through."

"I'll go write to my family then," Connor said. "It may be the last thing they ever get from me."

It was a final jab at the Captain and his decision. The statement may not have been strong enough to change anyone's mind, but it did land,

and Darius felt the sting. If they left the solar system and never returned, he would have taken every soul on board the *Jericho* away from their family and loved ones. He knew that. It was a terrible thing, but a necessary one if they were going to have any chance of surviving into the years and decades ahead. Darius was not the kind of leader who could turn his back when a threat was revealed. He didn't hide and hope that the enemy would pass them by. It wasn't who he was as a man and military officer. He wrestled with the decision, and then, once his mind was settled, he presented the data to his senior officers without any direct pressure. They had all confirmed his thinking and backed the plan of action he was already intending to take.

Still, even knowing that he was making the right decision, he was painfully aware of the risks involved. He left his office and made his way to his cabin. The alcohol was in his bloodstream. He imagined he could feel the heat in every vein and artery. Once he reached his berth, he felt a little more at ease. The last thing a line officer wanted was to be seen drunk. Darius hadn't imbibed enough to be drunk, but he knew that the warmth he felt would start to make his thinking fuzzy, and his coordination might be slightly off.

He did his best in his cabin to let go of any stress. His sleep chamber was his private space. In his berth, he wasn't a ship captain; he was just a man. He could turn off his sense of duty and unburden himself from all responsibilities for a few hours of privacy and rest in his cabin. It was surprisingly comfortable and more spacious than any berth on a regular Fleet ship. He went directly to his bed and kicked off his shoes. The alcohol had reached his brain. He knew it because his thoughts slowed, and his worries slipped away. In fact, he couldn't remember what he had been worried about.

He threw back the blankets and crawled between the sheets. The light switch was on the bulkhead. He could reach it without getting up. His muscles relaxed, and he felt himself sinking into the soft mattress. With one arm, he reached up and tapped the switch that turned off the lights. The ship's interior was pitch black, and the cabin was well insulated. There was no engine noise, no sound of other sailors with boots clomping on metal grates, and nothing from the deck above or below. Darius reached over and activated a small sleep machine. Normally, he used it to cover the noise of a ship, but on the Jericho, he didn't need it. Only the sounds the device made gave him comfort. His favorite track among the many on the device was the *Country Evening*, which he had rarely experienced in real life. But he knew there were places on earth where the crickets still chirped when the sun went down. The sleep machine had a variety of sounds on the track, like the occasional wisp of wind rustling the leaves in a tree, the odd croak from a frog, and the gurgle of a creek somewhere nearby. It was grounding for the Captain, who had spent nearly all his adult life in space. The sounds relaxed him, ushered him off to sleep, and reminded him of the beautiful place he was defending. Outside his cabin, he had to make hard decisions and think about others before himself. But in his private room, he could do what he wanted and indulge his desires. What he wanted was sleep. He needed it. The next day, they would be going where no human had ever been and maybe dying in the process. Those thoughts would have been popping in his brain like corn placed on fire. But the whisky had done its work. He closed his eyes and let the sweet river of unconsciousness carry him away.

CHAPTER 27

EVERYTHING HAD CHANGED for Master Sergeant Remmy Steel. He was still the same man, but no one else seemed to think so. They were stiff around him, wary, guarded. He had seen it before. Marines weren't superstitious but could lose confidence in a leader, and the results were never good. Lieutenant Colt had called a platoon meeting. They were gathered together in what was commonly called grunt country. The back three sections of the lower deck consisted of spaces for the Marine platoon. The armory was designed more like a locker room for a professional sports team. Each Marine had an extra wide locker with a padded bench in front of it. They were mostly sitting around, waiting for the CO to show up. Normally, Remmy would be engaged in conversation, but most of the platoon was lingering on the far side of the room. Only Staff Sergeant Laila McPherson and Gunnery Sergeant Chad Rand were near enough to him to converse, but they were talking to one another in quiet tones while trying not to make eye contact with the Master Sergeant.

Thankfully, before things got awkward, Lieutenant Micky Colt arrived. He stood just inside the doorway and put his hands on his hips.

"Looks like this is going to be more than just a pleasure cruise, people," Colt said. "As you may already know, the alien device has warned us of a threat. It shouldn't be surprising to know there are powerful enemies in the galaxy. We may not have met them face to face, but that won't be the case for much longer. So! The *Jericho* is going to make history once more. We are leaving the Sol system via a hyperspace jump and going to the Lawa system. There, our platoon will descend to the surface of a planet called Lawash. It's been bombed out and left to rot. The only survivors look like creatures from a toxic waste dump. They are hostile and dangerous, so that we won't take any chances. From this point forward, we will be on high alert. This ship is making a daring charge into history, and we are the tip of the spear. Whatever happens, it is up to us to defend ourselves and the ship from alien threats. So get your minds right. This is not an exercise or simulation. It's the real deal. Make your peace with that and get your gear ready."

"What's the op, sir?" Gunny Rand asked.

"Recovery operation," Lieutenant Colt replied. He was in his element. The young officer rattled off the details in a clear, distinct manner. "On Lawash is an ancient temple. There are tunnels under it, and somewhere in those tunnels, we will find an alien power core that is the main target of this mission. We find it and bring it back—simple as that."

"But it won't be a walk in the park," Remmy broke in. He didn't bother looking at Lieutenant Colt. He knew the man had suspicions about Remmy; the entire platoon acted like he had grown a second head. But that didn't change the fact that he was the senior NCO of a special forces platoon. He had a job to do, and the fact that GIGI had bonded to him only made him more fit to carry out the operation before them.

"The world is poisoned, so make sure your armored space suits are in optimal condition," Remmy said. "Bravo team will be our snipers. Get your long-range weapons dialed in. You'll need to use suppressors to avoid attracting more bad guys, called the Rake on Lawash. They're big, easily twice our height, and powerful. If one gets anywhere near our team, you have authorization to use deadly force."

"We'll also be in an unstable environment once we reach the temple," Lieutenant Colt said. "The tunnels where the power core is located may or may not have collapsed. We won't know until we are boots on the ground. Coms may be compromised. I want everyone carrying glow stickers and extra O_2 canisters. This is not a combat operation, nor should we burden ourselves with extra gear. Two spare air tanks, glow stickers, and your choice of firearms with noise suppressors. We get in, we get the power core, we get out and back to the *Jericho*. I want it clean, and I want it neat, people. No showboating, no unnecessary risks. Is that clear, platoon?"

"Yes, sir!" They responded in perfect unison.

"Very good. Once we hit the system, Master Sergeant Remmy will give us a more thorough mission prep with holographic data pulled from the planet's surface. Let's get our shit together, people. I want everyone back here in twelve hours with gear and weapons ready. Any questions?"

There were none, and the Lieutenant dismissed the meeting. There was plenty to talk about, and McPherson turned to Remmy with her questions.

"How dangerous?" She asked.

"Hostile territory," Remmy said. "We'll know more once we're in the system."

"Hyperspace? I thought that was just BS sci-fi mumbo-jumbo," Gunny Rand said. "They can't be serious."

"It's real," Remmy said. "Inter-dimensional travel. I don't understand it, but I don't need to."

"Yeah, tell us who is fighting and be done with it," Sergeant Hugo McManus said as he joined the little group facing Remmy.

"How long will it take to get to this alien world?" McPherson asked.

"Six hours once they make the jump," Remmy said, having already asked GIGI that question after the Captain's decision on the Bridge. He checked his watch, which was set to ship at the time. It showed the hour as twenty-two hundred. "My guess is they'll go in eight hours once the nav officer confirms the math. The ship then takes a couple of laps around the planet to get surface data, and we're in business."

"Better than just running sims every day," Gunny Rand said. "If we survive the trip through hyperspace."

"Anything we need to know about that?" Laila asked.

"Don't know," Remmy said. "I asked, but we'll be the first humans going through it. GIGI has no idea how it might affect us."

"So we could all die," Rand said. "Wonderful."

"Other people do this, right, Master Sergeant?" McManus asked. "Other aliens, I mean."

"Yes," Remmy said. "There shouldn't be any harm to us."

"Famous last words," Gunny Rand said.

"You scared, Gunny?" Laila asked.

"I'm not scared," he replied calmly, "but I will say this: I didn't sign up to go fight and maybe die on a world outside our solar system. Seems like we should have had a say in the decision, that's all."

"You'd rather run sims and fight dissidents on Mars or some lousy space station?" Hugo McManus asked. "Not me, man. I want to see what's out there. I have not been too impressed with space since I joined the Corps. It's been a lot of cramped ships and lousy food. I say we do something no one else has ever done before. Maybe something really important."

"Looks like you'll get your chance," McPherson said.

"Twelve hours," Gunny Rand said. "I got stuff to do before I'm stuck in a space suit for who knows how long."

"Ditto," Hugo McManus said.

They both left the armory. Most of the others followed them out. Laila stayed with Remmy. They had unfinished business, and he guessed that after they had avoided each other for their seven days of quarantine, she would be finally ready to hash things out.

"What's really going on here," she whispered.

Remmy liked being close to Laila, but he could feel a sense of anger coming from her, making him nervous.

"I'm not sure I understand what you're asking me," he said.

"The hell you don't," she snapped, then pointed at the side of his head. "Who's in there? Is it the man who boarded this ship with us three months ago? Or are we dealing with someone new?"

"I'm still me," Remmy said. "Always have been."

"Prove it," she said. "Prove to me that you're Remmy Steel, that won the Medal of Honor and saved all those civies on Mars. Prove to me that I can trust you, that you aren't under the control of some alien—"

Looking back, he could never say why he did it. Maybe it was an impulse, but Remmy had always been the type of man who prided himself on his self-control. Maybe it was her anger, which both baffled and scared him a little. He knew one thing for certain after their space-walk to get the artifact. And maybe he just felt like it was time to take it.

He reached out, grabbed Laila McPherson, and pulled her body into his. Her eyes went wide, and he kissed her. Their lips came together, and she was initially stiff, with surprise or maybe even shock. They had been flirtatious, but neither had spoken about their feelings for each other. Remmy knew the traditions of the Corps. He wasn't supposed to frater-nize with someone in his platoon, but he had spent three months denying his feelings and couldn't understand why. So he kissed her, and she kissed him after hesitation. Her arms came up to his shoulders and wrapped around his head. The heat of her anger and his pent-up desire kindled into a passionate blaze. It didn't hurt that they seemed to be a perfect match. Remmy had kissed girls before. It was usually awkward at first and sometimes even unpleasant. But Laila felt to Remmy like they were made for each other. When they finally broke apart, he looked into her eyes. The shock was still there, but also a contentment that let him know she wasn't mad. In fact, she seemed relieved.

"Did we just do that?" she asked, glancing around to see if anyone else was still in the armory.

"Yes," Remmy said. "I should have done it long ago."

She sighed, still unconvinced that Remmy was who he said he was. "I don't think the man I knew would have done that."

"You're right, but I've seen things, Laila. GIGI speaks to me in images sometimes, and I know we're looking at some perils that are bigger than anything we've ever faced before. Who knows how much time we have or if we'll survive the next mission? I don't want to meet my maker without telling you I'm falling in love with you."

"You are?" she said, her eyes widening with surprise again.

"Yes," he declared. "You are such an amazing woman. Maybe I'm moving too fast."

"Light speed, Master Sergeant," she said with a flirtatious chuckle.

"Yeah, well, I've let this job dictate my life for too long. You're not just a flight, Laila, or a shipboard distraction. You're the real deal, and I mean top-shelf quality. If there's any chance you feel something for me, I want to explore it."

"There's a chance," she said, her eyes shining. "But if we're facing long odds, are you sure we should? Can you love me and make the right call in combat if it comes to that?"

"I already care too much," he admitted. "I'll just have to do everything I can to make sure it doesn't come to that. But if we die, at least you know how I feel."

"No one has ever been in love with me before," she said. "I'm not sure what to think about it."

Remmy shrugged, not sure what he should say.

"And you're positive that alien hasn't corrupted your brain?" she asked, both playful and serious at the same time.

"It can speak to me," he admitted. "But it isn't running the show. I'm still making all my own decisions, Laila. You can count on that. And I'll make you this promise; if that ever changes, I will tell you."

"Okay, I can live with that," she said. "Now, don't get mad, but I've got to go see someone."

"Yeah," he said, wishing she wouldn't leave but knowing they couldn't flaunt their relationship without causing problems in the platoon. "I'll see you tomorrow."

"Count on it," she replied.

Laila left the armory, and Remmy sat down. He felt nearly overwhelmed but also happy. It had been a long time since he did exactly what he wanted. And their kiss had been so perfect that he wanted to lock it into his memory forever.

CHAPTER 28

HE HAD SLEPT SIX HOURS, showered, shaved, and eaten a light breakfast of toast and coffee. He felt good when Captain Zeke Darius stepped onto the bridge, but his nerves were on edge. They were about to do something that might cost him his career. Worst still, it might cost someone their life, or maybe even everyone on the ship could die as a result of his decision. If the *Jericho* was destroyed in the process of accessing hyperspace, it would cost the entire human race access to the artifact and its vast database of advanced technology. The risks were enormous. Supposing they survived the voyage through hyperspace, they could still come out directly in the line of fire of some hostile vessel with no time or ability to save themselves. Worse still, they could somehow reveal the human race to the Pratoreen Empire, who would undoubtedly enslave or destroy mankind.

"Good morning," he said to his senior officers and crew, who were already there and waiting.

"Morning Captain," Commander Lee said.

"Lieutenant Ramos, what conclusion did you reach?" Zeke asked.

"I've run all the numbers twice, Captain. The equations are flawless."

"Your recommendation?"

"Is that we proceed."

"Anyone have anything they would like to say?" Darius asked. "Any reason that we should wait?"

Darius cast his gaze around the room. Everyone met his eye, but no one spoke.

"Very well then," the Captain said. "Let's begin. Lieutenant Nash, bring the Prometheus engine online."

"Aye, Captain, bringing propulsion systems online," Henry replied.

"GIGI, are you with us?"

"I am always available, Captain. How may I assist you this morning?"

"You to tell me how this works, please?"

"Of course. The Prometheus engine was designed to propel the ship into hyperspace. There are what you might call portals that connect to the fifth dimension. They are thin places in the dimensional membrane that allow a ship of the right dimensions and power to pass through. A ship traveling at the correct speed and trajectory will pass into hyperspace briefly and then exit via a series of minor course corrections. I have enabled the ship's computer to tabulate the data and make the exact maneuvers using the autopilot feature."

"Sounds easy enough," Darius said sarcastically. "We're looking at a six-hour flight time?"

"From the moment the Prometheus Engine is engaged, it will take us forty-seven minutes and eighteen seconds to reach the proper speed and coordinates to pass into the hyperdimension. Another five hours and twenty-two minutes of flight time until we exit hyperspace in the Lawa system. From there, we should be within two hours of reaching orbit around Lawash."

"Outstanding," Darius said. "Lieutenant Best, what is the status of weapons?"

"We have a full compliment, Captain. The laser turret is charged and primed with a full power supply in the laser reservoir. Sonic shielding is at full power. We're ready for whatever we run into, sir."

"I hope you're right," Zeke said, settling into his captain's chair and checking the system readouts on his small, personal screens. "What's our plot look like?"

"Clear space," Ensign Jacee Bergtoli replied. "Radar and Lidar scans show us nothing in our path or approaching it at this time, Captain."

"Engineering?"

"Prometheus is primed and ready, Captain," Henry Nash replied. "I've looked at the course and speed requirements; we should be able to hit all the required milestones."

"And the computer pilot?" Darius asked.

Ensign Alex Stanislaus turned in his chair. "Captain, the ship's computer is ready. In fact, its functionality is higher than anything I've ever heard about. Even the supercomputers back on Earth don't operate this well. We're in very good shape, plenty of computing power."

"Outstanding. Alright then, let the ship's log show the order is given to proceed with the journey to the Lawa system."

"Aye, engage the computer's autopilot," Commander Lori Lee announced.

"Engaging autopilot, now," Alex Stanislaus said.

"Prometheus engine is engaging," Henry Nash said. "Ten percent, Captain."

"Very good. Let's keep an eye on the gages, people. I don't want any surprises," Darius said.

"Passing one hundred kilometers per hour," Vivian Ramos said.

There was a feeling of excitement on the Bridge. The wall displays showed the video feed from the exterior cameras. It wasn't immediately obvious they were moving at all.

"Five hundred kilometers per hour," Vivian called out.

"Prometheus engine is at twenty percent, and all is well," Henry Nash said.

"Fuel consumption?"

"Below estimates, sir. We're in good shape," Nash replied.

"Thrusters to begin course correction in three, two, one, engaged," Alex Stanislaus said.

"We're lining up for the big burn," Nash said into a small comlink. "All hands stand by."

"Commander Lee, crew announcement," Darius said.

"Aye, Captain, crew announcement."

A trilling chime let Darius know everything said would carry through the ship's speaker. It also alerted the crew to an announcement from the captain. In the mess hall, sailors put down their utensils and looked up; in the REC, crew members set down their playing cards and entertainment slates. Those on duty at various posts looked up toward the ship's speakers as if seeing where the sound came from would give them a clear hearing of the announcement.

"Now hear this, now hear this, Captain Zeke Darius to the crew of the S.D.F. Jericho. We are about to make a major increase in thrust. Please secure loose items and brace for an exponential increase in perceived gravity."

He repeated the warning. His chair automatically tightened around him, holding him secure. Nash gave a countdown, and the computer increased the power of the Prometheus engine from twenty to fifty percent. The *Jericho* shot forward like a bullet from a gun. She was already moving more than a thousand kilometers per hour, but with the increased thrust, the speed shot up so fast that Vivian had trouble keeping track.

"Passing ten thousand, correction, we have surpassed... well, that's thirty thousand and climbing fast, Captain. Forty thousand... fifty..."

"Just let me know when we pass one hundred thousand," he said.

They had gotten the ship to slightly over two million kilometers per hour on the trip through the solar system, but it had taken well over twelve hours to reach that speed, keeping tabs on the engines the entire time. Darius didn't like pushing the new Prometheus engine so hard, but it was built for speed and power. The computer was operating the ship's drive system well within the parameters it was engineered to function at.

"Man, we are humming," Nash said. "All systems remain in the green, Captain. No problems reported."

"One hundred thousand kilometers per hour," Vivian said with a note of triumph in her voice.

"Engine at sixty percent capacity," Henry Nash said.

"How's our progress, Ensign Stanislaus?"

"Right on target, Captain. We've hit every milestone so far. The ship and computer are in perfect sync."

The next half hour was tense. The ship's engines went all the way to seventy-five percent capacity. They were at one point three-eight-seven million kilometers per hour as they approached the target area. Everyone on the Bridge looked up. The view screens showing outer space with thousands of stars in the distance suddenly changed. A white light flooded the Bridge and made them all squint for a few seconds, but the light on the screens immediately dimmed to a dull grey.

"Are we..." Captain Darius asked.

GIGI, the alien-fabricated Galactic Information and Guidance Instrument, answered. "You have entered hyperspace," the alien device said.

"Holy..." Henry Nash started to say.

"Where no man has gone before," Pete Best said in a joking tone.

"Very funny," Vivian Ramos said.

"I don't get it," Jacee Bergtoli said.

"It's from an old television show," Vivian told her. "One that was ludicrous even in its time."

"We're making history, people," Lori Lee said. "We're the first people ever to leave the Sol system."

"Your statement is only partially correct, Commander Lee," GIGI said, her voice sounding like a human's. "You are the first humans to leave the Sol system willingly."

Darius felt a shiver run down his back. He was shocked at what he was hearing.

"What?" Lori Lee asked.

"There have been a total of thirty-seven humans taken from their home system," GIGI said. "They were collected for observation and study. This is how the Correll knew to send me to your system."

"Wait, you're saying that aliens were abducting people from Earth?" Captain Darius asked.

"That is correct, Captain."

"By the Correll?" He pressed forward, pushing for the truth.

"Among others," GIGI said. "Humanity has been watched and visited by at least six intelligent species."

"Well, this is surreal," Henry Nash said.

"History is full of unsubstantiated accounts of visitors from other worlds," Alex Stanislaus said.

"I guess it's not unsubstantiated anymore," Pete Best said.

"What gives you the right?" Commander Lee demanded. "You just kidnapped people, and you think that's okay?"

"My makers did," GIGI replied. "No suitable allies were found among those unreached by the Imperials. Finding a race with the capacity for intelligence and martial skill was necessary. I was built to recruit your race to the fight for freedom in the galaxy."

"That's still not right!" Lori Lee declared. "You can't just take people from their homes and lives."

"It was necessary for the greater good," GIGI said.

Captain Darius had another cold chill run down his spine. How many of history's atrocities were carried out in the name of the greater good? More than he could remember, and he couldn't help but worry that what GIGI had in mind for the *Jericho* would be just one more example of power gone awry.

CHAPTER 29

LAILA MCPHERSON WAS ON A MISSION. She found Donny Elgersma right after her kiss with Remmy Steel. Her mind was reeling from that kiss. It still shocked her to think that Remmy would break the unwritten rule for her, but she felt almost giddy that he had. But before she could take it all in and enjoy it, she had to end things with Elgersma. They weren't lovers, but they had been seeing one another. Donny was pushing for more, which wasn't surprising. It was an unusually long cruise, and he was a typical sailor. A little burly for most spaceships with cramped quarters and narrow gangways, but he was a munitions specialist, and his strength was useful for moving the heavy bombs and ammunition used by the Fleet.

She had found him to be funny and charming in his way. Donny was well-liked and popular among the ship's crew. Maybe on a different cruise, Laila would have felt differently about him. She liked Donny, but her feelings didn't go beyond that. And she wasn't looking for a fling. Perhaps, deep in the parts of her mind that she never admitted to anyone and rarely considered herself, she knew she was using Donny to make Remmy jealous. The one thing clear from the day she met Master Sergeant Remmy Steel was how strong her connection with him had been. He was stoic, but she believed he felt the connection, too. They were much alike, and she had never dated anyone in her platoon or even the same battalion. But her feelings for Remmy were undeniable. And so was her determination not to lead Donny Elgersma on for one second longer.

The break-up had seemed amiable to her. There wasn't a scene. She found him with a few of his friends. They were working their way through a bottle of whiskey that one of them had won in a bet. Fortunately, they were just starting, and Donny wasn't drunk yet. He took the news with a straight face and told her she could do whatever she wanted. Relieved, Laila had returned to her quarters. Being an NCO had its perks. They were few and far between, but on the *Jericho*, her rank earned her a private berth. She had a nice room with a sitting area, a small desk, and twice the normal locker space. Most importantly, she had her own bathroom with no time restrictions on showers.

After getting cleaned up, she forced herself to sleep. She could usually fall right to sleep, but her mind was too filled with possibilities that night. Remmy was at the top of her list, but so was the idea of traveling to a new star system and their mission on an alien world. Laila McPherson was a practical person. She hadn't signed up for the Space Marines out of a romantic sense of adventure. She was an athlete, and the Marines offered her the biggest challenge. She had risen through the ranks quickly, accepting every assignment and surviving the difficult training involved with becoming a commando. But she loved the hands-on aspect of being a Marine. Weapons, tactics, and fighting appealed to her and suited her. She was not a book learner, although she enjoyed reading for pleasure. And she wasn't into expensive clothes and jewelry. Laila McPherson was more fatigued at home than in an evening gown and more comfortable in combat boots than high heels. But the prospect of making history was exciting. They were going into the unknown, and that was enticing. It fired her imagination.

Eventually, she got in nearly six hours of sleep. When she got up, her first stop was in the gym to spend half an hour on the cardio equipment. Darcy Haynes was already there when she arrived. Darcy was a computer software engineer, and the two women were friends.

"There you are," Darcy said as Laila stepped onto her machine and adjusted the settings. "Have you heard?"

"About the mission? Yes, we got briefed yesterday."

"No, not the mission," Darcy said. "It's Elgersma; he's saying some things about you that are not pleasant."

"What?"

Darcy nodded. "He was drunk, of course, but he made up some awful lies about you."

Laila's blood began to boil. She didn't usually care about gossip and preferred to decide about the person rather than accept the stories that often circulated through a starship. But she had never been the source of such a story. She was careful about privacy, and her reputation had always been stellar.

"Last night?"

"Right now," Darcy explained. "They're still up. I passed them in the REC. Someone must have ordered them to sober up. They're drinking coffee and telling awful stories."

"I'll see you later," Laila said, leaving the cardio machine and her friend.

"Wait! Where are you going?"

"To set the record straight," Laila said.

She was determined and angry, but more than that, she was afraid. What if Remmy heard the stories, and the way he felt about her changed? It wasn't fair. She hadn't done anything wrong to Donny, but Laila knew some men couldn't handle having their pride hurt. The REC was the ship's main gathering space for crew members not on duty. There were all the usual games and entertainment options, along with snack machines and a drink station. When Laila reached the upper deck and entered the REC, her heart was pounding harder than if she had run for half an hour with Darcy.

It wasn't difficult to find Donny. He was still with his friends, although there was a larger group of them, and they were drinking coffee instead of booze, but almost as soon as she entered the compartment, the group burst into laughter. She went straight toward them, and a few caught sight of her. One sailor tapped Donny on the arm, and the big man looked up.

"Well, speak of the devil," Donny said. "Change your mind, sweetheart? Need a little something from your man?"

"I'm not yours or anyone else's," she snapped. "Just what lies have you been spreading, Donny?"

"Hey!" he said, sounding tough. "What gives you the right to come here all hot and bothered? You broke up with me, remember?"

"And you've been running your mouth ever since," Laila proclaimed.

"That's my business, sweetheart."

"Not if you're talking about me."

"I guess you'll just have to live with it," he said, standing up. "Ain't no one on this ship going to tell me what I can and can't do."

"If you say one more thing about me, Donny, I'll knock your teeth out of your lying mouth. Now, tell them that you are lying."

"About what?"

"About anything you've said about me," she snapped.

"I haven't said anything about you except how you like—"

She reacted so abruptly that Laila even surprised herself a little. Her hand darted out and slapped Donny across his stubbly jaw. The slap made a loud pop and left a hand-shaped red mark on his face.

"You are a liar," she said. "We never did anything more than kiss a time or two."

He reached up and rubbed his face. Laila had worked mostly with men in her career with the Marines. She knew all kinds and had learned to read their body language. There was hate and cruelty in Donny's eyes. It was so plain that she felt shocked that she had ever been friendly with him.

"You bitch!" he snarled. "I ought to break your arm for that."

"You're free to try," she said.

"See what I mean," he said to his friends. "She's a nasty little tramp. Likes it roug—"

She slapped him again, only the second time she lashed up with her hand and smacked him on the bottom of his chin. His teeth clashed together, and his tongue was caught between them. It was just a small bite but hard enough to break the skin.

"Ouch!" he shouted. "Damn it!"

He reached up and touched his bloody tongue. "You're gonna pay for that," he said.

His friends moved out of the big man's way. Donny was twice Laila's size. She was strong but lithe, while he was thick and burly.

"Better not hit a woman," someone warned the angry Fleet specialist, but Donny wasn't listening.

"You won't be so pretty when I'm through with you," he threatened.

Laila didn't respond. She set her feet and waited. During the weeks on board, she had sparred with nearly every platoon member and had learned a lot from Remmy. She timed her advance perfectly. Donny didn't bother trying to hide what he was planning. He rushed forward, cocking his arm back for a haymaker punch. Just as he threw his arm forward, Laila ducked and drove her shoulder into his midsection. With all his momentum going forward, her diving attack caused him to lose his balance. Like most men, his upper body was heavier than the lower half. He flopped forward, and Laila drove her body upward. Donny's legs flew upward and over her, as he crashed head-first into the deck. They weren't on the sparring mats. The floor in the REC was hard and unyielding.

Laila spun around fast. Donny was still on the floor, face down. She dropped down, landing on one knee that was planted right between his shoulder blades. The blow knocked the air from his lungs, and she grabbed his ears, pulling them back hard. He screamed in pain and tried to pull her hands from his ears, but that only made the pain worse.

"Tell them it's all lies," she said.

"I'll kill you!" he shrieked.

Laila knew she had to be careful. Donny was still very strong, and once he realized he wasn't helpless, he would roll. The maneuver would get his attacker off his back and free up his hands to put them on her. But she was ready for him. When he let go of her hands and put them on the floor, she slammed his head forward. His face was smashed into the floor. His nose took the brunt of the impact and gushed blood that smeared a crimson streak across the white tiles of the deck.

There was no time to bask in her small victory. Laila jumped to her feet and stepped backward. The crowd was closing in around them, and Donny started to get up angrily. She should have put him down before he was able to rise. He was taller than she was on his feet, with a longer reach. But as angry as she was with him for spreading lies about her, she didn't want to injure him. So she let him get up. He turned to face her. Laila was barely out of reach. Donny's nose and cheeks were swelling. Blood stained his lips and chin. He cleared his mouth and spit a bloody glob on the floor.

"I'm going to kill you," he threatened.

It was just the sort of thing a bully would do. Laila understood that she had dealt with her fair share of bullies in life and the Marine Corps. At that moment, when Donny was trying to intimidate her with a threat, she lashed out. She hit him square in the mouth with a hard palm strike. It was enough of a blow to make him stagger back and reach for his mouth.

"Tell them the truth, or I'll hurt you for real, Donny," she said. "I'm not kidding."

He reached up and felt his teeth. They were all intact but a little looser from her strike. She watched his eyes. They were dull, almost glassy, but when his eyelids squinched down a little, she knew he was coming after her again. With a bellow of rage, he stepped toward her. Laila was just out of his reach, but she had long legs. Fortunately for Donny, she was wearing trainers instead of her combat boots. The top of her foot smashed into his groin. The look of hatred in his eyes turned to pain, and he dropped to his knees.

"What is going on in here!" Commander Lori Lee's voice cut through the hubbub and caused the crowd watching to fall silent.

They also stepped away from Laila and Donny Elgersma. Donny was in so much pain he fell onto his side and groaned.

"We were clearing up a misunderstanding, ma'am," Laila said.

Lori Lee walked past the crowd. She looked down at Donny, then back to Laila.

"You picked a hell of a time to start a fight," she said.

"Yes, Commander, I'm sorry," Laila said.

"We expect more from our NCOs," Lee said before turning to a couple of Donny's friends. "Get him up and to the med bay," she ordered. "Then get to your posts. We'll be entering a hostile alien system soon. And the last thing we need is to get caught by surprise. I want everyone in the sound of my voice to report to their COs. Move people! And someone cleans this blood up."

Laila felt a wave of relief. She could have been charged with a crime for fighting on board a ship or at least taken from active duty right when her platoon needed her the most. She hurried from the REC and went straight to her quarters. There was just enough time to get cleaned up, changed, and grab some chow before she was needed in the armory. She was thankful again for the privacy of her berth. Standing in front of the mirror, she looked at her reflection. Her cheeks were flushed, and her hands trembled slightly. The adrenaline still coursed through her circulatory system, not fear. She had seen the hands of the most savage killers shaking and knew it was a natural reaction, but she still didn't like it. And she certainly didn't want anyone to see it.

Most of all, she didn't want Remmy to see her. She didn't want to see him. She wasn't afraid of the fight but of what she might see on his face. Would he be disappointed in her? Would he believe Donny Elgersma's lies? Would he think that revealing his feelings for her was a mistake? She didn't want to be rejected, yet they were about to depart on a very important mission together. The last thing he needed was her emotions. She had to push them down deep and pretend she wasn't scared or angry. Emotionally, she could feel the tension building, but there was no time to hash things out with Remmy. That would have to wait, and they would both have to survive. She resolved to feel nothing and almost achieved it before setting off on the most important mission of her life.

CHAPTER 30

"DID I MAKE IT?" Commander Lori Lee asked as she hurried back onto the Bridge.

"Just in time," Captain Darius said.

"Dropping out of hyperspace in sixty seconds," Alex Stanislaus said.

Normally, the navigator gave out readings, but the regular scanners and radar didn't work in hyperspace. It was almost like running a submarine or flying blind. They were completely at the mercy of the ship's autopilot, run by the computer. So, Ensign Stanislaus gave the updates.

Darius was relieved. They had been in the fifth dimension for over five hours. It was a relief to go back to normal space, even if they were in a completely alien star system.

"Everything all right up there?" Darius asked his executive officer.

"Fine, sir, just a meeting of the minds," Lori Lee said. "Munitions specialist bit off more than he could chew with one of the Marines. *She* took it easy on him. No significant injuries, just some wounded pride."

"I imagine so," Captain Darius said. "Which Marine?"

"Staff Sergeant Laila McPherson," the Commander replied.

Darius turned to Lieutenant Colt. "See that the Staff Sergeant gets an earful," he said.

"Yes, sir!" Micky Colt replied.

Beside him, Master Sergeant Remmy Steel cleared his throat but didn't say anything. Captain Darius got the impression there was something to the gesture, but it wasn't the time or the place to get into it. In fact, a fistfight wasn't unusual on a ship of war. It rarely rose to the level of a Captain's consideration. His subordinates would handle it.

"Lieutenant Best, I want a full scan of surrounding space the moment we come out of this dimension," Darius ordered. "Radar, Lidar, visual scanning is our priority. Let's make sure we didn't just jump from the frying pan into the fire."

There was a chorus of "Aye, Captain" from the fleet personnel. The Bridge was packed, and Darius couldn't blame his crew for wanting to see the alien system. It was a monumental achievement for the human race, although Darius didn't think they could take credit for it. They had built a ship and manned it, that was all. The ship had been designed by GIGI, who had revealed the secret to hyperspace travel, set their course, and told them what to expect in the Lawa system.

"Ten seconds," Alex Stanislaus said.

Darius didn't need to tell people to be ready. They were all leaning forward, eagerly anticipating what they were about to see. Suddenly, the dull gray that filled every video feed flickered and went dark. One more second of tense anxiety, and then the video feeds were normal again. Straight ahead of them was a huge star, and there were several dark spots where planets slowly rotated around the massive ball of burning gas.

"Anything?" Darius asked, his eyes straining away from the display screens to see his view of the radar.

"Negative," Pete Best said. "Lidar is clear in all directions."

"Radar isn't picking anything up," Ensign Jacee Bergtoli said.

"Visual scans, I want a full sweep," Darius said.

There was a pause, and then Vivian Ramos spoke up. "We're clear, Captain. There is no activity in the system at all. Not even radio signals."

"Distance to orbit?" Darius asked.

"Just under a million kilometers," Vivian replied.

"All right, let's turn this bird around and start slowing down," Darius said. "Lieutenant Nash, prepare to engage the Prometheus engine. Ensign Stanislaus, utilize thrusters, and get us turned around."

"Aye, Captain, beginning turn for retroburn," Alex said.

"Engine is primed and ready, Captain," Nash called out.

"Let's have all systems report in," Darius ordered.

"Navigation is green," Vivian Ramos said.

"Weapons are primed and ready, Captain," Pete Best called out.

"Life support systems are all in the Green," Henry Nash said. "Fuel level is still above fifty percent, not including emergency reserves, Captain."

"No other crew issues reported," Commander Lori Lee said, "other than the dust-up in the REC."

"Good," Darius said, feeling slightly relieved but surprised that GIGI hadn't said a word. The ship was completely unfazed by the inter-dimensional travel, and they were right where the alien device had predicted they would be. "Let's begin a survey scan. Recorders on."

"Aye, survey scan," Alex Stanislaus called out. "Recorders on."

"Lieutenant Ramos, can you begin mapping constellations, please?"

"Aye, Captain, mapping constellations."

"GIGI, do we have a return course plotted?" Darius said.

"Yes, Captain," the living computer said.

Darius turned to Lieutenant Colt. "You're Marines are up, Lieutenant. "We'll be in orbit in an hour and ready to launch the drop ship one hour later."

"Two hours," Colt said. "We'll be ready, sir."

"Thank you. Let's check your communication once you're in the drop ship."

The Marine stood up and saluted. Darius returned the salute.

"Five hundred thousand kilometers to orbit," Alex Stanislaus announced. "The ship has flipped, Captain. You can begin retro burn."

Darius just nodded to Henry Nash, who engaged the Prometheus engine.

"Ten percent thrust, Captain," Nash said. "Would you like me to increase that?"

"Not until we're closer. The quicker we get into position, the better our odds are," Darius replied. "I want a fast orbit. Ensign Bertoli, let's make sure the long-range surveillance cameras are ready."

"Aye, Captain," Jacee said. "Long-range cameras coming online."

The nose of the ship didn't rotate. It was divided between the sonic shield generator, a battery of laser cannons, and the ship's sensor suite, which included the radar, lidar, and a bank of long-range surveillance cameras on rotating mounts.

"On screen," Captain Darius ordered.

"Four hundred thousand kilometers," Alex Stanislaus announced.

A dull-looking marble appeared on the Bridge screens. Jacee Bertoli had to adjust the direction of the cameras and the focus. The marble was a swirl of colors. White clouds hovered in the atmosphere. There were swaths of blue from the oceans, and the land masses were green and rusty brown.

"The planet is much improved," GIGI announced.

"A few hundred years will do that," Captain Darius said. "What kind of toxins were left from the bombing?"

"Heavy metals, specifically Lead, Cadmium, Chromium, and Arsenic. The Imperials used solid-state bombs from orbit to devastating effect on the cities, and leaving the soil, water, and parts of the atmosphere toxic from the heavy metals."

"Scorched earth tactics," Henry Nash said. "They don't play around."

"All the more reason for us to find that power core," Darius said. "Until we do, the Earth is defenseless."

It took thirty minutes to reach orbit. The ship had slowed to under ten thousand kilometers per hour and settled easily into a high orbit. The surveillance cameras showed a world that was bright and verdant.

"Amazing how resilient planets are," Commander Lori Lee said.

"Time heals all wounds, Commander," Darius replied. "Ensign Stanislaus, I want atmospheric readings. Surface temperature and weather patterns, too, give this world a full scientific survey. You can share all that information with Connor O'Dell. Call it a peace offering, but keep a copy in the ship's records. The Brass will want all the information it can get about this world."

"Aye, Captain, beginning a full scientific sensor survey on Lawash," Alex said.

"Vivian, can you make sure the Marines in the drop ship are getting this video feed," Darius continued, giving commands. "And let's do a full communication check."

"Aye, Captain," the Navigation officer said.

The video from the long-range cameras showed mountains and valleys, sweeping grassy plains, and large, sandy deserts. The ratio of land to ocean was nearly fifty-fifty. In places, the land was covered with bright green flora: grass, trees, shrubs, bushes, and even flowers. One of the cameras could zoom down far enough to make out the leaves on the tallest trees. Unlike Earth, where conservation had been practiced for over a century, no dense forests existed. The green grass grew thick in places, but everything else was sparse.

"Looks like that used to be a city of some kind," Henry said, pointing at the display screen.

It wasn't obvious at first. The rubble had long been covered with new flora growth, but the terrain revealed straight lines and geometric shapes. Vines seemed to be the predominant flora over the ruins of once sizable cities. In other places, craters could be seen, and great bowls on the planet's surface were rarely covered in plant life. Some of the city ruins were barren, too, great jumbling heaps of rubble with everything covered in a thick, gray layer of dust. As the ship flew over the daylight side of the planet, there were no signs of animal life, but on the dark side, there was movement.

"Picking up life signs," Stanislaus said. "Looks like a herd of something."

"They're pretty big," Nash said. "I think they're grazing on the tall grass."

"Most herbivores aren't nocturnal," Commander Lee said.

"Not on Earth," Captain Darius said. "But that is definitely not Earth."

They slowed, the ship still under autopilot control, with GIGI feeding the nav computer the coordinates so that they fell into a geosynchronous orbit over the ruins of a major city. Most of the city was in rubble, but a massive pyramid was covered in green and brown vines.

"That's got to be it," Vivian Ramos said.

"The Jatoshi temple of light and hope," GIGI proclaimed. "It was once a great attraction for beings all over Lawash."

"Lieutenant Ramos, do we have solid communications with the Marine Platoon?"

"Aye, Captain, their coms are online and reading five-by-five," Vivian replied. "And they've got a signal booster on the drop ship."

"Commander Lee, let's begin the launch sequence. I want a permanent line of communication with Lieutenant Colt. And let's ensure they remember to turn their helmet cams on when they leave that ship."

CHAPTER 31

THE ENTIRE PLATOON was strapped into the drop ship. Lieutenant Colt and Gunny Rand were in the pilot and co-pilot seats, but the ship would be flown by computer. The two Marines at the controls were just safety measures with minimal training. They could land the ship if necessary or return to orbit, but they didn't have the experience or skill needed to fly in combat zones or to reconnect with an orbiting spaceship.

The rest of the platoon were in jumpseats in the cargo section. Master Sergeant Remmy Steel sat in what was called the *hot seat*. His job would be to direct the Marines off the ship in emergency conditions or lead them out of the ship in a combat zone. They all felt the big clamps lock onto the ship and pull it toward the massive airlock. Everything felt exaggerated. They had done dozens of sims that started in a drop ship, but haptics were nothing like a ship moving in launch position.

"Ronin One, this is Shogun Actual. Combat communications are initiated. Standby for the drop."

"Shogun, this is Ronin One. We are standing by for drop, over," Lieutenant Colt said.

Remmy heard it in his combat helmet. The rest of the platoon could hear it, too. They were strapped into metal seats with their weapons secured in racks between their feet. Everyone carried a rifle, but no one had the standard issue Spitfires they used on simulations. In real combat, the special forces had the privilege of carrying mission-specific weapons.

Bravo Team would be on overwatch, and they each carried high-powered laser rifles with telescoping digital aiming displays.

The rest of the platoon carried projectile weapons. Lasers were great for distance shots, but they required heavy batteries and didn't have the stopping power of a projectile. Remmy carried a Nelson LTX. It was loaded with armor-piercing, explosive shells. On impact, the thumb-sized bullet would explode on the back end, damaging whatever was hit and driving the tungsten point deep into the target. It also had a spring-loaded bayonet for close combat fighting.

"Ronin One, initiating drop in three, two, one, Mark!"

At mark, the clamps released, and a burst of pressurized air hurled the drop ship out of the airlock.

"Shogun Action, this is Ronin One; we are free," Lieutenant Colt said in a calm voice. Remmy couldn't feel the ship spinning, but he knew it was. If he had synced his battle helmet to the drop ship's exterior cameras, he could have seen how seemingly out of control the little shuttle was. "Activating autopilot, over."

"Copy that, Ronin one," a steady voice that Remmy recognized as belonging to Lieutenant Vivian Ramos said. "We have you on our radar. You are cleared to begin flight operations."

"Autopilot is engaged," Colt replied. "Next stop, Lawash actual. See you soon, Shogun, over."

"Be careful," Captain Darius instructed them. "I don't want any surprises down there."

"Roger that, sir," Colt replied.

Remmy could hear the thrusters firing. Inside the ship, it sounded like relief valves venting along the various sides of the ship, like a child letting air out of a balloon in short, staccato bursts. It took them less than a minute before the gravity of Lawash reached them.

"Oh, man, I hate this part," Corporal Al Van Winkle said. He was known as Rip because of his last name.

"Why do we always have to come in upside down?" Corporal Ricky Thompson asked in a wretched voice. "I get sick every time."

"Keep it in your space suit," Corporal Wendy Downs said.

The shuttle was sealed and had breathable air in it. Ricky Thompson slid the sealing latch on his space suit's helmet latch and popped open the transparent front. Sergeant Jay Thorne flicked open an emesis bag and held it out to his teammate.

"Don't make a mess," he ordered.

Remmy looked away. It felt like they were hanging upside down, and the feeling was becoming more pronounced. The shuttle would rotate through the atmosphere to keep one side from getting too hot from the friction. Remmy knew it would only be a few moments, and they would turn right-side-up again.

"The atmo is thicker than expected," Lieutenant Colt announced. "Hang on, it's going to be a bumpy ride in."

"Thicker than expected," Laila said. "Why is that always the case?"

"Never smooth sailing on a combat drop," Sergeant Hugo McManus said. "That's one thing you can count on."

Remmy felt the ship slowly turning, but it also began to shake. It felt like the drop ship was a rock skipped across a pond. The flight down took twenty minutes. Gravity did most of the work, and the shuttle's heat-deflecting tiles got scorched. The ship wouldn't be so pretty anymore, but it did the job. The autopilot circled the temple and surrounding area.

"Let's begin visual scans," Lieutenant Colt ordered. "Radar isn't picking up anything, but I don't want to take any chances."

"Copy that," Remmy replied via the comlink. "Platoon, activate vid feed from the ship's exterior cameras. Alpha team, take the bow feeds; Bravo team, you have the stern. Charlie team, you get the starboard video."

"That's the ship's right side, Tex," McManus teased.

"Very funny, Hugo," Corporal Tyler Fry said in a laid-back drawl, which was how he got the nickname Tex.

"Stay sharp, people. Delta has port-side vid feeds. You see something," Remmy warned, "you say something."

"Roger that," Sergeant Dirk Oliver, leader of Charlie team, said.

But there was nothing to see. The weather was calm. The sun was sinking toward the horizon, but there was still more than an hour of daylight left. The ruins were visible, although patches of weeds had sprung up in places. Remmy searched the dirt, looking for tracks or marks from some animal. There was none that he could make out.

"Bravo team, I want you to spread out and as high as you can get," Remmy ordered, marking three spots on his battle helmet's mapping application. He sent the locations to Laila to assign to her team.

"Roger that, Master Sergeant," Laila said.

The ship landed softly. The hum of the repulsor lifts died down, and Remmy unfastened his safety harness. It felt good to stand up, even though the gravity on Lawash was a bit stronger than he was used to.

Lieutenant Colt called in their status. "Shogun, this is Ronin One, actual. We are on the ground. I repeat, the drop ship has landed. Awaiting your go, no go, on egress, over."

"Ronin One, this is Shogun actual, we have you. All scopes are clear. You are going on a recovery mission. And good luck, Ronin, make us proud."

"Roger that, Shogun actual. Ronin One out."

When the Lieutenant stepped through the narrow passageway into the passenger compartment of the drop ship, Remmy was already at the controls of the rear hatch.

"Ready, sir?" Remmy asked.

"Born ready, Master Sergeant. Let's show the galaxy how the SDF Marines get things done!"

There was a chorus of *oorah* from the platoon, and Remmy hit the hatch release. His rifle was strapped across his chest on top of the nine extra magazines for the weapon. The space suit was bulky, and movement was restricted by it. The suit reminded Remmy of being a child and his mother bundling him up to go out into the snow. She sometimes put so many layers on him that he could hardly move. The space armor wasn't that bad, and he was thankful to have it as the hatch opened and the last of the ship's air supply was sucked out.

"Wow," Laila said.

"Would you look at that?" Corporal Downes added.

The platoon was crowding in, anxious to get a glimpse of the new world.

"It's spectacular," Sergeant Thorne said.

"And dangerous," Remmy reminded them. "Check your weapons, then make sure your helmet cameras are recording and transmitting."

"Sergeant Steel, let's form a perimeter around the drop ship," Lieutenant Colt ordered. "Bravo team, you can move to your positions. I'll need just a minute to ensure the ship's signal amplifier is working."

"Alpha, Charlie, Delta, let's circle the wagons," Remmy ordered. It was a common order, not an official one, but most NCOs used euphemisms from Earth for orders that were regularly issued, such as setting a perimeter around a drop ship.

He led the way. There was no slow egress or time to revel in the fact that Remmy was the first human being to set foot on a world outside the Sol system. He jogged down the ramp and took a defensive position beside it while the rest of the platoon filed off the ship.

"Bravo team is moving into overwatch positions," Laila McPherson said.

"Outstanding, Staff Sergeant," Remmy replied as the trio jogged away from the ship. "We'll wait here until you're set and can give us an all-clear."

"Alpha team in position," Gunny Sergeant Chad Bran said.

"Charlie, team in position," Sergeant Dirk Oliver chimed in.

"Delta team in position," Sergeant Jay Thorne reported.

Remmy was the only Marine left directly behind the ship; the others had spread out according to the same sides they had been assigned to watch from while the ship circled the area. Remmy had time to take in the planet's natural beauty for the first time. They were standing in an ancient city's ruins, yet time had softened the rubble. It looked like a desert vista from the ground level, with small hills, scrub brush, and some bright green vines snaking up between boulders. The sky was pink with streaks of gold. The light from the star was warm at that time of day, filling the world with a soft, white light.

But the most impressive thing was the ancient pyramid, which was only a hundred paces from the rear of the ship. Remmy had never seen the pyramids on Earth except in pictures and on screens. They were ancient, too, thousands of years old, with signs of erosion and looting. But the pyramid on Lawash was spectacular. It was almost entirely covered with vines that had bright green leaves. It was huge, and Remmy's helmet gauged the size of almost a thousand feet across the base. It rose nearly six hundred feet and starkly contrasted the dull grays and browns of the terrain around it.

"They won't believe this back home," Lieutenant Colt said as he descended the ramp toward Remmy.

"No, sir, I don't think they will."

"Communications are up. The *Jericho* has a good lock on our signal."

"Outstanding," Remmy said. "But if we're going underground, sir..."

"Yeah, we'll probably have to form a chain or risk losing contact," Lieutenant Colt said. "We'll leave Thompson at the mouth of the pyramid and do coms checks at regular intervals."

"Sounds like a plan, sir," Remmy replied. "You think the power core is still in there?"

"The odds aren't very good," the Lieutenant stated. "Even if it is down there, what's the likelihood we can get to it, or it isn't buried? A team of diggers could spend years excavating this site and still not find it."

"I suppose that's true, sir."

His helmet beeped to alert him to new information. On his HUD, a message appeared: The atmosphere scan was *complete. Nitrogen 57% Oxygen 29% Carbon Dioxide 9% Argon 5% Assessment: atmosphere safe for humans. Warning: high levels of Carbon Dioxide can lead to rapid breathing, confusion, increased cardiac output, elevated blood pressure, and heart arrhythmia.*

"You get that warning, sir?" Remmy asked.

"Yeah, the CO2 seems a bit high," Colt replied. "It's pretty warm here too. Ninety-four degrees."

"We knew the atmo was thick. It's probably holding in the heat of the day."

"I think it's better if we maintain the suits," the Lieutenant ordered. "No sense in taking additional risks, even if the air is breathable."

"Roger that, sir."

Laila's voice sounded clear in Remmy's helmet. "Lieutenant, the Bravo team is in position," she said.

"Any signs of life out there, Staff Sergeant?" Colt asked.

"Negative, sir. There's nothing moving within our sight. We have visibility for over ten klicks, sir. If anything moves in this direction, you'll know it."

"Very good, Staff Sergeant. We will maintain radio contact at all times."

"Roger that, sir," Laila replied.

"Alright, Master Sergeant, let's see if we can find a way into that structure."

CHAPTER 32

MORE THAN A DOZEN camera feeds were going simultaneously on the Bridge of the Jericho. They were all projected on the big wall displays. One showed the forward camera mounted on the ship itself, giving the officers a feeling that they could see out a windshield as if the Bridge was a cockpit rather than a command bunker in the very center of the ship.

Captain Darius had already minimized the camera feeds from the three Marines on overwatch. The cameras in their battle helmets were wide-angle devices that were good for close-up images but not for longer-range viewing. Lieutenant Vivian Ramos and Ensign Jacee Bertoli were monitoring all the communications from the Marine platoon. If the warriors on overwatch caught sight of something, Darius would bring their specific helmet cameras back online.

One of the camera feeds was the long-range surveillance shot from the *Jericho*. It gave the officers on the Bridge of the starship an unobstructed view straight down onto the ruins of the old city. The pyramid temple was fascinating from above. It looked to the naked eye to be perfectly constructed, with perfectly straight lines running down to the four corners from the summit and along the base of the structure. There was debris around it, but the overhead view looked very closely at where the building met the ground in most places. What Darius couldn't see was a way into the structure.

The rest of the cameras were from the Marines moving toward the pyramid. They were spread out in a loose formation. Their heads turned steadily from side to side, always watchful for danger.

"They're moving in," Darius said. "GIGI, do you have any idea how they could get inside?"

"The main entrance was five meters tall and five wide," the alien device replied, its voice coming through the ship's speakers. "The odds of it still being possible with minimal effort are very good."

"And I suppose there are signs that say, treasure this way," Henry Nash said.

"Negative Lieutenant Nash, the passageways leading down to the tunnels under the structure were hidden. I will have to lead Master Sergeant Steel to them."

"How do you have so much information on this place?" Vivian asked.

"Yeah, if it was supposed to be so secure, how do you know so much about it?" Pete Best added.

"The clergy of the Jatoshi faith practiced a martial art form called Jato."

As the alien artifact explained, it also displayed images via the plot table's holographic protector. Darius saw a group of four-legged beings. They had wide bodies and two short arms in the middle of their wide chests, just below their heads, which were angular and shaped like a traditionally cut diamond. They moved in unison as they performed some fighting display. They would stand on three legs and use the fourth to hit or kick, sometimes rearing on just two legs. They moved slowly, but there was a gracefulness to their motions.

"It was enough to keep most thieves away. And the temple itself was complex," GIGI continued the lecture. "Getting in wasn't as hard as getting out. Of course, the clergy guarded the structure, and there was a strong law enforcement presence in the city."

"It's all gone now," Vivian said sadly.

"Unfortunately, that is true. The Jatoshi understood the inevitability of that outcome. Most of their members volunteered to fight the Imperialist forces, which was part of the reason the planet was bombarded from orbit. Ground forces took heavy casualties fighting the natives on Lawash. The Jatoshi gave the Correll extensive maps so that it could be rebuilt if anything happened to the temple. Sadly, none of the Jatoshi survived the bombing, and their religion died with them."

"But the Correll included maps of the tunnels in your programming?" Darius asked.

"That is correct, Captain," GIGI said. The hologram of the Jatoshi aliens practicing their martial art disappeared and was replaced by a three-dimensional map of a multi-story tunnel system. "The Jatoshi had ventilation shafts and water drainage systems, but I have not included those in the map I am displaying on your plot device."

"This is the map of the tunnels under the pyramid?" Darius asked.

"Yes, Captain. Notice there are several chambers labeled Tango, Uniform, Victor, Whiskey, X-Ray, Yankee, and Zulu. These will be the treasure rooms, although no information about them exists in my records."

"In other words, you don't know what's inside those chambers?" Nash asked.

"You are correct, Lieutenant Nash."

"Are they booby-trapped?" Pete Best asked.

"I have no records indicating traps, but they may exist," GIGI said.

"Our Marines may be walking into a death trap," Captain Darius said. The Marine platoon was nearly to the structure. He pressed the transmit button and spoke directly to Lieutenant Colt. "Be advised, Ronin One, the tunnels and chambers under the pyramid may contain traps."

"Copy that, Shogun," Lieutenant Colt replied. "We'll be careful."

"I don't like this," Vivian said.

"They're professionals," Pete Best said. "Besides, they're going in with full armor. I doubt the Jatoshi planned for that kind of hardware when they designed their traps."

"If there are any traps at all," Nash added. "We don't know that they used traps. That kind of thing is great in movies, but in reality, they only serve to get your people hurt or killed. The risk is too high to have lethal traps where your people are working regularly."

"How did the temple get treasures?" Captain Darius asked.

"The Jatoshi accepted donations from pilgrims, as you might expect," GIGI replied. "The order, having renounced all attachments to material possessions, was seen as a trustworthy steward of highly valued items. And their martial skills made them ideal guardians. Throughout the centuries, many items were sent to the temple for safekeeping, first by the native people of Lawash and later by beings who visited the star system."

"Like the Correll?" Darius asked.

"Yes," GIGI responded. "My makers utilized the excellent steward-ship of the Jatoshi. It was a symbiotic relationship. We saved their construction secrets, and they held our most valued treasures."

"That's fascinating," Vivian said.

"Looks like our guys found a way inside," Pete Best said.

On the display screens, Darius saw the platoon removing a large piece of fibrous material that looked a lot like a wooden board. It was several feet wide and tall but with a rough section along one side. Darius guessed it had been broken or torn in half. The rough side had stiff fibers sticking out.

"That doesn't look like something left over after the invasion," Nash said. "But added afterward."

"Probably to keep the entrance closed," Darius agreed. "Something may be living inside."

The camera feeds showed a dark tunnel lined with debris and dust. The ceiling was arched, and the stones on the floor were cracked and rough. I guess now we find out if this was worth the time and effort, Darius thought. He was hopeful but not optimistic. Part of him knew that finding the power core was essential to the survival of the human race. But another part of him still felt like they were toying with something they couldn't understand. It seemed impossible that the key to an entire species' survival could be buried in the ruins of an old temple. As a boy, he studied the ruins of ancient Egypt. He knew the Great Pyramid was a mystery, with no real understanding of what the gigantic structure had been constructed for. No treasure had ever been found in all the years the human race had searched those ruins. And Darius feared that the same would be true of the pyramid on Lawash. It seemed like the kind of place that only took and never gave. If so, the only thing it could take was the lives of the Marines, and Darius feared that was a price much too high. But that was what the military was for: to take the risks that ensured freedom for the system and safety for the civilians back home. Darius just hoped that if anything happened to them, he would be able to live with himself under the weight of the guilt he knew would land squarely on his head.

CHAPTER 33

"HELMET LIGHTS," Remmy barked. "Low light amplification. Make sure you adjust the settings for your battle helmet cameras, too."

"Sometimes it feels more like we're making movies than waging war," Hugo McManus said.

"Nothing wrong with that," Corporal Leigh Ann Poh of the Alpha team said.

"Let's stay focused on the task at hand," Lieutenant Colt ordered. "This is a significant structure. The odds are high that it will foul up our comlinks, so I'm ordering Corporal Thompson to stay on guard here. The rest of us will continue, but I want regular communication checks. If the feed starts breaking up, we'll form a human chain to relay the signals to the *Jericho*. You understand that, Marine?"

"Yes, sir!" Thompson said.

"You stay here, and I mean right here," Colt told him, pointing at the dirt-strewn floor just inside the mouth of the tunnel entrance. "You keep watch, and you keep that comlink on high. Don't go falling asleep, Corporal."

Remmy thought the instructions were a little over the top. Ricky Thompson had completed Spec Op training like the rest of the platoon. That was a feat in and of itself. The Special Operations school had a graduation rate of less than thirty-three percent. Two out of every three Marines who volunteered failed to complete the course. And it wasn't

Ricky's first combat engagement either. He had proven himself on more than one occasion. In addition to that, there was the stimulation of being in an alien world, and there was no way that Corporal Ricky Thompson would get drowsy and fall asleep in his post.

"Yes, Lieutenant!" Ricky replied in a high-pitched voice.

"Alright, Sergeant Steel has a point," Lieutenant Colt continued. "Let's spread out a little people. No need to bunch up. Watch for danger."

Everyone acknowledged the cautionary warning, but again, it wasn't necessary. Remmy could tell by looking that the old tunnels inside the massive structure were dangerous. The outside looked impressive, but the massive stone blocks inside the pyramid looked jumbled and uneven.

"You know, Master Sergeant," Hugo McManus said. "I never heard a story about treasure hunting that went well for those involved."

"That a fact, Hugo?"

"It is, Sergeant. Just thought I'd put that out there."

"What's wrong with a little positive thinking on this op?" Rip asked.

"Seems like an easy mission to me," Wendy Downes said. "We aren't in enemy territory. I think we can handle whatever this world has waiting for us."

"Famous last words," Tex said, sounding solemn in his southern draw.

Remmy wasn't paying them any attention. His mind was focused on the tunnel ahead of him and the voice only he could hear inside his mind.

Hello, Master Sergeant. I will be leading you through the temple. There will be a corridor on your left in about thirty paces. Turn into it.

GIGI?

Yes, Sergeant.

How can I hear you when I'm down here and you're in orbit all the way up there?

The alien device said, *My communication focuses on your unique brain wave pattern. I can detect it from a great distance and project directly to it. Likewise, I can read your replies via those same brain waves.*

Great, Remmy said. *Nice to know you're with me.*

Always, the alien device replied.

It didn't give Remmy a feeling of comfort. In fact, he suddenly wished the living computer was out of his head completely. But there was no time to worry about it. He had reached the opening to his left.

"This way," he said.

"Hold on, Master Sergeant," Lieutenant Colt ordered. "Why are you leaving the main corridor? Shouldn't we search through it first before checking the side rooms and offshoots?"

"I've got the artifact in my head, sir," Remmy said. "I can't explain how, but GIGI is leading me. She says to turn into this room right here."

"Alright, we'll follow your lead then," Colt said. "But I want Sergeant Thorne and Oliver to continue exploring this place."

"Roger that, sir," Dirk Oliver said.

"Don't get lost," the Lieutenant warned. "Use your glowsticks and mark every room you search."

"Are we looking for anything in particular?" Sergeant Jay Thorne asked.

"Just make sure we don't run into any surprises. Lead away, Master Sergeant."

Remmy couldn't see his commanding officer's face, but Colt's voice was thick with trepidation. He was either afraid of what lay ahead or bothered that Remmy could hear GIGI speaking to him from so far away.

There was no time to worry about what Lieutenant Micky Colt was thinking or what terrors his mind conjured as they crept through the dark temple corridors. Remmy went directly into the room that GIGI had indicated. His hands ached from gripping the handles of his rifle so tightly. Fear was a constant in combat. Fear always looms over a person, even through the long, tedious hours when nothing happened. Remmy had feared bombs dropping, snipers shooting, and IEDs unexpectedly going off. He feared being maimed more than dying. Death was final and complete, like a light being switched off. The dead didn't feel pain and no longer feared anything. What happened to a person after they died was one of the great mysteries of the human race, who couldn't fathom the cessation of existence. Remmy had been raised to believe in God and the eternal reward that came from that belief, but the horrors of war had eroded his faith, and the logical side of his brain couldn't help but wonder if GIGI wasn't the ultimate proof that there was no God.

But his fears didn't keep Remmy Steel from doing his duty. At that moment, his duty was moving deeper into a cave-like chamber inside the pyramid temple. It was as spooky a place as Remmy had ever been. Spiderwebs were hanging from the ceiling and stretching to the walls. It is not fine, gossamer filaments with geometrical elegance in their design, but thousands of thick, faded webs hanging limp and tangled together. Fortunately, there weren't many webs in the center of the room to cling to his armor. Neither did he have to breathe the stench inside the ancient structure. Dust floated through the beam of light projected by his battle helmet. And he wasn't forced to feel the webs that occasionally crossed his path.

At the back of the chamber is a hidden doorway. It will look like stone and is probably hidden under a tapestry or behind a shrine.

How do you know this? Remmy asked.

It is in my database, Sergeant. The most likely type of doorway is a pressure release. When you find the door, press against it, and it should spring free.

The back of the chamber was like the rest. The entire room appeared to be empty. Only spiderwebs hung across the back wall. Remmy reached out with a gloved hand and swiped the webbing away. McManus joined him on one side and Gunny Rand on the other.

"Looks like a dead end," the Gunnery Sergeant declared.

"Hidden passage," Remmy said.

"Of course," McManus said. "That's exactly what it is."

"Remmy started pressing his hands against the stones. They didn't move, and they certainly felt solid to his touch. He stepped sideways and continued searching. Rand and McManus joined in.

"Hey, look!" Rand said, his voice pitched high with excitement. "It opened!"

Remmy pulled back the wall section, only to have the hinges fail completely. The door was wood, with large stones adhered to the surface. It was heavy and clattered to the floor. The wood, rotten after five centuries, disintegrated on impact.

"Wow, you don't know your strength, Master Sergeant," McManus said.

"What have you got up there, Remmy?" Lieutenant Colt asked.

The Master Sergeant leaned through the doorway. It was a staircase leading down into a dark underground chamber with more spider webs and dust, but nothing else Remmy could make out.

"I've got stairs going down, sir," Remmy said.

"Down is good. Head in that direction, and when you get to the bottom, give me a check on your comlink."

"Copy that," Remmy replied.

"After you, Master Sergeant," Gunny Rand said, clearly happy that he didn't have to go first.

It wasn't exactly dark to the Marines, with lights on their battle helmets and low light amplification giving them good close-range vision.

Still, the darkness closed in just beyond the light of their helmets, and the spiderwebs looked like they were straight from a haunted house. Remmy ignored his sense of self-preservation and set off down the steps. They were made of stone and still solid. They went down at least ten meters, thirty steps in all. At the bottom, Remmy found himself in what looked like a tunnel chiseled out of solid rock.

"It's clear down here, sir," Remmy said, relying on his comlink to carry his words into the temple proper. "Looks like a tunnel cut into solid bedrock."

"You get that, Corporal Thompson?" Colt asked.

The reply was laced with just the slightest static in Remmy's helmet. "Yes, sir. I heard every word."

"Alright, let's proceed," Lieutenant Colt said. "Gunny, I want the tunnels down there marked with arrows leading back in this direction."

"Roger that, sir," Rand said.

"Stay loose, people. Let's find this power core and get out of here."

"What if there's mounds of gold coins and valuable jewels down there, sir?" Rip asked. "We allowed to take any of that if we find it?"

"Van Winkle, you're as cracked up as your name, man," Hugo McManus declared.

"I'm just saying if there are treasure rooms, there could be treasure," Rip argued. "We wouldn't be the first people to take back spoils of war."

"We're not in a war," Wendy Downes pointed out.

"And who's to say that aliens even value gold or jewels," Gunny Rands explained as he pulled a roll of glow-in-the-dark stickers from his pack and slapped one onto the wall at the bottom of the stairs. "Maybe to them, lead is more valuable than gold. Maybe they value quartz crystals more than diamonds."

"Maybe what they love most is the blood of naive Marines," McManus added in a spooky voice. "Maybe they're coming for you, Rip."

"Cut that out," Rip replied.

"Let's keep a level head," Lieutenant Colt said. "There could be traps down here. We don't want to stumble into something that could hurt us."

"Copy that, LT," Rand said. "Head on a swivel platoon."

Remmy wasn't paying much attention to the conversation. His focus was on the tunnel. He hadn't gone more than twenty steps before coming to a four-way junction.

Is this on your records? Remmy thought. He didn't have to do anything for GIGI to hear his thoughts. The alien artifact was reading his mind from orbit, which, under the circumstances, he didn't mind.

It is, Master Sergeant. Turn to your right.

"Right turn at the first junction," Remmy said.

"Copy that, right turn at the first junction," Lieutenant Colt repeated. "Gunny, mark the turn, please."

"Yes sir," Rand replied.

"Com check," Colt continued. "Thompson, you read this?"

"Yes, Lieutenant, but it's getting sketchy," the static-filled reply was barely understandable to Remmy.

"Downes, take up station at this junction. Report anything you see or hear," Lieutenant Colt ordered.

"Yes sir," Wendy replied.

Remmy thought he heard a touch of trepidation in her voice and didn't blame her. As if being in an alien world wasn't strange and scary enough, there was something spooky about the old tunnels. They were wider than tall, but the thick spidery webs made them feel smaller. And soon, they came to a T-shaped junction. GIGI bade him go left. Remmy knew that anything could be lurking in the darkness. It was the stuff of nightmares, and it made him grip his rifle tightly, thankful that he had a powerful weapon.

"Sir!" Wendy Downes said a few minutes later. "Report of contact on the surface."

Remmy stopped his progress, as did the rest of the platoon. He hadn't heard anything from Thompson, which meant they were far enough into the tunnels that they were out of radio contact. They had to rely on Wendy to relay the information to them.

"What is it?" Lieutenant Colt replied.

"It's twilight up top," Wendy reported. "Overwatch is switching to night vision, sir, but it seems like they've seen a group of aliens."

"A group? How many, and what are we dealing with?"

The response was delayed. Wendy relayed the questions to Ricky Thompson, who then asked Staff Sergeant McPherson.

"Uncertain," was the eventual reply. "They aren't out in the open. Not yet, anyway."

"Alright," Lieutenant Colt said. "McManus, Poh, you're with me. Tex, Rip, you continue with the Master Sergeant. Rand, you keep marking the way so we can catch up."

"Roger that, sir," Gunny Rand said.

"And keep a check on coms. I don't want us to lose contact."

"Copy that, sir, we're on it," Remmy said.

"We're going back to help secure the drop ship. If whatever's up there damages it, we're in a world of hurt. Find the target and get moving, Master Sergeant. I don't want you down here a minute longer than you need to be."

"Yes, sir," Remmy said.

The Lieutenant and two members of the Alpha Team headed back. Remmy couldn't deny the pang of jealousy. He wanted to find the power core, but part of him just wanted to return to the drop ship. Being in the alien world left him feeling exposed and vulnerable. The sooner they were gone, the better, he decided.

"Let's move," Remmy ordered, completely unaware that the Marines weren't the only beings on the move inside the dark tunnels.

CHAPTER 34

LAILA WAS on top of a jumble of material that had collected dirt for over four hundred years. The dirt was powdery, not like soil on Earth or Mars. It reminded her more of ashes from a fire pit. She could make out the jumble of materials as she climbed up to the top of the heap. There were hard materials, maybe stone, maybe synthetics, she wasn't sure, metal beams, twisted bits of what appeared to be plastic, and other materials that seemed to have been under extreme heat. The materials felt solid under her as she got down on her stomach and did a sweep of the area with her rifle's sighting device. It was like a scope, only she didn't look through it. The narrow device was a set of tiny lenses in a long tube. They connected wirelessly to her battle helmet and displayed a clear image directly in front of her dominant eye. She could see through the faint display and make out anything around her with both eyes. But when she closed her left eye, the image from the sighting device took on more substance and focus.

After radioing in, she laid on her mound and kept watch. She was close enough to the drop ship that she could get a reading from its radar, which continued to scan the landscape. Laila didn't like being on overwatch. It was important but far from the action. She was the type of person who enjoyed the adrenaline rush of charging into a dangerous situation. Although, she thought of herself as a cautious, controlled force. She wouldn't go diving out of a third-story window the way Hugo

McManus had. But she didn't like being stuck keeping watch, even if she understood the duty's reason and importance.

But her frustration quickly faded in the beauty of the alien world. The sky was a magnificent display of colors. There were no clouds overhead. The pink and gold streaks soon filled the entire sky, with hints of the darkness of space peeking through. In the distance, beyond the city ruins, was a low range of ragged-looking mountains. A river flowed out of them, although it curved away from the city. She was only forty meters above ground level but had an excellent view. The drop ship was below and in front of her; beyond it was the massive temple. Everything about the alien world was exotic, and she realized that what she saw was unique in all the history of mankind. The rest of the platoon was stuck inside the pyramid, searching through dark tunnels. Her duty might have been boring, but at least she had an excellent view.

"Staff Sergeant," Jack Fortnoy said calmly. "I've got movement."

"What?" Laila replied. "Where? There's nothing on the radar."

"It's coming from that jumble of big rocks about three hundred meters from the pyramid to the east."

Laila was due south of the pyramid. Her two subordinates were on shorter hills to her northeast and northwest. They were far enough out that they could see around the pyramid between them. It was a standard military strategy. Jack was on her right side, and Izzy was on her left. They were both more than five hundred meters from her location.

"Where? I don't see anything," she said.

"Just keep watching. They're moving slow and staying close to the mound," Jack said. "They blend right in when they ain't moving."

Laila was suddenly frustrated by her inability to make out what was happening. Where there was no flora, everything was covered by the gray-colored, powdery dirt. In the low light of the evening, it all blended. Gray shadows, gray land, gray hills, and the ruins of what had once been buildings. How was anyone supposed to see anything?

"Ronin One, this is Bravo team," she reported over the platoon channel of her comlink. "We have movement on the surface. I repeat, we have movement on the surface."

"Copy that, Bravo Team," Ricky Thompson replied. "I will relay to Ronin One."

It took a moment to get the information to the Lieutenant and for his reply to reach her. Of course, he wanted to know what they were seeing.

"Unclear," she reported. "Switching to night vision."

She made the change, and the world went from gloomy gray to vibrant green. That's when she saw them. A group of what was called the Rake. They were big, misshapen beings. They covered their bodies in rags. Their skin, clothing, and features all blended with the ruins around them. There was still no indication of them on the ship's radar. They were too close to the mound of debris they had come out of to be seen on the ship's scans. With her rifle pointed at the mound, she could see movement but couldn't distinguish the individuals. They were too close together.

"We are seeing multiple bogies," she said. "Number unknown. At this moment, they are loitering around, staying close to their domicile. We're too far away to get a good read on them."

"Copy that," Thompson said. "Lieutenant Colt is on his way back up with McManus and Poh."

That was some good news. Laila didn't mind some extra guns in the situation. What she could make out about the Rake was their size. They were big-bodied creatures. Her laser rifle was a Hemlock Stinger, the preferred weapon of Marine snipers. It had a powerful laser blast that could penetrate an inch of solid steel. The battery was a heavy block she had on a tether attached to the back of her belt. It gave her eight shots with the laser rifle before needing to be recharged. And Laila wasn't sure what the laser beams would do to the aliens. It might take several shots to bring them down. And worse, she still didn't know how many there were.

"They have to know we're here," Jack Fortnoy said. "They're being cautious."

"I hate to think they were scared of something besides us," Izzy said.

"Pick up your visual scanning," Laila ordered. "Three-sixty... make sure there's nothing we haven't seen out here."

Lieutenant Micky Colt's voice crackled through the comlink a moment later.

"Talk to me, Staff Sergeant," he said. "Where are they?"

"A group of them, sir," Laila said. "They're staying close to that mound of debris three hundred meters from your position."

"I see the mound but nothing else," he said. "Are you sure?"

"They're on the far side, sir," Jack reported. "They're crawling all over each other like animals."

Laila heard the disgust in his voice. She had to remind herself that they weren't humans, even though she projected a sense of humanity onto them. She had to stop. They were targets and nothing more. Her job was to watch them and make sure none got too close to the pyramid or the drop-ship.

"Alright, three of us are coming out," the Lieutenant explained. "Cover us if those things move."

"On it," Jack Fortnoy said.

"Staff Sergeant?" Colt asked.

"You're clear, sir. We've got you covered."

"Alright, let's move," Lieutenant Colt said, his voice clear and loud in Laila's helmet.

In her peripheral vision, she saw the Marines sprinting across open ground toward the drop ship with their weapons ready. But Laila's focus was on the aliens. They stopped moving when the Marines made their dash for the ship.

"What are they doing?" Jack asked.

"Listening," Laila said.

Suddenly, one of the Rakes stepped away from the others. It was Laila's first clear look at the alien. It had long, skinny legs. She wasn't sure, but they looked bare. Its body was not symmetrical but lumpy with odd bulges. It walked as if one leg was shorter than the other, a strange, lurching gait. A baggy garment hung over its body. There were no sleeves. The arms seemed to Laila to be all bone and veins. And the head looked like a mutilated potato. The eyes were uneven, the mouth slanted, and the nose was a massive hump in the middle that hung down over the mouth. What stood out the most to Laila was the stringy shock of hair that hung from the top of its potato-shaped head. It was all a dirty gray, not just colored from the powdery dust that covered everything on Lawash, but the gray hair of old age.

"I got a bogey on the move," Jack said.

"Easy, let's see what it does, Corporal," Laila said.

They watched the alien, who was busy watching Lieutenant Colt and the two Marines with him.

"It's watching the LT," Jack said. "Permission to engage."

"Negative," Laila said. "Hold your fire."

"I thought these things were hostile?"

"That's the report we got, but it was over four hundred years old," Laila said. "And that thing doesn't have a weapon."

"Doesn't mean it won't attack."

"Just stand by," Laila ordered. "Lieutenant? Do you see the alien?"

"He's in my sights," Colt replied. "McManus, I want you up top. Poh, guard the rear hatch. I'm going in to prime the system. We may need to dust off if those things come after us."

"It's two hundred eighty-six meters from the ship," McManus said as he settled in on top of the dropship. "I'm tethered on and in a good position. I've got that thing in my sights."

"The others are starting to move," Jack announced. "I'm counting eight of them, and there's more still next to their mound of trash."

"Looks like they're carrying weapons," Corporal Leigh Ann Poh said.

"Agreed. They've got clubs," Jack said. "Eight fighters. They're spreading out, too."

"How do you want us to proceed?" Laila asked.

"I'm in the cockpit," Lieutenant Colt said. "Ship systems are coming online. Don't let them get near the ship."

"They're still out of my range," Hugo McManus said. "My rifle is only set for two hundred meters."

Laila knew that McManus carried a Tull Rapid Fire or TuRF rifle. It was a heavy, over/under dual ammo weapon. The upper barrel fired tactical shotgun rounds through a smooth bore. The high-energy buckshot pellets had a maximum effective range of only fifty meters. The lower barrel fired .44 caliber magnum rounds. McManus had loaded up with supersonic shredders made of a soft alloy meant to flatten into ragged-edged disks on impact. They were considered maximum damage ammo, but with a maximum range of two hundred meters before the heavy bullets lost all lethal velocity.

"Fire a few rounds anyway," Laila ordered. "Let these things know what they're facing."

It was nearly full dark. When Sergeant Hugo McManus fired his rifle, there was a flash at the muzzle from the explosive gel that was set off with each shot and hurled the bullets toward their targets. The shots dropped at least forty meters from the old alien, but it screamed in response to the rifle reports. And the others bellowed in fury and hurried forward, raising their clubs in a threatening manner.

"Now?" Jack asked.

"Fire away," Laila said.

She already had one of the aliens in her sights. The targeting crosshairs were centered on one of the alien's wide chests. She pulled the trigger. Lasers fired without any discernible movement to the shooter and covered the distance between the rifle and the target almost instantly. It wasn't pulled down by gravity or slowed by the friction in the air. It did,

however, show up as a flash of light as it burned up any microscopic parti-
cles in the air. Laila saw the flash from Jack's weapon just a split second
before she fired herself.

Neither of the aliens fell. Laila kept her left eye closed so that she
could focus on her target. It staggered back. The shot had hit just to the
left center of its chest. She saw the scorch mark on the dirty fabric and a
wisp of smoke from the wound. The alien bellowed in pain and slapped
his free hand to the wound, but didn't go down.

"They're not dropping," Laila said.

"Hit 'em again," McManus said.

"Should I move?" Izzy asked. "I could work my way around the
pyramid and flank them from behind."

"Negative, negative," Laila said. "Hold your position, Corporal."

"Copy, holding my position," Izzy Berry said.

Jack's second shot still didn't take the aliens down. They weren't
exceptionally fast on their feet, but they were running toward the ship.

"Tough bastards," Jack said.

Laila wasn't a good enough marksman to target the alien's legs.
Instead, she aimed for one's head. It was moving, and the shot was difficult, but she steadied her breathing and aimed low on one alien's face.
Her shot hit the big nose, and for a second, nothing happened. Then the
alien toppled forward, falling face down on the ground.

"That did it," McManus said. "They're in my range now."

"Aim for their head, Jack," Laila said.

She lined up a second target as Hugo McManus started shooting.
The man could be obnoxious and was certainly too gung-ho at times, but
Laila appreciated his grim determination. He fired his rifle on semi-automatic, squeezing off a few rounds at each of the remaining targets. Laila
hit another in the forehead. It dropped. The bullets had a more dynamic
impact than the lasers. The rifle reports were loud, too, echoing through
the ruins of the ancient city. The aliens hit by the sonic shredders wailed
in pain and immediately moved back the way they had come. One fell
and crawled back; the others managed to stay on their feet, even with
multiple shots ripping through their flesh.

Jack managed to hit one of the aliens in the head. It went down,
cutting their numbers in half. Laila felt a wave of relief seeing them
retreat. The older alien with gray hair was moving back, too, walking
backward. She couldn't tell if it could see in the darkness. Other than the
muzzle flash from their weapons, there was no light to see by. A million

stars glowed in the night sky, but their light didn't enough to illuminate the city, and Laila felt certain they wouldn't see the Rake again.

She was just about to radio in her thoughts on the matter when a strange, reverberating noise ripped through the darkness. No one spoke until the sound faded away, and then Jack asked the question they were all thinking.

"What was that?"

"Not the Rake," McManus said. "It came from back that way."

Laila didn't have to see Hugo to know what he was talking about. The sound had come from behind her, far to the south.

"It's not good whatever it is," Leigh Ann said. "I've heard lions roar like that."

"A roar?" Jack asked. "That's what it was? What roars like that?"

"Nothing we want to meet face to face," McManus said.

"What should we do?" Izzy asked.

"Hold your positions," Lieutenant Colt said. "Nothing is showing on the radar."

"The Rake didn't show on the radar either," Jack said.

"They did once they moved away from the hill they were hiding in," Lieutenant Colt said. "Let's all just stay calm. Corporal Thompson, let's have a report from Master Sergeant Steel."

"Yes sir, standby," Ricky Thompson replied. A few seconds stretched to nearly a minute, with no response from Corporal Thompson.

Finally, Lieutenant Colt spoke up again. "Well... Corporal?"

"Sir, I'm sorry. I'm not getting a response," Ricky replied. "Corporal Downes is offline."

The silence that followed was ominous. Laila had been on missions that had gone wrong before. There was nothing quite like fear and dread when someone failed to respond to a call on their comlink.

"What about Sergeants Thorne and Oliver?"

"Can't reach them either, sir. No one is responding," Ricky Thompson replied.

"Sergeant McManus," Lieutenant Colt said in a tightly controlled tone. "Will you return to the temple and check on Corporal Downes?"

"On my way," Hugo replied. "Off tether."

Laila checked her laser rifle's battery charge. It was at fifty percent. And she couldn't help but wonder if any of them would make it off Lawash alive.

CHAPTER 35

REMMY HAD GONE another two hundred meters through the tunnels. He and Gunny Rand left Rip at the section where the tunnel sloped down deeper. He was charged with ensuring that communication with Corporal Downes wasn't lost.

Tex was the first to feel the vibrations in the rock. They had stopped long enough for Gunny Rand to put more stickers on the walls. Tex was leaning against one wall, looking back the way they had come. The tunnels were like a giant maze. Remmy knew they would never find the power core if not for GIGI's guidance. And anyone exploring the tunnels ran the risk of getting lost. It was a frightening place. Remmy couldn't imagine being down there without a light source.

"Y'all feel that?" Tex asked.

"What?" Gunny Rand said.

"I dunno, some kind of vibration," Tex replied.

Gunny Rand had his rifle slung over one shoulder. He had a glow-in-the-dark sticker in one hand. He reached out with his other hand and touched the tunnel wall.

"It's hard to say," he replied. "Can't feel much through the glove of this suit."

"GIGI says we're only a few hundred meters from the vault," Remmy told them. "Let's keep moving."

"He's right. Anything could cause little vibrations in the rock,"

Gunny Rand said. "It could be magma moving below or a herd of animals running through a prairie a hundred kilometers from here."

"Could be something down here, too," Tex said. "Have you noticed there's very little dust here?"

"Plenty of webs, though," Rand replied.

"Let's get moving," Remmy ordered. "I'm ready to be done down here myself."

"Are you claustrophobic, Master Sergeant?" Gunny Rand asked.

"No, but I don't fancy being down here in the dark."

"My suit's got seventy-eight percent power," Tex said.

"Yeah, I'm at seventy-five, plus a backup that should add another hour to the suit's power," Gunny Rand said. "And all we've got to do is follow the stickers back up."

Remmy didn't want to talk about what they would do if they got lost in the tunnels. His rational mind knew they could follow the stickers right back out, but his emotions were convinced they were getting more and more lost in an endless maze with every step.

And then they heard something. All three men heard it. All three froze in place.

"You hear that?" Tex asked.

"Yeah," Gunny Rand said.

"There's something down here," Tex said, shaking his head sadly.

"Sounds like it's shuffling along," Gunny Rand said. "Something big."

"Big means slow," Remmy said. "Rip, you still read us?"

"Sure do," Corporal Van Winkle said.

"You hear something?"

"Just you guys," he replied. "It's quiet as a tomb up here."

"Unfortunate turn of phrase," Gunny Rand said.

"What about Corporal Downes?" Remmy asked. "You still got her?"

"She's been quiet. Let me check. Wendy? You there?" He paused for a moment. When there was no reply, he said, "Corporal Downes, do you read over?"

Still no reply. The hair on the back of Remmy's neck stood straight out.

"Oh, this is bad," Tex complained.

"Gunny, you go check on Wendy," Remmy said. "Maybe her coms are down."

"Or maybe whatever is making that shuffling noise got her," Tex suggested.

"Nice," Rand said. "Get a grip, Corporal. We've got a job to do. Can you you find your way back here, Master Sergeant?"

"Affirmative, Gunny. I've got a map in my head. Take Rip with you when you get to him. Let's move in pairs from here on out. No reason to take unnecessary chances if we don't have to."

"Copy that," Gunny Rand said. "See you guys in a bit."

"Hopefully, not in little bits," Tex said.

They all chuckled at his grim humor. Rand hurried back through the tunnel, and Remmy started moving forward again. He hadn't gone far when he and Tex heard something that made a chuffing noise. They both froze again.

GIGI, there's something down here with us.

I have no data on that, Master Sergeant.

Can you sense any other brain waves or seismic vibrations... anything that would help me out here?"

Negative, Sergeant; I cannot help you at this time.

"Wonderful," Remmy said.

"Not my assessment, but you do you, Sarge."

"Can you tell where the sound came from?"

"It's seemed to come from both directions at the same time," Tex complained.

"Well then, we move forward back to back," Gunny said. "Anything we run into down here that's bigger than a rat is a threat. But I don't want you shooting me in the back and vice-versa if we see something. Just walk backward and let me know what you see."

"Roger that, but don't make any turns without telling me first," Tex said.

They set off, with Remmy telling himself they only had a couple hundred meters left. He had no idea what to expect in the treasure chamber. It might be empty. Or they might be filled with junk, forcing them to search high and low for the power core. He didn't relish staying down in the tunnels any longer than he needed to.

And then it appeared. What it was, he could never say. It looked somewhat like a worm, only it wasn't solid. The thing was like living jelly. Remmy fired as soon as he saw it. His Nelson was set to semi-auto. It fired one round every time he pulled the trigger. The bullets charged straight into the jellyworm, which was mostly transparent. In the low light amplification his battle helmet gave him, he could see the monster and even the flashes as the explosives detonated inside it. The thing shuffled back at first, either in pain or frightened by the loud report of the rifle, which Remmy's helmet muffled to protect his hearing in the close confines of the tunnel. The report of the rifle shots echoed through the maze of rocky corridors. And he fired more than half his magazine before the jellyworm charged forward again. It seemed completely unfazed by the shooting.

"Go back! Go back!" Remmy shouted.

Tex didn't need to be told twice. He ran, and Remmy followed. The creature pursued them both. In his head, GIGI gave Remmy directions. He didn't want to lead the monster back to the others. Instead, they turned into a side corridor and ran hard. The jellyworm wasn't especially fast, but their shooting didn't slow it down. Tex carried an old M85 manufactured by the Sigfreid Company on Mars. It fired .223 rounds. A simple, rugged weapon that was deadly on the battlefield but which had no more effect on the jellyworm than Remmy's rifle had.

They turned to their left and then took an offshoot on their right. They would have been helplessly lost without GIGI. The alien device led the pair of Marines right to a treasure vault. Unlike the rest of the tunnels, there was a door with a simple sliding bar lock. Remmy pulled the bar and pushed the door open. The chamber beyond was much larger, with massive steel beams across the rock ceiling.

Tex came in, and they pushed the door closed. There was no lock on the interior side of the door, and the two men leaned their weight against it.

"Gunny Rand, do you read me?" Remmy asked between puffs of breath.

He wasn't breathing hard from the run but from his fear, which seemed to constrict his chest.

"They can't hear us," Tex said. "We're too far down."

"We need backup," Remmy insisted.

But to both men's surprise, the jellyworm didn't force its way into the chamber. It didn't even press against the door. It just shuffled on by, grunting and chuffing. After a few moments, Tex looked at Remmy.

"Is it gone?"

"I don't know," Remmy replied. "You want to look and see?"

"Hell, no," Tex said. "I'm good right here."

"Me too. Let's have a look around."

They let the light from their helmets play through the chamber. It was carefully arranged, although some items looked to have been knocked over in the past.

"Hey, get a load of this," Tex said, pointing to the corner.

Two skeletons lay there side by side. They had strange-looking clothing, and the bones were alien, too.

"Not human," Remmy said.

"No sir, not by a long shot," Tex said. "You reckon them two got trapped in here by that creature out there?"

"And just stayed in here until they died?" Remmy asked. "I hope not."

"I suppose that's why the monks here could be trusted with riches," Tex said. "Even if a person could figure the way through the tunnels, they wouldn't last long against that worm."

"How did the monks get in and out?"

"Beats me. But our bullets didn't do diddly squat to that thing."

"It just absorbed them," Remmy said. "Let's have a look around. See if we can find some answers."

"You go ahead," Tex said. "I'll guard the door."

Remmy walked over to what looked like a statue. Rip would have been impressed. The figure was on what looked like a polished granite pedestal. Whatever it was, Remmy had never seen anything like it. He counted six legs and eighteen short protrusions that were probably arms. It had a serpentine neck and three heads. Each of the heads looked completely different. There were wings on the statue, too, not like birds, but almost like something mechanical. They were folded over the statue's back, with hinges as if they could rotate out and extend in length. The statue looked to be either made from or plated with gold. And there were gemstones in the statue's strange clothing, although Remmy couldn't make out what type they were.

The next item he came to looked like a picture frame with a glass front. It was as deep from the glass to the back as his hand from the palm to his fingertips. Inside was filled with sand, or what appeared to be sand. After a moment, he decided there had to be protection for something delicate inside.

He moved on. Some things looked like ancient ceremonial weapons, armor, outfits on headless mannequins, and a few things carved into stone that looked simple but were probably very old.

"*Are you seeing this stuff?*" Remmy asked.

I get a sense of what you are seeing, Master Sergeant. Your mind is not adroit in communicating with images. Your emotions blur everything."

"*Yeah, that's humans for you,*" Remmy thought. He knew his fear was still coloring everything he thought and saw. *There are still treasures down here.*"

"*That bodes well for our endeavor.*"

"*Only if we can get to it. Tell me what that thing was.*"

"*I have no data on the creature that chased you, but I have some conclusions.*"

Remmy had all kinds of thoughts about the jellyworm, but nothing he felt he could bet his life on.

First, GIGI said, undeterred by the feeling of helplessness that Remmy was struggling with, *it is possible that the creature you saw made the tunnels. My supposition is that it must feed on minerals rather than organics.*

Remmy looked at the walls of the treasure cavern. They were different from the tunnel walls. Both appeared to be chiseled from solid rock, but the walls of the chamber were rough and uneven. There were also thick metal support beams to ensure the ceiling didn't cave in. The tunnels had grooves, but they were uniform and smooth. The floor was flat, but the floor of the cavern was uneven and rough.

That seems like a solid hypothesis, Remmy thought. *Go on.*

It's most likely blind, and I would guess it operates on sound. Most subterranean creatures use other senses rather than sight.

So, the sounds of our guns affected it.

Enraged it, perhaps. What if it was simply traversing the tunnels and was as shocked by your presence as you were by it?

I don't see your point.

The point, Master Sergeant, is that it may not be a threat to you. I propose that your fear is the threat. Did you see skeletons in the corner of this chamber?

They were hard to miss, Remmy said.

I suppose that the creature's flesh is caustic, perhaps even deadly. But you are in a fully contained space suit. It might be possible to let the creature pass over you.

Might be? This is my life we're talking about.

It would be wise to send your subordinate to test GIGI's proposed theory.

I will not! His life isn't worth less just because he's of lower rank.

I have studied your species for a long time, Master Sergeant. Throughout your history, with only a few exceptions, the population has been divided into a hierarchy. *Your military rank is based on that same notion.*

But we don't experiment with people's lives, Remmy argued.

You are ignorant of your own race's history if that is what you believe.

The alien's argument made Remmy furious, partly because it was true. He knew enough history to know that many times in the past, people thought of themselves above others. He could name more than a few politicians who considered themselves superior. But he wasn't going to send Tex out to see if the jellyworm was waiting to kill them.

Keep in mind, Master Sergeant, that if you perish, Corporal Fry will be lost in the tunnels. He will die either way. There is only one logical choice to be made.

Wrong, Remmy insisted. *We can go together. We can face whatever is out there together.*

And risk the future of the entire human race? GIGI asked. *That is not logical. You have found treasures in the vaults, Master Sergeant. That fact increases the odds that the Arodoni Power Core is still there. Putting yourself at risk unnecessarily is illogical.*

There are other Marines who can retrieve the damn thing.

They are no longer in contact. You have no data to rely on. The entire platoon could be dead. Those are the realities on which you must base a decision that could affect the future of an entire species.

She was right, but Remmy hated her for it. One of the reasons he held the enlisted ranks in such esteem was because they rarely had to make such philosophical choices. He would rather rush into danger than send someone else who might die in his place. As an NCO, he sometimes had to make difficult calls, but he was almost always in the heat of battle. In combat, he could think of the unit as a cohesive whole, so it didn't feel like he was sending others into danger that he was holding himself back from. In most instances, they were all in danger, and there was a bond in facing it together.

He walked back to the front of the vault. Tex still leaned against the door, but he looked calm.

"No changes?"

"None. It's not trying to get in here," Tex said.

"Hear anything?"

"Quiet out there, Sarge."

"One of us has to go and find out if the creature is waiting for us."

"I'll do it," Tex said.

Remmy felt terrible. It was the absolute worst feeling he had ever experienced. Every fiber of his being wanted to argue that he should go and Tex should wait in safety, but he knew GIGI was right. The alien device had bonded with him. He was the only person in the tunnels who could find the power core and get out again. And their mission, the entire reason they were on the alien world in the first place, was to get the power core. If they had returned without it, everything they had done would have been for nothing.

"Alright, Corporal, just ease out there and check the tunnel both ways," Remmy ordered. "Don't bother fighting. If it's there, just run. I'll hit it from behind. Something's got to kill that thing."

Tex didn't reply. He was stoic and brave. Remmy admired him. But there was no time to think about what was happening. Tex opened the door, and nothing happened. He slipped through, and there were no screams, no roars, no sudden death. He looked both ways, the light from his battle helmet illuminating five meters of the dark tunnel.

"Whew boy, that's a relief," Tex sighed.

"Nothing?" Remmy said, stepping out of the vault.

"It's all clear, Sarge. At least for now."

"Then let's go find the power core and get out of here before it returns."

CHAPTER 36

HUGO MCMANUS WAS SCARED. He didn't fear a fight; in fact, he sought conflict. Fighting was the only time he felt something other than self-loathing. His past was a hellish mix of abuse and bad choices. The Marine Corps had given him the discipline and direction he needed to put himself on a better path, but it couldn't keep him from reliving the emotions and horrors of his past. Some combat vets suffered PTSD from everything they had seen in battle, but Hugo suffered from the things that came before.

He wasn't scared of whatever horrible thing might be in the pyramid. What scared Hugo was that it had already attacked, and he wasn't there to face it. He was scared that more of his platoon mates had died, and he couldn't do anything about it.

Death didn't frighten Hugo. He had faced death many times as a child. It had left scars on his psyche that many experts predicted would ruin his life. But the Marine Corps had reached down, pulled him out of the pit of hopelessness, and given his life a purpose. Hugo wasn't a good man. He had trouble making friends and getting along with most people. He had never had a relationship with a woman that lasted more than a few days. And while he rarely found a way to connect with people, he could still earn the respect of his comrades in arms. In combat, facing death, he was valuable. And while that sort of respect didn't earn him enduring friendships or belonging, it did give him a brief respite from the intense feeling of shame that he had for being alive. Death would, in many ways, be a relief for Hugo McManus. When it came to him, it would not find him weeping or begging for more time. Hugo intended to ask the Grim Reaper what took him so long.

Dashing back across the open ground toward the Pyramid, Hugo glanced in the direction from which the Rake had come. Four of them lay dead. His night vision display showed their deformed bodies. Or maybe the Rake wasn't misshapen. They might have been simply a race of grotesque creatures. He wasn't the type to think too deeply about aliens. Everyone he ever met fell into two categories; they were either friend or foe. The discovery of aliens in the galaxy and his engagement with them didn't change his binary view of the universe.

Ricky Thompson saw Hugo coming. There was relief on the younger man's face. They weren't friends in the word's traditional meaning, but Ricky fell into the friend category. They were friendly enough, although Hugo knew some platoon mates talked about him behind his back. He knew and didn't even blame them because he disliked himself at least as much as they did.

"What do we do?" Ricky asked as Hugo climbed into the opening that led into the pyramid.

"You stay here," Hugo told him. "I'll go see what's wrong with Downes comlink."

"Okay, yeah. You want me to stay here."

"That's right, Corporal. You're the link back to the LT. Don't leave your post. Report anything you see."

"Yes, Sergeant."

"Good man," Hugo said.

He didn't blame others for being afraid. Fear was part of living. Fear was a gift that kept people from doing stupid, dangerous things. And there were layers to fear. Some people were afraid of everything. Others understood that danger, and even death, could be avoided under the right circumstances. However, most people just pretended the things they did regularly were perfectly safe. Riding in a vehicle, whether a land-based transport or aircraft, wasn't safe. More people died in vehicular accidents than in any other way. People were exposed to germs, chemicals, and unsafe situations daily, yet they were capable of going on with their lives without fear. Hugo didn't have a death wish. He didn't take unnecessary chances in life or combat. But he didn't turn away from danger either. And if it were between him and the people in his unit, he would rather it be him who died.

"Alright, I'm on the move. Let the LT know where I'm headed," Hugo told Thompson.

He heard the radio chatter. It was all normal, a nice, disciplined exchange of information. Dust rose in a cloud from his boots, hitting the floor with each step. Hugo was jogging through an alien temple. Strange designs were carved into the stone floor and walls. He thought briefly that it would surely fascinate most people, but it held no interest to Hugo. Without being able to decipher what the markings meant, it was just white noise to him. He had always been that way. Or maybe curiosity was beaten out of him as a child. Hugo wasn't opposed to learning, but he rarely sought information. It was better to go unnoticed; that was another lesson from his violent childhood.

The side chamber that led down the tunnels appeared out of the darkness. He dashed through the doorway and ran back to the opening in the rear wall. The Marines hadn't replaced the door. It had broken to pieces when it fell off the ancient hinges. They had pushed the bits of wood and faux stone out of the way and left the opening to the underground maze of tunnels unobstructed. He looked down the stairs. There was nothing but darkness.

"Corporal Downes, do you read me?"

There was no response. "Thompson, I'm at the stairwell. No sign of Downes. I'm heading down to investigate."

"Copy that, Sergeant," Ricky Thompson said. "Lieutenant Colt, Sergeant McManus has reached the entrance to the tunnels. There's no sign of Corporal Downes. He's going to investigate."

Hugo couldn't hear the Lieutenant's response, but he didn't need to. The LT was safe in the drop ship, with Leigh Ann Poh guarding it and the Bravo team in Overwatch. Staff Sergeant McPherson was more than competent. At least those five Marines should survive the mission, he thought as he reached the bottom of the stairs. One of Gunny Sergeant Chad Rand's stickers was ahead of him and to his left. It glowed in the otherwise pitch darkness of the tunnel. It wasn't bright enough for anything to show beyond it, but it was visible in the inky blackness where no sunlight ever reached.

Moving down the tunnel, Hugo saw no signs of Corporal Wendy

Downes, but when he reached the junction where she had been posted, he did notice that there was some type of glistening fluid on the ground and lower walls where the passageway passed the initial tunnel to his right and left. It wasn't much, but there was something there. It wasn't blood; in fact, the fluid was clear. He bent down and touched a spot that glistened in his helmet's light amplification.

"Thompson, you read me?"

"I do, Sergeant, yes. I hear you," Ricky replied, his voice muffled with static.

"Corporal Downs is not at the junction where she was assigned to wait," Hugo explained. "There's no sign of her, but I found some clear, viscous fluid. Pass that on to the LT and tell me what he wants me to do next."

"Got it, standby, Sergeant," Ricky said before relaying the news.

Hugo stood up. He shinned his helmet light as far down the passages as he could. There was nothing to see but thick spider webs and the glistening trail. He couldn't tell which way it was leading and didn't think he could follow it in hopes of finding Wendy. She was a pretty cool customer, certainly no pushover. If something had come through the passage, she would have reported it or, at the very least, fought it. But there were no signs of conflict. There were no chip marks on the walls that would indicate that bullets hit the stony surface. There were no empty shells on the ground from discharged bullets. If something had killed her, it would have been fast, yet there was no debris from her battle armor and no blood. It was a mystery.

"Sergeant McManus, hold your position," Ricky Thompson said. "Word from up top is that Master Sergeant Steel is alive and still on mission."

"How the hell could they know that?" McManus said.

"Beats me, but that's what the LT said. Just stand there and keep trying to raise someone on the comlink."

Hugo thought that was a waste of time, but the beauty of being an enlisted Marine was that he had no responsibility for the decisions made in most circumstances. He didn't trust himself to make good decisions. Unlike most people, Hugo didn't have an internal compass or a natural understanding of right and wrong. That's part of what had made his childhood so difficult. He had to learn to navigate a world he didn't fully understand because, from a very young age, the adults around him had abused any notions of what was good and what was evil right out of him. But he had learned to do what he was told, exactly what he was told. It was the only way to avoid pain as a child, making him a great Marine. So he took up his post, kept his head on a swivel, and waited for any signs that the rest of the platoon was still alive.

CHAPTER 37

"YOU THINKING WHAT I'M THINKING?" Tex asked.

"That this is too easy?" Remmy said.

"Yeah," Tex agreed. "This place is starting to make sense in my mind, except for the jellyworm giving up."

"I've been thinking about that," Remmy said. "There has to be a reason that it didn't bust down the door and eat us both."

"It didn't eat them other two fellas," Tex said. Reminding Remmy about the skeletons in the treasure vault wasn't unnecessary.

"I think the vaults are off limits to those things."

"Off limits? You mean to say you think that worm thing was trained?"

"Why not? We train dogs to guard places. We train dolphins to jump through hoops and monkeys to use sign language. Maybe the aliens who built this temple trained the jellyworms to guard their treasures."

"So the vaults are safe?" Tex asked.

"That's my thinking," Remmy said. "There are two between us and getting out of this place. The first one has the power core. The second one is closer to the exit."

"All we have to do is get to those before the worms get to us," Tex said.

"Yeah, simple, huh?"

"Piece of cake."

They were jogging through the tunnels. Remmy allowed GIGI to give him turn-by-turn directions. At one point, they felt the familiar vibration and heard the shuffling sound, so they turned back and took an alternate route to their destination's vault. When they found it, they were both relieved. Remmy slid the locking bolt aside, and they stepped in, relieved to be out of the tunnels.

"This it?" Tex asked.

"This is the place it's supposed to be," Remmy said. He couldn't keep the disappointment from his voice. Unlike the other treasure vault, parts of the ceiling had broken loose, and much of the treasure had been looted. Finding the power core wouldn't be easy if it was still in the vault.

"Think I'll just guard this here door, Sarge," Tex said.

"Yeah, okay," Remmy said.

"I mean, I can help, but I don't know what we're looking for."

"Stay at the door. I'll dig around a little. If something happens to me, you head back to the surface."

"Something happens to you, and I'll be lost in this maze of tunnels forever."

"Don't be so pessimistic," Remmy told him.

But they both felt the pressure. Maybe their entire world depended on them finding the Arodoni Power Core, and even if it was still in the treasure vault, it was probably damaged by the rocks falling from the ceiling. And if by some miracle it wasn't, they still had to survive long enough to get back out. The odds were not in their favor.

Remmy walked carefully through the rubble. It was impossible not to think about the massive pyramid over his head. He had no idea how much weight could be held up with tunnels running through the foundations. The treasure vault was constructed much like the first one. Metal support beams were along the walls and across the chamber's ceiling. They were intact, mostly, although two of them had snapped under the pressure and twisted. Big sections of rock had broken loose, probably during the orbital assault. Remmy knew that bombs set off on the surface of a world could wreak havoc on underground structures. Humans had kinetic bombs. They were massive pillars of tungsten steel loaded onto defense satellites in orbit. They were called the Rods of the Gods, an alternative to atomic weaponry with supposedly the same destructive power. Humans had never used them, but Remmy had learned about the concept in a book he had read on the history of warfare. One of those hitting the surface would disrupt underground facilities for hundreds of miles. It was a wonder that the pyramid and tunnels beneath it had survived.

To his surprise, he skirted a big pile of rubble and found what looked like a stainless steel hard case box sticking out of the backside. It was dented, but not deeply. The latches all looked intact, at least on the portion he could see.

That is it, GIGI said. *The Arodoni Power Core should be inside that case.*

Remmy went to the box and pulled on a handle fabricated into the side of the case just below the lid. At first, the box didn't move. He slung his rifle around his back and pulled on the box with two hands. It moved a few centimeters, then stopped.

"Find something?" Tex asked from the far side of the mound of rock.

"Found it, I think," Remmy said. "But it's half buried."

He started moving rocks. It was slow work. The stones were fragments of the bedrock from overhead. They had cracked and fallen, shattering to pieces. From what Remmy could see, the process had happened more than once. He knew he would get killed even in battle armor if the ceiling fell again.

It took several minutes before he felt like pulling the crate again. But when he did, he was rewarded with success. The box pulled loose, and part of the mound dropped into the void, pushing the crate away. A cloud of dust billowed from the shattered rocks and enveloped Remmy, but he had the crate.

"You okay, Master Sergeant?" Tex called.

"Fine," Remmy replied. "You?"

"A-Okay."

Remmy could hardly wait for the dust to settle and his vision to clear before flipping the latches and removing the lid of the crate. He was certain the box wasn't empty; it was too heavy to be empty. Inside was what appeared to be another box; only Remmy knew that it was the Arodoni Power Core. It didn't look like a valuable object, but if it worked, it could produce massive amounts of energy, enough to power entire fleets of starships for hundreds of years. Remmy had no real idea how it worked. But he felt a sense of giddiness looking at the device.

I have it, he thought. *Inform Captain Darius that we have the power core. All we have to do is return it to the surface and onto the dropship.*

I will inform Jericho's *crew*, GIGI replied.

"Tex, come give me a hand with this," Remmy ordered.

"You sure the ceiling ain't gonna fall on us?" the other Marine asked.

"The sooner you get over here," Remmy said, putting the lid back on the crate and flipping the latches closed, "the sooner we can get gone."

"Now, you're speakin' my language, Sarge!"

Tex joined Remmy, and they each took hold of the crate's integrated handles. Even with both men lifting the crate, it was heavy. They walked it around the mound of rubble and to the cavern door before having to set it down.

"Dang, boss, that's heavy," Tex said.

"Worth its weight in gold, according to GIGI."

"You talk to that thing like it's alive."

"It is," Remmy said. "Getting this thing to the surface won't be easy, though."

"Yeah, we ain't outrunning no jelly worms if we're toting this box, Sarge. That's a fact."

"I don't see any options."

"We should have brought us a repulsor sled or something."

"We'll manage. Get the door, Corporal. I'm ready to get off this rock."

CHAPTER 38

CAPTAIN ZEKE DARIUS WAS WORRIED. He had watched from orbit as a group of the Rake attacked the Marine platoon, and there was a herd of animals moving toward the pyramid, probably drawn by the sounds of gunfire. Worse still, the Galactic Information & Guidance Instrument had no idea what the creatures were.

"Ronin One, this is Shogun Actual. Be advised there are native creatures on the move. They will be in the city ruins in approximately ten minutes, over," Vivian Ramos said into the little microphone she was holding.

"Roger that, Shogun Actual. We heard them after fighting off the Rake," Lieutenant Colt responded. "As I'm sure you've heard, we've lost contact with our people inside the pyramid."

Captain Darius broke in on the conversation. "Lieutenant, can you give us an idea of your platoon's situation? Where are they, and who is out of contact?"

"I'm in the drop-ship with Corporal Poh. We have Corporal Ricky Thompson at the entrance to the pyramid and Sergeant Hugo McManus down in the tunnels. Master Sergeant Steel, Gunny Sergeant Rand, and five other Marines are missing or have lost contact with the rest of us."

"Captain Darius, I can confirm that Master Sergeant Remmy Steel is alive and proceeding with the mission," GIGI announced.

"Master Sergeant Steel is still in contact with GIGI," Darius said. "We've got to give your people more time, Lieutenant."

"Do you have any suggestions about the creatures moving this way?" the Marine officer asked.

Darius felt horrible that he couldn't be more useful. The *Jericho* had weapons, but they weren't intended for bombardment onto a planet. The animals, which was how Darius thought of the herd of creatures moving toward the city ruins, were a complete mystery. They didn't exist on Lawash when GIGI's database was assembled. The animals only seemed to move in the darkness, and they hadn't been seen during their two passes over the planet. Darius had no idea if they were herbivores or carnivores. They could be prey animals that were easily frightened away, or they could be something else entirely. For all he knew, they could be intelligent beings or bloodthirsty savages who sought only to kill.

"We don't," Darius said. "If your people aren't out of the pyramid in time, you will need to take to the air. The structure should keep the platoon safe from those creatures, but you can't risk the shuttle."

"Roger that," Lieutenant Colt said.

"I leave it to you, Lieutenant. Good luck. Shogun is standing by until you have more news for us."

"Roger that, Shogun," Colt said.

Silence descended on the Bridge of the *Jericho* until the doors swished open, and Connor O'Dell walked in. He looked around, not quite sure he was welcome on Bridge.

"Mr. O'Dell," Darius said. "It's good of you to join us."

"I appreciate the visual recordings of the planet, Captain. That data will be highly prized back on Earth."

"Are you here to help us complete the mission?" Darius asked.

"I don't know. I just couldn't sit in my room any longer. What's happening?"

"Our Marines have found the way into the tunnels under the temple," Darius said.

"Did they find the power core?"

"Not yet," Darius said. "And right now, we're concerned about these creatures."

The main video feed zoomed in. The night vision from orbit wasn't great. The surface of the planet was rendered in shades of gray that all blended and made things difficult to see clearly. There was movement by the herd of creatures, but the beings themselves could not be seen well enough to make out any details about them.

"They are headed toward the city ruins," Darius continued. "The Marines were confronted by a group of Rake, which they fought back, but the sound of the fighting seems to have drawn this herd."

"They changed course when they heard the fighting?" Connor asked.

"That's correct," Darius said.

Connor O'Dell shook his head. "That means they aren't prey animals," he announced.

"How did you figure that?" Nash asked. "They probably never heard gunfire before. They could just be curious."

"That's probably true, but prey animals rarely move toward loud popping sounds," Connor pointed out. "Think about it. A herd of deer, elk, buffalo, and horses would be apt to move further from the strange sounds. A pack of wolves, on the other hand."

"This isn't Earth," Commander Lee pointed out. "We have no idea what creatures on Lawash would do."

"Or what they're capable of," Vivian Ramos pointed out.

"We'll find out soon enough," Darius said.

The officers on the Bridge watched from orbit. Bravo team was called in, and the five Marines in the dropship lifted off just a few minutes before the first of the alien creatures arrived.

"I wish we had better visuals," Pete Best said.

"It looks like a swarm," Connor O'Dell said.

"Like bees?" Alex Stanislaus asked.

"Like locusts," Connor replied. "Perhaps that is why we see swaths of land with very little vegetation. Those creatures move through an area and consume everything."

The drop-ship lifted off and rose just over a hundred meters in the air. Darius brought up the video feed from the ship.

"Ronin One, bring the ship's floodlights online," Darius ordered.

"Roger that, Shogun actual," Lieutenant Colt replied.

Several powerful lights on the bottom of the drop ship lit the ground below. There was more movement from the Rake. Half a dozen of the mutated creatures appeared in the lights. They looked up, shading their eyes briefly, then returned to their business. Three were moving among the dead.

"What are they doing?" Vivian Ramos asked.

"Scavenging," Captain Darius said.

The survivors from the battle with the Marines took the clothing off the dead bodies. The three Rakes worked fast. The bodies were left lying in the dirt, and the scavengers hurried back to their abode.

"Where did the other three go?" Captain Darius asked.

"I'm tracking them, Captain," Pete Best explained. "They're running out of the city ruins, moving south."

"Okay, yeah, I see them," Darius said.

A few moments later, the swarm arrived at the city ruins. They moved like a swarm, bunched together, traveling swiftly.

"Guns are coming online," Lieutenant Colt said. "Target anything that gets near the pyramid."

"Belay that order, Lieutenant," Darius cut in. He didn't like undermining his younger officers, but the drop ship only had a single rotary barrel machine gun with ten thousand rounds. It wasn't enough to hold off the swarm of creatures. "Have your people secure the entrance to the pyramid and wait it out."

"What if those things break into the structure?" Colt replied.

"Then you are free to engage, but we aren't here to kill the native creatures if we can help. Let them pass."

The swarm flowed through the ruins. The only thing they didn't touch was the pyramid. No one could say why. The swarm left nothing in their wake. The bodies of the dead Rake were gone when the swarm finally passed. And nothing was growing that survived the swarm except for the vines on the pyramid temple.

"That's unbelievable," Henry Nash said.

"Look at the Rake," Pete Best said. "They're taking one of those things down."

It was true. At the rear of the swarm, there were a few stragglers. The three Rake rushed at them, brandishing clubs. They caught up with one of the slowest stragglers and beat it to death. As the drop ship lowered back to the ground, the three Rake dragged the carcass of the creature they killed toward the domicile in the city ruins.

"Life goes on," Connor O'Dell said.

"Even on what should be a lifeless planet," Vivian Ramos added.

"They've adapted to the conditions on the planet after the bombardment," Henry Nash said. "The bombs must have thrown up massive clouds of dust and ash, blocking out the sunlight for decades, maybe two or three hundred years."

"Your assessment is correct," GIGI suddenly spoke up. "There is news from Master Sergeant Steel."

"Go ahead, GIGI," Darius said.

"Master Sergeant Steel has located the Arodoni Power Core. He and Corporal Fry are attempting to remove the object from the caverns under the temple."

"Outstanding," Darius said. "Vivian, relay that information to Lieutenant Colt. His priority is to get his people out of there and back to the *Jericho*."

"Aye, Captain," Vivian said before speaking into her small microphone to send the order to the Marines on the ground.

"You were right, I suppose," Connor O'Dell said, although he sounded less enthused.

"We aren't out of the woods yet, Mr. O'Dell, but this crew is very capable," Darius said. "Why is it that you sound disappointed?"

"I'm not," Connor replied. "Surprised is all. I felt certain things would not go as planned."

"They rarely do," Darius confirmed. "But we're professionals."

"And once we have the power core, we can go home," the civilian said.

"That's the plan, Mr. O'Dell. It won't be long now."

They watched as the drop ship landed, and three of the five Marines on board headed for the pyramid. Darius felt a huge sense of relief. There was still the question of why some of the Marines had lost communications, but if they could round everyone up and get them out of the pyramid, all would be well. Despite his misgivings about the operation, he felt elated that they had successfully collected what was needed to protect humanity from a powerful alien force. They knew nothing, or next to nothing, about the other intelligent forms of life in the galaxy. But it wouldn't hurt to be cautious. And even though it seemed like the least important part of their success, he did consider that his superiors would have trouble court-martialing him for bringing back a rare and highly valuable piece of alien technology that would be the key to the Sol system's defenses.

"Captain, I have something on the radar!" Ensign Jacee Bertoli said.

"A ship?" Darius asked. "I thought we scanned the entire system?"

"Confirmed," Vivian Ramos said. "It's small, Captain, and moving fast."

"Where? Put it on the plot!" Darius demanded. He didn't often lose his cool, but he felt like he had let his guard down for just a moment to celebrate the success of their mission, only to be hit by a sucker punch he never saw coming.

"It's not headed this way," Bertoli said. "It's outbound... leaving the system."

"Where did it come from?" Henry Nash wondered aloud.

"Tracking," Pete Best said. "It's moving, sir. We might get a hit with the lasers."

"No," Zeke Darius said, regaining his composure. "It's not a threat to us. We can't shoot it down."

"I think it came from there," Vivian said, pointing at the next closest planet to the system star on the holographic plot. "It launched from the world."

"I thought this was the only habitable planet in the system," Darius said. "GIGI, what are we seeing?"

"According to the data collected by Jericho, it is a Wesset Courier Drone."

"A what?" Darius asked.

"Courier drones are used to send messages throughout the galaxy," GIGI explained. "They are small, unmanned spacecraft that can use hyperspace lanes to deliver important messages."

"Why is there a drone launching from a barren world?" Darius asked.

"Perhaps the people who attacked and destroyed Lawash set it up," Commander Lori Lee said. "It could be completely automated. Are the planets in this system in sync, GIGI?"

"The planet you are referring to is called Habash. It has a slightly elliptic orbit. It is at times closer and other times farther from Lawash. Still, within that differential, the two planets stay within five to six hundred thousand kilometers of one another throughout their orbit around the system star."

"That's close enough to monitor the planet," Lori Lee said. "It must have picked up the Jericho and launched the courier drone to warn whoever set up the station."

"They know about us now," Connor O'Dell said, shaking his head as if going to the Lawa system was a huge mistake.

"Who would that be, GIGI?" Darius asked. "Who attacked Lawash five hundred years ago?"

"The Imperial forces, led by the Prime Council," GIGI said.

"That's great, just great," Henry Nash said.

"Is it too late to shoot that thing down?" Darius asked Pete Best.

"It's moving fast, sir. It's at nearly a million kilometers per hour already. We could take a shot, but it's at the edge of our effective range."

"Do it," Darius ordered.

"Let's hope that's the right move," Lori Lee said.

"Targeting the object," Pete Best said. "Lasers are at full power. Permission to fire, Captain."

"Given," Darius said.

Lights flashed from the lasers, and the lights on the ship dimmed a little, then flared back to full strength.

"Recharging," Pete Best said.

Normally, lasers move so fast that the human eye can't follow. But in space at fast distances, it still took a few seconds for laser beams to move at the speed of light to reach some targets. The laser blast was bright red and zipped across space toward the courier. It took the beam three full seconds to reach the target.

"Hit, hit, hit," Pete Best said. "Target is destroyed."

"Vivian, can you confirm?" Darius asked.

"Yes, sir, the object is no longer on the radar," she said with a massive smile.

"That was too close, Captain," Lori Lee said.

"Agree Commander. Let's get our scan of that planet. What was it called?"

"Habash," GIGI's voice was feminine and artificial as it played over the Bridge speakers.

"I want eyes and ears on Habash. If anything else launches from there, we have to know it."

"You may have just started a fight we can't finish," Connor O'Dell said.

"What we did, Mr. O'Dell was buy the human race a little more time," Darius said. "What's the update from the Marine platoon?"

"No change, sir. They're still waiting," Vivian replied.

"Tell them to hurry, Lieutenant Ramos. I want us out of this system ASAP."

"Aye, Captain," Vivian said.

"Alright, people, let's get everything in order. Lieutenant Best, please run a full diagnostic on the weapons system. Commander Lee, let's get the crew in place for an immediate run back into hyperspace as soon as the dropship is back on board. And Lieutenant Nash prime the

Prometheus engine. I don't want us here one second longer than we have to be."

The orders were received, and everyone went to work while Captain Darius fought with his conscience over the decision he had just made. Perhaps they had no cause to shoot down the courier drone, but he didn't want the enemy, which was how he was thinking about the galactic Imperium, to know about humanity. It was inevitable that they would find out sooner rather than later, but he feared what the future held for his species if they didn't get the Arodoni Power Core back to Earth in time.

CHAPTER 39

THEY DIDN'T MAKE it to the next treasure vault before the jellyworm caught up with Master Sergeant Steel and Corporal Tex Fry. The two men were struggling with the weight of the power core. They were both strong men, but their grip strength waned the longer they held the crate. At first, they stopped and set the box down as frequently as needed. But both men had a growing fear of running into the alien in the tunnels again. Both hoped to reach safety before it did, but the longer the trek through the tunnels took, the more inevitable it seemed that the worm would return.

"You feeling that?" Tex said.

"I feel it," Remmy said. "Keep moving."

"At what point do we drop this thing and run?" Tex said.

"There's no point when we do that," Remmy said, teeth clenched against the pain in his forearms. "If the worm eats the power core, we're all as good as dead."

"Awesome," Tex growled sarcastically.

Behind them, the chuffing sound could be heard. Both men sped up slightly, but they were exhausted. The narrow tunnels, the spider webs, and the loss of contact with the rest of the platoon all combined into a terrible feeling of impending doom. And that stress did more to sap the Marines' strength than the physical toll of their mission.

"It's getting close," Tex said.

"There's a junction ahead," Remmy said. "I'll take the box into the right-hand tunnel; you take the left. There's no sense in both of us dying."

"You'll be a sitting duck trying to carry this thing yourself, Sarge. I say we stick together."

"Your funeral," Remmy said.

It seemed a terrible twist of fate to have come so far and to be so close to success, only to have the very prize they had worked to secure be the thing that cost them their lives. Remmy didn't know how long they could outrun the jelly worm in full armor. He wasn't about to take his off, and they couldn't afford to let the power core get destroyed, so it didn't matter. He knew their weapons had seemingly no effect on the worm. But that didn't mean he didn't flick off the safety on his rifle with his free hand as he ran.

"Almost there," Remmy said.

"So is the blob behind us," Tex said.

There was a note of terror in his voice that Remmy had never heard from the Marine before. He was so laid back and steady that it made the ordeal all the more frightening to hear him. They reached the junction, and Remmy pulled them into the corridor on his right. They were too tired to keep running with the power core. It fell from Remmy's grasp, his hand numb from the exertion. Tex jumped over the box and collapsed to the floor just as Remmy turned to face the worm. Only it didn't attack them. He was completely shocked as the worm raced by and continued in the direction it had come. Stranger still was what he saw inside the worm. The creature was easily six meters long. It wasn't as tall as the cavern, only coming up to about the halfway point, right where the spider webs ended. The creature's body was transparent, not like a glass of water, but more like a plastic bottle with undulations that refracted the light and made everything inside hazy. But Remmy saw things inside. Two of them were Marines in full armor.

"Did you see that?" Remmy said.

"Are we dead?" Tex asked.

"No, it passed us by."

"Why?"

"Who knows, who cares? But we're still alive."

"And the case... we still have the case."

Remmy hated admitting, even to himself, that the power core was truly more important than their lives.

"Yeah, we got it," Remmy said. "On your feet, Marine, this isn't over yet."

"Is it coming back?" Tex asked, instinctually checking his rifle even though he knew it wouldn't stop the creature.

"No, but we're going after it."

"What? Are you out of your mind, Sarge?"

"That thing had our people in it. I saw two of them."

They were both in space suits with full helmets. To save power, they rarely used LEDs in the lining so that their faces could be shown at night or in dark conditions. However, Remmy didn't need to see Corporal Frey's face to know he was shocked by Remmy's statement.

"You saw them?"

"The worm is transparent," Remmy said. "Probably because it exists down here in the dark. It doesn't matter why. The fact is, I saw two Marines inside that thing. It must have eaten them whole."

"Good Lord above," Tex said. "Tell me your plan."

"You stay here and guard the power core," Remmy said. "I'm going to catch up to the worm."

"That's insane."

"Maybe, but all I have to do is stay ahead. You have a combat knife?"

"Damn straight I do," Tex said. "Hand forged Damascus steel. Ole Jim Bowie would be proud of this one right here."

"Good, when the worm comes back, use it."

"You think a knife is going to hurt that thing?"

"I don't have time to speculate. It took every bullet we fired at it head-on, and my guess is it can run both ways up and down these tunnels, but hard turns it can't do. And I'm betting that the sides of the worm are vulnerable."

"So why not shoot it?" Tex asked.

"There's a possibility that our people are still alive in there," Remmy explained. "If we shoot, the bullets could hit them."

"Good point," Tex said. "I'll be ready, Master Sergeant."

"Good man," Remmy told him. "When I return, I'm taking the tunnel on the other side, just in case I'm wrong about it turning."

There was no time to waste. As tired as he was, Remmy Steel was a Marine. When he needed to run, even when he was bone weary, he could find the will to make it happen. He set off at a strong pace. The space suit made it difficult, but he had to make up time. When the worm finally came into view, his heart felt like a sledgehammer inside his chest, and there was a stabbing pain he had rarely felt in his right side. But he brought his rifle around, still running to match pace with the worm, and aimed high. The bullets hit the worm on its back and ran in straight grooves through the soft flesh.

There was a roar, maybe fear, maybe pain. Remmy got the impression that the creature didn't like loud noise. Either way, his attack had the desired effect. The worm suddenly reversed directions.

"Come on, you slimy piece of filth!" Remmy shouted, although his voice didn't carry outside the space suit.

The race was on. Remmy couldn't be certain, but he thought the worm was moving faster than before, and it took all his strength to sprint in the space suit. But fear was a powerful motivator. He ran hard, his fatigue and pain momentarily forgotten.

"I hear you coming, Master Sergeant," Tex said. "Don't slow down."

Remmy didn't have the breath to answer. He pushed himself a little harder the final forty meters and dove into the side tunnel. He hit the wall with one shoulder, and even in his armor, he knew his body would be bruised. But none of that mattered. He pressed the release on his rifle, and the eighteen-inch long, double-edged bayonet sprang forward. The worm was racing past his tunnel as Remmy turned and rammed the rifle into the worm's side. The creature's momentum did most of the damage. The bayonet cut deep, and there were no bones, no thick tendons, or dense tissue for the weapon to get lodged in. The creature wailed a high-pitched scream that shook the solid rock walls of the tunnels. There was no doubt its cry was one of pain. The worm kept moving. It was charging too hard to stop, and the bayonet cut down its side.

Hot liquid gushed out. It made the gloves and cuffs on Remmy's armor smoke and left grooves where it splashed onto the stone floor. It wasn't acid, but it was caustic, just the same. It ran completely past where Remmy and Tex had attacked in the junction, but it was slowing.

"That did it," Tex said.

"It's not finished yet," Remmy said.

They both chased after the worm, catching up quickly. The front, or rear, Remmy couldn't tell the ends apart, looked almost like an open mouth. He jumped on top of the creature and found that the skin on the top was thicker. He stabbed the creature again and again until it bucked him hard into the roof of the tunnel. He toppled backward and hit the floor. His suit absorbed most of the damage, but his ears were ringing as he sat up.

"It's dying," Tex said.

And indeed, the worm was flopping violently. The cuts in its sides had deflated it. Smoke from the caustic fluids burning into the stone walls filled the tunnel. The Marines had to wait until it stopped moving, then they pressed in. There was slime everywhere. They crawled on top of the beast and made their way down to the two Marines trapped inside. They cut their companions free. It was a messy business, and the caustic, internal fluids were ruining their armored space suits, but Remmy could see the name badge on the victims' chests.

"It's Wendy Downs and Gunny Rand," he said. "Check him for vitals."

Remmy pulled Wendy free and then bent over her suit. There were places where the digestive juices had eaten deep inside. He took a chance and pulled her helmet off. One look and he knew the truth, but he pulled a small med scanner from his belt and activated it.

"She's dead," he said angrily.

"I got a heartbeat here, Sarge. But his suit's in real bad shape."

"Get it off him and you, too," Remmy said. "We'll have to carry him out."

To his credit, Tex didn't complain. They pulled off everything but their gloves and their helmets, which were sealed against their shoulders and chest so that they could supply them with emergency oxygen even though it wasn't necessary on Lawash. There was enough oxygen to keep them alive without their suits, but Remmy feared the worm's caustic blood and digestive enzymes could poison them. They worked fast, but it wasn't a quick job. They could move a little easier out of their bulky space armor, but it was very hot in the tunnels. Remmy already felt the effects of dehydration, and they still had over two kilometers to go before getting back to the entrance of the tunnels.

There were times when Marines could rise above their perceived limits. Remmy and Tex did just that. Tex carried Gunnery Sergeant Chad Rand over one shoulder, and Remmy did the same with Wendy's body. He wasn't about to leave her behind, dead or not. Somehow, even carrying the weight of their comrades, the two Marines also managed to carry the crate with the Arodoni Power Core. They were soaked with sweat halfway to their goal, but when they heard the static-filled call of Hugo McManus, they felt such relief that tears filled Remmy's eyes.

"We're here," Tex said. "Master Sergeant Steel and Corporal Fry. We've got Gunny Rand. He's hurt but alive. And Corporal Downes..."

His voice cracked, and Remmy understood his emotions. The battle always ended with such powerful emotions that sometimes exhausted a person for days.

"I read you, Tex, hang on," McManus said. "I'm passing on your sit rep and coming to get you."

"Roger, thanks, man," Tex said.

"And pass on the fact that we have the mission objective in hand," Remmy added.

"Got it, Master Sergeant. Standby."

They didn't just stand around and wait. Both men knew and feared more jelly worms in the hellish tunnels. So, they kept moving, one trudging step at a time. McManus radioed in, then hurried to meet them. He took the crate, carrying it all by himself, which was no mean feat, but the big Marine was strong and anxious to help.

When they reached the stairs, they found Sergeant Thorne and Oliver. They took Gunny Rand and Wendy Downes, carrying them quickly up the stairs and into the side room where the secret entrance to the tunnels had been found. Remmy, Tex, and Hugo waited at the bottom of the stairs.

"We've got issues," McManus said. "There's a herd of alien creatures up top. The LT had to take the drop ship and wait for them to pass."

"At least we aren't stuck here forever," Tex said.

"What about Rip?"

"He's missing, but everyone else is accounted for," McManus said.

"Lieutenant Colt," Remmy said, utilizing his helmet's comlink, "this is Sergeant Steel. We have the power core, sir."

"Outstanding, Master Sergeant. It's truly astounding work. McManus updated us on your status. We get off this rock as soon as we can."

"Understood, sir. I'm requesting permission to leave the power core with Sergeants Thorne and Oliver while I search for Corporal Van Winkle."

"That's a noble endeavor, Master Sergeant, but why not let Oliver and Thorne go? You've got to be exhausted, man."

"I'm the only one that can navigate the tunnels, sir," Remmy pointed out. "Besides, Tex and I killed one of those damn worms. We can do it again if we have to."

"Fine, but you have until this swarm of alien creatures passes," Lieutenant Colt said. "And you take Sergeant McManus with you. We are here for that power core, and as soon as we can leave, I intend to do so. With Rip or without him. Is that understood?"

"Roger that, Lieutenant. Use GIGI if you can't reach us on coms. We'll come running, sir."

"Good luck, Master Sergeant."

Remmy turned to Tex, who was leaning heavily against one wall. "You up for this Corporal?"

"Try and stop me, Master Sergeant."

"My man, alright, let's go find Rip."

CHAPTER 40

REMMY HELPED Hugo carry the crate up the stairs. Sergeant Thorn was giving Gunny Rand first aid. It wasn't much, and they didn't want to remove his helmet. Sergeant Dirk Oliver returned down the stairs and followed the search party to the junction to act as the communications link. Remmy led the way, and they jogged through the hot tunnels. Remmy felt his tongue was twice its normal size, and his eyeballs were so dry his eyelids were stuck in place. But he was still sweating, and so he pushed on.

"Any idea where he might be?" McManus asked.

"He and Gunny were going to check on Corporal Downes," Remmy said. "My guess is they ran into the same worm that got her."

"I don't think I want to see a worm that can eat a full-grown man in a space suit," McManus said.

"You sure as hell don't," Tex said.

"Guns do nothing when one is coming right at you," Remmy said. "We must have fired fifty or sixty explosive rounds into the thing, and it just kept coming."

"Unbelievable," Hugo said. "Rip probably saw it get Gunny Rand and make a break for it."

"He's smart," Remmy said.

They called on the comlink every minute, eventually getting a response.

"I'm here," Rip said. "Oh, thank God, thank God. I'm here."

"Where?" Remmy asked. "Where are you, Corporal."

"I'm in a room," Rip said. "It's not like the tunnels. And there's a door. I had to get away from that thing. It got Gunny Rand. It just swallowed him whole."

"We know," Tex said.

Remmy got the location of the nearest vault from GIGI. It was the only chamber close enough to be in comlink distance with the amount of solid bedrock the tunnels were carved into. When they found Rip, he was shaking with fear.

"We tried to stop it," he told them. "I stayed as long as I could. We hit it with a hundred rounds. I'm not lying. Gunny Rand told me to run, and that's what I did. I didn't want to leave him, but it was eating him alive."

"You did the right thing," Remmy said.

"We follow orders and don't ask questions," Hugo added.

"Come on, we're getting out of here," Remmy said. "Stay with us, Rip, we're almost out."

"I... I don't know the way," he stammered.

"But I do, Corporal. Stay with us," Remmy assured him. "We're getting you out of here."

Rip was crying, but that was normal. Everyone cried who had endured the horrors of war. There was nothing more traumatic and downright awful to behold than battle. Seeing people die, not calmly in their beds, but ripped apart by bullets and bombs, was like spending an hour in hell. The shock of it always took a toll. The Marines with Remmy were strong, battle-tested veterans who understood the shock that Rip was experiencing, and none of them blamed him for his tears.

They were halfway back to the main junction when Tex felt the tremors through the floor.

"We've got company," he said.

"Oh, God, no. No, please," Rip cried.

"We've got this corporal," Remmy said. "Keep moving with him, Tex. Get him and Sergeant Oliver back up the stairs."

"Yes, Sergeant," Tex replied.

"We taking it down?" McManus said.

"Not if we don't have to," Remmy said. "I don't have the armor to protect me from the acids."

"I'll do it," Hugo volunteered. Just tell me what to do."

"We'll hang back at the junction. There's no guarantee that we know where it's coming from. Hopefully, it runs right past us."

"And if it's going after them?"

"Then we draw it away," Remmy said. "Can't kill it in the one tunnel that leads out of this place."

"Oh, yeah, good thinking," McManus said.

They didn't have to wait long. The shuffling and grunting sounds reached them. And just as he feared, the jelly worm was headed straight for the stairs.

"Can it get up top?" McManus asked.

"I doubt it," Remmy said. "And we're not going to let it. Tex, you read me?"

"Loud and clear, Master Sergeant."

"It's coming your way. Better hustle now."

"We're at the stairs. See you up top, Sarge."

"Be there in jif," Remmy replied.

"As soon as it passes us, we hit it from behind. Then we run. Stay right on my six, Sergeant. No heroics. All we have to do is stay ahead of that thing until we reach the next junction. It's about four hundred meters down that tunnel."

"Got it," McManus said.

Hugo McManus hadn't done anything nearly as reckless in the weeks since his stunt on their first simulation training, but his hard-charging attitude still showed through. Fortunately, he had bonded with Remmy. They weren't friends, but he had gained respect for the Master Sergeant.

The worm rushed by. Remmy felt McManus stiffen at the sight of the huge creature. It was taller and longer than the one he and Tex had killed. They saw into the worm. Remmy recognized the remains of the worm they had killed and the armored space suits left behind. They stepped out into the corridor and opened fire when it passed them. Their rifles blazed away, and the bullets punched into the worm. It roared in shock, if not pain, and stopped much more abruptly than either man expected.

"Damn, that was fast," McManus said.

"Get moving, Hugo. I'm right behind you."

To his credit, Hugo didn't argue or hesitate. He began to run, sprinting down the corridor. Remmy kept firing for just a few seconds, ensuring that the worm was going to come after them. Once it started in his direction, Remmy turned and followed Hugo.

In a foot race, Remmy had never been the fastest runner. But he was unencumbered and caught up with McManus easily.

"Faster," Remmy said, glancing over his shoulder. "This thing is coming, Hugo. Move it, Marine! Go! Go! Go!"

Hugo ran faster, but Remmy still grabbed the back of his armored suit and pushed him along. Four hundred meters is not a long run at a normal pace. Remmy normally put in eight to ten kilometers on the *Jericho's* cardio machines. But at a full sprint, with a monster chasing you, it seemed like a thousand miles. The worm was on their heels when they reached the next junction and dove to the side. It charged past the opening but slowed. And as it passed the tunnel, an appendage shot out. It hit Hugo's rifle, knocking it out of his hands and latching onto the chest plate of his armored suit, then yanked him toward the worm.

Remmy was shocked, but his training took over. He had his Nelson LTX rifle in both hands, and he hit the extender for the bayonet with no conscious thought. He dove forward and slashed at the appendage, slicing it cleanly in two with his bayonet. The jellyworm shrieked but kept going. Remmy waited until it was out of sight, lost in the tunnel's darkness.

"That was too close," McManus said. "Thank you, Master Sergeant."

"Forget it," Remmy said. "Let's get out of here."

"You don't have to tell me twice," Hugo said.

They stepped back into the tunnel they had just raced through and started back toward the entrance. They had done fifty or sixty paces when the vibrations started again."

"It's coming back," Hugo declared.

"Run!" was all Remmy had time to say before the chuffing could be heard coming up fast behind them.

CHAPTER 41

THEY WERE ALMOST to the first junction, and Remmy knew they could turn in and be safe from the jelly worms attack but feared it would trap them there. If it was smart enough to come back after them, was it smart enough to know they were trying to escape it? Remmy remembered the skeletons in the vault. Those thieves had known something was trying to kill them. Their remains testified to the fact that they had been pursued relentlessly. And Remmy didn't think it mattered to the jelly worm if they were dead or alive as long as it got to ingest them.

"Keep going!" Remmy shouted. "Fast as you can!"

Hugo McManus was in front of Remmy. The big man was not the fastest member of the platoon. Remmy was pressing him forward. They saw the stairs. There was light coming into the chamber from the opening above. They leaped onto the steps. There were thirty of them; Remmy remembered counting when he went down them. His legs were on fire, and every muscle ached. The worm was charging in fast, and Remmy didn't know how high it could climb to reach them.

"Go! Go!" he shouted.

But Hugo missed a step. He went down hard, and there was no time to yank him to his feet. The creature was right there; Remmy heard it roaring. In a split second, he had to decide whether to keep going or stay with Hugo. His reaction was mostly instinct. It was, looking back, a worthless gesture, but Remmy dropped onto the bigger man as if he could somehow shield Hugo from the giant worm with his own body.

At that same instant, thunder rolled above them. Not actual thunder, but the thunder of guns. The roof of the rocky chamber angled down from the stairs and gave the Marines on the upper floor just enough space to rain down a barrage of bullets onto the worm's upper body. At ground level, the bullets would just be absorbed into the creature. But from above, it was vulnerable. The bullets tore through its tough hide and brought the worm to a stop just a few meters from where Remmy lay covering Hugo. The beast chuffed in defeat, then retreated up the tunnel to escape the gunfire.

"Thanks, Master Sergeant," Hugo said as Remmy pulled the big man to his feet.

"We'll be feeling it tomorrow, eh?" Remmy replied.

"I meant for—"

"Yeah, I know," Remmy said. "I wouldn't have done much good without these guys. Nice shooting, Tex."

"I had help, Sarge," Corporal Fry said. "I'm just glad it worked.

"That makes two of us," Remmy said.

They left the tunnels, but the interior of the pyramid wasn't much different. It certainly wasn't cooler. And Remmy's helmet was nearly out of oxygen. It felt bulky and heavy on his chest and shoulders without the space suit to support it. After giving the pair a few minutes to catch their breath, the group started for the exit, carrying the wounded and the Arodoni Power Core. It should have been a victory march to safety, but they were all concerned for Gunny Rand, who was alive but hadn't woken up. And grieving for Corporal Wendy Downes. Remmy remembered her as a stalwart woman who didn't give up easily and didn't back down from a challenge.

When they got to the entrance, Ricky Thompson greeted them with enthusiasm.

"The animals are gone," he said. "Lieutenant Colt is returning the drop ship for a landing."

"Good. I'm nearly tapped on air," Remmy said.

"Glad you made it out alive, Master Sergeant," Sergeant Jay Thorne said.

"I'm glad there weren't any monsters up here," Sergeant Oliver added. "I doubt we would have fared as well as you, Sarge."

"Well, I suppose we won't neglect our running after today," Remmy said.

"Absolutely not," Tex responded.

"I haven't pushed myself that hard in years," Hugo said. "I feel like I'm back in basic."

"At least we're alive," Remmy said. "Let's get this thing to the drop-ship and go home."

The *Jericho* wasn't truly home, but it was close enough. The shuttle landed just long enough for the group to run out. They weren't moving fast. Sergeant Dirk carried Gunny Rand, and Sergeant Oliver carried Wendy Downes. Ricky Thompson and Tex each took a side of the crate with the power core, while Remmy and Hugo just worried about themselves.

Once on board, they strapped in. The air was pumped out so they didn't bring back microbes from the alien planet. Remmy attached an emergency air line to his helmet, and Tex did the same. For nearly half an hour, there was nothing to do but wait. Remmy slept through it and only woke when the *Jericho's* docking clamps latched onto the shuttle.

Gunny Rand was the first person off the ship. A team of techs in bio-hazard suits carried him out. Remmy had some minor burns from the jellyworm's digestive juices. Tex also suffered from some minor wounds. They were walked out and taken to a makeshift exam station. Remmy was disappointed that the Launch Bay was again transformed into a quarantine center. And the exam wasn't pleasant. They were stripped down, their clothes bagged up, their bodies poked and prodded. Remmy didn't know why they needed to have their skin scrapped, but the techs did their jobs. They even drew blood. The scanners showed no foreign matter but were forced to take cold showers in the Launch Bay's emergency stall, just a plastic curtain folded from the wall.

After getting cleaned up, they underwent another full body scan. The rest of the platoon, still in their space suits, were sent out. Gunny Rand was put into a medical tent and seen by the ship's surgeon. Tex and Remmy were fed mission standard MREs, which wasn't what either wanted to eat, but neither complained. They were back on the *Jericho*, and that was all they cared about. Remmy drank half a gallon of flavored water with electrolytes, found his cot, and slept for eighteen hours.

When he woke up, he could hardly move, but he was alive. Another medical scan showed him free of any foreign contaminants, and he was allowed back on the ship. But things weren't all roses there either, and he was called to an emergency meeting with the senior staff.

He was on his way up to the main deck when Laila McPherson appeared in the corridor. She was wearing standard-issue Marine fatigues and not a bit of make-up or jewelry, but Remmy thought she was the most beautiful woman he had ever seen.

"They let you out?"

"Yeah," he said, unable to keep the fatigue out of his voice.

"I thought you would come find me," she said, slightly disappointed. "Am I overthinking things, Remmy?"

"Not one bit," he said. "I wanted to find you, but the Captain is calling a meeting."

"What for?"

"Beats me."

"Doesn't the GIGI thing tell you what's going on?"

"Only when I ask," Remmy said.

"But it knows about us."

"I suppose," he said. "I've never really thought about it."

"What's it think about us?"

"Honest, I have no idea. It doesn't deal much with emotions. Says they blur things."

"What do you think?"

"I think how I feel about you clarifies things, Laila." He pulled her into a doorway just inside the simulator room. Her eyes were shining, making his heart beat faster in his chest.

"I'm so glad you were honest with me," Laila said. "But when we lost contact with you in the pyramid, I have to admit it was hard."

"I'm sorry," he told her.

"It wasn't your fault, but we need to figure things out between us," she said. "I'll admit I haven't felt this way about anyone in a long time... maybe never."

"It's a first for me, too," Remmy said. "I've got to go, Laila, but I promise I will come looking for you as soon as that meeting ends."

"You better, Remmy."

"Count it," he said.

Their lips brushed against each other, and then they continued on their separate ways, but Remmy knew that no matter what happened or what the future held, what he wanted most in all the universe was to be with Laila McPherson for the rest of his life.

CHAPTER 42

CAPTAIN ZEKE DARIUS had overseen the return of the Marine platoon. The medical team was ready. There were only five: Doctor Lanski, a surgical nurse, and three medical technicians. Most medical aid was done using robots and automated medical devices, so most ships had technicians who kept the machines calibrated and did some basic nursing work when patients were in the med bay. But every ship had emergency protocols in the rare event that quarantine was necessary. And Doctor Lanski had led his team well.

The *Jericho* was buzzing with news from the mission. Most important was the revelation that the Arodoni Power Core was fully functional. Henry Nash and his engineers had gone over it, but the alien technology was like a blank puzzle to them. GIGI had data on the device, but even her makers didn't know much about the power core. What was even more surprising was that in the designs for the Jericho, there was an alternate power slot that just happened to be a perfect fit for the alien power core.

Almost within an hour of the dropship's return, the debate began. GIGI had revealed that the power core could, in fact, power the ship. Some thought they should put it to use, others disagreed. Captain Darius wasn't in a hurry to make any decisions. His plan was to turn the ship around and go back to the Sol system, but before he could, GIGI laid another unexpected bit of information on them.

"There is an Arodoni battleship hidden in the Vangor Nebula," GIGI explained. "It has the weapons necessary to defend humanity's home system."

"We don't need it," Darius said. "We can build our weapons and ships."

He was in his office waiting for a report on Gunnery Sergeant Chad Rand. Doctor Lanski was supposed to update him as soon as the Marine could be examined and treated.

"That may be true in time, but please consider that your race is slow to act," GIGI said. "How long will they hesitate to build the equipment necessary to defend your people? They will want to study the Arodoni Power Core before using it. Please keep in mind, Captain Darius, that it took your race three decades to build the *Jericho*."

"I'm aware of all that," he replied. "But we have protocols for a reason, GIGI. You may not understand them, but I'm bound by my duty to the Space Defense Force. And getting that power core back home where it can defend our world is the highest priority."

"Agreed, but the power core isn't the solution to your problem, Captain."

"And what is my problem, exactly?"

"The Empire will soon be at your door, Captain. That is inevitable. And while your race is resourceful and certainly militant enough to put up a good fight, you do not possess the weaponry needed to stop an Imperial invasion."

"But you just happen to know where we can get that sort of weaponry," he said.

It was hard not to be angry and sarcastic. He was a Captain in the SDF Fleet and felt like he was being treated like a child. He knew humanity had weaknesses. They weren't perfect, but he would do everything in his power to save them. And while he had only been given a glimpse of what was out there in the galaxy waiting to enslave or eradicate the entire human race, he couldn't just pretend it wasn't a real and present danger to them all. Still, it angered him that GIGI hadn't just laid all her cards on the table. Instead, she only revealed her plan for them bit by bit. It made Darius suspicious, but they had started down the path, and he could see no logical way to turn back. Everything GIGI was telling him made sense on a strategic level.

"It isn't hidden like a treasure, but rather left unattended. It was one of the last ships in the Arodoni Fleet. The crew, feeling their destruction of much of their enemy was somehow immoral, committed ritual suicide.

They jettisoned the ship's power core. The Correll recovered it, and now we have it too. The *Jericho* was designed to link to the Arodoni battleship. In your language, the ship was called *Renegade*. Using the Arodoni power core, we can go to the Vangor Nebula, retrieve the *Renegade,* and return to the Sol system prepared to defend against all enemies."

"This was your plan all along, wasn't it?" Darius asked. "You weren't sent to our system to warn or recruit us. You needed bodies to carry out your bidding, and once we've synced up to that Arodoni ship, you'll have complete control of it."

"Technically, that is possible," GIGI said. "This course of action was not in my prime directives, but it is my strategy for marshaling the true strength of the human race. With the right weapons, you will be a threat to the Empire."

"With you leading us?" Darius asked.

"I cannot lead you. My function is to supply data to help you make informed decisions, Captain."

He didn't trust GIGI but couldn't shake the memory of the courier drone the *Jericho* had shot down. One way or another, the galaxy would soon learn about the human race. And while he hated to admit it, GIGI was right about them. If he returned with just the power core, it would be years before anything was done to prepare the system for an attack. Everything would have to be debated in sub-committees and voted on by the government. And even if they recognized the threat and decided to act immediately, it would take years of planning to build weapons that could use the power core's vast capability.

"Thank you for your input, GIGI. I have other tasks to see to at the moment."

"I stand ready to assist you in whatever way I can," the alien device said.

Darius didn't sleep for the next eighteen hours. He spent his time moving the ship out of orbit, getting updates on the wounded Marines, and wrestling with the decision of what to do next. And as soon as Master Sergeant Remmy was cleared from quarantine, he called a planning meeting. Everyone was assembled in the Ward Room when the Master Sergeant arrived. He was greeted warmly and ushered into a seat.

"How are you feeling?" Darius asked him.

"Sore," Remmy admitted. "I think I tweaked a hamstring, but I'll be fine with a few days rest."

"Yes, well, I'd like to give you all the time you need to recover, but we," Darius said, waving to everyone in the room, "have a decision to make."

He explained GIGI's suggestion about the Arodoni ship *Renegade*.

"You're saying we could capture and pilot an alien ship?" Pete Best asked.

"A ship that the Empire fears," Henry Nash added.

"That's a little hard to believe," Lieutenant Micky Colt said.

"Or an opportunity we can't pass up," Vivian Ramos said. "GIGI was right about hyperspace travel. She was right about the power core. Why wouldn't we believe her about the Arodoni battleship?"

"It's not a matter of trust," Darius said. "We have a duty and responsibility. I want to know your thoughts on what our next move should be."

"Go after the alien ship, or go home?" Henry Nash asked.

"Those are the options on the table before us," Darius said. "This isn't a vote. But I want your input before making a decision that affects us all."

"Are you leaning one way or another?" Remmy asked.

"I can find no fault in GIGI's logic," he admitted.

"What if GIGI just takes over this alien ship?" Micky Colt asked.

"She could do that now," Henry Nash said. "She designed the *Jericho*. With the alien power supply, she could go anywhere. The crew is just a redundancy."

"We aren't needed?" Pete Best said. "I find that hard to believe."

"On a regular Fleet ship, we are indispensable. But that's only because they're constantly breaking down. On the other hand, Jericho hasn't had a single issue. There's not one bug to work out or a single repair."

"But she can't load the weapons," Pete Best insisted. "Without us, she can't even connect the new power core."

"That's not true," Remmy said. "Remember how it got on board? She can project a gravity field. I believe GIGI could move anything on the ship, maybe even better than we can."

"That doesn't mean she isn't manipulating us," Pete Best insisted. "I'm just playing devil's advocate here, but can we really trust her?"

"Logically," Commander Lee said, "we have no reason not to."

"I think we all want to go home," Micky Colt said. "But not before the mission is complete."

"Agreed," Vivian Ramos said. "I, for one, would feel much better with a ship capable of resisting invasion."

"It worries me that everything we're doing seems part of someone else's plan," Pete Best argued.

"I can't say I disagree," Henry Nash spoke up. "But I also know that GIGI's right about it taking us years, maybe even decades before we could be ready to design something with enough power to fight across the distance of a star system. We're way behind in the technology department."

"Is there a danger to getting this Arodoni ship?" Remmy asked.

"Not that I'm aware of," Captain Darius said. "But we have to consider that as a factor. There are certainly dangers. The nebula itself might be a danger to the ship. We've never been close enough to study one, much less traverse it."

"I can't stop thinking about that courier drone we shot down," Vivian Ramos said. "Who was it supposed to report to, and what would it have told them?"

"GIGI could be lying about everything," Pete Best said. "Her creators could be the bad guys in the situation. How are we supposed to know?"

"We need time that we don't have," Darius said. "And no matter what angle I look at our situation from, I only see one way to get us the time we need."

"We have to have that ship," Remmy said.

"And the weapons on it," Henry Nash said. "With one move, we can defend ourselves and propel our technology further than anyone could imagine."

"It would be like fast-forwarding our entire culture," Micky Colt said. "Seems like we have to try."

"Then that's what we'll do," Captain Zeke Darius said, his mind made up. "We've come this far; let's finish the race. Lieutenant Ramos set a course for the Vangor Nebula. Master Sergeant, get some rest. We're going to need you at your best."

"Yes sir, Captain," Remmy said.

"Lieutenant Nash, you have permission to connect the Arodoni Power Core to the *Jericho*," Darius ordered. "All hands to their stations. Standby for hyperspace travel. Let's go get the *Renegade*."

EPILOGUE

AS HABASH ROTATED, the primary watch station came back online. It had been the first to pick up the arrival of the alien ship on its scanners and tracked its progress to Lawash. Its twin on the opposite side of the barren world picked up where the primary watch station had stopped as the world spun around. After a ten-hour cycle, it was back in full view of the planet and recording the strange ship as it headed out of the system.

A message that included all recorded data was being composed. A courier drone would launch soon, but not while the alien ship was still in the system. The destruction of one drone was enough for the automated watch system to learn from. The Imperium's Prime Council would know of the intrusion by the alien ship. And it's hostile nature. A new enemy had been detected. War was returning to the galactic empire, and a new race would soon bow to the Imperium or be destroyed.

AUTHOR'S NOTE

Thanks for reading this book. I have big plans for where this series could go. If you liked *Artifact* please leave an honest review on Amazon and/or Goodreads. And read on for an unedited sample of *Renegade* (Starship Jericho book 2).

RENEGADE CHAPTER 1

Emperor Vang stared out the viewport at the glittering world below him. Ashi Prime was the glorious capital of the Five Fold Empire. It was where the Imperium began, and after a thousand worlds were brought into the Empire and hundreds more burned for their resistance, Ashi Prime was rich from the taxes and tributes that poured in from across the galaxy. Entire cities were made of gold. The sunlight glittered on golden domes and flashed off the crystal spires. And all of it belonged to Vang, every Ashi citizen, every slave; everything was his, and yet no one could possess it all. He could go down and claim anything he wanted, but none of it made him happy.

He crossed his grand chamber in the Emperor's Eye. It was a massive space station. From the surface of the planet, it looked like a giant eye, fiery red and menacing. Fear was what kept the empire together, and for more than a thousand years, the Ashi Emperors had projected a ferocious demeanor onto the people of the Imperium. But Vang didn't want to just pretend. He wasn't happy basking in the glory of his forebears. And yet the Empire was so big, their armies so powerful, that no one dared resist them. Four hundred prior, there had been wars to fight, enemies to overcome, and worlds to conquer. But that had ended when the last Arodoni battleship disappeared. In the interval, there had been minor uprisings, a few weak fires that were summarily crushed by Vang's ancestors. They had left him an empire that was strong, wealthy, and at peace.

Vang despised peace. He was a warrior and eager for the chance to do battle. Only there was no one for him to fight.

"You called for me, sire?" a servant asked timidly from the shadows of the doorway arches.

"Dress me," Vang commanded.

"Yes, Lord," the servant said.

Ashi males were big, powerfully built creatures. They had once been warriors, first fighting in skirmishes between clans, then uniting into countries that warred across the planet. Eventually, as their technological prowess grew, they turned their martial aspirations onto other worlds.

The Dudonus were highly sought-after slaves. They were slender beings with long, delicate legs, tiny bodies, and four spindly arms. Their heads were triangular in shape, with long silver hair that grew out of the top point. Each one was worth a hundred thousand Imperial credits, and Vang had hundreds of Dudonus slaves across the various space stations, ships, and palaces on the more important worlds. He could kill them, snapping their narrow necks as easily as plucking a flower and with as little concern.

The servant brought the Emperor his fur-trimmed breeches and Angorian skin vest. From the shoulders was clipped the purple cap, and Vang preferred the slender crown first worn by the Emperors who marched into battle on alien worlds.

"Sheika Kahn is waiting for Your Excellency in the audience chamber," the servant said.

"Very well," Vang replied.

"Shall I have the harem prepared for you this evening, my lord?"

"I suppose. And have Konga prepare for sparring. We are getting fat and lazy. I will not have it."

"Very good, my master," the slave said, bowing low.

Vang strode through the ornate halls in the private part of the space station. His Audience Chamber was a huge room filled with treasures from across the Empire. It was decorated to show the power and riches of the Emperor, but it always reminded Vang who had been accomplished before him and how little he had done himself.

As a youngling, he had dreamed of being a great military leader. As he grew older and learned more about his father's rule, it seemed like his father feared losing the peace. There was no more talk of expanding the Imperium, no more worlds in open rebellion. Money was spent on things other than defense. To Vang, in his youthful ambition, it seemed that his father had grown soft. The difference in their point views drove Vang first to pity his father, and then to hate him. On his twentieth birthday, the Emperor threw a lavish party for his son, and that night, the son murdered his father. It was no rank assassination, no cowardly knife in the Emperor's back as had happened so many times before. Vang challenged his father, who tried to refuse combat, but Vang would not let him. They both had ceremonial daggers. Vang took his and sliced his father's chest.

The Emperor was bigger than his son, but where Vang was all muscle and bone, his father had gone to fat. Rage and lack of stamina were weaknesses that Vang counted on. His father, wounded and furious that his son would try to usurp the throne, charged at him, hacking and slashing in fury that quickly wore the older Ashi out. Vang had only to keep his guard up and wait for his opportunity. When the Emperor stumbled, Vang lashed out, knocking his father to his knees with a shoulder charge and then sawing his dagger across his father's throat.

The next day, Vang was named Emperor, and his mother was sent away. She lived in isolation on a world that Vang couldn't even remember the name of. He would have no one around him who judged his actions in taking the throne or who harbored any reason why he shouldn't rule. But Vang quickly learned that there was little to do. No wars presented themselves. Explorers and slavers plied the hyperspace lanes in search of new worlds, but there were no worthy adversaries to be found. Vang realized that it wasn't so much his father's fear of combat or loathing to break the peace as a lack of opportunity to do so.

"Your Excellence," Sheika Kahn said as Vang entered the Emperor's Audience Chamber. "I have news."

"What news?"

"A report from the automated surveillance station in the Lawa system."

"Remind me of that place," Vang ordered.

"Lawash was a resistance world," the Kahn said. "Pounded by Emperor Vega nearly five hundred years ago. All intelligent species were eradicated. The world is tainted with heavy metals."

Vang stifled a yawn. He cared very little for the administration of the Imperium. That was left to ministers and the five Consuls. Vang's focus was expansion and, if the need ever arose, defense.

"A ship was seen in the system," Sheika Kahn continued. "It went straight to Lawash and sent a shuttle to the surface. Who they were and what they sought, we do not know."

"Every ship in the galaxy is in the database," Vang said. "Where was it from?"

"That's just it, my Lord. This ship was not in the database and had no transponder code."

"Are you saying it is from an unknown race?"

"That is possible, sire."

"Speak plainly, Kahn, or I'll have your tongue removed."

"Sire, it was an ancient design. Part of the old Arodoni Fleet."

That got Vang's attention. The Ashi Imperium had been a near-unstoppable force. The only technology greater than the Imperium's was the ancient Arodoni ships.

"That is impossible," Vang said. "None still exist."

"It is believed," Sheika Kahn said, leaning closer to the Emperor, who had gone from slouching on his royal throne to sitting up straight. Vang's face was pinched in deep thought. The Kahn, his most trusted advisor and liaison to the Five Consuls, leaned closer. "We would have gotten word of any new ship constructed in this manner."

"Is it a ship of war?"

"Not exactly, your Highness. It appears to be the power drive of an Arodoni ship of war."

"A power drive?"

"Yes, sire. And before the highly esteemed Emperor Vega destroyed LaWash there was an ancient temple there. It still stands. A Jatoshi pyramid temple still stands, my Lord. A quick search in the archives revealed that it was a treasury."

"The unknown ship is searching for treasure?"

"Perhaps, but sire, please bear with me while I take a moment to explain. The Arodoni were seen as mortal enemies of the empire. As such, their technology was destroyed anywhere it was found. And anyone with plans of or possessing Arodoni tech was summarily executed. The only race who had a grasp on the advanced designs was the Correll."

"I am not familiar with them," Vang said.

"Because they were enemies of the empire and stamped out of the universe," Kahn continued. "They no longer exist, but before their demise, they sent out devices with the secrets of the Arodoni stored inside. No one knows how many, or to whom those devices were sent, but it does appear as though perhaps that a technologically advanced race has utilized those plans. It may be possible that one of the treasures in the forgotten temple was some bit of Arodoni technology that survived the purge."

"I'm sure you are driving toward a point, Kahn, but spit it out."

"It might be possible, Highness, that someone, somewhere, knows of an Arodoni ship."

"A ship of war?"

"That would make the most sense," Kahn said.

"They possessed the power to destroy entire star systems," Vang said. "A world possessing such a ship would be a formidable enemy."

"Indeed they would sire. Which is why I thought it prudent to share this information with you."

"Are they still in the system?"

"No, sire. The ship was making for the hyperspace portal. Subsequent investigation shows that the system is empty."

"Do we know where they went?"

"Not yet, your Highness. But with your permission, I will alert all systems."

"Do it," Vang ordered. "We must know if there is an enemy at the gate."

"Indeed," Sheika Kahn said. "Any race willing to utilize forbidden technology could be a threat to the Empire."

"Yes," Vang said, getting to his feet. "Yes... it might mean war."

He was clearly excited by the prospect. At last, there was a glimmer of hope. If he could win glory in battle, his name would be remembered for a thousand years. It was lost on Vang that he couldn't remember the names of his ancestors who crushed rebellions only a few hundred years previous. After months of stupendous boredom, he might actually have an enemy to fight. And that was the best news he had ever received.

"We will find them, Your Highness," Sheika Kahn promised.

"Find them, yes, but do not engage. We must not press in until we know everything about this new enemy."

It didn't matter to Vang if his Kahn knew that all he really wanted was for the potential threat to have the time to require his full attention. Vang would begin assembling an armada that he would personally lead. Eight ships of war, three troop carriers in the event that the battle went to ground. Oh, how he hoped that it would. Nothing else in his duty as sole Emperor of the Five-Fold Imperium even came close to the thrill of mortal combat.

"As you wish, my Lord," Sheika Kahn said.

"Yes, this is what I want," Vang said. "Send word to have my personal battleship prepared. I will take command first thing in the morning. You will see to all concerns here, Kahn. Destiny is calling. I will answer the call."

"For glory, my Lord!"

"For my glory," Vang said, already imagining the carnage that he would be lord over.

RENEGADE CHAPTER 2

"Attention, crew of the *Jericho*, this is Captain Darius speaking," the voice boomed through the ship's speakers. "We are about to come out of hyperspace. We have not reached our destination. This a transit change, and we have no alarms or warnings, but we will run a full diagnostic check on the ship before making our next jump. And, as we are in foreign space, we will go to Red Alert status. All crew are to report to battle stations just in case we encounter alien resistance. That is all."

Zeke Darius returned the hand held microphone to the nook in the side of his captain's chair. They had been in hyperspace for nearly thirty hours. And, according to GIGI, the alien device that the *Jericho* had picked up just beyond Saturn's orbit in the Sol system, they had two more stages of their hyperspace journey before reaching the Vangori Nebula. He looked over at Lieutenant Vivan Ramos. She was clearly tired. They all were. Darius didn't have to order his senior officers to put in overtime on their watch duties. It was only their second trip through hyperspace, and while everyone seemed in favor of their current plan of action, their nerves were on edge as well. Vivian was the ship's navigational officer and was keeping tabs on the computer's progress as it guided the ship through the galaxy.

"How long, Lieutenant Ramos?"

"Six minutes," she replied.

"How long will we be at the transit point?"

"According to the course set by GIGI, we're looking at just under an hour before making the next jump."

"I want to run full diagnostics the moment we complete a security scan," Darius said. "Lieutenant Best, are your weapons ready?"

"Aye, Captain, we are locked and loaded," Pete Best replied. "Missiles in their launchers and our lasers all fully charged."

"What about the sonic shielding?" Darius asked.

"GIGI says we don't need it in hyperspace, but it's up anyway," Lieutenant Best said. "And with the additional power boost from the alien energy device, we could probably deflect a full-on laser barrage, sir. The sonic shields aren't built for that, but my calculations suggest it is possible."

"Nothing wrong with a little extra protection," Commander Lori Lee said.

She was Darius' second in command, his executive officer, and one of the best he had ever worked with. Not every Fleet officer had the administrative gifts to keep a ship running at optimal levels, but Commander Lee was certainly up for the task. It made his job as Captain of the *Jericho* so much easier.

"Roger that," Darius said. "Lieutenant Nash, are we still good?"

"Green across the board, Captain," the tall, black man said without looking up from his console. "This ship is a well-oiled machine, sir."

"Good, let's make sure it stays that way," Darius said.

"Three minutes," Vivian said. "All stations standby for transition from hyperspace."

"Captain, I'll go to Red Alert with your permission," Commander Lee said.

"Granted," Darius said.

Red lights began to flash in the corridors of the ship. On the Bridge, the regular overhead lights faded, and red battle lights came on. Darius checked the radar screen built into the armrest of his chair. It was ready to go but wouldn't activate until they dropped from hyperspace.

Three minutes wasn't much. It passed quickly. And the transition back to normal space was smooth. The radar and lidar systems went live, and their plot was soon projected by a holographic table in the pit directly in front of the big main screens that showed the video feeds from the ship's external cameras.

"Contact!" Ensign Alex Stanislaus announced. "Two hundred thousand kilometers out, Captain, bearing two-three-seven degrees."

"Mark it," Captain Darius said.

"Contact is labeled Lima One, we have another ship. It's way out there sir, half a million miles, but pinging on lidar. Designating Lima Two."

"Are they talking?" Darius asked.

"I'm getting electronic transmissions from both ships," Ensign Bertoli said. "I can't make sense of them."

A voice from the Bridge's hidden speakers spoke up.

"May I assist in the translation?" GIGI asked.

Darius glanced at the slab of stone that was settled on the Bridge just in front of the plot table. It reminded Darius of a tombstone. The markings on the surface were completely foreign. They didn't light up like a neon sign, but there were occasional moments where the figures on the surface glowed slightly. GIGI, as the alien device called itself, was a Galactic Information & Guidance Instrument. It claimed to be alive, although it was constructed of non-organic matter. It had been in the Sol system for several hundred years before the *Jericho* made contact with the device. It had even sent the construction plans for the ship so that it could be reached so far from human habitation in the inner system.

"Yes, please," Darius said.

"Very well, Captain. Lima One is a Feringian Cargo vessel, completely automated. The transmissions from both vessels are transponder codes in the Imperium's common language. Lima Two is a gas harvester. Neither ship is armed and should present us no problems."

Darius felt a slight sense of relief. They were at an exchange point where there were multiple portals into hyperspace. It was all a bit over the Captain's head as a pure science, but the ideas were easy enough to understand. Hyperspace consisted of long streams, not unlike Earth's old Interstate highway system. In places where the hyper dimension touched real space, a ship on the right trajectory, traveling at the right speed, could slip into hyperspace, which allowed for faster-than-light travel through the galaxy. This depended on a knowledge of the hyper dimension lanes which GIGI had provided for the *Jericho*. Darius didn't like depending on anything, not even his ship's own computers. But they had no choice. GIGI served a dual role, first as a hyperspace navigation system and secondly as their encyclopedia of knowledge about the galaxy at large. She, Darius thought of the alien as female, had informed them of two major threats to the human race. The first were slavers, independent vessels crewed by nefarious aliens who raided planets for the sole purpose of capturing intelligent species to enslave. The unfortunate beings captured by the slavers were then taken to new worlds and sold as slave labor. Humanity had spent centuries stamping out slavery, first in the institutional sense and then in the outlawed practice of human trafficking. The *Jericho* was on high alert for any sign of a slaver vessel.

Second, and even more dangerous, was the Ashi Empire. Officially, it was the Five-Fold Imperium, led by representatives of the five core worlds. But, of course, there was an Emperor who was the real power behind the Imperium. No habitable world and intelligent species were safe from the Empire, who insisted on claiming every world as their own and every race as indebted to the Imperium. It was only a matter of time before the human race and the Sol system was discovered. When that happened, humanity would need a way to defend itself, which was the reason for their mission across the galaxy.

"No threats on the board, Captain," Pete Best announced.

"Continue scanning," Darius ordered. "New contacts could drop out of hyperspace at any moment."

"Aye, Captain. Continuing a scan of space surrounding the *Jericho*."

"Lieutenant Nash, begin a diagnostic scan of the main drive systems," Darius continued, giving his crew instructions. "Ensign Stanislaus, you're on life support systems. I want computer diagnostics and crew member visual inspections. Let's make sure we're in good shape before making the next jump, people. We're on the clock."

It was a tense hour. The computer checks went smooth and fast. GIGI had upgraded the ship's computer systems. The hardware engineers were still trying to figure out exactly how the alien artifact had done it, but their computer's processing speed was faster than any known computer made by humans, and its storage capacity had increased exponentially.

The crew inspections took longer, but everything was done within half an hour. Even the Marine platoon had reported in. There was no reason not to make the next jump through hyperspace.

The only real difficulty in traveling through the galaxy via the hyperspace lanes was Captain Darius' ability to visualize it. There were no markers outside the solar system that he could look to and get his bearings. It was like being blindfolded and led through an unfamiliar home. He had no way to link the places they arrived at or passed through to a larger understanding of the galaxy as a whole. He couldn't give the proper context, which left him completely reliant on GIGI. And Captain

Darius had yet to conclude that the alien device wasn't using them for a purpose he wouldn't approve of.

"We're ready to make the jump, Captain," Vivan Ramos said. "Sixty seconds. Ship is at optimal speed to enter hyperspace."

"Nash?" Darius asked.

"The Prometheus engine is at sixty percent," the Chief engineer said. "All systems green. She's purring like a kitten, sir."

"Power?"

"More than we could use in our lifetimes, Captain," Nash said. "The Arodoni Power Core is providing so much energy we're having trouble measuring it."

"Let's stay at Red Alert until we're in hyperspace," Darius said.

"Fifteen seconds," Vivan Ramos said.

"How long will this leg of the journey be, GIGI?"

"Ten hours, twelve minutes, and thirty-one seconds, Captain," the alien device said.

"Three, two, one," Vivian counted down the final seconds.

The transition into hyperspace was uneventful. The ship's external camera went dark, and the plot disappeared, but otherwise, nothing happened that the crew could discern. Traveling through the galaxy seemed almost too easy. And Captain Zeke Darius of the SDF Fleet wasn't sure how he felt about that.

RENEGADE CHAPTER 3

Master Sergeant Remmy Steel was with the Spec Op platoon in the armory during the Red Alert. They treated every call to battle stations with the respect and professionalism of veteran Marines because that is what they were. But the mood on the *Jericho* had shifted for the platoon. They had lost one of their own in the mission on Lawash. It was a wake-up call for all of them. The cruise had seemed like a vacation of sorts. The ship wasn't going into a hot zone. They weren't expected to be running missions that might require the ultimate sacrifice, but everything had changed since getting the alien artifact.

"Not sure how I feel about all this," Lieutenant Micky Colt said.

"All of what, sir?" Remmy asked.

"Going after the alien ship," the LT said. "It's hard to believe something so valuable could just be out there waiting for us."

"The power core was," Remmy said.

"From what I hear, it's the real deal, too," Staff Sergeant Laila McPherson said quietly. "Unlimited free energy."

"That's my point," Colt said. "Something that valuable should have been taken home. What happens if we come under fire?"

"This ship has weapons," Remmy said.

"But it ain't no battleship," Sergeant Hugo McManus pointed out.

"That God for small favors," Laila replied. "At least we have a little room on this tub."

"Don't get me wrong," Lieutenant Colt said. "I understand the stakes. And I don't mind leading our platoon into battle if it comes to that. But if we lose, it isn't just a bunch of jarheads that get wiped off the board. We could lose the power core, and the folks back home will have nothing to show for our losses."

Remmy wanted to say no one was going to be lost, but he couldn't. Not after losing Corporal Wendy Downes. And not with Gunnery Sergeant Chad Rand still in the med bay.

"Red alert has ended," Commander Lori Lee's voice boomed through the ship. "I repeat, red alert has ended. Return to regular duty schedules. That is all."

"All dressed up and no place to go," McManus said.

"That's fine by me," Sergeant Dirk Oliver said. He had been Wendy Downes' team leader. He took her loss hard even though he had nothing to do with it. She was standing guard when an alien worm attacked and ingested her. Remmy had managed to retrieve her body and save Gunny Rand, but Dirk still felt responsible. He was close with the pair of Marines on his fire team. It was the way the system worked, the rule of threes, NCOs looking after the enlisted Marines under them. And losing a friend was always hard. Just because they were Space Marines who put their lives on the line regularly didn't mean they were immune to the grief that threatened to overwhelm a person when they lost someone they cared about.

"Stack 'em and rack 'em," Renny ordered, referring to their combat armor and weapons. Everything had to be secured in the armory lockers before the platoon could be released back into the ship. Normally, Gunny Rand saw to the armory, but his duties had fallen to the Master Sergeant. "Let's keep it clean. We want things all squared away when Gunny Rand comes back."

The platoon was down to just an even dozen without Corporal Downes and with Gunny Rand out of commission.

"You seen him yet?" Laila asked Remmy.

He hadn't. After their mission on Lawash, he was kept quarantined for nearly a day. After that, he had just enough time to attend a senior leadership meeting before the ship began making preparations for the jump into hyperspace. He hadn't even had time to talk with Laila alone. Their friendship had grown into a romance, but they were careful not to let that secret out to the rest of the platoon. Marines fraternizing together on a cruise was seen as bad luck. The ship's crew was fair game, but relationships within a platoon could lead to problems in a combat situation. And Remmy was the Master Sergeant. It was his duty to set an example for the platoon, but he had risked his life on the cruise and wasn't going to hide from his feelings. He wanted desperately for Laila to know how he felt before something happened to either one of them.

"Not yet," Remmy admitted, pulling off his battle helmet. "You?"

"I did. He was unconscious, though. The surgeon said he has burns over twenty percent of his body. The creature's stomach acid ate its way into the seams of his space suit."

"His helmet kept him alive, though," Daniel said.

"Yeah, that and your quick thinking."

"I didn't do it alone. Tex did the heavy lifting."

"I doubt that," Staff Sergeant McPherson said.

She glanced at him. It was nothing, not even a smile or a wink, but it was enough. Remmy felt like he could have walked on air. There was something to be said for impressing the girl you liked.

"How long to the next transition, Master Sergeant?" Lieutenant Colt asked.

Remmy didn't know, but he had a source of information that no one else had. The alien artifact, GIGI, had bonded with him. It mapped his neural pathways and kept a telekinetic connection with him. The device claimed that it didn't read his mind. But it was always there, always listening. That bond had caused some concern for the rest of the platoon. They weren't even sure he was still the same man as before. But his actions on Lawash had cleared up any doubts about Master Sergeant Steel. He had not only saved Gunny Rand and found Corporal "Rip" Van Winkle, who was trapped in one of the treasure vaults under the Jatoshi temple, but he completed the mission, finding and getting the Arodoni Power Core out of the tunnels and back up to the surface. Not that he had done it all alone, but his leadership and valor were uncontested.

"Let me check," Remmy said.

GIGI, you there? he thought.

I am Master Sergeant.

How long till we transition from hyperspace on this leg of the journey?

Approximately ten hours. We will pass through a portion of the Kadish system, then begin the third and final hyperspace jump that will take us to the Vangori Nebula.

How long is the third jump?

Thirty-seven hours and fifty-two minutes, the alien artifact said. Its voice only registered in Remmy's head.

"Ten hours, Lieutenant," Remmy explained. "After that, we've got another jump that lasts a day and a half."

"Alright, let's get some chow and then some rest," the Lieutenant said. "We meet back here in nine hours, people. No excuses. Platoon, dismissed."

Remmy closed his weapons locker and headed for the door. He stopped beside it, letting the rest of the platoon go ahead of him. Laila McPherson was one of the first ones out. She didn't even look his way.

They passed from the Armory, through their simulator training room, and into the cargo hold of the ship. The after section of the lower deck was officially grunt country. The ship's crew didn't have much reason to be down there. On the other side of the cargo hold was the galley and then the Mess Hall. The Marines ate. They sat together. There were three women and nine men. Lieutenant Colt took his meal up in the Officer's Ward Room. Remmy could have done the same thing. He was considered a senior officer on the ship, partly because he had won the Medal of Honor, which made him a minor celebrity among the military, and partly because the Marine Major assigned to the *Jericho* had fallen ill before she could report for duty. But he preferred to eat the highly processed ship food with the rest of the platoon. Remmy didn't mind rubbing elbows with the senior officers of the ship, but he felt more at ease with his enlisted comrades.

After his meal, Remmy went to the Med Bay. There was only one occupant, Gunnery Sergeant Chad Rand, but the ship's surgeon, Major Mishta Lanski, met Remmy just inside.

"Ah, the Sergeant has been asking for you," the Surgeon said. "He is sleeping now, but you can wake him, I think. The pain medication is strong."

"Is he in much pain?"

"He would be, but not while he is here. The burns were not extensive enough to need grafts. Time and therapy will do work, Master Sergeant. Boredom will probably be the hardest part of his convalescence."

The doctor led Remmy over to one of the pods and gave Gunny Rand's chest a light touch. The Marine's eyes fluttered open. Even high as a kite, it only took the slightest touch to wake the Gunnery Sergeant. It took him longer to focus on Remmy and recognize the Master Sergeant.

"You can talk," the doctor said. "Five minutes is enough, though. Sleep is the best medicine."

"Remmy," Chad Rand said in a soft voice that seemed very unlike the gregarious Gunnery Sergeant.

"How you feeling?" Remmy asked him.

"Like I'm floating on a cloud," Gunny Rand said. "Whatever I'm on, it's the good stuff, Master Sergeant."

"I'm glad."

"Heard what you did," Gunny Rand said. "Thank you."

"Forget it. Besides, I think it was Corporal Fry who pulled you out."

"Sure, he came by, told me the truth," Gunny Rand said with a chuckle. "You hadn't done that, and I would be dead."

"It'll take more than a giant worm to kill you, Gunny."

"Never seen anything take that kind of punishment and just keep coming," Rand said. "I must have emptied two mags into that beast."

"And saved Rip in the process," Remmy pointed out.

"It's what we do, ain't it," the Gunnery Sergeant said, his voice starting to slur. "All we know how to do."

"That's right," Remmy said. "I'm glad to be doing it with you, Gunny. Get your rest, Sergeant. We're all pulling for you."

"Thank you, Remmy. I owe you. Think I'll close my eyes now. Just for a minute..."

Remmy stayed by the pod until he was certain that Gunny Rand was sleeping, then he headed for his own cabin. Having private quarters was the biggest perk to being on the new ship. Remmy had never bunked in his own room on board a Fleet vessel before, and he liked it.

On his way to the upper level, he thought about what Gunny Rand had said. He wasn't wrong in Remmy's opinion. He was duty bound and really didn't know how to do anything other than his best. It was what he had been taught, trained to do, and practiced with every platoon he had been part of. There wasn't anything to think about. He saw a task that needed doing, and he did it. It was as simple as that. There was no need to celebrate it. No medals or commendations ever came into Remmy's mind when he was down range in a hot zone. He just did what needed to be done and never even wondered about the risks he was taking or how it scared his soul. Remmy Steel was a Marine, and that's just the way it was. He wouldn't have had it any other way.

ABOUT THE AUTHOR

Toby Neighbors is an emerging author of steampunk cookbooks. This is Toby's eighth book.

www.ingramcontent.com/pod-product-compliance
Lightning Source LLC
Chambersburg PA
CBHW052029240626
47153CB00006B/2016